K.C. Hall Looks to the S

Cameron McVey

Published by Cameron McVey
Kindle Edition
Copyright © 2022 Cameron McVey

http://www.amazon.com/author/cameronmcvey

http://www.cameronmcvey.com

Cover design by Cameron McVey and Molly Wilson
Kindle Edition, License Notes

To my wife,
Thank You for
Everything

1.
It's been a while since we last talked. That's on me. I've been busy. I'm still busy. The busiest I've been in my career. I have the weight of an entire universe on my shoulders, after all. The Hall-iverse as it's been dubbed by the media. MDB, of course, thinks it should be called the DuBont-iverse. Or the Madeline-iverse. But, yeah, my last name is better suited to the contraction. So, Hall-iverse it is.

What is the Hall-iverse?

So glad you asked. No, really, this is just what I need. To talk about the multiple interconnected series and movies in which I feature and/or am a producer and/or am referenced (the character I play, that is). Multiple. Interconnected. Series. And movies. See previous note about my level of busy-ness. I'll say this now just to get it out of the way. It's too much. I'm starting to burn out. I've never felt this way about working, about acting. But I do now. Please, don't tell anyone. I've kept this to myself so far. I've kept my head down and just kept working, working, working in hopes that this will pass. This tiredness. This dreading of getting in front of the camera. This…I don't even know what to call it. I just want to go hibernate in a cave for several months. A nice, warm, tropical cave with a totally private beach where paparazzi are not allowed with just Scott and me and NO ONE ELSE.

Yeah, it's been a long year.

Almost exactly a year since we last talked.

This week should be different though. It's K.C. Hall Week on Kincaid Live! The Sequel! We're on Luisa's ranch. Which is way outside of Hollywood. Which is where I need to be. Desperately. MDB warned me. She did. So, too, did Shawn. I thought I was ready. I thought I was prepared. But (low key drumroll) I wasn't (rimshot). Not even close.

I'll get to all that in due time. What happened. What I said and did. What other people said and did. What was reported that I said and did. And…yeah, I'll get to that. But now, just for tonight, let's focus on K.C. Hall Week. Is that self-centered? Actually, I don't think so. The name - yes, of course. But you have to tell the viewers what they're getting and calling a week of me co-hosting Kincaid Live anything other than K.C. Hall Week would be disingenuous. More to the point, the show allows me to focus on others: the guests, primarily. Yes, I'll be the face, the host, the constant, the through line. But it won't be about me. Not about me. Which is what I need after…

No, I'll talk about that later. It's been talked about to death these past few months. I'm not sure that I have anything new to add. But I do understand your curiosity. All I ask is that you be patient with me. Let me build up to that conversation. Because this week, here, away from Hollywood feels like the first time that I've taken a breath in several months.

What's that? You want me to say what happened? As if you didn't know?

Come on.

Everybody knows.

Everybody knows.

So, why not say it?

Because it hurts.

Let's get through the first show and some recapping of the year. Then we'll talk about it. This is supposed to be my "week away from it all." I can't get away from it all if I start right out talking about it, can I? No, I can't.

2.

The crew has set up a stage in one corner of the largest field on Luisa's Ranch. The weather (fingers crossed very tightly) has cooperated so far. They are prepared to cover everything in tarps and such should it rain. Some are already in place for shading/lighting purposes. And we have a backup set inside the barn. Yes, inside the barn. Luisa keeps only three horses there these days. So, the smell isn't too bad. And the horses actually seem to like the attention. One of them, Zephyr, mugs for the camera whenever there's one around. I swear he does. Mr. Ed's country cousin that one is.

But we won't go into the barn unless things get really bad weather-wise and so far that hasn't happened and isn't predicted to happen. Small miracles. I could use a few more of those.

Later this week, a decent size (not too big, not too small, very Goldilocksish) tent will be put up in a field just over from the barn. That's where Scott and I will finally have a reception for our wedding. More on that later.

Luisa called me up after my first Kincaid Live! show last year. I, of course, had told her that I would be talking about dad. She was more concerned for me than anything else. "Are you sure, K.C.?" She must have asked me that a dozen times on the phone. "Are you sure, K.C.?" I was sure. But I shouldn't have been. Because opening up about my father to the nation is what eventually led to…everything that happened this past year. What's the phrase? "The devil you know?" Something about knowing the nastiness being better than not knowing? Something like that.

I'm not sure that's true. Not if everybody in the nation knows, too. And then decided you're the devil as well. Because that makes them feel better about it all. Having someone to point at. Someone to blame.

Ok, fine. I'll say it. It's more tiresome not saying it, jumping around it, mentioning it indirectly than just coming out and saying it.

My dad had an affair while he was overseas in the Army.

That affair resulted in a child.

4

This betrayal is what crushed mom back in the day. This affair is why we kept moving when I was young. Dad was running away from it all. The pain. The truth.

No, that doesn't make logical sense. But it makes emotional sense.

So, when I got on stage last year and talked about my dad and how I missed him and how I'd dealt with his death over the years, sometimes successfully, other times not so successfully, the truth about what he did - truth that I had no idea about - came out. Not right away. But eventually. And painfully.

Yes, that kid from the affair, you guessed it, he's the VP at GMG who wants nothing to do with me. No matter how many times I've reached out. Absolutely nothing to do with me.

You'd think not being able to talk to a person I've never met wouldn't be a big deal. But it is. It haunts me.

And, yes, I know. Another half-sibling. Just like Kalindra. But, no, not like Kalindra at all. She, Shawn and Lucius, their baby, are doing great, by the way. They've been in the Caribbean ever since Lucius was born. Shawn owns an island or two down there. They can stay completely away from the media down there. Yes, I am jealous. I can't tell you how many "news segments" on various shows have opened up with aerial views of my building in L.A. Shawn's old building. Scott's and my new building. After the Nth time seeing the building from a helicopter, Scott said, "Well, they definitely know where to find us."

Back to the topic at hand.

Connor Elroy wants nothing to do with me. Nor does his mother. Who is still alive. She is the woman who had the affair with dad when they were "over there." She was a consultant of some sort at the time. Connected to a USO tour. An agent or something for one of the performers. A musician who did a little acting at the end of her career. She passed away a decade ago. The musician. Connor's mom came back from the tour and that's when she discovered she was pregnant. She reached out to dad and dad ignored her. He was at the end of his tour and heading back home to mom. I was born almost exactly nine months after he came home. So, yeah. He wanted a family. He just didn't want one with Connor's mom.

But Connor's mom - her name is Riley, Riley Elroy - persisted. She tracked dad down. Not in a stalker manner. In a "he's your son and deserves to know who you are" manner. Letters. Phone calls. That's how mom - my mom - found out about the affair. She picked up the phone one day. Instead of hanging up like she had so many times before, Riley introduced herself. Best I can figure, I was two, maybe two and half years old when this happened.

How do I know this?

Letters. From Riley. For dad. To Mo.

Yes, Riley got involved in Hollywood when she got back home. Her connection to the musician opened a few doors for her. She set up a publicist office. Made a nice little living for herself. Of course (because the universe has a twisted sense of humor,) at some point she crossed paths with Mo who had come back after the Army and gone to Hollywood himself. The letters say Riley bumped into Mo at a party. They didn't recognize each other at first but started talking. Like you do. Mo mentioned his time in the Army. Riley mentioned her time on the tour. Not many people from the military end up in Hollywood. So, they talked some more. Riley did the mental math (two plus two equals you know the man I had an affair with) quicker than Mo but Mo got there, too. It was the first Mo had heard about dad's dalliance.

Dalliance. That's such a crappy word. Such a CYA word. Such an avoidance. But, no, I won't go off on that now.

Riley put Mo on the spot. She asked him to send the letters on to dad as her calls clearly weren't working. I'm not sure if he did or not. I want to believe that he didn't and that dad put his past behind him and somehow convinced himself that this woman who had called and called and called for a few years was just some crazy nut nut making stuff up, some delusional woman obsessing over him and telling lies to get him back into her life. That's what I want to believe. But I can't.

Because Mo wrote back. I don't have those letters. I suspect Connor does. Or maybe Riley still has them. That makes more sense. They are referenced in subsequent letters

6

from Riley to Mo. I want to believe - no. PART of me wants to believe Riley Elroy was and is delusional. That my dad did not have an affair with her. That Connor Elroy is not my half-brother. PART of me wants to believe that because that would allow me to think of dad without getting angry at him. So, so angry.

But...

That's why I originally wanted to meet Connor. To get a DNA sample so we could settle this question with science. I know. How the tables have turned. I'm the one wanting a DNA test now. Not Kalindra. Yes, my life is a badly written soap opera. Half-siblings popping up everywhere. A father killed by a robber. A mother who writes a tell-all book. Which now I have to consider in a new light. Because she didn't tell all, not everything, did she? Assuming that the letters are true (and, to some extent, relying on my own childhood memories), then mom did find out about dad's affair when I was young but she didn't put that revelation in her book. Why not?

Because she had forgiven him?

Because she was ashamed?

Because she...wanted to protect me?

3.
        So, yeah, I wanted a DNA test. But Connor didn't. Still doesn't. So I'm told. I've yet to talk to him directly. He very clearly wants nothing to do with me. That's why he didn't want me involved with GMG. He must think I'm just like dad. That I'll break things then walk away. Or maybe he's super angry at me because I got to grow up with dad and he didn't. Or maybe he just doesn't fucking care. He's lived his whole life not knowing (I assume) who his father is and he's made a success of himself in an competitive industry (yes, I did stalk him online; Scott stopped me after a very obsessive week) and he doesn't need and/or want any of the crazy publicity that is part and parcel of being K.C. Hall focused on him.
        Or his mother.
        That last one makes sense to me.
        The most sense
        It's both honest and childish. "Your dad didn't want anything to do with me so I don't want anything to do with you."
        Honest. Hurt.
        So…
        So, now what?
        So, now here I am working, working, working and Scott is doing his graphic novel and the Hall-iverse is about get going (So. Much. Preparation.) and everything professionally is hunky fucking dory and Scott and I are great, really great and Sophie's working, too and Miley has been tremendously helpful and the twins have taken over the bookstore in Wayside and Hannah (I hear from the twins) is madly in love in Wyoming and Josie, Kelsey and Sasha are flourishing with their company and Levan Walker and Stciky Kyler are in Europe so I don't have to worry about them and I'm about to co-host for a second week on *KinCaid Live!* And by all rights I should be happy, happy, so damn happy.
        But I'm not.
        Scott understands. As much as he can. Which is to say as much as both he and I can together. We're going to start a family in a few years. We've planned that much out. The Hall-iverse will take five years to build up to a point at which I can

step back from it and take time off from my career. Which is what I want to do when we have kids. Did I say that I'm jealous of Kalindra and Shawn? I think I did. Because I am.

So, why don't I just stop now, have kids and get back to acting later?

I'd like to blame Hollywood.

Youth and beauty and double standards and all that stuff.

I would really like to blame Hollywood.

But I can't.

The truth is I'm terrified of becoming a mom.

I'm terrified of becoming my mom.

And, now, I'm terrified of becoming my dad, too.

4.

Scott is, too. Terrified of becoming like his parents. Not his parents now. But his parents back when he was growing up. There was a "bad decade" as he calls it. From when he was twelve to when he got out of college. College allowed him to escape the worst of it. His brother, Sam, wasn't so lucky. Scott won't ever come out and say directly that Sam's history of mental illness is a result of that bad decade. But Sam will. And does. Not in a vindictive manner. In a "this is what happened and you have to accept it, Scott" manner.

Because I wasn't part of it, I can see it clearer than Scott can. Sam's right.

Because he wasn't part of it, Scott can see my parents clearer than I can.

So, yeah, we've put family off for a few years because of my work and his graphic novel but really so we can get to a better place with ourselves. A better place with our parents. No. A better place in which we are comfortable that we will not turn into our parents. No, that's not it either. Too wordy. Our concern is not that wordy. Our concern - our fear - is more direct than that. We don't want to hurt our kids like our parents hurt us. There. That's it.

We're still young. We have time to figure this out. So, that's what we're doing.

5.

Before we get to the show, I want to clear up how this all came out. This stuff with dad, Riley, Connor and Mo. It started when Mo died and Jon went through all of Mo's stuff. That's when Jon found the letters from Riley. He held onto them for a while. He tells me that he seriously considered never showing them to me or telling me about them. Had it not been for me talking about dad on Kincaid Live! and the subsequent digging into my past (which I really should have seen coming but I didn't - Sometimes I'm stupid.) by various entertainment reporters (cough bloodsuckers cough) he probably would have kept the letters to himself. But then the first report that mentioned an old friend of Riley, a friend she had confided in about the affair with dad, came out. That's when he decided to show me the letters.

A (not quite) tell-all book. My mom's journal. And now letters from my dad's spurned lover. My life is so damn Gothic I can't stand it. Once I got over the initial shock of this revelation, a few big questions came to mind.

One: is avoiding Riley why we moved around so much when I was young?

Two: did mom's discovery of dad's affair drive her over the edge?

Three: did Mo quote keep me under wraps unquote because he feared that Riley would seek me out at some point?

Four: Did dad send me to Mo knowing I might encounter Riley and her son while working in Hollywood?

Five: Why can't things just be simple for once in my life?

6.
Let's talk about something fun for a change. Luisa called me right after my first night co-hosting Kincaid Live! She loved that I talked about dad. She was concerned about how it would come off but she said I did a great job and she wanted me to know that I did a great job and, also, she said, "I just love that man." That man = Sal Kincaid. So, the next time I was in a meeting with Kincaid, I asked him if he'd be so kind as to speak to Luisa. He was very gracious about it. He spoke to Luisa at length. She's been watching him for decades. Who knew? Not me. Anyway, when Sal handed my phone back to me, he winked and said, "Next year, we're going to do the show from Luisa's Ranch."

Ummmm...what?

But, yeah, once that ball started rolling there was no stopping it. Kincaid and I and MDB had been meeting to talk about the feasibility of doing a second week of me co-hosting the show. Ratings for my initial week were good. I enjoyed doing it. Kincaid was willing to make it a yearly thing. K.C. Hall Week. Like Shark Week. But we were still figuring out if that was the best way to go. One week is an interesting novelty. A week every year could come off as gimmicky or stale or forced. So, we were talking about that. Maybe we should, maybe we shouldn't. Tossing ideas back and forth. Then Luisa and Kincaid spoke and Kincaid came back and said, "Let's do this at Luisa's Ranch. Get all the way out of Hollywood. Don't even have any guests from Hollywood at all for the entire week. Instead, we have more librarians - the ratings were great for the librarian segments - and other people from other jobs and places and lives that have absolutely nothing to do with Hollywood. That's what we need to do."

So, that's what we're doing. We're on Luisa's Ranch and we're talking to librarians and tourists. The librarians were selected via an online process. They were recommended by their peers. The tourists...that's a different story. Luisa's Ranch is in a part of the country where tour buses filled with people from the Midwest pass through on a regular basis. The tour buses go to Mt. Rushmore, Crazy Horse, Medora, ND (look it up), Devil's Tower and various state and national parks scattered through the great expanse of the intermountain west.

Kincaid's people have set up a new stop on the tour routes for a few of these tourist buses. One bus for each show. The people on the bus agreed to go on this "mystery stop" when they signed up for the tour. They know that they don't know where they're going. But they don't know that they might end up on national television. When Kincaid first proposed this wrinkle, he said to me, "You're good with the scripted material. But you're better at ad libbing. Let's play to that."

So, that is indeed what we are doing. Or are about to do. Tonight's the first night of K.C. Hall Week. We'll film the shows in the afternoon. That's when the natural light is the best. We start a couple of hours from now. A couple of short hours. To be fully honest, I'm more nervous than I thought I would be. But it's only five days and I have something big to look forward to at the end of the week: Scott's and my wedding reception.

Yup, Miley made our un-wedding legal and good by getting the rector to sign a license. California law allows for a wedding license to be…okay, I won't bore you with those details. Just imagine Miley given the task of making the impromptu wedding ceremony at the hospital fully legal and binding. Yes, she made that happen. But, of course, we still need to have our reception. The celebration of our wedding. Yes, it was supposed to be May First. But when K.C. Hall Week, the Sequel was set for Luisa's ranch, it just seemed natural to have the reception at the end of this week's production. Our friends and family wanted to be here for this unique event. Luisa was more than willing to house everyone in the bunkhouse, the main house and a few of the cabins. So, that's what we're doing. One big, happy mass of private and professional life all right here this week.

Big T used to talk about proper boundaries. Proper emotional boundaries. Proper boundaries between work and home. Proper boundaries between me and mom. This was back when mom was alive, of course. I choose to view this week as an experiment with boundaries. This will be either a dream come true or a nightmare waiting to happen. I can't tell which. And, if I'm honest with myself, I wouldn't have it any other way. How could I turn this down? A perfect storm of my life centered on Luisa's Ranch where my father is buried. Where would I rather be? Right? Where would I rather be instead of here with all the important people in my life and, also, hosting a great, fun gig?

7.

So, we'll start each show (after the monologue, of course) with one of the librarians. There are actually three librarians and two professors. College professors. Somehow they got mixed into the, uh, mix. Sal's team did that. They set up and ran the online vetting process for these guests and somehow stumbled across the professors when they did the interviews with the potential librarians. One is a professor of creative writing. That should be fun. Sal told me his team chose him precisely because of my interest in being a writer. Someday. Down the line. When everything in my life settles down. Please, don't laugh.

The other professor specializes in the Classics, specifically The Aeneid and Dido. She, the professor, has been digging around in the old, old Carthingian dirt and has a new book coming out that reportedly - I haven't read it yet, bad host, bad host! - provided a "startling new picture of the Queen of Carthage." Sal said one of his team heard me and Scott joking about giving Dido a new story and thought that would make a nice little segment. In other news, Sal's team is good, very good.

Also, during the shows there will be short cutaways from the main stage to Sal schmoozing the tourists as they, uh, tour Luisa's ranch. Those parts will be filmed earlier in the day and shown as we come in and out of commercial breaks. We'll film the show as if we're broadcasting it live. We aren't. But we'll do that anyway. Sal said that "keeps it real." When Sal said that, Marcus stared at him and said, "Stop trying to be one of the cool kids." Those two.

The ranch is now a "bee ranch" (that is, the grounds are devoted to harvesting honey; all the cattle have been moved south to another ranch with less intense winter weather). There is a large, circular driveway that is more than big enough to accommodate the size of the tour buses. It is usually used by the two midsize trucks Luisa has purchased to ship the honey down to Rapid City retail outlets.

Sal joking around with the usually white-haired tourists as they step off the bus will be good. That will play, as he likes to say. That will play. So, monologue, librarians and professors, then Sal and the tourists then bringing some of the tourists on stage to sit and chat with me then, in case we need material to fill out the hour, we have some pre-recorded bits done back in Hollywood regarding the set up for the Hall-iverse. More details on that later. Also, at some point I will walk through the other large field where the wedding reception/much delayed party will be held at the end of the week. That will serve as a nice cap to the end of the week.

So, that's it. Let's go.

8.

One more thing. Scott, the girls, Jayson and Jaxson are all driving up from Wayside with Alonsha. They have Alonsha on a trailer behind Missy Von Van and one other car following. Miley's car. Because she insisted. Don't ask. At last report, they were heading up from Durango along the western side of Colorado. Relocating Alonsha has become a bit of a thing. She's been in storage for several months ever since the company purchased the resort in Wayside. Storage = in the center of the bookstore draped in tarps as Jayson and Jaxson refurbish the interior. World's worst interior design show ever. Scott's told me stories but I can tell he's kept the worst details from me. Somehow I agreed to let the twins redo Hannah's bookstore once I purchased it and hired them to staff it. After their comic con circuit tour they had all sorts of ideas about "what to do with the space." Foolishly, I gave them carte blanche to implement their vision. I should not have done that. The pictures Scott has shared with me show more paint on the faces of the twins than on the actual walls. Also, the "laid back, cool lounge" vibe they were shooting for looks far more like a used furniture store than a bookstore. A bad, scraggly used furniture store. Also, they want to call the place "Jay Jays." Because of their names. To me "Jay Jays" sounds like a roadside dinner. Or a seedy bar. Or a barber that gives notoriously bad haircuts to kids. But Scott tells me I should go with it. "Let them have some fun," he says. Fine.

The important thing out of all of that is that I am here alone for most days this week. Well, Luisa is here, too, but I hardly see her as she's still working her honey business and setting up for the reception. Luisa keeps pushing to make the reception bigger and bigger. I prefer smaller, more intimate. But how can I refuse her? It's her ranch, after all.

So, there you go.

Time to go talk to Sal about tonight's show.

9.
　　Sal, Marcus and I meet in Sal's cabin which is the largest one on the ranch. Luisa insisted on that. I would have had she not. Being the largest, Sal's cabin has become the de facto headquarters of the show for this week. My cabin is across a small field tucked in some trees and is about half the size. So, no room for meetings, discussions, planning and such. Darn! All that happens in Sal's cabin. That's some good boundary-ing on my part if I do say so myself.

　　Marcus and Sal are sitting at the main table when I walk in. They have coffee mugs in hand. Sal hands me a mug as soon as I sit down. He says, "Today's flavor is Highland Grog from Dakota Coffee Company." We'll feature a number of products from local companies. And by local I mean "'the Dakotas." It's not so much "South Dakota" and "North Dakota" in common parlance out here as it is "the Dakotas." There's a pretzel company, a coffee company, Luisa's honey, a bookstore in Rapid City (no, not the one with the danishes) and, of course, Scott's comic bookstore which is now Sam's comic bookstore. That's where Scott and I met. Yes, those are hearts in my eyes as I think of this. Thank you for noticing.

　　I take a sip, sound my approval of the groggy flavor then say, "So, where are we?"

　　Marcus is attired in an L.A. Kings hoodie and clasping both hands around his mug. His thin, Los Angeles, perpetually warm blood is not handling the crisp chill of weather in the Dakotas this time of year. He makes it seem like we're living at Ice Station Zebra (you should watch that movie!). I point at the hoodie and say, "Are you wearing that ironically?"

　　He shoots me a confused look as he says, "I don't get it."

　　I say, "The L.A. Kings. Hockey. Ice. Cold. You've been cold all week." He stares at me dumbfoundedly. He's too cold to get the joke. Not that it's much of a joke but…anyway.

　　Sal chips in with, "That's not really what irony is." I shoot him an eye roll. He waves it off then launches into the notes for this afternoon as he looks at a sheet of paper, "My agent inside the tour has sent us some interesting information." Sal has a person riding along on the tour bus as it progresses up from Custer State Park to Rushmore then to Rapid City for an overnight then up to Luisa's the next day. One person for each tour bus that will head our way. Like an embedded reporter. Like a secret agent. Have I mentioned that Sal's team is good? By the way, Sal loves saying "my agent."

"It turns out we have an actual brain surgeon, retired, on the tour. A man named Arnold Holmes. He's traveling with his grandson who is in his early twenties. Apparently, Arnold's wife…"

"Dr. Holmes," I say as if greeting him for the first time. Then, trying out different pronunciations, "Dr. Holmes," I say melodramatically. Then, "Dr. Holmes, I presume." Then, "Yo, Dr. Holmes."

Sal shoots me an eye roll now then forges ahead, "…Arnold's wife died a couple of years ago and they had always said they would go to see Mt. Rushmore but never did. His job as a surgeon kept getting in the way. So, now that he's retired he's doing it. His grandson is accompanying him because his two kids, full on adults now, are worried about him traveling alone. So his son's son, Jake, is traveling with him." Sal takes a sip from his grog then looks up at me, "Think you can work with that?"

"Sure," I say, "the brain surgery jokes write themselves. And, yeah, the passing of his wife. I'd have to ease into that. Maybe avoid it all together. Maybe have both the grandson and the doctor together so I could shift back and forth between them. Does your agent," pause for melodramatic moment, "have a sense of how open the doctor would be about his life?"

"She thinks he'd take some warming up but, once he got going, he'd be entertaining in a somewhat unintentional way. He apparently has no qualms talking about the details of brain surgery. Just launches right into it when you ask him."

"Okay," I acknowledge. "What about the grandson? Will he just be a lump on the log or…"

"My agent says he's a quirky guy. Done some traveling on his own. Seems to really care for his grandfather. He could be a nice counterbalance to the young people as disrespectful of their elders meme that's out there."

I say, "That's not really what a meme is."

Sal holds back a smile. He knows I'm playing with him. He loves it. I love it. He goes on, "There's also a couple of other people that might be interesting on stage." Sal slides the top sheet of paper to the back of the thin stack of typed up notes then takes a moment to scan through the second page before saying, "Right. There's a woman who owns her own department store in a small town. Apparently, she got fed up with having to travel to the big city back in the day and decided to set up her own department store in her town. Natalie's. Natalie's Purveyor of Fine Goods. That could be interesting."

"Yup. I can play with that," I agree.

Sal goes on as he shuffles the third page to the top of the pile, "Ahh, here's a veteran, Army, who has decided to visit all the national parks. He lost his lower left leg in the desert." Sal flips the page over then back. "That's all it says. 'In the desert.' Hmmmmm."

I add, "Sometimes vets don't like opening up about those types of details." I met a few of dad's army buddies over the years. A couple of them had similar injuries. I'd sit and talk with them if they showed up at our place before dad got back from after school meetings. Damn, I haven't thought about that in a long, long…

My phone buzzes in my pocket. I confess I'm wearing a hoodie, too. But mine's far more stylish than Marcus'. Yes, I have a fancy hoodie and I like it. It's silky and slimming and shiny and fun. Not bulky and heavy and rumply like Marcus' black and white one. Mine's a silvery gold. Scott calls it my "space hoodie." A friend designed it for me. Someone MDb introduced me to. I pull the phone out of the koala pocket and look at the screen. I say to Sal because he's waiting for me to tell him, "MDB. She's got a script she wants me to look at." I look up at Sal. I know what he's thinking. "I know. I know. I'll tell her to wait until this week is over. But you know how she is." I tap my response into the phone then send the text.

Sal clears his throat then says, "You two are the oddest of couples. I never would have predicted you'd end up working together. Never."

"She's not like you think," I say. Marcus and Sal refuse to believe me. I add, "She's much worse than you think." That gets a laugh from both of them. "But she's also much better than you think. Seriously." Nope, they still don't believe me. Oh well.

MDB sends me a text back that reads, "Your Scott will like this one."

That's how MDB refers to Scott. As "my Scott." I tuck my phone back in the koala pocket (yes, I like saying "koala pocket") and refocus on Sal. He shuffles through his stack of notes once again then says, "Those three, four with the grandson, should give you plenty to talk about, yeah? You might not even get to all of them."

I nod and say, "Agreed." I look at Marcus hunched over his coffee mug like it's the source of all the warmth left in the world. I ask him, "How's the weather looking?"

He says through clenched teeth, "Good. Mostly. But there's a chance it will cloud up for the second half of the show. So, we might want to consider moving to the barn. The artificial lighting is much better there. The outdoor lights make you look…"

"Like a ghoul," I jump in. Because they do. My skin looks sickly yellow. I hate that. I add, "We could break between guests and shift into the barn quickly if we need to. Or maybe do a walk and talk with one of the guests. Natalie. Not the old surgeon. Or the vet with half a leg. Unless…well…what do you think, Sal?"

He muses silently for a moment then says, "Just cut to the barn after the break. You'd have to hustle over there but you can hustle. That way the guest can already be there. And if you're late getting there, we just film that. Show you on the golf cart going around the fields, waving at the horses as they munch the grass outside, avoiding the bee hives. That sort of thing. Play it up silly and fun."

Marcus says as he taps a note on his phone, "Okay, I'll make sure both sets are good to go and have the golf cart in place. The bus will be here ninety minutes before the broadcast starts. That will give you and them time to meet a bit. Also for Sal to warm them up and show them around. So, that's it for now. You good with your monologue?"

"I am, I am," I say because I am. After last year's nervousness, I'm feeling much more at ease opening the show. Especially the first night. Half the monologue will simply be telling people what guests will show up. Then I'll mention the reception at the end of the week. Then make a few jokes about myself. Done and done.

"Okay then," says Sal as he stands up. "Off we go."

I exit Sal's cabin and head to the main house where the stylist, Greg, has set up in one of the first floor bedroom suites. Greg has been working with Sal for a decade or so now. He's good. This week he's doing my hair and my outfits. The usual wardrobe person couldn't make the trip to the Dakotas so Greg is taking over. He said, "You'll be cowgirl chic all week, honey." Then he laughed. He's got a great laugh.

As I head to the main house I take a moment to look out at the surrounding valley. It's stunning. Even with the fields and trees free of their summer greenery and preparing for winter, the landscape is still beautiful. Mountains in the distance. The clear, crisp, enlivening air. There's a sense of solidity in this part of the world. A sense of permanence that L.A. just does not have. I close my eyes and breathe in deeply. Yeah, when Miley gets here we'll have to do a meditation down by the pond.

As I start walking again, my phone buzzes once more. It's another text from MDB. A follow up to her last one. This one reads, "It's got sasquatch in it."

Oh, no. Scott's going to want to read this script for sure.

10.

As I get close to the main house, I see Clara walk by with an armload of boxes. Black Hills Bee HIves boxes. This is Clara Thompson, daughter of the man who killed my father. She's been working here with Luisa for a few months now. Ever since she turned eighteen. She doesn't see me at first as her sight is blocked by all the boxes she's carrying very carefully from the back of a golf cart into the main house side kitchen entrance. She's having trouble opening the door so I call out to her, "I'll get that for you."

I can see (or do I imagine it?) her arms and hands tense up when she hears my voice. I step around her, swing open the outer screen door then ease open the inner wooden door with my toe as I say, "Hey, Clara. Is that you? How are you? It's me, K.C."

I haven't seen Clara since I briefly met her in Wayside. That's when she ran away from home to bring a bouquet of flowers to me. A bouquet of flowers that my dad would have brought back from the convenience store to Luisa had Clara's father not shot and killed him. The bouquet should have gone to Luisa but Clara couldn't find an address for her. So she brought them to me instead. It was a bittersweet gesture. One I'll never forget.

I haven't had much contact with her since then. She and Jayson have had an on again/off again long distance romance/flirtation/friendship dynamic going for a while now. Last I heard through Sophie, it was in the off again stage. Sophie is the one who tells me these things. The twins don't reveal much about themselves to me. I'm fine with that. Trust me, I'm fine with that. Sophie, even though she's just a year or so older, mother hens the twins somewhat. She has since they all grew up together in Wayside. She even manages to do that all the way from Hollywood which is where she is these days following up on her third place finish on Hollywood Boot Camp.

Spending some time with the twins is why Sophie wanted to be part of the drive Alonsha to the ranch road trip. Miley tagged along as she and Sophie have become fast friends over the past year. After all, they live just down the

23

hallway from each other in the new building. Scott wanted to drive Missy Von Van with Alonsha because he doesn't quite trust the twins to do so without having an accident. Neither do I. It's not that they're irresponsible. They're just young. And Alonsha is important. Very important. In a way that I can't put into words. Especially since Benny passed.

But I can't talk about that now. I have to talk to Clara now. The first thing I notice (is this a good thing or a bad thing?) about Clara is that she's in much better shape now than when I first met her. The muscles in her arms are more defined and the soft doughiness she had about her torso is gone. That's both the fitness fanatic and the actron/writer's brain in me noticing this. Those parts of my brain are always taking notes, keeping an eye on details that might help me with a role or story somewhere down the line.

Clara doesn't respond to me until she's inside and puts the boxes down on the large, wooden side table. There's three other stacks of boxes there. She brushes cardboard box detritus off her work shirt. I can tell it's her work shirt because it's denim and has a nametag on the upper left chest. The nametag is sewn on (that's Luisa for ya) and reads, "Clara T." Clara looks at me for a half-second then stares at the floor as she says, "Hi, Ms. Hall." Pause. "Or is it Mrs. Langle now?" She looks up with a look of genuine curiosity/did I just fuck that up on her face.

I say, "It's not Ms. Hall. Or Mrs. Langle. Technically, it *is* Mrs. Langle. But I want you to call me K.C. Please."

Clara stares back down at the floor as she says, "Okay." Then very tentatively, "Hello, K.C."

She obviously is nervous around me. Anyone with a half a brain could see that. But I don't know why. Is this the same girl who ran away from home just to present me with a bunch of flowers? That's hard to believe right now. She seems so withdrawn and meek as she stands in front of me. I wonder if... "Has anything happened with your dad?"

The words are out of my mouth before I can stop them. Stupid, K.C.! You went right there, didn't you? You had to. Why? Why not let Clara interact with you without bringing up the massive elephant in the room. But, nope you couldn't do that, could you?

Clara looks up with eyes wide as saucers when I ask my question. We look at each other in silence for several moments. I don't know what to say. She doesn't know what to say. Finally, I whisper, "I'm sorry. I didn't mean it like that. It's just…you seem different somehow."

For some inexplicable reason all of Clara's defenses fall away and she opens up to me. But only for a moment. She says, "It's not dad. It's mom. She's been using a lot lately. Especially since I left and came to work here. That's what I hear from Sherry. My social worker."

Such a sad story is so few words. I hesitate for a second then I take a step forward to give Clara a squeeze on the shoulder. But she sidesteps me and rushes back outside as she mumbles, "I'vegottoworknowMsHallgoodtoseeyoubye."

11.

It's a bit later now. Greg has me all ready for the show - hair, makeup and outfit-wise. I'm wearing a long, fringey, black suede skirt over basic black cowboy boots and a simple but snazzy white, blousy top. He wanted me to wear a black suede cowboy hat when I first walked out on stage but I tried it on and said, "Nope, too much."

I'm on the set going over my monologue and getting a feel for the stage itself. I like to familiarize myself with the space I'm working in as much as I can before the cameras turn on. That's a little more difficult when I'm doing movies and TV shows as the sets change up with different scenes. With the talk show it's much easier. I sat in the chair behind the desk and adjusted it a half-dozen times to make sure it's just right. I checked and rechecked my marks on the stage for the monologue. I checked and rechecked my mic pack. I've spoken with the crew. I know most of them from last year but not all. I like to introduce myself to the crew, get to know them as much as I can. They probably have a harder job this week than I do making this all work on a ranch in the Dakotas instead back in a Hollywood studio.

I confess that Clara's reaction has thrown me a little. I wanted to comfort her when she told me about her mom but then she took off. I sought out Luisa after Greg got me ready. But I was told she was out at the hives supervising something or other. The fields with the boxy hives (you know the ones, we've all seen them on some mystery show or another that has an episode with someone dying from multiple bee stings) are about a quarter mile away from the main house. I didn't want to risk getting messed up making that short hike. It's down a small, packed dirt path after all. Greg would kill me if I messed up his work. And rightly so. He's got to get Sal and the guests ready, too. Sal he can do beforehand but the guests from the tour bus he'll only have a few minutes with before they go onstage so he's focused on getting ready for that. That's why I went in a bit earlier than I would have had we been doing this back in Hollywood.

Everything is different back in Hollywood.

As I stand once again center stage and walk through my monologue half-whispering/half silently remembering my lines a thought pops into my head for the hundredth time in the past couple of hours, *Not everyone wants a hug or a shoulder squeeze, K.C. Some people just want to be left alone with their pain.* It's a thought that I don't quite believe. Someone said it to me years ago. I think it was in high school. Maybe middle school. A teacher maybe. Or the school receptionist. Someone like that. The details of the incident are blurry. Who was involved. What was the matter. I can't recall any of that now. But I do recall that line. *Not everyone wants a hug...*

That's not me. I'm a big hugger. I'm probably an over-hugger. That comes from mom not being a hugger. I can count on one hand the times my mom hugged me. So, as I grew up, I sought out hugs from others. But I was smart enough to do so judiciously. To get hugs in hug-appropriate scenarios. Because there was that one time when that one school play director hugged me for just a little bit too long and it got creepy. Thankfully, that didn't turn into anything. I think he was more embarrassed than I was. At least, that's what I want to think. That did teach me to keep my radar up which has served me well ever since. There are a lot of creepy people who want to over hug young actresses in Hollywood. So cliche. So creepy. So true.

So, I find myself wondering how many hugs has Clara gotten from her mom? My guess is not many. But maybe she's got someone else in her life to give her hugs? Do social workers give hugs? How could they not? Working with kids in tough situations it seems like you'd have to be a hugger. But maybe they aren't allowed to. Maybe there's some regulation that stops them from...

Okay, I need to focus on my monologue. I need to clear my head. Let's go for a little walk. Just not on the dirt paths. Stick to the gravel covered paths.

12.

I walk to a small alcove (that's not the proper term but I don't know the proper term for "alcove of trees outside in nature" so I stick with just "alcove") along one of the gravel paths that extends away from the field with the stage. There's so much of Luisa's ranch that I have yet to explore. I've only been here a couple of times before and those times I stayed mainly around the, uh, main house. I pull out my phone and give Scott a call. I should have done this earlier. He's the world's greatest expert on stopping K.C. Hall from overthinking things. But I didn't think to do that as I was very busy overthinking the whole incident with Clara. See how that works? You get caught up in worrying and forget what works to help you stop worrying.

My call goes to message instantly. I thought that might happen. The reception has been spotty on their road trip. They (i.e. Miley) planned a route that takes them through the mountains as much as possible. They all wanted to "go the back way" and see "the real sights" on this trip. So, no big interstate roads if they can help it. Which means smaller roads winding through the mountains and the backcountry. Which means spotty phone service. Scott's been good about checking in whenever they stop for the night. He's been good because he knows I'd kill him if he didn't. And, yeah, he loves me so that's why he checks in, too. But mostly because I'd kill him if he didn't.

I say into the phone, "Hey, hon. Just thinking of you surrounded by all those younguns. I hope they aren't driving you too crazy. And that you aren't driving too much. See what I did there? Give me a call when you can. Ohhh, right. I need to tell you that MDB has a sasquatch script for me. Yup. Sasquatch."

Then I hang up. Ha! That will peak his interest. He swears when he was ten years old and out with his boy scout troop that he saw a sasquatch across a small lake. It was there for just a few seconds before disappearing back into the woods but he hasn't seen anything like it since then. He didn't tell anyone until a number of years later. And, of course, those friends laughed at him. Like people do when things they don't understand or can't explain come up. So, Scott doesn't talk much about sasquatch but he does talk about it with me. We make jokes about it now. Because, well, a big, hairy, human-like animal that lives in the woods. How could you not joke about that? But when he first told me about seeing what he saw we didn't joke about it. That was actually one of our first tender moments as a couple. He opened up about this weird thing and I listened and asked questions. I took him seriously. I wanted to know how the sighting made him feel. I wanted to know what he felt about it now that he was older and knew more.

I walk a little farther down the path past the alcove very deliberately counting my steps and counting my breaths. This will help me focus. This will help me clear my head. It does. I've turned around and am about halfway back to the set when my phone buzzes. I pull it out of my koala pocket (I've draped my space hoodie over my shoulders just in case a bird tries to poop on me) and am surprised when I see it's Thad who sent me a text. I haven't heard from him in a few months. He and Miley tried turning their friends with benefits thing into a more serious thing for a while. But that ended up not working out. Thad took a month or so off from our weekly, online meditations but then he came back. Neither Miley nor he spoke about what happened and I let it be. Because Scott told me to let it be. And, this time, I listened.

Thad's text reads, "Hey, K.C. Hope you're good. I know you're in the Great Midwest somewhere now but I'd like to talk to you when you have time. If that's when you get back, that's cool. Nothing pressing. I just need some advice."

Hmmmmmmmm. I text back, "Let's do lunch when I get back. I'll have Miley set that up. If that works for you."

He fires back, "Let's keep Miley out of this for now. If you don't mind. I can swing by your place or your offices sometime when you get back when she's not around. I know this is a little weird but I swear it's not a bad thing."

Double Hmmmmmmmm. I send back, "Okay. I'll have to wait until I get back to see what my schedule is like. So, next week sometime? Does that work for you?"

He sends a thumbs up emoji. I send one back.

13.

Marcus is on set when I get back. He comes right up to me and says, "So, I know this is a sore subject but I've got some interesting news. Well, potentially interesting." He looks me dead in the eye as he says the next few words, "Mighty and maggie." He stops there to gauge my reaction. I cringe only a little. He adds, "I know they didn't do too well."

I quip, "Everyone knows they didn't do too well." Oh, wait. You don't know this yet. "Mighty and Maggie" is how Marcus refers to my two projects from last year: Mighty Martie and Zenda the Magnificent. "Mighty Martie" is the very bad name they finally chose for my giant ape woman movie. It's a play off the Mighty Joe Young movies from way back and the remake with Charlize Theron from a while back. My character's name was Martie. The name was supposed to be a call back to those movies and, also, a female empowerment thing. But instead it ended up just being crap. A crappy title and a movie to go with it. Not that the movie is actually crappy. I think it's a decent film. The version that came out in theaters. I think the director's cut is even better. The plot is tighter. There are a couple of added scenes that really pull it all together. Scenes that the studio insisted be cut from the theatrical release. Because reasons. Marketing and focus group reasons. Whatever.

"Maggie" refers to my character "Zenda the Magnificent" in the Curated Worlds spin off, "L.A.ser Boy," that I did with Gyrin, MDB's son. That was a six episode streaming show. Josie Steans played the main character in the Curated Worlds movie. L.A.ser Boy was a minor character in the movie. Gyrin played that role in the spin off show. I played L.A.ser Boy's superhero mentor/love interest. The show got some good reviews but not many eyeballs. That is, not many people watched it. This was blamed on making a minor character from the movie the focus of the show. "People want more of Alva. Not more of L.A.ser boy. Wait until the sequel movie comes out before you take a trip to this universe again." Yes, that is the review that sticks out for me. Because, honestly, it makes sense. I didn't think of it before taking the role but it makes sense. You don't make a Robin movie. You make a Batman movie. That was the fatal flaw.

Marcus says gently, hesitantly, "They're trending up this week. It's a slight but definite uptick for both of them. Rentals and watches." I look Marcus in the eye. I don't have to say anything. He goes on, "Sal thinks it's because people think you'll poke fun at them this week on the show. That's one of the things people like about you as a host. How you make fun of yourself. So, Sal thinks they want to be in on the joke when you do that this week." Marcus pauses then adds, "But maybe…" Then he shrugs.

I know what he means. But maybe Mighty and Maggie have finally found their audiences. Or the audiences have found them. Maybe they're slow burn projects that have finally at last been discovered by the public. Especially the director's cut of Mighty Martie. Because it is genuinely better than the theatrical release. Because Shelli had the right vision for the project and the studio should have trusted her but didn't. I want to believe this. But… "Maybe Sal's right," I say. "Maybe people are watching them ironically."

"That's not really what ironically means," Marcus says then chuckles at his own joke before adding, "Sure. Sal's been around awhile. He may very well be right. But if he's not and people do like those projects and then you stand up on stage this week and really make fun of them then…"

"…then I'd be shooting myself in the foot," I say. Because he's right. So, the question becomes… "You want me to back off making fun of Mighty and Maggie?" I've gone over my monologues with Marcus and Sal. They know what I'm planning on saying. I have several exoskeleton jokes planned. And pew, pew laser jokes. And tight spandex jokes. And… you get the idea.

Hmmmmmm. I need to think on this. I say to Marcus as I look at the time on my phone, "I'll go over my monologue. See how I can soften those jokes."

Marcus says, "Good, perfect." Then, "I'm off." He walks towards the barn, I assume, to check on the set there that we will switch to halfway through tonight's show. I center myself on my mark on the temporary stage and once again mentally run through my opening remarks.

14.

I'll start out with a simple greeting and thanks then list off the guests that will appear this week with some jokes about the viewers not knowing a single one of them. I tie the librarians for this week back to the librarians we had on the show last year and, yes, to Stack Life (soon to be airing its fourth season, thank you very much; Mac Waid will be here at the end of the week to talk about that, love him) then I segue from that to Mighty Martie. See how that works: greeting, guests, last year's librarians, this year's librarian, the library show I'm part of and then the movie that I'm part of. It all ties together rather nicely. One thing leads to the next.

Now, I was going to say, "Mighty Martie…not so mighty, apparently" as a way to set the audience up for me to make more jokes about the giant ape woman movie. Jokes using turns of phrase like, "the beauty is a beast…of a movie," "you can't make an old ape do new tricks," and "sometimes you just need to get away from it all…which is how I'm feeling on stage right now." That last phrase would be paired with a clip from the movie in which I see the betrayal of my best friend and lover then fall off the cliff and disappear under the roiling waves never to be seen again. I planned on saying, "So, sequel?" and shrug my shoulders really high up, hold my hands out palms up and twist my face up like a kid asking for something that she knows she shouldn't ask for. The point I wanted to make was, "Ooops, not a good movie so I know that the public doesn't want a sequel but maybe if I act cute enough I could get one." It's hard to describe the tone. It comes off far better as an interaction with the studio audience than it does on paper.

That joke assumes the movie is truly bad and, of course, it doesn't deserve a sequel. But maybe there's something there I can play with. The "So, sequel?" question. If I put that up front instead of saving it for the end that could work. I put it up front, make a light-hearted joke about the movie along the lines of "I hear there are some people who didn't like this movie." Then stare at the camera like "Really? You didn't like it? I worked my ass off in an exoskeleton and you're telling me you didn't like it?" A bit in the face of the imagined audience out there in the viewing world who didn't like Mighty Martie.

I start to riff. If I go with that then I can change the "So, sequel?" question from a silly kid/aren't I so darn cute thing into a more serious "let's see who wants a sequel" thing. I can even jokingly ask, "Sequel or no sequel?" to play off the "Deal or No Deal" game show from a few years back. It's important to tie the monologue jokes back to phrases or situations that the audience (most likely) has heard of/knows about. That way the collective memory of the audience, all those neurons firing at once as they tune into the show and take in the same material all at the same time in exactly the same way (if I do my job well enough) and there's a burst of laughter energy that spreads across the nation at night when the country is either falling asleep or already in bed.

That's my theory, at least. I told it to Scott when we were lolling around in bed one morning. He said, "Hon, I love you but that's ridiculous."

"No, it's not." Pause and scowl. "You're ridiculous."

"There's no such thing as laughter energy," he said.

"People laugh. Yes? You agree to that?"

"Of course, yes, people laugh," he gives me an eye roll.

"And that requires muscles contracting and breathing and probably some chemicals or hormones or dopamine or something like that in the brain, in the neurons."

The look on his face lets me know that he highly regrets telling me about the science articles he reads on the regular. He sighed then said, "Yes, all that is generally true but…"

I cut him off, "So, muscles, breathing, neurons, hormones. Imagine ten thousand people doing all that at exactly the same moment when they watch the show. Laughing with all that going on. All those little brain sparks, muscle sparks, laughter sparks. That's what I mean by laughter energy." I am so proud of myself when I say this.

Scott is not as convinced by my theory as I am. Sometimes he's stupid. This is one of those times. He sees he's not going to change my mind so he diverts the conversation, "Only ten thousand? You're only going to make ten thousand people laugh? I thought the audience was in the millions for Kincaid Live!?"

"That's just one of the early jokes. It takes a few minutes to warm up the audience. Since there are a lot of people like you out there. Un-funny people. People who don't understand laughter energy. It takes a few minutes to get past their defenses, make them relax, get them to turn off their I'm a teacher and I can't joke about stuff algorithm and to turn on their laughter algorithm and just relax a little bit."

I stare at him. He stares at me. He has nothing to say. So, I continue, "By the time I do that, there will be millions of little laughter energy explosions going on out there across the nation. Then the laughter explosions will turn into laughter fireworks which will light up the sky with invisible laughter aurora boring atlases."

"You mean 'aurora borealis.'"

"Yes, Scott. I know. That was a joke."

I stare at him. He stares at me. This time he says, "Sorry, I didn't have my laughtron-o-meter turned on. I'll do that now." He holds a hand to the side of his head and pretends to twist a knob. Then he says with a very robotic voice, "There. Now I will comprehend your very advanced humor messages."

I stare at him. He stares at me. Neither of us say anything. Then he says, "I'll go get you some coffee now."

"That's a very good idea," I say as he walks out of the bedroom.

Okay, back to the present moment which is me rehearsing my monologue which I'll actually say a little bit into the future as I talk about a movie and TV show that I made last year but have only been available to the public for a month or so. So, yeah, the past, present and future are blending together for me. Just then one of the audio techs tests the speakers on the far side of the stage with a burst of music. It's one of the jazz standards that Sal's band often plays. I asked about it last year after I'd heard it a few times. It's from Art Blakey and the Jazz Messengers. It's a short part of a song called "Moanin."

This music clip and my temporally jumbled up sense of time does something odd in the center of my brain. I feel like I'm back on stage that first night last year and like I'm standing right here, right now rehearsing my monologue for tonight's show and like it's already tonight's show and the lights are on me and I'm doing the monologue already before the live, tourist bus audience. This moment lasts only for a split second then I snap back to the actual present when the music clip cuts out. There's silence on the stage. The sudden absence of music accentuates how quiet it is. That's when I see the new version of my monologue in my head. No. I don't see it. I know it. Just like that. Boom. I know what I'm going to say.

The audio tech comes out to adjust the life-size cardboard stand-ins for the band. The band couldn't make the trip. Sal never asks them to go with the show when he takes it on the road. "That allows them to stay at home and go play gigs in the area. Get back to their roots of performing in truly live settings," he explained to me one time. "On the show they're a canned band. In the club is when they really let loose." I made a mental note to go see them sometime when they're in the club. But I haven't done that yet. Because…. because life.

The audio tech sees me as he walks out from the back to fiddle with the cardboard stand-ins. He says, "Ohh, sorry. I didn't realize anyone was out here."

"It's all good. Just running through it all one last time," I say. He nods and stands in front of the cardboard stand-ins then moves one slightly to one side and another slightly to the other side. I ask, "All good over there?"

He (I think his name is Colin) says, "Yeah. I'm just being a perfectionist. I want the sound to come out of the speakers behind the stand-ins as clearly as possible." He shrugs when he turns to look back at the stand-ins. "I'm sure I'm the only one who'll notice it but…well…" Another shrug.

I understand. I say, "Yeah, I hear you. But you have to do it. Because you know that's what needs to be done."

He points at me as he keeps his eyes on the stand-ins, assessing their placement, "That's exactly it." He reaches out and slides one of the stand-ins a fraction of an inch to one

36

side. Then he claps his hands together, waves at me and walks backstage.

15.

Greg's come to do last minute touch ups on my makeup and outfit. He tsks at me then says, "I knew I should have saved you for last. Can't sit still for one simple hour, can you."

"It was over two hours. And you know it," I say back at him as he does something magical with my hair.

"One hour, two hours. You just need to stop messing up my work. Here, sit still and be quiet." He starts doing more things with my hair. I do as he says. Note: not even Scott can get me to sit still and be quiet. But Greg, like all good stylists and makeup people, has a special power that way. They'd be really good kindergarten teachers. They'd be able to put snotty, grubby kids in time out with no problem.

Greg tsks some more and digs deep into the roots of my hair near the back. I stay silent. I know this is going to take a few more minutes. He says, "Did you actually go roll in the dirt? What happened back here?" I do not respond. I know better than that at this point in my career.

Instead, I let my thoughts drift back over the past year. Back to the end of the first K.C. Hall Week on Kincaid Live! Shawn Muze was my last guest on the last night. His appearance was supposed to coincide with the online release of the first three chapters of his book. His book was, yes, about his life and career in Hollywood. It was strongly rumored (not by him, by the usual media gadflies) to be a tell-all book, one that named names and cast many people still in the biz in a very bad light.

But that didn't happen. The publishing company got cold feet. Or someone important in the publishing company did. I'm still not sure about those details. Long story short, when Muze was on the show the chapters weren't released. He said to viewers, "For legal reasons the publisher and I have agreed to rework my book as a roman a clef. That way I can say everything I want to say and not get sued." He played the line for laughs. He got a lot of them. But I could tell that he was disappointed with the whole scenario. Big time. I heard from Kalindra a little while later that Shawn strongly considered releasing his book on his own. Maybe starting a publishing company for the sole reason of publishing his book and other books about what really goes on in Hollywood. But she said she talked him off that ledge. She said she told him that she doesn't want Lucius to get targeted when he grows up. She said she told Shawn, "You know someone will do that. You know they will. And you won't be here to defend him." So, yeah, Shawn didn't start a publishing company. He agreed to go ahead with the roman a clef version of his life story.

Roman a clef - the truth thinly disguised as fiction. Hmmmmmmm. I wonder what the first, famous roman a clef was? I'll have to look that up. Or, better yet, save that one for when Miley is bugging me with too many questions and tell her to look that up. Scott did tell me later that night, the night Shawn made his announcement on the show, that roman a clef translates literally as "novel with a key." How very French of the, uh, French. Ha. Miley. Depthen. Ha.

Greg snaps me back to the present moment as he stands in front of me and tells me to turn my head this way then that way then back then back again then he says, "Okay, Miss Thing, you only have a few minutes before you go on stage. Don't go for a hike or whatever you did earlier. Stay right here and continue to look fabulous." Greg sweeps out of the little shed that serves as my prep room for this week. A little space for me to get ready before I go out on stage. When I told Scott about it he called it my "she shed." I did not like this. "Man cave." "She shed." No. Just no. I said, "No, it's my super shed. It's like Superman using phone booths back in the day to switch from being Clark Kent. I go into the shed, switch from being little, ole me and turn into K.C Hall, Hollywood star then I go out on stage."

He said, "Like Beyonce and Sasha Fierce."

"Exactly. K.C. Fierce."

"Or Garth Brooks and Chris Gaines."

"No. Not Chris Gaines. Because I will never have a soul patch."

"Do you spin around like Linda Carter and turn into Wonder Woman?" Nerd alert. Scott just went full comic book guy.

"No, I don't spin. I do magic karate kicks." That made Scott laugh which made me laugh which is what I needed.

But that was a few days ago. Now it's just me in here waiting for the production assistant to come get me so I'll be ready to step into the spotlight.

Breathe. Just breathe.

Ki-yah!

That was a magic karate kick executed in my imagination.

Ki-yah!

That felt good.

Ki-yah! Ki-yah! Ki-yah!

16.

      The sunlight is at the perfect angle when I walk out on stage. The smaller than the Hollywood studio live audience section is off to my right as I look out. I see Marcus and Sal off to the left. There are two stationary cameras, one fewer than in the studio. But there is one man with a steady cam strapped on which we'll use for the bit when I leave this stage and go to the barn. I do see the leading edge of the clouds Marcus was worried about off to the south. I know that the first librarian guest is in the wings as I chatted with her briefly just moments ago and now it's time.

      "Hello, America, it's me, K.C. Hall once again. Yup. I'm baaaackkk!" I say that like Randy Quaid's character says his line in Independence Day when he sacrifices himself to blow up the alien mothership. Love that movie. I have no idea if anyone in the audience will make the connection. But then I see a few chuckles from the tour bus audience. Good. They did get it. Ki-yah!

      I run through the guest list. You already know that so I'll skip over it. Oh, I haven't mentioned musical guests. That's because there are no musical guests. No one wanted to come out to the Dakotas to do the show. Well, no one that Sal reached out to. I suspect that I could have gotten a band or two to make the trip. But Sal likes to be in charge of the musical guests. Seeing as he's letting me take over his show, I figure he can keep the musical guests for himself.

      I walk over in the direction of the stand-ins and pretend that they are the real band and I'm having a conversation with the band leader, Keeley J., just as Sal does every night when the show is in non-K.C. Hall Week mode. This little bit was a suggestion from Sal. It's good. The whole unheard conversation allows me the freedom to say pretty much anything I want. Well, not anything. Anything PG rated. I promised Sal and Marcus that I wouldn't swear (cough as much cough) this year at all. We'll see how that goes.

      I ask the cardboard Keeley J. how he and the band are doing. I pull a face as I "listen" to pretend Keeley J.'s anwer. Then I say, "Ohhhh, so you stepped right in it? Well, this is a ranch so you have to watch where you're going." Drum roll, rim shot. Thank you, I'll be here all week. No. Really. I'm doing this all week long. I ask the fake band, "What do you think of this view, huh? Isn't it fantastic?" I know the cameras will show the truly stunning view south from the stage. The mountains in the distance. The thin (but growing) line of clouds. The sweeping grass fields extending out as far as the eye can see. Then the camera cuts back to me as I react to the fake band once more, "What? No. Ahhh, I think the nearest Starbucks is about a hundred miles away." Yes, Starbucks did buy some ads this week. We're going to riff on how far away we are from one as part of that. I add, "There's a whole urn of fresh coffee in the barn. We'll go there in a little bit. See the horses, stay dry as that storm comes in."

Again, I pretend to listen to a question from the band. "The clouds? What are they? Is that what you're asking? Well, they're clouds. And they look like rain clouds so that's why we'll... What's rain? Is that your question? Boy, you have not traveled outside of southern California, have you?"

That's the pivot point. I turn to camera one and say, "That's what we'll be doing this week, just to be clear. Getting out of California, away from Hollywood and out here to the center of the country. Or, close enough at least. Apologies to Centerville, OH. I know you like to claim that title. But when you include Hawaii and Alaska then Belle Fourche - which we're not too far away from - is actually the geographic center of the United States. So, sorry Centerville." I hold a hand to my ear as if I'm being told something by the producers. Then I say breathlessly, "Oh, my apologies. Apparently, it's not Centerville that claims to be the geographic center of the United States. It's some spot in the middle of Kansas." I twist my face up then turn to Sal and Marcus as I ask, "Why didn't we go there?"

Sal and Marcus bend in and whisper to each other then stand back up as Sal shouts out to me, "We couldn't afford the tickets." Drum roll, rim shot.

I say right into the camera, "Okay then. In just a moment we're going to sit down with a charming woman who works at a library to talk about, well, library stuff. No, don't fall asleep just yet. I promise you'll never think about libraries the same way ever again. But before that I need to ask an important question. An important question about one of my movies. Feedback. I need feedback. Honest feedback. Since I'm not in Hollywood right now, this is my chance to get it."

I look into the camera and hold it for a couple of seconds, take a deep breath then say as if I'm talking to a close friend about a delicate situation, "We need to talk about Martie. Mighty Martie."

There are a few polite claps from the tourist bus audience but that's it.

I cringe but continue, "Yes. Mighty Martie, the giant ape woman movie that I played the lead in. It came out a few months ago and let's just say that it was not a giant at the box office."

There are a couple of polite claps. More cringing.

"But," I hold up a triumphant finger to emphasize this point, "the numbers for its first week out on digital - rentals and purchases - are strong, are good, are way better than expected given how poorly it fared in the theaters. Normally, a movie wouldn't be released on digital so soon after it was in theaters but Covid changed all that and since Martie didn't do all that well," I mug for the camera in a self-deprecating manner, "and I am hosting this very popular late night show this week, the powers that be decided to rush little Martie back out into the public domain, so to speak. And, as I just said, the numbers for it are better than expected."

I pause for a moment here with my hands at waist level, parallel to the ground and fingers spread. It's like I'm playing a game of freeze tag and I just was tagged. I hold the pose for several seconds while staring out at the audience. Then, as the tension builds to a slightly uncomfortable point, I say, "Sequel or no sequel? That," I drop my hands and turn to camera two with a smug look, "is the question."

Then I relax, smile and clasp my hands behind my back as I continue, "Seriously, that is my question. I think Mighty Martie, despite its noted lack of financial success at the box office, is a quality movie. I'm not saying it's the Godfather or Citizen Kane or Giant but it is a solid story about a giant ape woman." I turn to Sal and Marcus with finger pistols and say,

43

"See what I did there? Giant. Giant ape woman. That was good. Go on. You can laugh at that. It's okay."

Sal and Marcus stare back at me stone faced and shaking their heads.

I take a step towards the band stand-ins and say to fake Keeley J. in a more pleading tone of voice, "Come on. You got that, right? Giant. Giant ape woman. That was good."

The whuh-waaaahhhh of a sad trombone sound comes from the band. You know the one. The sound of cartoon failure and rejection. The sound when the character (sometimes literally) falls flat on her face. I did not expect this. It catches me off guard. It's perfect and hilarious and I can't help but genuinely laugh. Perfect, perfect, perfect. I'll have to thank whoever did that after the show.

I once again turn back to camera one and say, "I'm not sure how we'll get the feedback from everyone out there. Twitter or Insta or Tiktok or whatever your preferred social media messaging service is. Maybe the show's website can have a..." I look over at Sal and Marcus. They are pointing fingers at each other in mock anger like you go do that, no you go do that, no that's your job, no that's your job. I turn back to camera one, "We'll figure something out. It can't be that complicated. And, ahhh, we'll have results...of some kind...by the end of the week. Mighty Martie. Sequel or No Sequel. Okay. After the break stay tuned for more than you ever wanted to know about the secret courier system that sends library books across the country and around the world."

17.

"Welcome back, everybody," I say as I'm sitting behind the "rustic country" desk. It has fake brands burned into its sides. A woman named Heddy Standel is sitting to my right. She gives a little wave to the audience. Some of her friends and family members are sitting out there. They, of course, cheer for her. She's a middle aged woman in a dark brown pantsuit with a matching dark brown (chocolate, let's call it chocolate) top that has a bright print design on it. It takes me a second to realize that the bright images are books. Small, bright, partially open books are splashed across her torso. That's fun.

I lock eyes with her and study her face for a moment. Her skin color is almost exactly like mine. Slightly more than tan. Slightly dark. A light mocha. Yeah, I've never come across a good term to describe my skin tone. Whatever I come up with it always feels like I'm trying to avoid saying, "Hey, I'm part black." But I'm not. Not avoiding that, that is. See, this is already awkward. Back to the show. Her hair is a delicately frizzed medium brown streaked with light brown bordering on blonde. Backstage she told me it's a dye job. She told me this as she gently touched the side of my head right where my hair starts and said in a very grandmotherly manner, "Mmmm Hmmmmmm." I'm not sure what she meant by that but I felt all warm and tingly inside. Sisters of the hair. It was good.

All this flashes through my head as I introduce Heddy and she gives another wave and there is another burst of cheering and applause from her family and friends. When it dies down I turn to Heddy and say, "You've got quite the fan club out there."

"That's my boys," she says as proud as she can. "My two sons and my husband. They came all the way here to see me tonight."

"Let's start there, Heddy. Where are you from and where is your library?" I ask.

She says, "Lincolnton, North Carolina. It's twenty miles outside Asheville right in the Smoky Mountains. Small town, right around five thousand and it's got a great little library.

That's where I work. Chester Gunding Library. Named after one of the founders of the town from way back in the day. He was a big man and a big reader. Just before he died he donated all his books, about ten thousand, to the town as a way to start the library. And it's only gotten better since."

There's another cheer. Just one. Heddy waves quickly at one of her sons then says, "Stop that now and let Miss K.C. and I talk."

I wave at her family as well. Then turn back to Heddy, "So, you and I talked a little bit earlier and the aspect of libraries that surprised me when you told me about it is the courier service. The book courier service. You're in a small town in the mountains and you often have to request books for your patrons from…"

"The patrons make the requests themselves. Via our website," Heddy clarifies.

"Okay, sure, then the requests go out into the digital ether and sometime later…"

"Usually a week. Maybe a little longer," another clarification.

"…the book shows up via this courier system. Is that right?"

"That's correct. Most books come from the Asheville libraries but some of the more rare and/or older items will be shipped from libraries in other cities, other states." She nods then adds, "It's a good system. Most all libraries in the country have something like it."

"So, there are librarians driving books…"

"And movies and TV shows and maps and all sorts of archival records. Not just books, K.C." Heddy waggles a finger in my direction as she corrects me. I feel like I'm in second grade and forgot to say "please" and "may I."

"Sure, books and all sorts of other items. But I need to be clear on this point. There are librarians who drive all these items all around the country. Every day. This is happening every single day. Like a secret library transportation network. Is that right?"

46

"Well, every weekday. Not on the weekends. And it's not librarians themselves doing the driving. The librarians stay in the libraries. The libraries hire courier services to…"

"Courier services?" I interrupt. "Not just like the U.S. Mail or FedEx?"

"Well, a few books do get sent to us through the mail. Or FedEx or UPS or what have you. But most go through the courier. And the couriers don't transport just our books. Our books are only part of their business."

"What else do the couriers ship? Along with the books?" I ask.

"All sorts of things. Could be anything that one business needs to get to another business in a day or a week. Oftentimes its medical material. Drugs getting shipped from a hospital or pharmacy. Or blood tests. Or, well, you know there was a driver we had a few years back who lived in Colorado a number of years ago before marijuana was fully legal. The laws back then allowed for medical use and such and there were many marijuana dispensaries around the state and a number of marijuana companies who needed to ship their products to the dispensaries. None of the established courier services would touch their stuff because, well, you understand. This man used to be a courier for the marijuana companies back then. Boy, he told me some stories about late night driving that sent shivers down my spine. Over those tall mountain passes in all that snow and such and he had to get to the dispensaries by a certain time of night or legally they weren't allowed to take the product from him because that's how the law was back then. He likes to say 'books are a lot easier to ship than bud.' Ha. I always did love that line. Books are easier than bud."

Heddy and I chat breezily for a few more minutes about her library and her town and a bit more about the courier system and I finish up by telling her, "I think there's a movie in there somewhere. I really do. I'm not quite sure if it's a contemporary setting or maybe a post-apocalyptic setting. Like a cross between The Transporter and The Postman. That would be the post-apocalyptic setting. But if we stayed with a contemporary setting I see it more as Big Lebowski meets one of the On the Road films with Hope and Crosby. A Dude like character as the driver. Maybe a little singalong as the driver drops off the books. Get the librarian characters into it. Do you sing, Heddy? You look like you might be a singer."

"Only in the choir. And not that well. I stand up and look proper but I don't sing so well," she says.

I turn to camera one to send the show to break but Heddy interrupts me one more time. She leans towards me and grabs my arm as she says, "I just want to thank you for having us librarians on the show this week. Your show, Stack Life, we just love it to death. It's so clever, so clever."

My heart melts a little when Heddy says this. This. This right here is what I love about acting, Hollywood, movies, TV shows, all of it. This type of interaction and feedback from the fans is what keeps me going. I say, "Oh, Heddy. Thank you for saying that. That's very sweet of you. So sweet." I turn back to the camera and say, "When you come back, I'll be in a barn."

18.

I'm sitting on the back seat of an extra long golf cart. One of the production assistants is driving the cart while the steady cam guy is braced awkwardly in the front seat as he films me. I wave when he tells me that we're live. I wave and say, "Since the clouds are thick now and it's going to rain any second, I'm on my way to the barn where I'll interview an actual brain surgeon. He was on the tour bus that stopped by the ranch today. But right now as you can see I'm riding in a golf cart as the barn is on the far side of the main house from the stage I was on before break. It shouldn't take but a minute more to get to the barn."

I stare into the camera for a few seconds then look out over the fields we're passing through then crane my neck up to the clouds as I hold my hand out to feel for the first drops of rain. I turn to the camera just as the cart hits a big bump and I almost get thrown from my seat. I barely manage to hang on and I need the help of the steady cam guy as he lunges his hand towards me to help me pull me back in. I stare into the camera with a mildly shocked look on my face. But I don't say anything. I just make a long exaggerated exhale.

A moment later, the golf cart pulls up in front of the big barn doors. Camera guy helps me step off in order to avoid a nasty little puddle and then he steps back to show me framed by the big open doors. I hold my arms out wide and exclaim, "Welcome to the barn. Come on in." The steady cam follows me as I walk towards the chairs and desk set up on a small riser a dozen feet inside the big doors. I see the two guests sitting and waiting for me. I walk right up to them to introduce myself and shake their hands. Dr. Holmes and his grandson, Theo. I sit down at the desk, the steady cam guy stands a few feet in front of us then gives me the thumbs up. I say to the viewers at home, "So, here we are. To my right are Dr. Arnold Holmes who is a retired brain surgeon and his grandson, Theo Holmes."

I talk to Dr. Holmes for a few minutes about his career: how he got started and notable cases and a few funny incidents. There are only a few. Brain surgery, once the obvious jokes are said, is a fairly serious deal. I have a few other questions at the ready for the good doctor but he insists on me talking to his grandson. In fact, Dr. Holmes says, "You know my grandson here, Theo, he is very single and he is very bright. Maybe you and he…"

I can see Theo blushing hard. I think I'm blushing a bit, too. I did not expect this from a brain surgeon. But, yeah, I can see a grandfather doing this now that I think about it. I smile gently as I say to Dr. Holmes, "Oh, sir, that's very sweet of you but I'm married."

Dr. Holmes' eyes go big as saucers when I say this. Then he drops his head for a moment before looking back at Theo and saying, "I tried. I tried." Pause. "Maybe you should give Rita a call, yes? Just one call. What could it hurt?"

Rita? Who's Rita? I have to ask. "Is Rita an ex, Theo? Is that the vibe I'm picking up on here?"

Theo, blushing even harder now, looks at me as he clenches his jaw. He maybe really doesn't want to talk about this. Maybe I should find a way out of this moment. But before I can think of anything, Theo says, "Yes, Rita is my old girlfriend. Not that she's old. She's young. Not that she's too young. She's my age. Not exactly my age. Dammit. Rita was my girlfriend. Yes. That's correct."

Theo's nervous. Which can play well on TV. But I have to be careful not to embarrass him. "So, is this a recent break up? Did she break up with you?" I see a flash of pain in Theo's eyes. Yes, Rita broke up with him. But he doesn't want to say so. So, I say, "No. You know what, Theo. Forget those questions and just look at me. Look at me and pretend I'm Rita. Tell me what you want to tell Rita. I can see in your eyes there's something you want to tell her. What is it? You're not going to have another chance quite like this. So, if you're comfortable, if you want to, look at me and tell me what you want to tell Rita."

I hold my gaze softly on Theo. I can't see it but I'm sure steady cam guy is focused solely on Theo right now. Theo looks down at the floor. He's debating whether to say anything. His grandfather pats him on the knee a couple of times as he says, "Speak up. Speak up. Tell her what you told me on the bus yesterday. Don't miss your chance."

Theo clears his throat as he looks up at me. I can tell he's seeing Rita's face and not mine as he begins, "Rita, I'm sorry. I was forgetful. And selfish. I was. I apologize. I don't expect anything in return for this. I'm not looking for anything from you or asking anything of you. I just want to tell you that I'm sorry."

That's all Theo says. I hold my gaze on him for a few seconds in silence. He looks at me in silence. Then Dr. Holmes leans in between us and looks at the steady cam as he says, "Rita, call him. Call Theo. He loves you. Call him."

I wave to the camera guy then hold still for a couple of more seconds. Camera guy says, "Okay, we're clear."

I look over at him and ask, "How was that? Did you get that?"

Camera guy says, "It was good. Yeah, I got it. I got it."

"Thank you," I say. Then, "Tell me your name."

"Al," he says. "Alfred but please call me Al," he says.

"Thank you, Al. That was great." I turn to Theo and Dr. Holmes, "And thank you, Theo for opening up like that. I'm sorry if I put you on the spot…"

Theo shakes me off, "No. That was fine. I've been…"

Dr. Holmes interrupts again, "He's been dragging his feet. He should have apologized a long time ago. So, thank you for giving him this opportunity." He turns to Theo and slaps his grandson's knee.

Theo nods his head in agreement, "I should have apologized sooner." He looks at me with a smile, "You have no idea. Rita…she's a huge fan of yours. Huge. When she sees this…she'll freak out a bit. Like a major bit."

I ask, "Can I call her for you? Tell her to watch the show tonight?"

Theo's eyes go big as saucers now. I can see the family resemblance between him and his grandfather. He says as he looks at his phone, "She's probably on her way home now. She usually talks to her sister when she drives home. And she hasn't been taking my calls lately so…" His voice trails off in disappointment.

I say as I hold out my hand for his phone, "Perfect. I'll leave her a message."

Theo looks at his grandfather. Dr. Holmes says, "Do it, you fool. Give her the phone."

Theo hands me his phone after punching up Rita's number. I tap to call. It does indeed go to voicemail. We all wait for the recording to start then I say, "Hi, Rita. This is K.C. Hall. I just met Theo. You remember him, right? Well, he has something to say to you but he said it to me instead. You can see what he said on Kincaid Live!. Yup, tonight. Check your local listings. And thanks for being such a big fan. Give me a call at this number tomorrow if you want to chat. Bye!"

I hang up and hand the phone back to Theo. A sudden fear pops into my brain. I ask Theo, "You didn't treat her really badly or anything, did you?"

Theo shakes his head as his grandfather says, "The young man forgot her birthday. Three years together and he forgot her birthday."

Dr. Holmes and I say at the same time, "Not good, Theo. Not good."

Al speaks up, "Hey, Sal wants you back at the first set. We have to go."

19.

This time the golf cart driver swerves to avoid the bump. This time the sudden swerve almost sends me flying out onto the ground. But I was prepared - enough. I held on to the vinyl-covered seat with both hands. Those endless burpees, downward dogs and Turkish Get ups with a kettlebell all paid off as I leaned and leaned and leaned and clung and clung and clung and managed to stay on the cart. When the driver jerked the wheel and got us back on the gravel pathway, my weight shifted back under me and I let out a little whoop. That's when I saw Al had filmed the whole thing. I broke out laughing, pointed at him and said, "That'll make a good promo shot. Hold on, K.C. This week's going to be a wild ride."

Al said, "That's good. Sal will like that."

I turned to the driver, "Tell me your name. Because that's twice now you've almost sent me flying. If this happens a third time I might start getting suspicious."

The young woman (short, straight black hair, an oval face, a slightly upturned nose) turns back slightly and only for a moment as she says, "Kendall. Kendall Holtzmann." Then, "Sorry about that. I didn't mean to turn so sharply." Then after a swallow, "I'm a little nervous."

"Well," I add, "me, too." Al and Kendall both nod their heads agreeing with the sentiment. I say to Al, "Do you know why Sal wants me back on the stage? I see that the clouds have blown over but…"

Al shrugs his shoulders. He doesn't know. Kendall offers up as she points to her earpiece, "I heard something about feedback on Mighty Martie. Some of the audience members talked to Sal about that." Then she shrugs to indicate that she's not sure about what she just said. We complete the rest of the ride back to the main stage in silence. I let the wind blow through my hair and across my face as I look once more up at the now clear sky.

20.

     While I was interviewing the brain surgeon and his love-lorn grandson, Sal stayed with the tour bus audience and did his Sal thing. He joked with them, chatted them up, got to know them, told them stories about old Hollywood and so on and so on. Kendall brings the golf cart as close to the edge of the stage as she can. I wait for Al to hop off, check the camera then give me a thumbs up before I step off the cart and walk the short distance to the stage.

     Sal's waiting for me and bends down to whisper in my ear, "I want you to ad lib with the audience about your movie. A few of them have some strong opinions. You good with that?" He squeezes my elbow as he asks this question. This means that if I'm not good with this I need to let him know. But I am good with this so I say, "Let's do it."

     Sal and I walk side by side across the stage and over in front of the audience section. Sal has rearranged a few of the people. The three audience members sitting in the front row on the left end are the ones he wants me to interact with. He introduces them to me: Sally, Frank and Michael. Two of them are roughly the same age (I'd guess 45 - 50) while one looks much younger. They are all solidly middle class Midwestern.

     Sal and I turn to camera one which is angled now to show us standing by the edge of the audience section. Sal takes the cue from Marcus as we go live. He says to the camera, "Welcome back. Yes, it's me, Sal Kincaid. As you can see, K.C. has not killed me off and I am still very much alive." There's a soft chuckle from the audience. I shake my head like I'm disappointed in myself for not getting rid of Sal. He goes on, "Earlier, K.C. asked for feedback on her recent movie, Mighty Martie…" he bends down and whispers, "Did they really call it Mighty Martie? I mean, that's probably why no one went to see it. That's a horrible name."

     I respond, "Well, you see, my character's name is Martie and I turn into a giant ape so that's the mighty part. So, Mighty Martie. Get it?"

     Sal says, "But you're a giant ape. You need a giant name for a giant ape movie. Mighty Martie is not giant. It's pipsqueak. You should have gone with something like King Kong. Now that's a name."

Sal's use of the word 'pipsqueak' throws me for a second. That's what Sasha used to call me when I complained about her workouts years ago. But I can't think about that now. I can't think about how Sasha and I haven't hung out nearly as much as I thought we would when I moved back to L.A. Because reasons. Stupid reasons. Nope. I definitely cannot think about that now. So, I should go ahead and stop thinking about that now. Yup. I should.

Sal sees I'm swimming and says, "When you were making the film, was there any talk about King Kong? The original King Kong. The movie that created the giant monster genre."

Okay, good. I can focus now. Thank you, Sal. I say, "Ummmm, not any direct talk about that movie, no. We were so focused on the script and the scenes and changes we made...there were a number of changes made as the production went along. That's not unusual for a big budget film. So we were focused on our story, not the original King Kong. Not consciously anyway. When you make such a movie it's hard to not be aware of all the other giant monster movies that have come before you. The same was true when I made Big Fin X. On that set we definitely talked about Jaws and how that movie started the whole shark attack genre. We were very consciously aware of that comparison. Of that precursor. Jaws set the standard."

Sal angles his body toward the audience seated just a few feet away as he says, "That's good. Thanks for answering that. Now, here are a few people who have some other questions about the movie they'd like to ask you." Sal steps back a bit and holds a microphone that a production assistant has just handed him out towards Sally who is seated on the end of the row. She's wearing a floral print jacket over a white top. Her hair is very puffy. Bright red lipstick. She should not have gone with that color.

Focus, K.C. Focus.

After Sal has Sally introduce herself he prompts her to ask her MIghty Martie question, "I want to know why you didn't go more along the lines of King Kong. Like Sal here said. King Kong is a classic. You should have just copied the classic, in my opinion. Switch up the man and woman roles but stick to the story. The classic story. Beauty and the beast. That's what I wanted from the movie. But instead there was this investigator character. I didn't understand that at all."

I wait a beat to make sure Sally has finished then, thinking on my feet, I say, "Well, there are a couple of elements that are similar to King Kong. For example, the scene at the end when I climb up the cliff then see my lover with my best friend. That sense of loss and betrayal right before I fall back off the cliff and into the sea. That was most definitely an homage, a reference to the original King Kong falling off the Empire State Building. So that, uh, is in there. And there was some talk in the very beginning of the project about flipping the male and female roles, as you said, but we all agreed that we wanted to do something more, something different than a beauty and the beast story. The mad scientist slash technology changing people and, more specifically, changing how people interact with each other, how it's easy to view others as metaphorical monsters when our interactions are so often mediated, that is, not face to face, not one on one but with an intervening technology be it phone or internet and how that technology can be and is very powerful, monstrously powerful, if you will, but we have to be careful how we use it or we can end up hurting people, sometimes on accident, sometimes on purpose. So, ummm, that was the way we used the monster aspect in our film."

I study Sally's face as I talk to her. She seems to shift from disagreeing with Mighty Martie, from not liking it to maybe, maybe seeing it in a different light. But I'm not sure. She looks more confused, perhaps, than convinced by my explanation. So, I risk a joke, "Plus, King Kong never did Flashdance moves."

There's another soft chuckle from the audience. This one takes me by surprise. I assumed that only these three here had seen the movie. But this response to my joke makes me think many more of them have seen it. Otherwise they wouldn't laugh at my joke. This encourages me. I look up at the rest of the audience and ask, "Show of hands, how many of you have seen Mighty Martie." About two thirds of the hands go up. So about fifty people. I ask, "Great, okay, keep your hands up if you saw it in movie theaters." A little over ten hands stay up.

Sal speaks up at that point, "Interesting. Good to know. Now, K.C., this next gentleman is named Frank and he has a question for you, too." Sal maneuvers around the front of the audience section and holds the microphone close to Frank (thin, long face, mostly bald, blue blazer over peach button down shirt, no tie, sharp, probing eyes). Frank says with soft and rounded tones, "I couldn't help but notice that there are several homages, as you said earlier, to classic Gothic literature stories. For example, your character is a lab assistant and how you portray her as intelligent but trapped in a menial role while the bloviating and smug doctor, the geneticist who makes the serum that transforms you into Mighty Martie, is obviously a parallel to the stuffed shirt upper class characters that run rampant through the classic, Gothic novels. The choice of an English actor to play that role only reinforces this connection. Indeed, the hidebound brittleness with which the geneticist character interacts with and, you might say, lords it over everyone who works for him in his laboratory makes it quite inescapable to see the scenario in any other way."

Frank obviously just wants to hear himself talk. I get it. I mean, look at me. I'm hosting (correction: co-hosting) one of the more successful talk shows of the past thirty years so I have no ground on which to stand in terms of criticizing Frank. The problem I have is that he doesn't have an actual question. He described a couple of characters in the movie and, in essence, gave a review of them. But...there's no question. I was expecting a question. I was told there'd be questions.

I glance up at Sal. He understands my difficulty. He asks Frank, "Interesting. So, do you have a question about that Gothic element, Frank?"

A flash of confusion passes across Frank's face. He realizes he doesn't really have a question. So he says, "Was that…written into the script specifically or…did it come through organically?"

Okay. Technically, that's a question. Let's see what I can do with this. I lean forward a touch and place my hand on the railing in front of Frank as I begin, "I can't speak for the writers. I need to say that first. And there were a total of, I think, six or seven writers by the time the project was finished. So, to really answer your question we'd have to talk to them. But, having done this whole movie thing a few times now, I can make some decent guesses." I pause and purse my lips. Thinking, thinking, thinking. Okay. Here we go. "Let's put it this way. It's hard to write a monster story and not have some Gothic elements. It just is. Gothic and monsters go hand in hand - whether they be vampires or giant apes, Frankensteins, werewolves, invisible men, invisible women, heck, even killer sharks and kraken and other sea beasties. Monsters are all about our collective fears, our repressed fears and, also, suppressed desires. That's Gothic territory right there. Dead center Gothic territory. The woman trapped in the attic. The giant ape trapped," I use finger quotes here, "inside our DNA. The shark lurking just below the surface just as our fears and unspoken desires lurk just below the surface. Yeah, it's all there. It's all right there. So, Frank, if I had to guess, I'd say the writers, pros that they are, did insert those Gothic homages, as you call them, into the movie in a deliberate manner. I'm willing to bet they did so as a hat tip to that body of work, an acknowledgement that while this is a modern, big budget, special effects laden, big screen movie its bones are old as the hills, its bones are as old as these mountains that surround us here on the ranch."

Sal looks impressed with what I just said. Hell, I'm impressed with what I just said. I'm not sure where it came from but it sounded damn good. Sal touches his ear then turns to the camera for a moment before turning to me as he says, "We do have to go to break for a quick moment, K.C. King Kong and gothic novels. Not bad. Not bad. I think I might actually rent your movie now."

58

I smile. I just thought of something. I'm going to say it but first I have to set up Sal. "Well, you know what they say, Sal."

Of course he doesn't. But he'll play along, "No, K.C., what do they say?"

I turn to the camera, puff up my chest and ready my deepest, most aggressive voice. I punch the words out just like Denzel Washington in Training Day, "Jane Eyre…ain't got nothing…on me."

Cut to commercial.

21.
    When we come back from break, we take the last
question. Sal once again does his hold the microphone over
the railing thing as Michael (the younger man - early twenties?
- a bit overweight, long sleeve denim shirt, painfully shy, as he
speaks he stares at his hands which are in his lap) says, "I
don't have a question about Mighty Martie. My question is
about L.A.ser Boy. A question and a comment." I look quickly
at Sal. He winks at me. He set this up. Sneaky man. Michael
goes on, "Ummm, in L.A.ser Boy you play Zenda the
Magnificent who has special powers but her powers are never
really defined. They are mysterious and the audience never
quite knows what she's capable of doing as she keeps her
powers secret even from L.A.ser Boy himself. I think that's sort
of cool but I was wondering if you could tell me are we ever
going to find out what Zenda's powers really are and how she
got them?"
    Michael's description of Zenda the Magnificent is spot
on. The nature and origin of the character's super powers
were deliberately left unclarified in the series. This was a bit of
a risk as so many fans of superhero stories like to have these
details mapped out for them at the beginning of the adventure.
That way they can spend the rest of the story figuring out
exactly how those powers will be used to defeat the villain.
This twist gave Zenda a mysterious and playful edge that
worked well - in my humble opinion - with Gyrin's L.A.ser Boy
character who was young and seeking guidance and trying to
figure out his own life and powers and just how far he wanted
to go with the whole superhero thing.
    But some viewers of the show complained that Zenda's
unknown powers were simply a shoehorned, deus ex machina
plot device that robbed the scary moments of any real tension.
Nothing's at risk, really, if Zenda can just do something to
either escape the scenario or beat up the bad guy with a wave
of her hand. Or nod of her head. Or tap of her maybe/maybe
not magic wristbands. And so on. So, I understand Michael's
question and the dissatisfaction that is behind it. Narrative
dissatisfaction. I look at him and say, "I can tell you this."
Pause, look down at the ground, shake my head, look back

up, "Yes. I shouldn't tell you this. The producers will get mad at me but since you asked so politely I am going to tell you. When the next season comes out, by the end of the next season, Zenda's powers will be explained." I hold my hand up like I'm swearing to tell the whole truth and nothing but the truth, "And it will be good."

[Note: I have no idea if this is true or not. So, it's a little bit of a risk to say so. I think that's the direction the writers were going. But I'm not sure. Not sure by any means. But this little give and take between me and Michael, this clip will get Youtubed ten thousand times by the superhero fan community and it will be the source of endless speculation and theories. This will lead to more viewers. At least, I hope it will. So, yeah, this is more than a little self-serving of me. But...well...yeah. We'll see what happens. If the writers can't come up with a satisfying explanation for Zenda's mysterious powers, one that ties all of the varied effects she's created to one source, then I'll have Scott come up with something. I'm sure he can. He could probably do it in fifteen minutes flat. Yes, L.A.ser Boy is Scott's favorite project of mine. Because he is such a nerd.]

22.

It's a few hours later. The rest of the show went well. Very well, in fact. Sal and Marcus were happy with how it turned out. As Sal says, "Once the lights go on, you never know what's going to happen." That's the beauty and terror of live TV. Live performances of any type, really. Public speaking, theater, dance, sports. All that. You plan and you practice and you plan some more but once you get out there - once the lights go on - you never know what's going to happen.

What happened tonight was good.

I called Scott as soon as I changed and got my makeup off. I was walking back to my cabin for a little alone time when I did so. There's a long, circular gravel path that extends out from the main house, works its way through a thatch of trees, up a slight incline then through a field and back around to the main house coming back at the opposite side from which it started. Several cabins are situated along the pathway. The cabins here today are not the original cabins from when this pathway was first put in place. Luisa told me a little bit about the history of the ranch a day or so ago. But I'm sure there's more to learn. I'll let Scott get into that when he arrives. What I know now is that Luisa and her brothers refurbished (i.e. overhauled almost completely) the seven cabins along this path. There are a handful of other cabins and a bunkhouse past the barn, as well. Luisa said that she's thinking about adding an experiential, hands on element to her bee company. Her vision is to have people pay her to stay in the cabins and work the beehives and the rest of the production steps of getting her honey ready for market.

I said, "So, people are going to pay you to work for you. That's clever."

"I'll provide them a wonderful ranch B&B experience: food, nice accommodations, horse rides and bike rides in the afternoon. All they have to do is help with the honey in the mornings."

"You think people will sign up for that?" I asked because I have no sense of what people will sign up for anymore.

"I do. I just have to sell it the right way. We have the cabins now. Your crew will be a test run for them. Work the kinks out. Then we'll figure out the rest," she said.

She hasn't implemented this program yet and there are a few kinks to work out. At least, in my cabin there are. The lights are a little hinky. They flicker randomly. The pipes have some issues too. When you turn the water on in the morning it sounds like winds from the Great North are blowing through them. That lasts for about ten seconds then the water spits out of the faucet like it's running away from something. That lasts for only a few seconds but it's a little disconcerting. So, yeah, Luisa needs to work all that out before she advertises for guests/worker….[I really want to say "worker bees" but I'm not going to].

Not that I'm complaining. Luisa opened up her ranch to us this week and it's been a wonderful experience so far. It's been good to spend time with her. It's been good, even, to spend time at dad's grave site. I don't like calling it a grave site though. Dad's place. Dad's spot. I usually say one of those terms. Grave is too grave a word. Ha. I'm such a little girl sometimes. "Don't say grave. That's not nice. That means he's dead." Which, of course, he is. Sigh.

There's acknowledging someone's dead then there's living your life as if that person is dead then there's living your life fully accepting that someone is dead. I slipped into that last stage at some point these past few days. I didn't realize I wasn't in it until I finally reached it. Death comes suddenly into our lives. Sudden and hard. He shows up unexpectedly. Then he hangs around for a while on the fringes of your life like an uninvited guest. Then you finally go "ohhh, fuck it, come on in" and he sits down at the main table. He doesn't say much. But when he speaks, you better pay attention. Death at the Dinner Table. Sounds like an Agatha Christie mystery. Write that down.

The first day I was here, I spread some of Mo's ashes on dad's spot. Old army buddies together again. I filmed my shaking out the small packet of ashes over the grassy nook in the thicket of woods past the barn then sent it to Jon. He called me as soon as he got it, "How you doing, Case?"

I sniffled through some tears as I said, "I'm okay. I'm good, actually. Just a little sad."

"Yeah, me too. Me too," said Jon. We talked for a bit. He's finally looking to get back to work. Mo's estate has given him enough that he doesn't have to work if he doesn't want to but, as he says, "I'll go crazy if I don't focus on something." So, he's taking the Chester/Charlene script to producers looking for backing. That's the story of Chester Zelnick, one of the forgotten founders of the Hollywood movie business back in the early twentieth century. It's part revenge story, part…nope, now that I think of it it's all revenge story. Revenge story with a possible twist. The book the script is based on strongly suggests (though does not definitely prove, imho) that Chester was actually Charlene. That the person known as Chester Zelnick was actually a woman named Charlene Zelnick who presented herself in public as male, as Chester, in order to do business back in those backwards times.

Where was I?

Right, I called Scott. He didn't pick up. Crappy reception. Yup, crappy reception in the mountain ranges he and the crew are driving through. Definitely crappy reception and not something horrible like a car accident. Nope, definitely not a car accident. Okay, so I called and left a happy, happy message so he and the crew know tonight's show went well and that I'm excited to see them and all that. Then I rounded the bend and saw my cabin and saw Clara sitting on the front steps.

23.

    She looks up as soon as she hears my footsteps on the gravel. Which is actually a little later than I thought she'd look up. She was lost in thought. I give a little wave as she stands up. She returns it and steps out from the cabin. She looks over her shoulder down the path and I know that she's thinking very strongly about running in that direction. I stop and wait. Clara holds her gaze down the path, looking away from me for several heartbeats. Then she turns slowly back to look at me. That's when I see the tears flowing down her cheeks. I step forward her then stop. I really want to hug her right now. No. I really want to over hug her right now. The pain rolling off her is palpable. Her eyes are burning with grief. Her shoulders are trembling. I hold my arms out to her and she comes to me. She collapses into me. I hold her tight as I can and rock her gently side to side. I say nonsense phrases like, "There, there," "shhh, shhh now," and "i'm here, I'm right here"

    Over the course of a minute or so, I walk Clara over to the cabin steps and we arrange ourselves side by side sitting down. She's wiped the tears away for the most part but every few seconds a new one issues forth unbidden from the corner of her eyes. I wait as long as I can in silence. But eventually I ask, "Did some…"

    "Mom's in the hospital again." Clara spits this out like she's disgusted that she has to say the phrase. I look her in the eye. She nods once as she says, "Overdose."

    "What…" I begin then realize I'm not sure what to ask. I don't want to ask Clara what she's going to do because there is nothing for her to do. I know that. I know that painfully. As much as you want to do something - scream at the heavens, scream at the person using, walk away from it all and swear never to come back, swear that you'll stop caring - you can't. You just can't. So, I say, "…state is she in?"

    Clara wipes another tear off her cheek like it's an insult, like the tear is a sign of weakness that she simply can't have if she's going to survive this, "Stable." Pause. "She'll have to stay in the hospital though. She's stable but weak. She doesn't eat well. She never has. Never…" Another tear comes. It's chased by several more. Clara wipes furiously at each one. I can see she's boiling with anger. Her wiping away of tears quickly turns into her slapping her own face.

As soon as I see this, I grab her hands in mine and yank them down into her lap as I say, "No! No! You will not do that. This is not your fault, Clara. This is not your fault. You're just a kid, Clara. This is not your fault."

Clara's eyes are bottomless pools of rage as she looks at me. Rage at her mother. Rage at her father. Rage at life. Rage at herself. I hold her hands even more tightly as she tries to pull them away from me. I won't let her go. I say again, "No. Not until you swear you won't hit yourself. No." I'm hard and strong outside as I say this. Because that's what Clara needs right now. But inside I'm wailing for her. I'm wailing for her, for myself, for my mother. For all of it. For everything.

Clara lurches up into a standing position. I follow along. She tries to yank her arms free. She succeeds with one hand but I hold onto the other with both my hands now. She tries several times to break free from my grasp. But I clamp down with both hands on her forearm as hard as I possibly can. This sad, silly tug of war lasts for a dozen seconds. Then, exhausted more than just physically, Clara goes limp and collapses into me once again. She lets the tears flow freely now. I hold her gently, pat her back. She cries and cries and cries some more.

A few minutes later we're once more sitting on the steps. Clara takes a deep breath and looks straight ahead as she says, "I'm sorry."

"It's okay," I say. "I get it. Probably more than most. I get it."

That's when she turns to look at me. She asks, "How did you do it?"

I know what she's asking. But I don't have an answer. There is no magic answer. Clara wants to know how I survived growing up with a mother who was an addict and all the chaos that addiction brings. She wants to know how I lived through that, how I coped and how I made the life for myself that I have now. I've been asked various forms of this question for a few years now. It was a standard one for interviews during my Shadows of the Moon 1 appearances and articles and such.

66

It's my turn to take a deep breath as a wilderness of childhood memories gather around me. I say to Clara, "I made do. I kept going. I kept putting one foot in front of the other. I raged out for a while. It felt really good to rage out. In the moment. The rage makes you feel powerful. But when it's gone - and it always goes away, even though it feels like it never will - things are still just the same. I'm not telling you not to do it, not to rage out. I'm just saying that it's not going to change anything. It'll feel good but it won't change anything. What changes, in the end, is you."

I hold my gaze on Clara. I look right into her eyes. She wants to believe me but I don't think she can at this point. It's all too fresh, too raw for her in this moment, which is all the moments that her mother has betrayed her piled on top of her all at once. Yeah, I know that moment. It's not fun. It's the opposite of fun.

I keep talking. Clara needs me to keep talking. She doesn't need me to say anything particular. She just needs me to stay right here and keep talking. "When I got to Hollywood I drank and did other drugs for a while. Which, if you knew me in high school, would have surprised you. I was so tight, so controlled, so self-contained in high school. I had my little emo journal in which I wrote about typical sad stuff - oh, johnny doesn't like me, oh suzie's mad at me - but I never put the real stuff into words. Not like that. I tried writing. Fiction. I tried making up stories using the real stuff. But I was so young. The stories just became rehashing real life with different names. And I could never figure out a good ending. Not once. So, I stopped doing that. I threw myself into my studies. But not because I liked school. Because it filled my brain with details. It distracted me. Plays helped. Theater. Speaking other peoples' words. Being part of stories that had definite endings, definite conclusions. That helped. Watching a lot of TV and movies helped. That was part distraction, part searching for guidance. I figured if all these fake people can survive all these calamities then I could survive my mundane traumas. Huh. Dad never understood that. But...yeah. Dad helped in his own way."

I risk a question, "How are you and your dad? I know he's..."

Clara speaks up before I say "in prison." She says, "I try to talk to him once a week. But sometimes he misses the phone call. I want to go visit him. Luisa says she'll go with me. But...it's a long way away. And the trip would be hard on her. She's older. So..."

"Do you have a car?" I ask. This is a detail I'd never even considered before.

Clara shakes her head no.

"I'll get you a car," I say matter of factly.

Clara gives me a stunned look, a pained look. I know what she's going to say. She's going to say I shouldn't do that. She's going to say she doesn't deserve it. She's going to push back against receiving any help because she doesn't want to get close to anyone because she doesn't want to disappoint anyone by ending up like her mother. Because that's what we all think. That's what we all fear. That we'll turn into the thing we despise. That our own weakness will take us over and we'll become just like the person who has betrayed us so many times. That's the big secret. We don't hate people for what they do to us. We hate people because they show us what we're capable of doing to others. We just don't admit that. Ever. And that's how the cycle continues.

I reach out a hand. I hold it halfway between me and Clara for a moment. Then I rest it gently on Clara's shoulder. She lets me do that. It's hard for her but she lets me do that. I take another deep breath then say, "It's the least I can do for you, Clara. Please, let me help you in this way. You've been through some shitty stuff in your life. Stuff that no one should have to go through. I'm not saying you're special. There are others out there who go through shitty stuff, too. Even worse stuff. But for whatever reason you and I and your father and my father are all tangled up. We just are. So, let me help you this way. Let me help you untangle all this. Or, at least, smooth it out a bit. Please."

That's when I pull my hand away. That's when Clara stands up, bites her lower lip then looks me in the eye as she says, "Okay. Yes. Thank you."

I stand up and we shake hands. This hand shaking is not violent. This one is good, honest, equal. This one is two people helping each other out. Because as much as I'm helping Clara, she's helping me. I know that sounds silly but it's true. Being able to help someone in need in such a simple way - that keeps me sane. It keeps me grounded. When all the Hollywood nonsense swirls around me it's moments like this that keep me going. "Where're you sleeping tonight?" I ask as we let our hands fall back to our sides. A thought-fear has just flashed into my brain. I don't think Clara should be alone tonight.

She says with a questioning look, "In my cabin. Like usual. With Kaley."

I nod and say, "One of Luisa's...interns? Is that the term?" Kaley is one of a handful of young people who are working on the ranch for a semester for college credit. Luisa told me a little bit about them. But I confess those details went in one ear and out the other. "You two get along?" Listen to me! I sound like a concerned mother on a sitcom.

Clara shrugs and rolls her eyes, "Kaley's...fine. She's boy obsessed. So..."

So, Clara is not boy obsessed. So, she and Kaley probably don't talk to each other much or connect in any solid way. I gesture vaguely to the cabin, "You can crash here tonight. If you want. There's a really big couch." Pause. Clara's eyes flare large then shrink back down to normal size. Her brow furrows up. The moment is awkward now. Somehow my saying what I just said has become the strange part of this interaction. "Just know it's an option. That's all."

Clara folds her arms across her chest and stands up a little straighter as she says, "Sure. Okay. Thanks." Then she says, "I've got to get back. Or I'll miss dinner."

Luisa makes dinner for the workers who live on the ranch. Besides Clara and Kaley who are, essentially, interns (no matter what their official designation is) there are four other young people (two guys, two girls) who all attend Black Hill Community College. The details are coming back to me now. Apparently they didn't fall completely out of my head. The interns are spending the semester working here on the ranch under Luisa's supervision as part of their college education. That, in fact, is where Luisa got the idea for her (I can't resist) worker bee program. So, these students are a couple of years older than Clara which at her age is sometimes a huge gap. Plus, I'm guessing none of their parents are in prison. Or drug addicts. I imagine Clara finds it hard to connect to them. Maybe. But maybe not.

I say to Clara, "Sure. Right." I point at the cabin again, "I'm going to call some people." I study her face for a moment more. She seems calmer now. She seems like she's not going to run away or hurt herself. She smiles for a split second then turns on her heel and walks back down the gravel path. As much as I'm relieved that the whole scene with her is over now, I'm a little sad that she's walking away.

Hmmmmmmm.

24.

Big T asked me early on in our sessions - way early - if I ever engaged in any self-harm behavior. I joked, "Like trying to be a Hollywood actress?" He actually laughed at that. One of the few times he laughed at my jokes. Then he went on to describe cutting and abusive relationships and way too far over the edge thrill seeking and a few other patterns of behavior that are, according to him, various ways in which people either cause themselves pain directly or put themselves in positions in which pain is a likely outcome.

I listened but I was defensive. Like I said, this was early in our sessions. I still didn't quite trust Big T yet. I made another joke, "No. That's not me. I'm more into other harm, not self harm." Other harm. As in hurting other people. I know. It was a bad joke then and it's a worse joke now.

Big T didn't reprimand me or even raise his voice. He simply told me a story. He told me about a client he'd had years before. He kept the names out, of course. To protect client/therapist privilege and all that. The client was a firefighter, he said. Visions of hunky guys doing dangerous and sweaty things filled my head immediately. And I do mean FILLED my head. Big T had my attention.

He went on to describe how the client knew he wanted to be a firefighter ever since he was a young kid. He loved watching any movie or TV show that featured firefighters. As he grew up, he read as much as he could find about being a firefighter: the training, the history, the engineering details of different fire trucks and breathing apparatus - all of it.

This was not one of those childhood infatuations that dies out over time. This was the real deal. He got his associates degree (to appease his parents) then went right into a firefighter training program. He loved it. He felt like he was finally doing what he was put on this earth to do. Moreover, he was good at it. Dedicated. Thorough. Professional. "He was a lifer," said Big T. This is a term he used to describe people who'd found their life's calling. This guy, Big T used the fake name "Paul," was a lifer firefighter.

Then, over the years and multiple experiences of rushing into burning buildings, showing up at horrible car

71

accidents, being on scene for one tragedy after another, Paul started to hurt himself. More explicitly, he started to burn himself. Big T said, "Being in the buildings when they're on fire is the most alive Paul ever felt. The most present and engaged with his world. Being in imminent danger often brings out this sense in people. But, of course, for Paul those scenarios were also where he experienced significant traumas. Not being able to save people. Losing fellow firefighters. Horrible images and emotions. Feeling powerless - despite all his training and experience. That's why he started burning himself. He felt compelled to recreate the traumas, to recreate the pain. He said, 'If I can just feel enough of the pain, absorb enough of it then I can't hurt anyone else.'"

Big T fell silent at that point. I waited for him to continue. But he didn't. So, I asked, "Were you able to help him? Did he stop burning himself?"

"Yes. It took time but yes, eventually, Paul stopped burning himself. I got him to see the connection between the flames and the trauma and he was able to emotionally separate one from the other. To maintain a healthy respect for fire and flames and its danger and be able to address the traumas associated with his job in a more healthy, a more healing manner." Pause. "That's what it's all about, K.C. Finding a way to channel all that energy, all that emotion - whatever its origin, wherever it comes from - in a way that helps us heal. That's all self-harm really is. Misguided attempts at healing. That part of us wants to heal. It just doesn't know how."

The story stuck with me. I referred back to it several times when I was auditioning. I asked myself, "How does this character want to heal? Does he/she know how? Given what she/he knows, what would he do with that healing impulse? How would she channel it? How would it manifest in his/her life?"

Then, of course, I realized that acting was a way for me to heal. That's what Big T wanted me to realize all along. A few months after he told me Paul's story, I asked, "What's Paul do now? Does he still run into burning buildings?" I needed to know.

"Yes," Big T said. "He does. He's still active. But he also trains other firefighters. And he makes sure to share his experience with them. He's very good at it."

25.

As I wait for Scott to pick up, Paul's story flashes through my mind once again. I wait and wait as Scott's phone rings. Once. Running into burning buildings. Twice. Saving people's lives. Thrice. Seeing co-workers die. Then Scott picks up, "Hey, hon! We just pulled into Delta now."

"Delta?" I ask as my mind comes back to the present moment, leaving Paul's story behind. I'm not sure what Delta is. A hotel? A campground?

"Delta, Colorado. Decent size town. They have a real old west thing going on here. Miley wants to see the tour guides dressed up in period costumes. So, that's what we're doing. She's got it all planned out."

Of course, Miley has it all planned out. I ask, "You're still on schedule then?" This is what I want to know. I want to make sure Scott will be here at the end of the week. I miss him.

"Yeah, still on schedule. It's a little hard to roust the twins in the morning. But otherwise the trip's been smooth."

"Alonsha's okay? She's not cracked more or anything?" I ask.

"Ha! I'm checking on her right now while the crew grabs their bags and Miley handles check-in. Yeah, Alonsha's fine. Jaxson rigged up a system here that would make NASA jealous. You should see Jaxson and Miley together. Miley's got a thousand questions. Jaxson's got a thousand answers. Just wait until you see them interact. You'll probably want to turn it into a script. Your writer's brain will love it. How was the show tonight?"

I tell him.

"So, now you're going to need me to come up with an explanation for Zenda's powers? A good one." he asks.

"If the show writers can't, then I'm sure you can," I say. Because I am sure he can. He may not be. But I am.

"If I do, will this get me a credit? Like the one I have for the Hall-iverse? Or will have when all that kicks in?"

"I'll make sure you do, hon. I'll make sure you get an even bigger credit. I'll make sure your name is three times as large as everybody else's."

74

"You know that's not why…" Scott doesn't like it when I tease him about this. But I just can't resist. When Hugh Summers (formerly known as Writer Mysterioso) was brought on by MDB to oversee the Hall-iverse I happened to mention in passing one day very casually yet very precisely that I knew a guy, yes - my husband, who's writing a graphic novel and it has a story element that could be just the thing, just the right detail to tie together all these different projects. Because it was. I could see that once Summers started talking about his vision for the Hall-iverse.

When I told Scott that Hugh wanted to meet with him about using his graphic novel idea as part of the Hall-iverse, he was both excited and pissed off at me. The excited I understood. The pissed off I did not. I asked him why he was upset. He said, "It's my story. I wanted to make it. It's my thing. Now it's going to be part of your thing. The Hall-iverse."

Then I understood. His pretend world was getting merged with my pretend worlds. He was going to lose his thing. It was going to get subsumed by my thing. I said, "I hear you and I promise that you'll get full credit for the story idea. That's usually how that works. Then, when your graphic novel is done, I'll make sure you can link it to the Hall-iverse. To help with marketing and sales." He frowned. "If you want to."

He frowned some more than said, "I know I'm being silly. Childish. It just feels like the story is slipping away from me. I wanted to work on it, make it good, get it perfect then…then…"

He didn't know how to put it into words. But I did. Because I've been through this with acting. I said, "…then you wanted to present it to the world and be hailed and praised and have songs sung about your amazing genius." I gave him a look that said you know I'm right, don't try to deny it.

He tried to deny it, "No. That's not it. I wanted to…to…to…"

I did not jump in this time. I did amp up the intensity of my look.

He finally succumbed, "Okay. Yeah. Maybe you're right"

More amping up.

"Okay, okay. Yes. Yes, I do want to be hailed as the greatest graphic novel writer to have ever lived on planet Earth. I…do. Because that's how it feels when I'm writing this story. It feels so good, so right, so…cool." He laughed at himself at this point. "God, I sound like one of my old students."

I jumped in at that point, "That's a good thing. That young, childlike feeling. I've found that most good stories require that, have an element of that in them somewhere. That sense of the creator/writer/director/actor wanting to tell the story because you think it's cool. Because it lights you up inside when you tell it. Because it shines in its own special way and you want to share it with others so they realize how cool it is, too. It's like stumbling across the most beautiful sunset in the world. You want to share it with everybody. You want everybody to see it. But, you also want to keep it to yourself. You want to keep it as your special thing. Because it's so cool."

"Yeah. That's it. You just put words to my thoughts, Case. Wow."

Scott was really impressed with me in that moment. So, I had to make fun of him, "Well, I am a genius actress, after all. Just ask me. Go on. Ask me."

"No. No, I will not as I fear that asking you that question will only add fuel to your already significantly sized ego fire," he said.

"Hello! Ego inferno!" I said very melodramatically. Then I tackled him. That's what he gets for teaching me football.

Anyway.

Ever since, Scott's had to fight the I want to share my stories but I want to keep them as mine creator's dynamic anytime something like this comes up. Which hasn't been often - yet - but I suspect will become more of a regular thing for him. The longer we live in L.A., the more he's going to get involved in the industry. I can just tell that's going to happen. So, he's got to get used to sharing his stories, his ideas, his input, his suggestions. Films are a collaborative enterprise, after all.

Scott says, "Ummm, Miley's yelling at me now. Yelling and waving at me to hurry up. So, I better go. Love you."

"Love you, too."

When I hang up, I realize I'm starving. Did I eat lunch today? I don't think I did. Time for food. Which means either go back to the main house or stay here and eat some of the tiramisu servings I've hidden in my fridge.

Hmmmmmm.

I decide to be good and head back to the main house. About halfway there is when MDB calls.

26.

"Has that Thad boy talked to you yet?" That's the first thing she says when I anwer. Not "hello." Not "hi." Not "It's nice to talk to you, K.C." None of that. This is standard operating procedure for MDB. I'm still getting used to it. I confess that part of me likes it. The whole no bullshit, no time to waste, let's get things done approach is a refreshing change from the usual, pseudo-laid back but really extremely anxious and neurotic Hollywood approach to things. The say one thing to your face then another thing behind your back approach. There's no fear of that with MDB. She will say whatever she wants right to your face. I asked her one time if she grew up in NYC. She said, "What the fuck does that matter?" I took that as a yes.

I respond, "Yes, Thad called earlier today. I'm going to talk to him when I get back." Pause. Sudden realization. "How did you know about that?"

"Because I told him to call you. Because he's going to be the new L.A.ser Boy. For next season."

?????

It takes me a moment to digest this information. "The new L.A.ser Boy? Why do we need a new L.A.ser Boy? Gyrin…" Gyrin Halto. The actor who plays L.A.ser Boy. The actor who played the investigator character in Mighty Martie. Also of note, MDB's son.

"Because I fired Gyrin yesterday," says MDB matter of factly.

"Wha…why did you fire Gyrin?" I ask. I shouldn't be surprised. But I am.

"Because he isn't strong enough to carry the next season. I've got the scripts. They're good. Very good. Hugh has done a fantastic job bringing them together. The various storylines. You'll love them, I'm sure. But Gyrin is not the right fit for them. So, I fired him. We'll say his L.A.ser Boy got sucked into another dimension or something. Thad will take over. You won't know this at first. Your character, that is. Zenda. But then she'll figure it out. We'll do some CGI stuff with Thad's face for the first few episodes next season. Make him look like Gyrin. Then there will be the big reveal. That's why I had Thad call you. I watched Big Fin X. You and he are good on screen together. I watched a couple of his other movies. He's good. The films are crappy but he's good. So, I want you two to talk. I want you to bring him along, K.C. I know you tried with Gyrin. But it didn't stick. Not your fault. He's just too resistant. So, now it's time to shift to Thad. I've talked it over with Hugh. If Thad does well in the second season of L.A.ser Boy then we'll work him into other Hall-iverse projects. Both you and he and your relationship in all these different stories, different time periods will be the foundation for the Hall-iverse. But he's got to do well in L.A.ser Boy first. If not then…"

I see it now. I say, "Then you'll replace him with some other actor. The multiverse storyline makes that simple, gives you a way to do that. In the story."

"Precisely," says MDB. Like I'm a child who's just realized Santa Claus isn't real and she doesn't have time for me to be upset. The magic isn't magic. It's people lying. A split second after this realization sinks into me, she adds, "Also, I sent you the Losing the Race script. That one you wanted from those women." "Those women" are Sasha and Kelsey. Sasha was my agent. She still is my friend. Mostly. It's just that we never, ever see each other. Even though we don't live that far away from each other. But this is not the time for that.

"Lastly, Jasmine, from Heroes Plus, wanted to go out there sometime later this week. But I've postponed that until next week when you're back. I liked the interview she did with you, Miley and Thad about Big Fin X. I promised her I'd keep her in the loop about season two of Curated Worlds and other Hall-iverse details if she agreed to hold off on this next interview. So, there's that," says MDB. Then, "Go over the script. I see some simple ways we can make it better. But, of course, dear heart, we'll need your feedback, too. That's it." MDB hangs up.

"That show" is Kincaid Live! Sal and MDB have a slippery relationship. Or should I say sticky? No, it's both: slippery and sticky. It's like they're two old boxers who have bumped into each other on the sidewalk and they don't know whether to hug or fight. It feels like something happened between them in the past but neither of them has said word one about it.

I draw up the script in my email. I'm tempted to read it right now. But, first, I need food. And I need to use my tablet. I hate reading scripts on my phone. Too small a screen. Ideally, I'd like to have it printed - pages in hand. I still get a thrill from that. Being handed a script and told, "Okay, K.C., this is your movie." Yeah! I still get goose pimples like it's the first time. Good. The magic isn't gone then. MDB just chased it away for a moment.

I walk up to the main house and head inside to the kitchen. Luisa is there hovering over the massive, ancient, cast iron stove. Clara and another young woman are at one end of the long, wooden table. Luisa flashes me a knowing smile. Clara looks supremely put off by the other woman. That other woman jumps up from her seat when I come in and walks right over to me. She holds out her hand. I shake it. She says, "Hello. My name is Kaley Tonsich. I'm Clara's roommate. If you don't mind, I'd like to interview you for my college newspaper."

27.

I let go of Kaley's hand and look over at Luisa again. She says as she fills a bowl with two ladles of chili and walks over towards me, "I know I said I wanted as few press people at the ranch as possible. But this is part of Kaley's internship. If she doesn't do this then she'll be marked down. Kaley's not press like those people from L.A. She's a student. And a very hard worker. So I said she could wait and you two could do the interview here."

I nod and think, think and nod. This past year MDB has been in charge of all such interviews, articles and appearances. She's the co-founder, along with me, of Whirled Rainbow Productions. As soon as she did some testing and learned that my name for our studio was more appealing to the 18 - 35 demographic she was more than fine dropping her request to call it Midnight Dancer Productions. All business - that's MDB. She does it all: script procurer, fashion adviser, restaurant recommender, bespoke travel guide (yes, we traveled together for a few weeks, a mini press junket for the launch of our company: NYC, Miami, London, Paris; no, it wasn't horrible, much to my surprise; MDB on the road and away from Hollywood is a different creature, a far more personable one), makeup brand selector, music aficionado (everything from pop to classical, even jazz), architectural enthusiast, art critic (okay, that one isn't surprising), cultural commentator and, lastly (please don't tell anyone) a mother figure. Yes, in her own way MDB is very motherly. Yes, that does add a big wrinkle to our relationship. Yes, I am still learning how to navigate that. Navigating the Wrinkle. Write that down.

I take the bowl from Luisa. She says, "Spicy today. Turkey, not beef, like you requested." She shakes her head. She doesn't understand why I don't eat red meat all day every day. But she's willing to go along with it. I hesitate to think how she'd react if I were a vegetarian. I thank her then say to Kaley, "Let's sit and talk first. There are a few things I need to know." As we sit down I see the stoic expression I used to wear a great deal of the time when I was in high school settle across Clara's face.

Hmmmmm.

I hold up a finger to Kaley and phone MDB. She picks up immediately. This is one of the reasons I like working with her. No phone games. I tell her about Kaley and the student newspaper interview request. She, as I knew she would, wants to talk to Kaley to set the parameters of the interview. I say to Kaley as I hand her my phone, "You should step outside. This will take a few minutes." Kaley smiles, takes the phone, says hello to MDB and pushes through the side door. I look up at Luisa. Luisa nods to Clara. I say to Clara, who is a couple of spots down on the opposite side of the long table, "How did that come about?"

Clara, doing her best to keep the stoic expression plastered to her face and failing, says through clenched teeth, "She followed me here. Saw me and followed me here and acted like she's my best friend ever and hey let's have dinner together. But the entire time she was just waiting for you to show up. She was so obvious about it." Pause. She chews over the next words deciding whether to say them or not.

I say them for her, "You hate her, don't you?"

"Yes," says Clara as she slaps her thigh for emphasis. "She's a user."

This term confuses me for a second. A user as in drugs? But...no. I get it. A user as in Kaley uses people. I turn to Luisa for confirmation of this assessment. She shrugs and waggles one hand in the air. Maybe yes, maybe no. Then she says sweetly, "She's just young. She needs to grow up. That's all."

I turn back to Clara who shoots daggers from her eyes at Luisa then says to me, "She's not just young. She's conniving. She usually eats with the other interns, the other students. They all hang out together. But today she was like 'Oh, Clara, I want to get to know you, let's be besties.' But it was so obvious she just wanted to wait here until you came in. All she did was ask me questions about you. She...she...she didn't..."

"She didn't try to get to know you?" I ask.

Clara's eyes flare. She's really good at the eye flare. I need her to tell me how she does that.

82

I say, "Well, sometimes people are just that way. Especially at your age." I shrug. I can tell Clara doesn't like hearing this. "I know. It sucks but it's true. A friend of mine with a new kid - she's going crazy, she's purchased all the kids books in the world even though her kid can't walk let alone read at this point - told me about one of the books. It's about a llama who gets into trouble. Or something like that. The other llamas don't like him. You know how those stories go. But this one has the phrase, 'We all must deal with the annoying llamas of life.' That's just how it is. Right now, Kaley is your annoying llama. Be thankful that she doesn't spit. Because that's what llamas do. They spit on you."

I'm very proud of this comment. It came spontaneously and fit the moment perfectly. I'm half-expecting a round of applause. [Note: yes, the friend is Kalindra.] But I can tell by the expression on Clara's face that she strongly disagrees with this assessment. She not only doesn't want to give me a round of applause, she wants to stab me with a knife. Maybe. Perhaps just yell at me. Ahhh, youth. I'd forgotten what it's like to be a teenager. Everything is so...much. So very muchly much.

Clara peels her eyes off me and looks down at her empty plate. She doesn't say anything for several seconds. Then she says in a whisper, "You sound like my social worker."

It's clear by her tone of voice that soundling like her social worker is not a good thing. She starts to get up from her seat. I know she's going to storm off again. I say sharply, "Hold on. Hold on." Thinking, thinking, thinking. "If you stay here for this interview - it won't take but a few minutes - I promise I'll make it worth your while."

Clara eyes me suspiciously for a moment then asks, "Are you going to make fun of her? Because I don't believe that. That's not your..."

"No, I'm not going to make fun of her." I look to Luisa then back at Clara. "She's young. She'll grow up. But I will *have* a little fun. But it'll only work if you stay here. Okay?"

Clara looks to Luisa for help. Luisa shrugs. She has no idea what I'm up to. Clara relaxes in her seat, taps her fork into her dish a couple of times then says, "Okay."

Kaley comes back in a half minute later. A half minute of silence and continuing suspicious looks from Clara. Kaley sits across from me and hands me my phone back. I can tell by the stunned look on her face that MDB has been very MDB with her. I look at Kaley expectantly. She swallows hard then says, "Mrs. DuBont says it's okay for me to interview you. But I need to send her the interview before I post it on the school site. If I don't..."

Kaley's voice trails off. I know why. MDB has threatened her in some way. MDB has a very colorful way of phrasing her threats. She, of course, doesn't think of them as threats. She thinks of them as "clear guidelines." We were sitting in a studio in NYC waiting to do a morning show when she first said this to me. I almost spat out my coffee. MDB took note of my reaction and said, "People prefer to know where they stand, don't you find?" It was not a question that needed an answer. MDB: love her/terrified by her.

I pick up Kaley's sentence, "...if you don't she'll make sure you never do that again." I say this matter of factly. Kaley nods. I look at Clara for a moment. I see a hint of a smile on her face. But only a hint. I say to Kaley, "Okay. Let's go."

Kaley pulls out her phone and says, "I'm going to record this to make sure I get your answers word perfect."

That's an MDB phrase: word perfect. I knew she'd tell Kaley to do this. I place my phone down on the table, "Great. Me, too. For my own records." Yes, I admit it. MDB has taught me how to be more professional in regards to interviews. More professional, less off the cuff. It's one of the many little lessons that I've taken in over the past year.

Kaley asks several, basic questions. I've answered all these a hundred times before. How did you get started in Hollywood? What's the craziest thing that's happened on set? Who's your funniest co-star? And others along these lines. FYI: you know how I got started in Hollywood, the craziest thing that's happened on set is...seeing a UFO from the top of a hotel in Puerto Santibel and my funniest co-star has been

Miley but that's slightly unfair because she's my personal assistant now so I'm sure there's some familiarity and constant exposure bias mixed in with that assessment. But, come on, "depthen" is a classic. Almost as good as my "buffalo om" joke. Almost. So, yeah, actually I'm the funniest co-star. But I don't tell this to Kaley. I just give her the needed, somewhat canned, somewhat boring but still interesting enough answers so that she'll have a decent interview for her school newspaper.

Towards the end of the interview, Kaley asks the question I knew she'd ask, "What's your next project?"

I say, "Well, I just received a script for a potential movie. The working title is 'Losing the Race.' I'm going to go over it tonight with Clara here and see if it's as good as I think it is or if I should pass on it. It might not be the right fit for me. That's why I need Clara. To help me make that decision."

Kaley's jaw drops open. But only for a second. I'd hoped it would be longer. I give her credit for quickly regaining composure. She says as she looks kindly in Clara's direction, "I didn't know Clara…helped you like that. How…"

Before she can finish her question, I cut in with, "I've known Clara for a couple years now. I've asked her to keep the relationship between us quiet. On the down low. She's sharp. I trust her. Let's just say, I value her input and leave it at that. Some things have to remain secret, after all." Kaley blinks at me, looks again at Clara then looks back at me. I say, "Thanks for the interview. That was fun."

I stand up and look over at Clara as I say, "Do you have time now to go over the script or should we…"

Clara stands up, too, as she says, "Let's do it now." She walks around the end of the table and comes up to me. I offer my arm out and she hooks her arm through. I wave and say goodbye to Luisa. Clara does the same. I bend my head close to Clara and whisper, "Don't look back." We ease ourselves through the doors and walk about a hundred feet away from the main house before we break out laughing.

Clara unhooks her arm from mine and we continue walking as she asks, "So were we the annoying llamas there? Is that what we just did?"

I say, "I think maybe we were the smug llamas. Condescending llamas? Petty llamas? Yes, that's it. We were the petty llamas." We both laugh again.

Then Clara stops in her tracks and says to me with a serious tone of voice, "You didn't have to do that."

I say, "I know."

"Then…why?" There's genuine confusion on Clara's face. In that moment, I realize she's not had this experience in her life yet - someone helping her just to help her.

I say, "Because…I could. Because it was fun. Because Kaley needed it. Because…you're worth it."

Clara stares at me for a moment then starts walking again. We walk several paces before she says anything. Then, as she looks down at the ground, "Is there really a script?"

I say, "Yup. I received it right before I got to the main house."

Clara looks up at me. Her face is so wide and open and hopeful it almost hurts to look at it. She asks, "Can we really go over it together?"

I smile and say, "We have to go over it together. Otherwise, what I told Kaley would be a lie. And I, K.C. Hall, never lie."

For a split second, Clara believes me. Then she realizes I'm joking and says, "Shut up."

She says it in a way that lets me know she doesn't want me to shut up. In fact, she wants to hear more from me. Ahhh, youth. So, I say, "That's called acting, dear heart. Acting." I laugh at my own joke. Clara laughs along with me. Yes, I did hear a touch of MDB in that statement. I'm sure you did, too.

28.

It's a bit later. Clara and I are in my cabin. I'm sitting in the leather wingback chair. There's a special place in my heart for leather wingback chairs. Clara is sitting on the couch. Correction. Clara is supine on the couch holding a printed copy of the script up in the air with one hand as she reads through it. Yes, I have a printer in the cabin. Like I said before, I prefer printed scripts for reading. The printer was my one demand for this week at Luisa's. As stars go, I'm fairly low-maintenance. Cough, most of the time, cough. And, no, don't tell Scott I said that. Unless you want him to burst into laughter. Okay, fine, you can tell Scott. Just do it when I'm not around.

There are two cups apiece on the coffee table between me and Clara. So, four total. Four now empty tiramisu cups. It was delicious. But it got me thinking. How far away is the bookstore with the best danishes in the world? If we drove down there tomorrow and I bought a car for Clara would we have time to get danishes before heading back for the show? I think we would.

Hmmmmm.

Before I make this suggestion, Clara drops her arm and the script down and keeps staring upwards as she asks, "So, the main character has no idea her family was killed by a serial killer? Not until the end?"

I say, "That's correct."

"But why have a serial killer in a movie and not have anyone know about it?" she asks.

Decent question. I say, "Because it's not really a serial killer movie. It's a movie about growing up and figuring out who you are when you don't have the usual structures in place to help you with that." Then it hits me. Oh shit. I look at Clara. She turns her head in my direction. I say, "Sorry. I didn't mean…"

She says, "Nah. It's okay. It's not the first time I've seen similarities between my life and some TV show or whatever."

I nod. Good. I didn't think it through when I asked Clara to read this script with me. The main character grew up without a family. That's close to Clara's situation. Maybe too close.

Clara goes on, "I tell myself..." She pauses. She wants to reveal something to me. But she's still hesitant. She decides to do it. That's the power of tiramisu right there. It can work miracles. Clara says, "...I tell myself I'm almost a superhero."

I don't get it. I cock my head at her and say, "How's that?'

She closes her eyes but keeps her head turned in my direction as she says, "Because my parents aren't dead, like so many superheroes' parents are. But they really aren't in the picture either. Aren't in my life. So...I'm almost a superhero."

Dead parents.

It's Clara's turn to not think it through. Then she does and sits upright all of a sudden as she says to me, "Ohhh, I'm so sorry. I didn't think..."

Her father. My father. My mother. Yeah.

I look her in the eye, "It's okay. Really. I've been through years of therapy." I nod then I add, "Besides, that makes me the superhero, right?"

Clara stares at me. She's doing her best to figure out if my reaction is genuine or if I'm brushing things over. She's still not used to me. She lies back down on the couch and says, "I don't know. Can you fly?"

"When I'm Zenda, I can." Another shrug, "Sort of. It's more like teleportation. Short distance teleportation. Something like that."

"Okay, I see it now," says Clara. She holds up the script again and pretends to read it as she says, "You're not a superhero. You're a superdork."

"Took you long enough to figure that out, girlie," I retort. We look at each other. Nothing needs to be said. We look back at our scripts. We sit and read in silence for several minutes more. I yawn. A moment later, Clara yawns. She puts the script down and turns to me once more, "So...the car thing..."

She's hesitant. A bit unsure. She wants to know that I'm really going to actually truly and for reals buy her a car. I say,

"If we get our asses in gear tomorrow morning we can go down to Rapid City and buy you one. Then we can go get some amazing danishes. What do you think about that?"

She sits upright like she's just been jolted by electricity, "Really? You're not lying? You're not fucking with me?"

I hold my gaze on her face for several seconds before saying very slowly, "No. I am. Not. Lying to you." Pause. "Let's go get you a car tomorrow." Sudden thought, "You do know how to drive, don't you?"

She assures me, "Oh yeah. My uncle taught me a couple of years back. But then he moved to Florida and no one's heard from him since. He and mom..."

She doesn't say anything more about that. I don't ask anything more about that. Instead, I riffle the pages of the script and say, "So, what do you think?"

She scrunches up her face as she says, "There are some nice scenes in there but..."

Once again she trails off. I can tell she's not often been encouraged to share her views. Not encouraged, not told she can, not shown how. That's unacceptable and I'm just the one to help with it. "Go on," I say.

She looks away for a second then back at me as she finally says, "...but what's the point? The killer - which we don't even know about, not really - doesn't get caught until the very end and then all she - Trixie, which is a terrible name - does is hang out with some people in her neighborhood."

"Well," I push back - gently, "she doesn't just hang out. She comes to realize that her life which she thought was so damaged and twisted and incomplete is actually full of connections and warmth and the kindness of others."

Clara screws her face up even more, "Yeah, whatever. Sounds like upper class problems to me. I mean, no one died. Yeah, her family died when she was very young, boo hoo, and it's haunted her ever since. Okay, sure, I feel sorry for her. But she's smart, she's got a job, she lives in a hip area of the city. All she needs to do is...is..."

"Is what, Clara?" I genuinely want to know what she thinks the character (yes, Trixie is a horrible name) should do.

"Sack up," Clara spits out. "All she needs to do is toughen up. The past is the past and it can't hurt her anymore. All she needs to do is move forward. Maybe go get drunk and screw someone. Take her mind off things. That's what bothers me about her. She's always just sitting around feeling sorry for herself. Until the blackout. And even then she's pretty selfish. At first. Until that one guy yells at her."

"I agree," I say, "Until [checks script] Howie yells at her to help the old lady up the stairs, she is pretty selfish. Or is she still in shock from her family's death? I think the writer wants us to think she's in shock. That the disappearance - that's right! It was a disappearance. They vanished. We only find out that they were killed at the end. So Trixie, ugh, never knows, never has closure on what happened to her family. I think that's why the writer has her so disconnected, so self-absorbed. Until she gets yelled at in the blackout by Howie."

I look up from the script to see Clara flipping through her copy. She reads a few lines, flips the pages, reads a few more lines. Her lips move as she gets to the dialogue. She reads and rereads it a couple of times then looks up and says, "So, after years of being in shock or whatever all it takes is a guy yelling at her to snap her out of it? I don't buy it."

I look at her and say, "You're a tough critic. I like it. What do you think should happen? What should Howie do to snap Trixie out of it?"

Clara reads through the scene once more then says, "Howie should grab her by the shoulders and shake her as he yells at her. And the old woman should have fallen down or something. Have a cut with blood. Something dramatic to emphasize the moment."

I say, "Ohhh, I like that. Punch up the scene a bit like that." Pause. "Emphasize the moment. Are you sure you're not a movie critic?"

Clara jokes, "Oh, I'm a critic alright. I criticize everything. In my head. It's just no one has ever asked me my opinion before."

I can see by her face that she's surprised those words came out of her mouth. She let her guard down for a second and now she's expecting to be jumped on. Because that's what would normally happen. But I don't jump on her. Instead, I say, "Well, I'm going to need you to keep speaking up, Clara. We'll take the script with us tomorrow and go over it as we go to the car dealership."

"How will we get there?" says Clara, glad to talk about logistical details and not emotional ones.

"Sal and Marcus have production assistants and fleet vehicles they can spare. I'm sure it will be no problem." Then I stretch my hands over my head and yawn again. "It's time to go to bed. You're welcome to crash on the couch there or…"

Clara stands up and says, "Thanks but I'm going to go back to the cabin and act like I have a big secret because I know that will drive Kaley crazy."

"Well done," I say. Clara gives a little wave, says thanks and heads for the door. A thought. "Be ready to go at 7AM. I'll come by the cabin, yeah?"

Clara understands instantly that this is more teasing of Kaley, "I'll be good to go." Then, she exits.

29.

Sal's an early riser. Marcus is not. This fact has been the bane of Marcus's existence for several years now. Back home, Sal wakes up full of energy and ideas and instantly calls Marcus who is definitely still sleeping. Thankfully, Marcus' wife, Tanesha, is an early riser, too, and loves to tease her husband when his boss calls at the butt crack of dawn. So I'm told. I only met Tanesha once and very briefly. But she has a good vibe, a playful vibe. A nice balance to mister organized and focused Marcus.

All this is to set up the scene that follows. It's 6AM. I've been up for an hour already and finished my workout. I call it the tiramisu workout. I do the workout, I get to eat tiramisu. Perfectly logical. Lots of body weight stuff. Jumping jacks, squats, lunges (I hate lunges), some plankish moves on all fours on the floor suspending my weight on hands and feet and then a brisk jog interspersed with fartlek intervals. What's fartlek? You can look it up. The word is Swedish for "speed play." Essentially you run slow then you run fast. Some people are very organized, measured and precise about how and when they run fast. Me? I wing it. Out here on the ranch there's a nice loop of a gravel path near the main house that makes for perfect fartleking. Ha. I love that word. Fartlek, fartlek, fartlek.

So, post-fartleking but pre-showering, I knock on Sal's door. He opens a moment later. He's beaming and has a huge cup of coffee in his hand. He says, "Ahhh, good to see you up. Come in, come in. Coffee?"

I step inside his cabin. It's the big one as mentioned before. It, too, is rustic western design and furnishings down to the bone. Antlers on the wall, bear skin rug, rough hewn timbers support the ceiling. A painting of a bison looming in tall grass dominates one wall. The morning light is just starting to seep in through the windows. Yes, I was careful. I brought a headlamp with me when I fartleked. Ha. That sounds messy. Sal is already in jeans and a white button down oxford. This is his casual look. I asked him one time if he ever owned a velour tracksuit. He whispered conspiratorially to me, "I have one in every color." Then tapped a finger on the side of his nose and winked at me. I still don't know if he was joking or not. Part of me wanted to see him wearing one this morning. Alas, it was not to be. He hands me an empty coffee mug - a howling coyote design wraps around it - then spins around then back again and pours very fresh, very strong smelling coffee into my cup. I take a sip. It's delicious. I don't even have to say so. Sal can tell by the expression on my face. He says, "Excellent. That's one of the local companies we're working with. I love seeing genuine approval of the products we endorse. That lets me sleep easy at night." He gestures to a wingback chair. His cabin has four of them. I sit on the edge of one. I don't intend to be here long. He says as he sits in a wingback opposite me, "What's gotten you going so early in the morning?"

"Tiramisu guilt," I say. He knows of my confectionary proclivity.

He nods sagely as he says, "Ahhh, yes. I used to call that tequila compensation. But that was years ago. What else?"

"I need a p.a. to drive me and Clara down to Rapid City so I can buy her a car and, also, get some danishes." I feel completely relaxed with Sal. There are not many people in the world I feel completely relaxed with. So, I'm enjoying this. Really enjoying this. A good workout, better coffee and talking to a respected and acclaimed entertainment professional who respects me so much he lets me co-host his show once a year. It's a beautiful thing.

Sal looks up as he says, "Clara? Clara? Is that the young woman who…oh…right." I can tell he's just remembered the nature, no, the occasion for Clara's and my relationship. Her father. My father.

I push past this by saying, "Her mom's in the hospital. Weak but stable. Clara's several hours from home. She doesn't have a car. Luisa…can't travel as freely as Clara needs to. I'm helping her out." I've learned to be direct with Sal. That's what he prefers. Me, too. "If we leave at 7AM then we should have plenty of time to go down, buy the car, get the danishes and head back here. I'll be back in plenty of time to get ready, go over the guests and do all that before the show."

Sal rolls his eyes up again as he runs the day's details through his head. Then he looks at me and says, "Would you mind filming the car buying? And the danishes? This is the place that AM LA showed a video of you at years ago, right?"

He's right. Damn, his memory is good. "Yes, exactly. That place."

He says, "That could make for some good clips. The whole helping out the kid thing. You wouldn't have to divulge the whole story of your connection to Clara. And Clara would have to be on board, too, of course. But at least take some one - hmmm, Al would be good - to film you at the danish place. It would be sweet if the same girl were working there but I suppose that's too much to ask."

I shrug, "I don't imagine she'll be there. But who knows? The world is funny that way. So, yes, Al can drive and film the danishes. I'll talk to Clara about filming the car buying. No promises though. That wasn't part of what I told her would happen today."

Sal says, "Great. Perfect. You better drink up and get your butt in gear."

30.

I'm at Clara's cabin at 6:58AM. I knock. She opens the door immediately. We smile at each other. In the background I hear a confused moan. That's Kaley. I say to Clara with exaggerated tones, "Come on. We've got to head out now to buy your car."

"I'm ready. Let's go," she says far more loudly than she needs to. I step back from the door. She steps out, turns to close the door behind her and says, "See you later, Kaley." We do our best to hold in our laughter as we walk from the cabin to the main house. We do not succeed.

I see Al standing out front as we walk up. He gives us a wave. I wave back. When we're a few feet away, he points at one of the SUV-ish vehicles that the show rented down in Rapid City to schlep various pieces of equipment and personnel up to the ranch. It's midnight blue, boxy, shiny. In other words, it's hummer-adjacent. Which reminds me, I need to keep an eye on Scott in that regard. He's been whispering about getting a Hummer for "self-defense purposes." By this he means that the traffic in L.A. is so bad he wants a big bruiser of a vehicle so he feels safe. He's exaggerating, of course. But only by a little.

We three get in the vehicle and buckle up. Al, of course, is driving. I insist Clara take the front seat and I kick my legs out on the back seat. Al checks the mirrors, enters the name of a car dealership into the built in GPS of the vehicle, looks at each of us in turn and says, "Let's ride!"

Oh, wait! I know this one. I say to Al, "Are you a Broncos fan?"

He smiles as he looks at me in the rearview mirror, "Ab-so-lutely! You?"

I say, "My husband is a Vikings fan but I don't really have a team. I didn't get into football when I was young so Scott, that's my husband, has been educating me for the past couple of years. Trying to get me to like it."

Al says, "And what do you think so far?"

I squeeze one eye shut and tilt my head to one side as I say, "I'm...getting there. There's no doubt the players are incredible athletes. And I do understand the games, the plays

95

a bit better now. But it takes so much time between plays. It's like go, stop, go, stop, commercial, flag, go, stop, penalty, replay review, go, another penalty. So, it's hard to watch sometimes. I'm more of a, mmmm, I guess I'm more of a story person. I like movies and TV shows. Good stories. So, sports are hard for me to watch."

Al says, "You know Game of Thrones?" I nod into the mirror. He goes on, "Just think of each team as its own house. House Bronco. House Patriots. Because in many ways that's what they are. There are trades and free agency - lords and soldiers changing their alliances. There's the much despised king. That's Godell, the commissioner. There's..."

"But there's no dragons," Clara interjects.

Al says, "No, I guess you got me there. There are no dragons. But there are various mascots. The Broncos horse, Thunder, that rides down the field before every game is, clearly, the best of all the mascots. In my humble opinion."

Clara looks at him. I can tell she's assessing him in her head. She waits a moment or two then she says, "So, I'm going to buy a car. I've never had a car before. What kind of car do you have? At home? What do you drive?"

Al looks at me in the rearview once again. I nod. He says to Clara, "Back in L.A. I have your basic sedan. Nothing fancy. Good gas mileage. Good handling. Good for taking road trips with the family because it's got a big trunk. Most cars these days don't have big trunks. I remember the car my parents had when I was really, really young. Its trunk was so big. My brothers and I used to play sardines. You know that game? It's like hide and seek but when you find the person who hid you squeeze in with him wherever he is. One time there were five of us squeezed into the trunk of that car. It felt like we were in there forever. Then six. Then seven. That was ridiculous. We were kids so we were short and skinny but still. It was like those old clips you see of college kids squeezing themselves in phone booths back in the day."

"Phone booths? People squeezed themselves into phone booths?" Clara says dubiously.

I chime in, "Oh yeah. That was big for a while after World War II. Sort of like planking. It was a fad thing." Clara turns to look at me to make sure I'm not pulling her leg. I say, "Look it up. I swear it's true."

Al waits a moment then goes on about cars, "But what I drive isn't important. This is going to be your car. So, what kind of car do you want?"

Clara stares out the windshield at the road and the landscape around us. After a few seconds she says, "That's just it. I don't really know."

"Well," says Al in a very dad-like way, "what are you going to be using it for? City driving? Rural driving? Long trips? Short trips? A combination?" He nods back towards me as he stage whispers to Clara, "Normally, I'd ask what your budget is but with this one back here, I don't think that's a concern." He looks at the road then at Clara, at the road then at Clara, at the road then at Clara. Then he says, "You do realize how lucky you are, right? Most kids don't get cars purchased for them. I mean, sure, some do. But not most." Clara nods and looks down into her lap. Al looks at me in the mirror again, "This is a very nice thing you're doing, Ms. Hall. If you don't mind, I'd like to share this story when we get back to L.A."

I tense up, "On social media? Is that what you mean? Because I don't..."

"No," Al cuts in, "Not social media. Not anything like that. Just with my wife, my kids, my neighbors. Like that. I'm asking because working with Sal on the show there are plenty of things we see, all us staff members, but sometimes the stars don't want us to say anything about it. I understand that. I respect their right to privacy. Even though some of the stuff I see in the tabloids I know is an outright lie. I know things about stars, good things mostly, that never get reported. Never. So, that's why I ask if it's okay for me to tell my neighbors and such. Because I don't think it's fair that the stars get treated that way when most of them are just simple, regular folk underneath it all. Sure, there are some prima donnas and assholes. But no more than any other industry I've worked in over the years."

I lean forward and put a hand on Clara's shoulder. She looks at me. She has a tentative smile on her face. I say as I lean back, "No, Al. Thanks, but no. I'd like to keep this just between us."

Al holds his gaze on me in the mirror for several seconds. I can tell he wants to say something but he doesn't. Instead, he turns to Clara and starts talking about cars again, "Having been through this with my kids a few years ago and seeing other parents go through it with their kids, I suggest you get a brand that is reliable in terms of maintenance. So, personally, I'd go with a Subaru. Great track record. Especially their Foresters. Good mileage, good handling, good in terms of reliability. They have that all wheel drive feature which is great in snow." He asks, "Are you going to be driving in snow? In a snowy part of the country?"

Clara says, "Yeah. And I'll be doing long trips, a few hours, most likely at least once a month. All year round."

Al nods and slaps the steering wheel, "Well, if it were up to me, I'd say get a Forester. Go on and look them up on your phone there. See what they look like. Get a sense of them. But, like I said, for your situation - first car, young driver, long trips, snow - I don't think you can do any better."

Clara soaks up Al's words. I can tell she's done this with other adults over the years. Other parent-like adults. Asked them for advice that any normal kid would have taken in from her own parents. So, this is a mixed bag of emotions for her. She wants the advice. The parental advice. But having to ask a stranger for such advice serves to highlight the fact that her own parents aren't very parental. Which, of course, cannot feel good. No matter how long she's dealt with that dynamic, no matter how normal and usual and familiar it is to her, it can't feel good.

We ride in silence for a few minutes as Clara looks at Foresters on her phone. She shows a couple of the pictures to Al who nods and says things like "ohhh," and "that's nice" and "interesting." Very dad things to say to a young woman purchasing her first car. For a moment, just a moment, I flash back to my dad and my first car. It was a pickup truck. I used it to drive to school and to work. It was a hand me down, essentially. Dad gave me the keys one day and said, "Okay. She's yours now." I loved that truck. I had it in Oregon the year before I made my way to Hollywood. I left it behind with dad. Then he moved to Luisa's ranch. Then… I wonder what happened to that truck.

As Clara is showing Al yet another picture of a Forester, her phone buzzes. She looks at the screen then turns to me as she says, "My social worker." I nod. She answers the phone. She says "okay," and "good," and "uh-uh," and "I'm getting a car," and "no, a friend is helping me," and "no, I won't," and "I promise," and "okay, goodbye."

Clara stares at the phone as she rests it on her lap. She takes a few slow breaths then she turns back to me, "My mom is out of the hospital. She's gone back home. She's better now."

Part of me wants to be really cheery/happy/peppy when I hear this news. But I can tell by the look in Clara's eyes that she's been through this a hundred times with her mom. So, I keep my response muted, "That's good. That she's back home"

Clara shrugs off my comment. Her mom is what her mom is. Then she says, "I told my social worker - Stacy - that I'm getting a car. She didn't believe me at first. She got all curious. She wanted to know if it was a man - a man! - buying me the car. She's funny that way. Protective. I…I told her it wasn't a man. I told her it was a friend helping me. I didn't use your name. I hope that's okay."

I realize - again - as she's speaking to me that Clara has never had anyone help her who isn't contractually obligated to help her. She's never had someone simply do her a favor. A simple favor. Because of her parents' absence and instability, Clara's never been tied into any social network long enough to develop those types of reciprocal relationships. Her time at Luisa's ranch is the most she's ever had in that regard. And - maybe? - her muddled relationship with Jayson. She puts on the tough girl exterior often. At least, I imagine she does. That's what I'd do if I were here. And I - sort of - was her for a while when I was younger.

I say to her, "That's perfectly okay. I like that Stacy looks out for you. And, if you want, we can take a picture together with your new car and send it to her. Just to prove that I'm not a man, of course."

Clara smiles at this comment. But the smile disappears quickly as she asks, "When do you...when should we...when should we tell my dad?"

This is obviously an emotional minefield of a question for Clara. I'm not sure why. So, I ask, "Do you think he won't like this? That I'm buying you a car?" I ask this as gently as I possibly can.

"He always tells me to not owe anyone anything. To make my own way. To buy my own stuff. He says owing people big and not being able to repay them is what got him into trouble. The trouble that led him to steal. So he tells me every time I talk to him to make sure to not owe anybody anything and, if I do, make sure I can pay it back as quickly as possible." She looks down at her hands again, "I don't know when I'm going to be able to pay you back for this, K.C. I really don't."

Uff. A sucker punch right in the gut.

Al and I share a pained look in the rearview. The kid just doesn't understand. She thinks she has to pay me back for the car. All along she's thought that she has to pay me back in some way, somehow. Because that's the lesson her father taught her. Of course, she thinks this way. It's the only way she knows. I reach a hand out to Clara's shoulder once more. I say, "Oh, honey. That's not what this is. You don't have to pay me back for this. You really don't. I...admire that you want to. That's a credit to you. It is. I understand why your dad taught you to pay back what you owe. That's a very good lesson. An important lesson. But it doesn't apply here. It just doesn't. Sometimes..."

I'm searching for the right words when Al says, "Sometimes people help other people because it's the right thing to do. And that's just how it is." Clara looks at Al. Her eyes are brimming with tears. I can tell she wants to believe us but it's been ingrained into her by her life and her father's words not to.

Al goes on, "You remember that big hurricane and flood in Houston a few years back?" I do. Clara doesn't. Al goes on,

"Look it up on your phone. Go on. Look up Houston hurricane flood and people helping. Something like that. It'll take you just a moment. There are a bunch of videos online."

As Clara taps the search terms into her phone, Al turns to me and whispers silently, "Thank you." I put a hand on his shoulder, squeeze it and mouth back the same phrase.

Clara holds up her phone to Al and asks, "Which one…" There are small previews of various videos from that emergency. Al does his best to stay on the road and look at the videos. After a few seconds, he says, "That one on the right there. Play that one."

I lean forward as Clara holds the phone in the space between the front seats so we can all watch the video. An aerial view of a line of cars several miles long appears on screen. The voice of some reporter comes through but it's hard to hear with the noise of the car. So, Al takes over, "You see all those cars, Clara? You see what they have in common?"

Clara tilts the screen towards her a bit and studies the image. Then she says, "They all have boats behind them."

Al nods and says, "Why do you think that is?"

Clara looks closely at the screen again. Her face is blank for several seconds then she gets it. She says, "They're going to help people with the flooding. They're heading back into Houston to use their boats to help people who are flooded."

Al beams at her, "That is one hundred percent correct. And you know what government agency organized that?" Clara shakes her head. "NO government agency organized that. No one person or company or charity organized that. That right there is simply people saying 'I got a boat. Let's go help.' That's it. They saw a need. They knew they could help. So they went and helped. It's that simple. And the people who didn't have boats did other stuff. And the people who weren't close enough to help gave money."

He turns to me, "JJ Watt played for the Houston Texans back then. As soon as people realized how bad the storm was, he set up a donation thing online. He was hoping to get a million, I think, was the first goal. He got that right away. He

101

ended up with something like forty million dollars donated to help the people who suffered in that storm. So, there's your football story right there. Think about that when your husband wants you to watch a game."

He turns back to Clara and the video which is still playing, "So sometimes you don't need to pay a person back. Sometimes you just help people because they need help. Sometimes you need the help. Sometimes you give the help. That's how the world works."

Al turns to me. I add to Clara, "The best thing you could do with your car is go visit your father as often as you can. And go to work. Wherever that is. And take a fun trip to some place you've always wanted to go. And go visit friends. And…well, hell, just go for a drive, see the sights, have some fun. And send me pictures. I'd like to see the pictures. But you have to promise to smile in each one. If you don't smile…well, I don't know what I'll do but I'll do something."

31.

As we pull into the car dealership, my phone buzzes. It's a text from Sasha saying, "Got time to talk, pipsqueak?"

I'm a little pissed when I see her use her nickname for me. She doesn't get to use that name anymore, I think. Because…because I don't want her to. But, in reality, I do want her to. I want our relationship - me and Sasha - to be good again, to be like it was again. Then she could call me pipsqueak and everything would be fine. But now when I see that word in the text it's just a reminder that things aren't fine between us.

I look up from my phone and see Clara showing more pictures of Foresters to Al. They've been doing this for the past twenty minutes or so. Clara, once she realized that she doesn't have to pay me back for the car, really dove into figuring out what she wants. Al has been a great help to her this morning. A great help.

I look around the sprawling lot of cars that surrounds the main building of the dealership. There are several people - couples, individuals - walking around the lot looking at vehicles. We're not the only early risers who want to get a car today. I look back at the main building. I see a couple of what I assume are car dealers (Car agents? What is the proper term these days? Car advisors? Car specialists?) waiting to work with customers. A thought. I say to Al and Clara, "Why don't you two go on in and start the process. I'll stay here. I think that's best. Otherwise…" I hold up my phone, "I have to make a call anyway, so…"

Al gets it before Clara does. Clara looks disappointed. She really wanted to go car shopping with me. And I do with her, too. But that would eventually (quickly) become about me. Someone would recognize me and we'd do the whole autograph and picture thing and the whole focus would shift from Clara buying her first car to OMG, K.C. Hall was buying a car today! No! I swear! I was there! Al sees Clara's disappointment as well. He says to her, "Come on. Let's go get you the best vehicle here and when we're ready, we'll drop the K.C. bomb on them. That'll make their heads spin."

Clara takes a moment to process Al's comment then smiles bigly, so bigly. She says to me, "You don't mind? I don't want you to feel like I'm using you…"

I assure her, "No, really, it's good. If I go out there with you now it'll be a mess. You and Al go. I'll make my phone call then you guys let me know when you're ready for me to come in at the end."

Clara smiles, thanks me again and pops out of the car. Al follows a moment later after he looks at me in the rearview again and says, "You're a good person, K.C. Hall."

His comment hits me in the soft spot. He's out of the car and the door is closed behind him before I let the tears come to my eyes. Sometimes I feel like a good person; sometimes I feel like an asshole. Right now, with Sasha, I feel like an asshole. I text back to her after wiping the tears from my eyes, "Yeah, actually, I do have time to talk. But no pipsqueak. Not anymore."

A moment or two passes as I stare at my phone. The three bubbles come up. Sasha's typing back a text. The three bubbles. Three bubbles. Three bubbles. My god! Is she writing a book? Come on, send the text! Three bubbles. Three bubbles. Three… no, the three bubbles disappeared. But there's no text. Wha… I nearly jump out of my skin when my phone rings. Oh my god, K.C. Chill the fuck out, calm the fuck down. It's just Sasha. Of course, it's Sasha.

I pick up and say, "Hey." I say that as neutral and calm as I can manage. But my voice does squeak a little.

Sasha, thank god, does not notice my voice squeaking. She simply says, "Hey back." There's silence for a few moments. I'm not sure what to say. She's not sure what to say. This never happened between us before. This is the opposite of how we were before. Yeah, we mended bridges after I left her company and Sasha and Kelsey signed Josie Steans and then signed a big deal with GMG. We mended fences, yes, but the fences are still there. There didn't use to be fences. Which caused its own problems. And now there are fences and, I think, that's what's messed things up. We don't know how to talk to each other over the fences. Around the fences? Through the fences? Fences, fences, fences. Fartlek,

fartlek, fartlek. Ok, that made me laugh in my head a little. I'll start.

[Note: I think I'll make 'fartlek' my new F-word.]

"So, what's up?" Good. Simple. Ask a question. Get the ball rolling.

Sasha says, "No 'pipsqueak,' huh? How about I call you T.A. then for tiramisu addict?"

She's trying to be funny. Should I go with it? Okay, why not? "Ow, that hurts because it's true. But I think T.A. is taken already. T.A. T. and A. Right? That might be confusing."

"Fair point," Sasha concedes.

Then she takes a deep breath. I know that breath. It's Sasha's let's get down to business breath. But I'm not ready to get down to business - whatever that may be today - just yet. I'm still a few feet away from that fence. So, I say quickly, "I need to thank you for those bodyweight routines you showed me a while back. I've been using those to counteract my tiramisu intake."

Sasha sighs, lets the deep business breath go and asks, "Which routines?"

"The ones with the groundwork. The all fours leg sweeps and ab twists and get ups and whatever those other exercises are called. The plyometric ones. They work. They really do. Especially when powered by Dakota coffee."

Sasha catches the geographic reference, "Right, you're out there this week. How is that going? I confess I was really busy last night. I didn't see the show."

Ow. That hurt. For real. Because, besides Mo, Sasha was my biggest cheerleader. For years. And now she didn't even watch the damn show? Really? Then, of course, I get really mad at myself. Like, really, K.C.? You need Sasha to stay current with every little project you do? She has her own life, you know? She's not your agent anymore. That, in fact, is why you left her company - so your career and your friendship with her could be separate. Duh!

I manage to say without my voice breaking, "It was good. It's more fun than I realized. Doing the show. The first time I did it - last year - the whole experience was so new and overwhelming that I didn't let myself enjoy the process. You know how that is. But this time, a little experience under my belt, I'm letting myself relax a bit more, enjoy the process more."

Hmmmmm, I hadn't realized that before I said it. But it's true. I'm not making it up. This time with Kincaid is more enjoyable. Maybe because I know it's just a week. It's Sal's show. Sal's universe. I'm just visiting. Before I dive into my own universe.

"That's good to hear. Really. I'm happy for you. I'll make sure to watch last night's show when I get home," Sasha says.

Right. She recorded the show so she could watch it later. Duh, K.C. There is this stuff called technology. Of course, she recorded the show. Does that make me feel better? Yes, not going to lie. That makes me feel better.

"You good to really talk now?" Sasha asks.

"Yes. Yes, I am. So, what's up?" I say. This is a more serious "what's up."

Sasha says, "I know I've been distant these past few months. So, first, I want to apologize for that. I'm sorry. I am. But I need you to know that you were never far from my thoughts, K.C. Seriously. In some ways, you've been all I've been thinking about this past year."

Dammit. More tears. Dammit, dammit, dammit. Don't say anything because she'll hear your voice cracking instantly. But you have to say something. Say something! Say! Something! "Yeah," is all I can manage. That "yeah" sounded like a hostage agreeing to some point her captor is insisting upon as he holds a gun to her head. Let's try that again, "Sure." Okay. That was…better. That was…not pathetic. That's the best I can do in the moment. Sasha will have to understand. Damn, I missed talking to her. I've missed her.

Sasha takes another deep breath. She really means business. This is really getting serious. I hold my breath as she says, "Here's the thing. You're going to be happy for me. I promise you will. When I tell you what's been going on with me this past year. Personally. But you're also going to be mad at me. Like maybe really, really mad. So, that's why I've been distant. That's why I haven't called to check in with you. And all that. So, here are your options. I know you love options. Scott pointed that out to me one time. He said…no, forget that. I don't want to get distracted. Here are your options. One: I tell you the thing that you'll be happy about first. Two: I tell you the thing you'll be mad about first. Three: I tell you both things all at once in the same sentence." Pause. "So, how do you want to do this?"

I need more information. I like options AND information. That's true. I say, "On a scale of me playfully calling you a bitch at the low end to me hanging up instantly on the high end how bad is the bad thing?"

"Ummm, you'll probably hang up instantly and even, maybe, throw your phone across the room. So, if there's anyone else around, you might want to give them a heads up that there will be projectile danger shortly." Sasha manages to say this in a tone of voice that is both light and honest. Forthright. With a touch of humor. Just enough humor to make it palatable. I really missed talking with her.

"Okay. And on a scale of say 'oh, that's good to hear' on one end and me jumping up and down like a lunatic and saying 'OMG, yes, yes, yes, she did it' on the other end how good is the good thing?"

Sasha says, "Well, that depends on how selfish you're being today. Are you in good K.C. mode today? Or pissy-grumpy K.C. mode? How selfish are you being today, Miss Thing?"

That comment was a risk for her. I'll let her get away with it. I look out the car window as a couple with a car agent (I'm sticking with 'car agent' as that sounds more Hollywood) walks past. This, of course, makes me think of Al and Clara out there buying a car. Clara's first car. I say to Sasha, "Today, actually, I'm being so good. Like notably good. Like tell this story for years good."

Sasha says, "Ohhhh. I wish I was there. I like you whole bunches when you're like that, K.C." Pause. "I miss that, K.C. I do."

"Me, too, Sash." We let the moment rest between us. Nothing else needs to be said.

Except, of course, for whatever it is that needs to be said.

I ask, "You really think you can tell me both things at once in one sentence?"

"I know I can. Because they're tied together. Like…weirdly tied together," says Sasha.

I hear a voice in the background. But I can't make out the words. I ask, "Are you in your office?" I assumed she wasn't. I didn't realize that until just now but I did. I figured she'd be at home or in a car when she called me like this. Not her office. At her office, she'a all Amazon warrior, let's go conquer the world Sasha. This phone call doesn't match with that Sasha. The content. The tone. The whole thing.

"No. I'm in the car. Heading to Malibu, actually, for a little get away," she says.

Curiouser and curiouser. A get away and someone is in the car with her. I can't be sure but it sounded like a male voice. Oh. Oh, I get it now. Sasha's in a relationship. That's the good thing. Okay. Okay, okay, okay. Yes! I am instantly happy for her. I know that part of her life has been hard for her for the past few years and if now indeed she's found someone and is serious about this someone… I need to know. "Okay, tell me the good thing. Then give me time to respond. Then tell me the bad thing."

Sasha asks, "Are you sure?"

"Yes," I say instantly. Then just as quickly, "No." Then, "Shit, Sasha, I don't know. I want to be happy for you and I definitely don't want to be angry at you. But you're telling me that I'll be both. So, I don't know. So…you decide. You know me, Sasha. You do. More than most people. So, you decide. I trust you. I do. I trust you." It feels good to say that last part. I do trust Sasha. Even though our relationship is strained. If shit went down in my life right now, I'd reach out to her for advice and help. I realize that now. So, I do trust her and it feels good to know that.

Sasha says, "Okay, here goes. I'll tell you the good thing now." Pause. "I'm on my way to Malibu with my boyfriend. No, wait. With my fiance. I have a fiance, K.C. I'm engaged."

YES! Yesyesyesyesyesyesyesyes! "Ohhhh! Sasha! I'm so freakin' happy for you! So! Happy! What's his name? Who is he? How'd you meet? How did he propose? Tell me! I need to know everything. Tell me, tell me, tell me."

Sasha takes a really deep breath. Uh-oh. Then she says, "It's…it's….ohhhh…."

I hear the phone get handed off to someone else. I realize in a flash that she's in the car with her fiance and instead of telling me who her fiance is Sasha is handing the phone to him so he can introduce himself. Okay. Let's go. Say you're damn name whoever you are new person that I'm excited to get to know because you'll be in my life as long as you're in Sasha's life which better be forever since you're getting married and that's a vow, buddy, a lifetime vow so don't fuck that up with any Hollywood divorce philanering bullshit because I swear if you hurt Sasha I will reign…

"Hello, K.C. This is Connor Elroy."

…

…

…

What?
The?
Fartlek?

32.

I stammer, "Is... Is this... Is... Ummmm... Put Sasha back on, please."

Once again, I hear the phone handed off. Then Sasha's voice comes through, "Hey."

I reach back a few years for a word I made up in my head. I told Sasha about it. And Scott. Maybe Sophie. But I haven't used it in a while. I say, "I'm so very pisspressed with you right now. Like the most pisspressed I've ever been with anybody. I think I'm in shock. No. I am in shock. Like shock shock. I don't even know how to respond. I need...I need to know how this came about. No. Wait. Put Connor back on the line. I need to say something. I need to say a million things, really. But let's start with just one thing."

The phone gets handed back. Connor says, "Hello, again, K.C. First, I'd like to apolo..."

"No! No, no, no. That's what I was going to do. I was going to apologize to you. You don't get to apologize first. I apologize first. So. Yeah. I'm sorry. Take that. I mean. There it is. I'm sorry for sending multiple messages to you trying to get you to meet with me when you very obviously didn't want to meet with me when the whole thing about my dad, I mean, our dad, I mean... I mean... Ohhh, fuck, I don't know what I mean. But, whatever I mean, I do mean I'm sorry. Really. Sorry."

There's silence on the other end of the phone. Then Connor says, "Yeah, I don't think I could have put that any better myself. I'm sorry, too. Really. Sorry. For being a dick to you professionally before you even knew who I was. I am really, tremendously sorry for that. I am. I don't know if I'll ever get over how guilty I feel about that. But, I guess, this is a start. Maybe. I hope."

Wait. He's.... What? He's sorry? He feels guilty? I am so confused right now. But, let's put a pin in all this. This is not about us. I mean, it is. But it isn't. We'll have time to hash this out later. Most likely. Let's get back to Sasha. I say, "Okay, Connor, okay. I have to say this has been weird. Very weird. But I need you to..."

"Yeah," Connor says, "here's Sasha."

"Hey, Case," Sasha says. It's the most beautiful thing she's ever said to me. Her voice is full of light. I can feel it.

"Hey, Sasha," I say back. More silence. Comfortable silence. The fences have opened and we're all in the same field of silence. Beautiful silence. Finally, I say, "So, sounds like you've been busy, yeah?"

"Ha!" Sasha barks out. A barking laugh. A laughing bark. Then she says, "So, this started, all of this started with a fucking business meeting. How un-romantic is that, Case? I met Connor at a business meeting. That was a while after you did your bit on Kincaid about your dad but just shortly after AM LA did their piece on your dad and…"

I can tell she doesn't want to say it. So I do, "His affair. With Connor's mom."

"Yeah. That. Anyway. I'd talked to you briefly around then. But you were really busy with Curated Worlds. Then I ended up in this meeting with Connor and I knew who he was instantly. He looks like you, K.C. Have you realized that? I guess you both look like your dad. I saw it as soon as he walked through the door. It's impossible not to see it. Anyway, I was pissed. So pissed. I waited until the meeting was over and then I pulled him aside and read him the riot act about you. Because I'd been informed by then by let's just call them reliable sources that Connor had been the one who didn't want you associated with GMG. I lit into him, K.C. I mean, you've seen me. You know me. But this, this was even a bit much for me. I don't know where it came from. Except, I guess, feeling protective of you. I was like 'how dare you' and 'didn't you even think' and 'what gives you the right' and 'if you ever do that with her again'….yeah, all that and more. Just lit right into him. And he stood there. He stood there and listened and nodded and let me go on and on and on. Then, the fucker, at the end of my tirade he asked me out on a date. Fucker. I had to say yes. I just had to. If he could listen to me rip into him and then calmly ask me out on a date I had to get to know him better. So, I went on a date with him. And…yeah, here we are months later driving to Malibu and I have a ring on my finger. Fuck. The world is strange, Case. Stranger than fiction."

My phone buzzes. I look at the screen. Clara has just sent me a funny-faced bomb emoji proceeded by my initials. Ahhh. Time for the K.C. bomb. I say to Sasha, "Look, I have to go now and I'd rather continue this conversation in person anyway. With both of you. You two Malibu lovebirds. Ohhh, I'm so happy for you Sasha. Truly. So happy. But I do have to go now. I have to buy a car for a kid."

"Come again," says Sasha.

"Long story. I'll tell you when you and Connor come over for dinner at the penthouse," I say and smile.

"You love saying that. 'At the penthouse,'" says Sasha.

She's right. I do. "How can you not love saying that? I defy anyone to not have a smile on their face when they invite a friend over to their penthouse. Can't do it. Not possible." More comfortable silence. Non-fency silence. "Okay, I really do have to go buy a car."

"Love you, pipsqueak," Sasha says.

"Love you, too," I say back.

33.

I stride through the front doors of the car dealership and see Al and Clara right away. I give them a quick wave and head over to them. They're sitting in front of a desk. On the other side of the desk is a slightly upset middle aged woman. I can tell she thinks that this kid and this guy are messing around with her. As she looks in my direction when Clara waves at me, her face goes from slightly upset to slightly confused to majorly confused to OMG, I know that person.

[Note: "know" here in this context really means "recognize" but very few people point at celebrities and say "I recognize you." Instead, they point/gawk and say, "I know you." So, now you know about "know."]

Clara is bursting when I get to the desk. Al is smiling like a proud dad. I guess that makes sense. This whole process has been very parent-ish. I'm happy to see that Clara's happy. I stand between their two chairs as I address the car agent (yup, sticking with it). She's standing now. She's wearing a business casual outfit of a very nice, maroon polo shirt and khaki pants. Instead of having a polo player on it, the shirt has a stylized car. That's when I realize her outfit is de rigueur for employees of the dealership. By the way, I'm in a nice blue and green watercolor-ish long sleeve silky top, a pair of A jeans, simple black ankle boots (suede) and my hair is pulled back in a ponytail. Also, sunglasses. Big ass sunglasses. Which I've just taken off.

The car agent woman is now one hundred percent sure that I am, indeed, K.C. Hall. I reach a hand across to shake her hand. She extends her hand but she's really focused on my face. Focused on my face and not saying a damn thing. I shake then let go of her hand. Her hand remains extended in the air for several seconds as she continues to stare at me. I wait. I've learned to be patient in moments like this. When they aren't annoying, they can actually be fun. After a few more seconds, I say as I look down at Clara then Al then back up at the woman, "So, is everything ready to go?" I reach into my small, shoulder bag of a purse. Did I mention the purse? Probably not. I usually don't carry one. But this morning I did. I reach into my purse and pull out my small wallet then pull out my purple credit card. Shiny, metallic purple. I love it. I flash the credit card and say again, "Is everything ready to go?"

The woman snaps out of her trance and says as she sits down, "Yes, of course. Excuse me. I didn't mean to be rude. It's just..." She doesn't finish her sentence. She looks at the paperwork in front of her then at her computer screen then says, "Yes," she looks at my credit card and reaches for it tentatively, "so the entire purchase is going on here. Do I have that correct?"

I extend the card to her. She takes it gently from my hand and somehow manages to not stare at it. Most retail people stare at my credit card when I hand it to them. I think it's a form of validation for them. Or maybe they're checking to see if my stage name matches the name on my card. It does. K.C. Hall is my name. I made it up. But I, also, made it legal. Years ago. But most people don't know that so they stare at the card. At least, that's why I think they stare at the card. As she scans the card and taps on her keyboard, I ask Al, "Did you get all the bells and whistles? All the extra insurance and service policies? All that?"

Al says as he looks up from his phone, "I figured you'd want the whole ball of wax, so, yeah, we had Susan here add all that to the package."

"Full roadside assistance? Satellite link calling? All that stuff?" I ask as I turn to Clara.

Clara hops up and gestures for me to sit down. I wave her off but she says, "No, please. I'm too excited to sit." Fair enough. I sit in Clara's seat and she stands on my left side. Now that she's mentioned it, I can feel how buzzy she is. Buzzy with excitement about getting a new car. I look at Susan, the car agent. She's zipping through a series of computer screens making sure all the ducks are in a row. Then she hits the print button and the grinding whine of the printer next to her desk kicks in. I look up at Clara and grab her hand. She smiles down at me and squeezes my hand back. I look over at Al. He's once again staring at his phone. He's frowning. I wonder wh...

Susan, car agent X952, says to me, "Here's your card, Ms. Hall and here for you young lady is the paperwork that needs to be signed. I've marked each spot with one of those, yup, those little sticky notes so if you could just…" Susan looks at me then at Clara. I get it. I stand up and Clara sits back down and pulls the chair closer to the desk as she goes through the paperwork signing her name. After a moment, she looks up at Susan and asks, "So, this is my car not…" She looks back over her shoulder at me.

Susan assures her, "Ms. Hall is paying for the vehicle. But it is one hundred percent legally your car. It is yours. You are the owner." She finishes with a sharp nod. I smile at her when she looks up at me. She gives me the same sharp nod. Clara beavers away at signing her name for several more seconds then hands the stack of pages back to Susan. Susan goes through them separating out the dealership copies and Clara's copies. Al asks me as he remains focused on his phone, "The danish place. Is that called Bidwell's?"

"Uhhhh," I say, "Yes." Then, "Huh. I always think of it as the 'danish place.' For a second there, I forgot its name. Bidwell's. That's it." Al nods and continues to stare at his phone.

Susan stands up, neatens the pile of pages then sticks it inside a sturdy, plastic folder thing, hands that to Clara and says, "There you go. You are now the obviously very proud owner of a brand new car." Clara takes the folder thing and shakes Susan's hand. Then Susan says, "Oops, forgot the most important thing." She grabs a set of keys from her desk and hands those to Clara.

Clara's eyes go even wider, even bigger. She says to both me and Susan, "So, I can just go out there and drive it off, drive away?"

Susan says, "Our technician will have it out front for you with a full tank of gas in just a minute and then, yes, absolutely, you can…you should drive it off. It's your car now."

Al is standing now as Clara turns to him and bounces on her toes for a second then wraps her arms around him as she says, "Thank you, Mr. Curial. Thank you so much."

Al returns her hug as he says, "You're welcome. And I told you to call me Al. Please, just Al." He looks into Clara's eyes then says, "Let's go out front and wait for your car." Clara all but runs for the front door. Al hurries along after her. I take a moment to watch then I walk after them.

That's when Susan calls to me, "Excuse me, Ms. Hall."

Ahh, right. I should have expected this. She wants a picture or autograph or both. It's all good. I turn back to her and say, "Yes?"

Susan's hands are clasped over her belly. She looks me directly in the eyes as she says, "I met your father once. He was a very sweet man. Very sweet." Her eyes flick over my shoulder to watch Clara for a moment. When she focuses back on me, she adds, "I can see his sweetness in you. That was a very nice thing you just did. Very nice, very sweet."

Bam. Another blow to the soft spot. First, Al. Now Susan, car agent X952.

I'm speechless for several seconds. I can feel the tears welling up in my eyes. I blink them away. Finally, I say, "You met him…?"

Susan says, "He traded in a pickup truck. Years ago. Rickety old thing. But I could tell he hated to part with it. He almost didn't sign the papers. But then he did. She adds gently, "I wouldn't have remembered except that it was shortly before…" She stops and looks me in the eye. She goes on, "There were pictures in the paper. That's when I recognized him. Also, a couple of years back when you came out this way for your mother's funeral. That brought it back to mind, too. Then that story about his affair. That one that came out a while back. I…I'm sorry but I need to say this. I hope this doesn't offend you. I told myself if I ever had the chance to tell you this that I would. Don't be mad at him. At your father. I only met him briefly. But I could tell he was one of those people who beat themselves up for doing wrong in the past. They do something and regret it for the rest of their lives. And, sweetie, that's just not fair. It's just not. We're human. We make mistakes. And the worst mistake is never forgiving ourselves for some stupid, hurtful thing we did years ago. So, there you go. I said it. I hope I didn't offend you. I hope you think of him as I think of him, as a sweet man doing the best he could."

Susan's eyes flick over my shoulder again. I turn to see what she's seeing. The Forester has been brought up front. The technician has stepped out. Clara is bouncing around the car, patting it, running her hand along its side, jumping in the air and doing a happy dance. Susan says from behind me, "He would have liked that."

I keep my eyes on Clara who is now posing for a picture in front of the car as Al gives her directions on how to catch the light just so. He is a cameraman, after all. I say, "Yes. Yes, he would have."

34.

It's a few minutes later. I made sure to wipe my tears away and smile, smile, smile as I walked out to Clara and Al. Al says to me as Clara hops in her car (it's blue, by the way, excuse me, horizon blue pearl), "So, now that that is all done and good, I do have some bad news." I wrinkle my forehead as I look at him. He pulls a frown then says, "Bidwell's went out of business a few months back."

I study his face. I don't want that to be true. But I can tell Al's not lying to me. Why would he? So, I say, "Dammit. I liked that place."

Al nods his head in commiseration with me then says, "Is there any place else you want to go, to try for danishes?" Then, "Didn't you say the other day your brother-in-law has a store somewhere in town?"

I actually thought of Sam before I headed out here. But he's away at a comic con in Lincoln, NE this week. I shake off Al's suggestion, "Yeah but he's out of town."

Al frowns again, "I'm sure there's someplace we could get donuts or whatever."

He's doing his best to finish out the trip holding to some semblance of our original plan. I look at Clara in the driver's seat. She's playing with the controls. The wipers go. The windshield gets sprayed with cleaner fluid. The direction signals go. Then the emergency flashers. She cranks the stereo so loud we can easily hear the lyrics to some syrupy, pop song. I can't help but laugh. Al does, too. I say to him, "I think we're good here. Let's head back to the ranch."

He smiles, "I agree. So, you ride with her and I'll follow along, okay?"

"Okay," I say. Al walks off towards the fleet vehicle. As I get in the passenger seat, I turn to Clara whose eyes are still big as saucers. I say to her, "Let's ride!"

35.

Sal calls me when we're about ten minutes out from the ranch. After I pick up and tell him we're almost back, he says, "Ahh, excellent, good. I've just heard from my agent inside today's bus group…"

Agent. That's where I got that from. Right.

"…and it sounds like there's some potentially really interesting interviews. I thought you were going to be gone longer so I was calling to tell you to give you a chance to think about them. But since you're so close, I'll just wait until you get here."

"Okay, Sal. Sounds good. Thanks for the heads up. I'll see you in a few," I say. A thought. "Any feedback on last night's show?"

Sal says, "Early returns are very good. More viewers than the first show of the week last year. So, very good. People seemed to like the old man and his grandson."

"Which librarian do we have on today?" I ask.

"Ahhhh, good," says Sal. "Glad you asked. Change of plan. We're shifting the librarian to later this week. Tonight, because of a scheduling thing, you're going to interview the Classics professor."

Oh. "Jodi something or other, right?" I ask Sal.

"Jodi Whitmore. Yes. Good memory. She'll actually be here in an hour or so. She wanted to come see the ranch, the whole bee hive set up. She says it ties into her work. Bee metaphors or something like that. Who knew?"

"Who knew?" I echo back to Sal. "Okay, see you in a few." I hang up.

Clara asks, "All good?" as she mechanically moves her eyes from the rearview to the sideview to out front through the windshield for several seconds then starts the cycle all over again with the rearview. She is a very deliberate driver. Very focused. I remember that stage.

"All good," I say. "Just the usual changes."

Clara's eyes are on the road in front of us as she announces, "I'm going to call my dad tomorrow and tell him that I'm going to visit him at the end of the month." When she finishes her statement, she grips the steering wheel so hard her knuckles go white. She turns to look at me for a quick moment and says, "I can't thank you enough for this, K.C. I just can't."

I rest a hand on her shoulder and say, "You already have."

36.

Let's cut right to the show. Oh! First, my outfit. When I went to see Greg to be coiffed and dressed for the show, he said, "We're doing a little stretch from cowgirl chic tonight. I know, I know. But when I saw this I knew I had to put you in it." At that point he flourished a sparkly tuxedo in front of my eyes. But not quite a tuxedo. It was more the bastard love child of a tuxedo and one of Elvis' Vegas-era jumpsuits. I say so, "Isn't that a bit too Vegas for the vibe this week?"

Greg looks at me, looks at the suit which he's now hung on a rolling rack in such a way that we can admire it like a piece of art in the museum. He looks back at me then back at the suit. He brushes a hand down its length of encrusted gems (large on the lapel, tapering down in size as they flow down the sides of the jacket and extend in a similar decreasing in size arrangement from the waist of the pants down to the cuff of each leg. The material is silky black with embedded sparkles. The pinpoint light reflections of the sparkles highlight the large gleams that come from the facets of the faux gems. The gems add texture to what is a fancy, yes, but simple, classic tuxedo.

Greg says, "Hold on. You haven't seen the best part." He disappears behind another rolling rack of clothes for a moment then comes back bearing the cummerbund and shirt to complete the outfit. He says as he holds them in front of the jacket, flicking the side panels out a bit so I can get a sense of what I'll look like once I put the ensemble on. The shirt is the lightest pink I've ever seen. The studs that run down its centerline are similarly light pink versions of the smaller black gems that encrust the jacket and pants. It looks good. But it doesn't compare to the cummerbund.

The cummerbund has a leather sheen to it. It is stiff and looks heavy. It is, in fact, a miniature version of a WWE championship wrestling belt. It has thick, bright pink stitching done in a flowery, cursive style lettering that says "K.C." right in the slightly bulging center. There are swirly/spiky patterns flowing around then trailing off to each side of the cummerbund done in the same bright pink thread. Between the K and the C is an elongated, pointy, diamond-shaped, pink crystal. Bright pink crystal. Greg hooks the hanger of the shirt over the main bar of the rolling rack, drapes the cummerbund championship belt over the same bar, holds up a single finger in my direction then disappears once more only to return a moment later with simple, mid calf length black cowboy boots with pink stitching that matches the cummerbund belt perfectly. He places the boots down in front of the pants then stands back to admire the whole thing.

He's standing next to me as we take in the sight of the outfit. He says without looking at me, "This, honey, is buckaroo sparkle times a million." Then, "This, honey, is K.C. the Magnificent." Then, "This, honey, is a classic outfit which is what you wear when you talk to a Classics professor."

Greg, once again, is correct. And I love it. It's the outfit I'd wear if I could perform at my own funeral. I have only one suggestion. I say to Greg as we both keep our eyes on the outfit, "I need a matching top hat."

Greg grabs my shoulder and squeezes so hard it hurts. He says, "You are so right. I will make that happen."

Long story short, he made that happen.

Now, on with the show.

37.

I walk out on stage in front of tonight's tour bus audience and the crowd goes wild. They give me and my outfit a standing ovation. Yes, it's fancy. It is, in fact, gaudy. But it's the flashy, damn right I look this good gaudy that everyone wants to pull off at least once in her life. It's cocky gaudy. It's I am in charge fancy. It's don't tread on me sparkly. It's modern day Rat Pack fresh. It's welcome to my world, let me take you on a tour you will never forget brazen. I. Love. It.

When the clapping and cheering die down, I raise the top hat (black satin with a matching light pink hatband) off my head and bow slightly. The crowd bursts into another round of applause. When that fades away, I turn to the side and give a wave to Sal and Marcus. They are genuinely surprised. No, neither Greg nor I told them about tonight's outfit. In our preparation meeting, they didn't ask and I didn't tell. I love the looks on their faces. It's a mixture of admiration, shock and oh, no, what have we done?

"Evening, Sal, Marcus," I say with a shit-eating grin on my face.

Sal says the only thing he can say, "All you're missing is a cigar." I can tell by his tone of voice that he's surprised but happy with the outfit. Sal is not one to shy away from a little flash, a little showmanship. I say as I wave a hand down the length of my outfit and do a little spin to show it off, "You like it, Sal. I can tell you like it. I can talk to my people and get you one just like it, if you want."

Sal puts up his hands in mock surrender as he says, "Oh, no, K.C. That outfit is for you and you alone. I couldn't pull that off. Not in a million years."

Sal turns to Marcus. Marcus says to him, "Not in ten million years."

The camera focuses back on me as I start the show in earnest, "Welcome to our show. I'm K.C. Hall and I will be tonight's ring leader. You see, we're mixing things up a bit. Instead of the originally scheduled librarian I'll be talking tonight to one Jodi Whitmore who is a Classics professor at…" At this point, I pretend to forget the name of the university Ms.

Whitmore works at. So, I turn to Sal and say, "Ummm, ahhh, do you guys remember where she's from? What university?"

When the camera shows Sal and Marcus, Sal has on fake moose antlers and is wearing a Wossamotta U. sweater while Marcus has draped on his head a pair of olde time aviator goggles. This, of course, is a reference to the Rocky and Bullwinkle show from back in the day. From way back in the day. I confess that I've only seen a couple of clips. But Sal and Marcus love it. They're the ones who wanted to do this schtick. I honestly have no idea if it'll get a good...

The tour bus audience is roaring with laughter. Sal and Marcus say a couple of Rocky and Bullwinkle's catchphrases then pass it back to me. Score one for nostalgic humor. I'll have to watch that show when I have some free time. Which may be five years from now but whatever. Hollywood is as Hollywood does.

Picking up the joke, I snap my fingers and say, "No, no, that's not it guys. It's not Wossamotta U. where Ms. Whitmore works. It's Grayson University." I wait a beat as if I'm expecting a huge round of applause for mentioning Grayson University. As really expected, there is utter silence. I pretend to be stunned by the lack of response from the crowd. I say, "No, I know they don't have a football program. But, come on, we've all heard of the Fighting Grayson Tigers, right? We all watched them take down the Parvard Crimsonettes in a sudden death overtime of the K-Nowledge Bowl, right? I mean, talk about a nail-biter." I shake my head as if remembering a hard-fought contest of wills.

I say "knowledge" with a hard "K" sound, like "Kuh," then drag out the "N" sound like "Nnnnowledge." This leads me into my next joke, "Little known fact, my initials, K and C, actually stand for 'Knowledge College.' Yup, that's right, my full, legal name is Knowledge College Hill."

This elicits, as we all knew it would, a pained groan from the audience. I turn to Sal as I raise my hands out to the sides, palms up as if I'm offended by the audience's reaction. Sal says, "I thought the K and the C stood for Kuh-Nnnnobody Cares."

I press a hand to my chest and wince at Sal's comment. Then I flash a smile and say to camera one, "Seriously, though, folks, I will be interviewing Ms. Whitmore about her research into Dido." I take a step closer and hold a hand to my face as if whispering to a friend and say, "Now would be the time to look up just who the hell Dido is so you can pretend with your friends tomorrow at work like you knew all along about the ancient Queen of Carthage." I step back, hesitate then step forward again to whisper once more, "You should probably also look up Carthage. That's Car-thage. Not gar-bage. Car-thage. Carthage."

I step back and say in a normal tone of voice, "We'll also be talking to a couple more people in the audience just as we did last night and I'm told that we have some feedback from the very pleasant and well-mannered inhabitants of the internet about the question I posed last night regarding Mighty Martie. That's right, all week long we'll be presenting the well-formed, well-argued, patiently stated and extremely eloquent comments generated by frequent fliers of the website comment section. The question at hand, of course, is Mighty Martie: sequel or no sequel? So, we're going to take a break now but we'll be right back with Professor Jodi Whitmore." I look over in exasperation at the life-sized cardboard stand-ins for the band and say to them, "Come on. Do something."

Cut to commercial.

38.

When we come back from commercial, Jodi Whitmore is sitting in the chair as I sit behind the desk. She's wearing a black pantsuit with a white top. It's a good look on her. She has very sharp, alert features. Her eyes feel like they're poking at me, trying to ferret out all my secrets. Her hair is short, brassy blonde and parted on the side. She has a surprisingly robust voice for someone so small. Did I mention she's shorter than I am? Not that I'm short. Scott is entirely wrong about that. I am not short. I am perfectly average height. Perfectly. Also, Jodi (she insists that I call her Jodi and not "Professor") is wearing a pair of overly large John Lennon glasses. That style of perfectly round, simple, wire-rimmed eyeglasses. Hers have clear lenses. No distracting tint to them whatsoever. The better for her ever-searching eyes to see-thru. Lastly, she's wearing thick-soled, black leather, slip-on shoes. In fact, her entire outfit is the more sedate, more academic, more business version of my own. I'm all flash and pizzazz tonight while Jodi is all let's talk turkey.

[Note: I've never understood that expression. I need to look it up.]

After tossing Jodi a couple of easy questions about what drew her to Classics and how she started her career in academia, I ask her about her interest in the bee hives, "So, Sal told me just before the show that you actually came out here to the ranch extra early because you wanted to take a look at the whole bee hive and honey operation here. Is that right? I mean, WHY is that right? I mean, what's up with that?"

I keep the tone light and slightly confused. Jodi says in a straight-forward manner, "Well, in fact, there is a scene in the Aeneid when the main character Aeneas washes up on shore after surviving a horrible storm at sea and this is his first encounter with Carthaginians, the people Dido rules over, her people, and they are very busy building and bustling around the very city of Carthage and the way Virgil describes the this mass, organized and very intricate activity is to compare them to bees working in a bee hive. So, when I received the invitation - thank you, and you, Sal and Marcus, over there for having me on, I'm going to be the biggest thing at the next

Classics conference, let me tell you what - first, I was flattered, I almost didn't believe it then when I found out about this location, that there were working bee hives here on the ranch I simply had to come take a look at them. It seemed very auspicious to me. I simply had to see the hives."

Bee imagery with Dido and the Carthaginians. Okay. I did not know that. I wonder if Scott did. Scott. Right. I say to Jodi, "I'll be honest here. You seem like a person who can handle honesty. This whole thing started a couple of years or so ago as a joke between, well, he was my fiance back then and now he's my husband. I forget the exact details of our conversation but somehow I was talking about a script or some movie thing and he, Scott, said - he's far more educated than I am, he used to be a high-school teacher - he said something like 'oh, that sounds like Dido's story.' I told him to explain Dido's story to me as I had never heard of it. Dido, to me, was a pop singer from a few years back. So, he told me, quickly, about Aeneas and Dido and the wedding in the cave and Aeneas abandoning Dido to go found Rome or some bullshit like that. And I just knew Dido needed a better story. I'm all about stories and Dido's story - can I…can I be blunt here, Jodi? (she nods as she hangs on my every word) - okay, good, Dido's story has a really horrible ending. It's got a great start and decent middle but it has a really crappy ending." I quickly look over at Sal and Marcus as I say, "See, I told you I wouldn't say 'shitty.'" Of course, I just did say 'shitty' but the techs were warned and bleeped it out for the broadcast. Sal and Marcus both do exaggerated face-palms.

I turn back to Jodi, she says to me in a very earnest, very professorial voice, "I couldn't agree more. Simply couldn't agree more."

I follow up with, "I understand you have a new version of Dido's story? A new interpretation? Something you and your students have worked on for a few years now?"

Jodi clasps her hands together as if she's standing in front of a full lecture hall. She looks up for a moment as she gathers her thoughts then turns and looks right into my eyes as she launches into her explanation, "Grayson prides itself on its interdisciplinary offerings. As a professor there, one is required to teach a course outside of one's area of expertise. I'll be honest. When I was offered the position at Grayson I almost turned it down because of that very requirement. I almost went to Duke instead where I would have pursued more traditional Classics research. Which I still do engage in. To some extent. But over the past few years I've been focused on a new interpretation, as you call it, but not just of Dido's story. It's a new interpretation, a re-visioning of the development of world history using Dido and Aeneas' admittedly failed and fictional relationship as a starting point."

"And," I break in for a moment because I sense that Jodi needs a moment to take a breath before she continues, "this re-visioning is in the form of a video game? Do I have that correct?"

"Not so much a game as a virtual simulation of world civilization. In fact, a few virtual simulations. They follow the same rules, which I'll explain in a minute, very simple rules, but they run, they progress at different time settings." I shoot Jodi a very confused look. She says, "Let me start at the beginning. Following Grayson's requirements, I developed a Creative Writing course, a course that I would teach as an elective English course. So, a course outside my own discipline. To be honest, I did this very begrudgingly at first. I slapped together a few ideas and did it simply because I had to. But about halfway through the first semester of teaching this course, I became absolutely fascinated with the ideas the students were generating. The idea for the course was this: I as Classic professor present to these budding writers several ancient stories, some fictional, some factual, some of the more well-known ones but also some of the lesser-known ones and then give them some simple writing prompts, some simple guidelines and say write a horror story based on Daedalus and Icarus or write a creative non-fiction account of the Battle of Actium or write a series of haikus about the killing of Julius Caesar. So, they had to take their creative writing skills and blend in the knowledge of the ancient world which I had just passed on to them and come up with something…well…something novel. Something new. A blend of known elements and structures to produce new stories. It

128

ended up being quite marvelous. Once the students were grounded in a deeper, fuller understanding of these stories of which, prior to the course, they knew only a little bit about - for example, the Trojan Horse - once they had a better, fuller, deeper understanding of the cultural context and specific sequences of events involved then were set free to play around with those elements to come up with new narratives, new narratives based on classical material, well, as I said, the results were quite marvelous, astounding, truly astounding."

"Can you give us an example?" I ask.

"I mentioned the Trojan Horse. We all have some sense of that story. Well, when you read the original version of that story, the version that we have a full record of, is, indeed, the Aeneid which, of course, ties us back to Dido but let's not go there just yet. So, one set of students - following the interdisciplinary nature of the course, I had the students work in groups of three, triads - produced this simply lovely version of the Trojan Horse story that had the Greeks building a Trojan Flower instead of a Trojan Horse. So, imagine a giant, wooden flower being wheeled up to the gates of Troy and instead of warriors lurking within ready to sack the city once its people are asleep for the night you have gifts of gold and bread and wine and honey and meat and religious artifacts. This triad of students flipped the basic premise of the Trojan Horse - an act of duplicitous sabotage - and turned it into something more akin to a potlatch, which is one version of a Native American gift-giving ceremony. So, the Trojan Horse became the Trojan Flower which was this giant gift laden with smaller treasures of food and precious gems and so on and so on. Everything a city surrounded by an opposition army for ten years could ever ask for. As I said, a simple twist, a simple flipping of the basic premise of the story - turns the story of this bloodiest of wars, The Trojan War, a ten-year long siege of the city of Troy that really, at the end, no one wanted to keep fighting but the forces of pride and vanity and, of course, since it was Ancient Greece, the meddling of the gods kept it going well past the time when it served any real purpose, if it ever did serve any real purpose which is very much open to debate, the changing of the premise of the well-known ploy of the Trojan Horse morphed the story from one of revenge sought in a bloody and underhanded manner - true bloodlust - to a story of self-sacrifice and insight and changing from the old ways, a giving up of the old ways in hopes of finding a new way whatever that might be. Truly beautiful. Truly."

"Amazing," I say. "I'd love to read that story. But…how does this all tie into Dido?"

"Well, the flower imagery of the new story reminded me of the bee imagery of the scene I mentioned before when Aeneas first sees the gleaming, wonderful, stunning city of Carthage. Carthage. Dido's city. Dido's kingdom."

I take this moment to say to Jodi while half-looking at camera two, "On that note, let's take a break. But you have to promise to tell me specifically about Dido's new story when we come back, Jodi."

Cut to commercial. The outro music is the chorus of Blind Melon's "No Rain." I wouldn't get the connection until later in the week when Scott and crew showed up.

39.

"Welcome back, people of America and all the...unknown countries," I say as camera one settles on me after spinning around full circle to take in the crowd, Sal and Marcus and the mountains washed with sunset in the distance.

"Unknown countries?" Jodi can't help but ask. "Is that a Shakespeare reference?"

"No. I wish. No, that was me slipping up. I meant to say 'Welcome back, Mr. and Mrs. America and all the ships at sea' like Walter Winchell used to say on the radio. That was way before my time but my father used to say it often. He joked around whenever we watched TV together, which wasn't often but sometimes, and when the shows would come back from commercial break he'd say that line. So, here I am, on the other side of the that experience, so to speak, and the line popped into my head but I couldn't quite remember it so I inserted 'unknown country.'"

"Gossip columnist, Winchell? Right?" Jodi asks.

"I believe so. But, let's not get sidetracked. It's time for you to give me the straight dope about Dido."

"The straight dope?" Jodi pauses for a moment. "That used to be a newspaper column a few years back."

Right. I remember now. I read it a few times in one of those alternative weekly newspapers that were big in the late 1990s and early 2000s. That was when dad and I lived in Albuquerque. "Oh, yes. I remember that now. I read that when I was young." Jodi and I stare at each other for a moment, each caught up in our own memories. Then I say, "Okay, enough of that. Let's get to Dido. Tell me all about that."

"Right. Yes. Well, so my course evolved over a few years. It took on another interdisciplinary element. We included a hard science element. A computer programming element. I'm sure you won't have heard of this but back in the early 2000s a researcher named Stephen Wolfram put out a book called 'A New Kind of Science.' As a Classics professor - student back then - that book was way outside my usual purview. But I had a few techy friends who geeked out over it big time. One - one, there were many - element of Wolfram's book was what are called 'cellular automata.' Which is really just a jargony way of saying 'simple rules' or 'simple algorithms.' At least, that's how I, a non-sciency person, understand it. If you've ever played minesweeper, you'll have a sense of this. You know, that game that used to be included on phones. There's a certain spatial layout - usually a grid display, often called a lattice - and certain rules that each cell or square in the grid has to follow. And those rules are dependent on what is happening in adjacent cells. The status and development of neighboring cells. Over time - development over time is the key here - the cells will evolve or take on different states. While each cell is following the same set of simple rules, the large-scale design and interaction of the cells becomes quite complex, often at a fairly fast pace."

"So, you applied this to the new stories the students were writing? To create a virtual world?" I ask this question verbatim from the notecards I've been supplied with.

"In a sense. The big takeaway is that simple rules followed by each cell in the lattice plus time equals a complex and often surprising development of patterns, highly complex patterns." Jodi is really warming to her subject now. She obviously loves her work, "So, imagine taking the imagery of the Trojan Flower and the concept it embodies of flipping the premise of a well-known story on its head and applying that to Dido and Aeneas to create a new story then encoding the basics of that new story, that new relationship into a virtual environment that operates on a set of simple algorithms dictated by this new story. I know. I can see your eyes glazing over. At this level, this is all fairly abstract. Hold on. It gets much better when you put some flesh on it, so to speak. When you make it specific and concrete. Which is what the relationship between Dido and Aeneas, that myth, does."

"How so?" This is the part I've been waiting for. Also, I can't believe I'm using Kincaid Live! to have this conversation. But, hey, this was Marcus' idea. He knows far more about the late night world than I ever will.

"In the Aeneid, Virgil does Dido dirty. There's just no way around it. There she is queen of her world. Undisputed ruler and, yes, hero of her people. Along comes Aeneas who we as the readers know has a duty, a divinely assigned task, a destiny to found Rome which is essentially a copy of what Dido has already done in founding Carthage. In the Aeneid, Virgil has Cupid shoot Dido with one of his infamous arrows so that she swerves from her duties and responsibilities to her people and falls madly in love with Aeneas and they have a weird sort of wedding in a cave but then once more the gods stick their podgy fingers into the story here and Aeneas quote remembers his destiny unquote, dumps Dido hard, sails away and Dido is so hurt, so pained that she commits suicide."

Jodi throws her hands out in front of her to show how upset this turn of events is to her, "Like I said, Virgil did Dido dirty. Now," she holds up a single finger, "take that scenario, Aeneas and his looming destiny meeting Dido, a woman who has already accomplished what he needs to do, get rid of the stupid cupid's arrow and have them meet as equals, as peers. Imagine Dido learning from Aeneas about his destiny and in the spirit of cooperation offering him the benefit of her experience. Imagine Dido and Aeneas, each ruler of their respective burgeoning empire, working together in mutual respect and friendship, working together as allies in the ancient world. Then," Jodi raises her finger high in the air like an olde time lawyer making a dramatic point for the jury, "translate all that into simple computer algorithms, insert those algorithms into a virtual world which has the details - the geography, the resources, the seas, the armaments, the food capacities - all those concrete details that computers are so wonderful at keeping track of - then letting that new world, a new version of the ancient world evolve over time - virtual time in the virtual environment - and what you get is amazing."

"This sounds like a very complicated game of Sims," I joke lightly. "As fun as Sims is, what makes this so different, so amazing as you say?"

Jodi relaxes a bit in her chair. Both her hands are on the arm rests now. She looks like the storyteller who has finally led her audience to the culmination of the grand tale and she is taking a moment to reflect on her own journey. She is content to be the bearer of this story. Content, satisfied, existentially justified. She smiles at me, "I hear you like to watch football." This isn't quite true but I'll go along with it. I nod. "You know how various companies will run virtual versions of the entire seasons or the playoff matches?" I nod. I don't know this but I'm sure Scott does. "They'll run through a season or the playoffs or sometimes just the Super Bowl itself literally thousands of times, sometimes tens of thousands of times. Then they average out the results to tease out the most common, most likely results which, of course, they use to predict the outcome of the actual, real-life football games."

"Okay. I think I get it. You set up this new version of the ancient world based on Carthage and Rome, Dido and Aeneas being allies instead of enemies and you ran thousands of…"

"Over one hundred thousand simulations," Jodi interjects.

"…simulations and…what? What did you discover? What did you predict?"

Jodi pauses for several seconds to gather herself. Then she carefully proceeds, "Understanding that this is quote just a simulation unquote. Understanding that the outcome I'm about to detail did not happen all the time. Nor did each version of its success include all the same, precise details. Though this particular scenario was the result more than sixty five percent of the time which if you were a gambling person you know is very good odds. Understanding…all that, all the potential limitations and knocks against this type of analysis and data processing - because I have been told about those limitations ad infinitum over the past few years by many of my fellow academicians - I find the scenario that arises most often from the simulation more than compelling. I find it enthralling."

"Jodi…you have to tell us now. What did the simulation produce? What's this new vision?" I say. I can almost hear the tick tock of the clock hurrying us along to the next commercial break. If she doesn't reveal the details before the next break, I know we'll lose the audience completely.

"K.C., imagine, if you will, two glorious city-states united, founded on a mutual admiration, respect and, yes, even a little heat, as the kids say these days. Instead of warring nations we have partner nations, instead of swords at each other's throat, we have hands clasped in union. We have trade facilitated from Germania down to the Sahara and beyond. Imagine a relationship between two equals - equal rulers, equal kingdoms, equal lovers - so strong that it shapes history, shapes economies, shapes the exchange of knowledge and scholarship, shapes culture itself, which we all know is the driving force of history. Well, at least I know that. My colleagues in the sciences will, of course, disagree with me."

"Imagine a partnership so powerful that it influences all of society to engage in similar partnerships on all levels, in all contexts. Envision a world in which Europe and Africa, working together, eradicated the slave trade hundreds if not thousands of years earlier. Imagine a world in which the technologies - plumbing and irrigation, food storage, crop rotation, monetary exchange - of the Roman Empire spread across the African Continent. Imagine a Green Sahara providing food for millions upon millions of people. Imagine the representatives of this Cooperative Empire, the new C.E., the crews of its sailing vessels, encountering native tribes of North and South America and spreading their vision of cooperative engagement and cultural exchange, C.E. and C.E. again, a sharing of knowledge and insights, spiritual practices and…and…everything. That's what the simulation produces. Far more often than not. When you flip the dynamics of Aeneas' and Dido's relationship on its head and proceed from there. That's what happens. The world, literally, changes. For the better."

"I know, K.C., that this is a pie in the sky vision. A utopian vision, if you will, and will be disregarded by many as such. But don't we deserve to at least consider it? Yes, I'm well off the track of standard Classics scholarship. But why do we study the past if not to help us shape the future?"

Cut to commercial.

40.

When we come back from break, Jodi is shown sitting in the audience. There are a fair number of history buffs in tonight's tour bus group. Well-read and very curious history buffs. As soon as we went to break, they had a thousand questions for her. Experienced lecturer and teacher that she is, she went right over to engage with them. With her brassy, blonde short hair and her black outfit, she looks like the early 1990s version of Madonna sitting amongst her adoring fans. She's been walking them through her findings in a step-by-step process for the past few minutes. They, clearly, love her. And her message.

I checked in with Sal and Marcus during break, "How was that? It felt like it got a little out of my control there?"

Sal shrugged off this concern and said, "That's what happens when you have a guest that is a good speaker, a good storyteller. You as the host take the backseat for a while. It's not a bad thing. This next segment will focus back on you. The comments section segment. Keep it punchy, keep it quick. You're good at that."

Marcus agrees and adds, "The comments alone will lighten things up a bit."

"Are they as nasty as I think they are?" I ask with a wince.

Marcus shakes his head, "No. I mean there are those out there for sure. There always are. But we found an interesting little thread, a back and forth exchange amongst a few commenters that was really interesting. So, that's what we're going to throw you when break ends."

"What did they say?" I ask Marcus.

Sal cuts in, "Nope. You surprised us with your outfit so now we're going to surprise you with the comments." I stare him in the eye. I can see he's being playful, not mean. I relax. But only a little. He adds again, "Don't worry. You're good at this."

I say just before I head back to the desk, "Just because I'm good at ad libbing doesn't mean I have to do it every show."

Sal shouts after me as I turn to walk away, "That's precisely what it means. That's what the viewers love about you, K.C."

Okay. NOW we're back from break.

I'm at the desk. Camera one once again does its spinny thing. The viewing audience sees Jodi embedded in the audience talking at length with the history buffs. When the camera settles on me, I wave like a little kid trying to get attention from very busy adults. I shout over to the audience and Jodi, "Hey! Hey ho! Over here. We're over...hey!" I drop my hand down and stare into the camera, "I guess they don't want to be disturbed. So, let's leave them alone for now while we talk about Mighty Martie. The question at hand is, yes, sequel or no sequel. I know what I think. I want Mighty Martie 2: Electric Bugaloo. Mighty Martie 2: it's still not safe to go back in the water. Mighty Martie 2: the ape strikes back. Mighty Martie 2: Fast Times at Gorilla Ridge High. Mighty Martie 2: this time the ship doesn't sink. Mighty Martie 2: The Shrekoning. Mighty Mar..."

Sal shouts at me from off-stage. I frown and say, "Okay. I've just been told I need to stop. So, let's check in with the Freudian-Jungian mishmash of a collective communicative consciousness that is the comments section of the Kincaid Live! website to see what's being talked about there. I wonder, given what Dr. Whitmore has just shared with us, will it be combative or cooperative?"

I stare down at the tablet recently placed on the desk by one of the production elves. On that screen I see what the viewers at home will see later tonight on their screens. It's a graphic showing the comments thread that Marcus mentioned during the break. I read the comments out loud. My voice will accompany the graphics for the home viewers.

"SexyApeGirl22: Mighty Martie will be viewed as an underground classic in five years time. Prove me wrong."

"GigantoPlayacus: Agreed. But I do wish the ending were less ambiguous. Don't pull your punches, Hollywood. Take a stand with Martie."

"SexyApeGirl22: I loved the is Martie dead or not element. Ambiguity is part of life. The world is gray. Embrace it."

"LonerStonerMovieGoer: Less ape, more Martie. I love her character. She deserves more screen time as a human. Make the whole thing a sitcom."

"GigantoPlayacus: Five years from now, we'll all be living in Mighty Martie's gene-edited world. CrispR is coming for all of us. Whether we like it or not."

"LonerStonerMovieGoer: Just as long as CrispR brings the super dope dope."

"SexyApeGirl22: CrispR is not the key. It's the humans using the CrispR that's the key. I'd give Martie the rights to my CrispR anyday."

"LoneWolfette@lonelyheart: Bottom line, we deserve a sequel in which K.C. gets to strut her stuff and Shelli Turndale gets complete creative control. Did you see her director's cut on the bluray? It's effing awesome! So much better than the theatrical release. So. Much. Better."

"SexyApeGirl22: Can't wait.

LonerStonerMovieGoer: Me neither.

GigantoPlayacus: Have to wait. But won't like it.

LoneWolfette@lonelyheart: Ohhh, squirrel!

SexyApeGirl22: ???????

LoneWolfette@lonelyheart: No, seriously, I just saw a squirrel outside my window."

That's the last of the comments. I look up from the screen into camera one. I say, "Sal wants me to ad lib off that but, come on, there's no way I can do better than those comments..." I smile as big and bright as I can, "...and at the risk of sounding self-serving here...I love them. I agree with everything they said. Except I don't know what CrispR is so I'll have to work on that. Also, Shelli Turndale is a fantastic director and I sincerely hope I get to work with her again whether it's on a Mighty Martie sequel or some other project. Okay, let's go to break."

The camera lingers on me for a few uncomfortable seconds. I glance over in Sal's direction. Then I look back at the camera and rattle off as quickly as I can, "Mighty Martie 2:

138

Ape Nation. Mighty Martie 2: Beyond Thunderdome. Mighty Martie 2: In the jungle no one can hear you scream. Mighty Martie 2: The Princess and The Ape. Mighty Martie 2: So Long and Thanks for all the Bananas. Mighty Mar..."

At this point, Sal and Marcus have come over to the desk. Sal is standing in front of me waving off the camera while Marcus is dragging my chair out from behind the desk. I shout one more time before I'm pulled off screen, "Mighty Martie 2: the Ape Wears Prada."

41.

I'm laying on the couch in my cabin when Miley texts me. It's not even half an hour after the show. I didn't give my tux back to Greg. I kept it. I saw him immediately after the show ended. He pointed at my tux and said, "You should…"

"…I'm keeping it," I said. We both laughed. He gave me the "right" hangers and a clothes bag. The tux is now hanging in one end of the large, rustic style wardrobe in the far corner of the cabin. When I got back here, I carefully took it off making sure to keep all the studs and cummerbund together and that it hung nicely inside the protective bag, placed it in the wardrobe then came over here to the couch.

I must have fallen asleep without realizing it. The sequential buzzing of multiple texts woke me up. Multiple Miley texts. I rub my eyes and prop myself up on a stiff pillow as I read through them. I confess that my first thought is, *If Miley can send me texts, why hasn't Scott called?* But then I realize that Miley could have sent the texts in a short window of reception which Scott might have missed. Or something. My brain's still sleepy.

Anyway.

The texts read, "MDB just contacted me!!!" Note the three exclamation points. Miley and I have developed a "text code" of our own over the past year. There was some story about some Hollywood exec's phone getting hacked and his texts about, well, everything were leaked online. They were harmless and vapid for the most part. There were a couple of judgy ones that the media blew way out of proportion. The exec didn't like working with this person. The exec really wanted to work with that female star. That very attractive female star. Yes, I am sanitizing the content of the texts. You don't need to know what he really said.

Anyway.

This whole incident made Miley a touch paranoid about our texts. Since it made Miley paranoid, it made me paranoid. I need my assistant to pay attention to stuff like this. And, yes, Miley can "wind me up," as Scott puts it. So, one day during my breaks between scenes for L.A.ser Boy, we developed our code. We are so clever. Here's how it works. For each level of importance of a message, there will be one exclamation point. So, one exclamation point equals a normal message, no hurry, get back to me when you can. Two exclamation points means sort of important, get back to me within the hour. Three exclamation points means this is something of concern and could turn out to be important, get back to me within a few minutes. Miley added, "within a few minutes or I'm going to start text bombing you." Ok, fine. Four exclamation points means call me now. Five exclamation points means the world is about to blow up. Miley, again, clarified, "Not literally blow up but Hollywood scandal blow up." So, there you go. That's the basics. It works because focusing on the exclamation points keeps us from actually using incriminating phrases, names and emojis.

We took our cue from Scott on that. He was there when we came up with the code. He wanted to see the L.A.ser Boy superhero meeting room set. I'd told him about it the night before and he totally geeked out. He asked if he could come see it by saying, "That would be like sitting where Superman sits in the Hall of Justice." His voice was so soft and reverent when he spoke that I couldn't refuse him. Not that I would refuse him but when he spoke like that I understood on a different level how much silly superhero stuff means to him. We all have our things, right? Fashion, superheroes, music, our favorite teams, politics, sasquatch, aliens, favorite TV shows, crocheting, baking, gardening, video games. We all have our things that we get wrapped up in. Mine are acting, stories and…Scott. Yes. I know. I'm a helpless, sappy romantic. So sue me. Actually, no, don't. That would bring the wrath of MDB down upon you and you definitely don't want that.

Anyway. Where was I?

Right, Miley's messages. The three exclamations points meant that MDB contacted her with a message that she, Miley, needs to talk to me about. The next several texts from Miley were one word repeated with a few variations:

"Thad?"

"Thad?!!!"

"Thad, really?"

"Thad, just no."

"We need to talk about Thad."

Then the last one was, "Thad will be an issue."

Ok, Miley, ok. I get it.

I call her hoping that the crew has reception now. Maybe she typed the texts earlier and they just came through because they got into an area with reception. I think they'll be staying in Steamboat Springs tonight. When Scott et al planned this trip, I reached out to an author who once had a bit part on Stack Life. Nell Hatch. She offered the use of her cabin in Steamboat if I ever needed it. I double-checked with her and she was so excited. She's not in town as she's on yet another book tour - the life of an author - but she sent all the needed details for the cabin. She, also, recommended going to Strawberry Park Hot Springs. The idea of a hot spring nestled in the Rocky Mountains was too much for Miley and Sophie to resist. Jayson and Jaxson were nonplussed. As was Scott. Those three wanted to drive farther on that stretch of the journey, get up into Wyoming. But the girls overruled them. So, they are staying in Steamboat for the evening.

Miley's phone rings. She picks up instantly, "Good, you got my texts. So, MDB told me - amongst several other things that she wants me to have set up by the time you set foot back in L.A. - about Thad taking over for Gyrin in L.A.ser Boy. First, yeah, something needed to happen there. Gyrin was a bit of a dead fish in that role."

In the background I hear Sophie say, "He wasn't dead. He was...flat. He was a flat fish."

Miley says in response to Sophie, "Fine, he was a flat fish not a dead one." Now she's talking to me, "So, yeah, a change there would be good. But bringing Thad on is... going to be hard for me. He and I did not part on the best of terms. As I'm sure you know. So...that's what I wanted to talk to you about."

I hear another voice in the background now. It's Scott. I hear a rustling as Miley holds her phone out in his direction. I think she has it on speaker mode now. He says, "Hey, hon, we're about an hour from Steamboat. We're getting in a little late since a few of our party did not get up on time this morning. Names will not be mentioned in order to give them a chance to bribe me handsomely."

Miley and Sophie chime in at exactly the same time, "Not going to happen."

I can't help but laugh. Then I hear Miley's voice close to the phone. She says, "So, Thad and I…all I need is to not be on set with him. You can work with him all you like. And I'll still be your assistant but I can't be on set with him. I just need to put that up front right now before we get too far into this. I know it won't be happening for a while yet but I needed to let you know."

"So, you're fully on the Bad Thad bandwagon still?"

"I am driving the Bad Thad bandwagon at excessive speed down the highway needing to jump the gap in the bridge just like Keanu."

"Hmmm, is this because he is a creep of some sort? Should I be worried about working with him? Because, honestly, I've never gotten that vibe from him. Not even close."

"No. He's not like that. He's a perfectly good guy like that. You're right. It's just… shit. It's just that we went separate directions and I didn't think I'd be involved with anything he was involved in so soon after we went our separate directions so MDB took me by surprise when she said what she said today. About you and Thad working together."

"So, to be clear this is just a Thad and you issue and there's no red flags that I need to be worried about?"

"No, no red flags for Thad. No, he's a very sweet guy. He's still the guy you met down in Puerto Santibel. Yes, it's just a Thad and me issue."

"You do realize that you can't hide from him forever, right?"

"I'm not hiding from him. I'm…I'm…"

Sophie says, "Miley…you're hiding."

Miley, "Fine. I'm hiding. And I want to hide for a little while more. And, damn it, maybe I won't have to hide anymore by the time you and Thad start working together. Fine, just fine."

"So, is that it?" This three exclamation point scenario seems to have de-escalated very quickly. I need to make sure, though.

"Yes." Pause. "Yes. I guess I'm just tired."

Sophie adds, "We may or may not have been out line dancing last night and there may or may not have been several attempted flirtations with a certain personal assistant who may or may not have rebuffed - excuse me - needlessly rebuffed - excuse me - needlessly and angrily rebuffed said flirtations because said personal assistant has still not gotten over said Thad."

Ahhh. I get it now. I wait for Miley to speak. There's a long, silent pause. I hear the hum of Missy Von Van's tires on the road. As I wait, I can't help but think Clara could use a little of this. A little of being on a road trip with peers, going line dancing, working through personal issues in a safe and light-hearted (but still very effective) way. A new car is great and all but what she really needs is a crew, a group of friends, people to share her daily life with.

At last, Miley says, "Sophie's right. As usual. So, sorry. I will put on my big boy pants and be on set whenever you need me when you and Thad do L.A.ser Boy."

"Okay, Miley. That sounds good. Now, please hand the phone to Scott."

Rustle, rustle, rustle, possible drop of the phone, more rustling sounds then finally, "Hey, hon. I'm driving. Jaxson's holding the phone. We're all a little tired."

I ask, "Did you go line dancing, too?" This seems like an impossible occurrence. But Miley and Sophie together can be persuasive. Very persuasive.

Scott says, "Ahhh, hello, this is Scott Langle speaking. Not Billy Ray Cyrus. No, I did not go line dancing. But the boys and I were up late watching the stars. There was some meteor activity last night. And we got talking and…"

His voice trails off. I say, "Okay. Well, I don't want to distract you from driving. I just wanted to hear your voice."

"Yeah. Me, too." Then he adds, "We're going to the cabin, unpack a little, then the girls are set for the hot springs while the boys and I are going to get a burger. Looks like there are lots of burger options in this town. We may…may end up spending two nights here. So, heads up in that regard. Driving Alonsha on the trailer and being careful with her is slower going than I predicted. Slower and a little nerve-wracking behind the wheel."

"Are you being a road martyr?" I ask. Scott has told me stories of various road trips he did when younger. First he told me about the trip to go get the wingback chairs which I love so much. Then he told me about several more. I noticed a pattern and asked him, "Why did you always end up driving the most? Why didn't your friends help?"

Scott winced when I asked this question then said, "I just didn't trust them to drive safely. I guess that's my version of paranoia. Besides, I like being a road warrior."

"Sounds like you were a road martyr," I joked.

He frowned and fell silent but then said, "Yeah, I think you're right. I was a road martyr."

Here he is doing it again. This time being careful about Alonsha is the excuse he's using. He always has "a good reason" to drive the most and longest. Always. But I need to point out to him what he's really doing. That's our deal. We point out to each other when we're lying to ourselves. I think for a moment then say, "Then, yes, you should spend another night in Steamboat. Rest up. Relax a bit. Steamboat's not that far from here. A couple of days. Even if the driving is slow. And you can let other people drive, you know?"

"I'm an excellent driver. Excellent driver," says Sophie mimicking the line from Rain Man.

Good. Yes. Of all the members of the crew, Scott would trust Sophie to drive. They've known each other longest and best. I echo this sentiment, "See? So, yeah, take a day then you and Sophie split the driving duties. No more martyring. Bad driver, bad driver." I say that last part with a playful tone.

Scott laughs. Then says, "Okay, yes, you're right, you're right."

Jaxson speaks up at that point, "There's a college with an observatory in Steamboat. Maybe we can get in there."

Then, because Jaxson said something, Jayson feels compelled to say something (Twins!), "Clara texted me that you bought her a car."

The voices of all the others inside Missy Von Van fall into stunned silence for a long moment then they all say in unison, "You did WHAT?!?!"

I say quickly, "I'm going through a tun...an't hear wha...breakin...can't..." Then I hang up.

42.

After dodging the Clara's car inquisition, I head over to the main house to grab some food. When I get there, I'm surprised to find Jodi and Clara sitting across from each other having a very serious conversation. I wave at Luisa who flashes me a big smile then points to a plate on the kitchen island. It has a cover on it. When I lift the cover off I see a down home cooking classic of honey-baked ham, creamed corn, peas and mashed potatoes. I shoot Luisa a look but before I can say anything she says, "Just eat your food and don't make me tell you that was your father's favorite meal because I just might start to cry."

She's joking but only partially. I do remember dad eating this or, at least, something like this once a week or so. I say, "Why..."

Luisa cuts me off with a nod towards Clara. I don't get it at first but then I do. The Clara sitting across from and engaging with Professor Whitmore is far more animated and focused, far more alive than the Clara that sat in the same spot last night. Luisa steps closer to hand me a knife and fork. She whispers so the pair at the table can't hear her, "You did good. You listened, realized there was a problem and offered up a solution. Just like your dad would. Well, maybe not just like. You have your own Hollywood flare but underneath it was just like your dad. Which, of course, got me thinking about him so..." She clinks the cutlery on the plate to finish the sentence. His favorite meal.

I side hug Luisa and walk over to Jodi and Clara. For a moment as I approach they look like older and younger versions of the same person. It isn't their hair or their eyes or their makeup. Or anything like that. It's the gestures and the facial expressions. I'm not sure if Clara is copying Jodie or if Jodi is copying Clara. They're like actrons reflecting each other's movements. Jodi, bless her, is locked in on Clara's comments. As any good teacher will do, she's tracking not only what Clara is asking but at the same time figuring out the best way to answer. Jodi has a way of sensing what phrases and context, what imagery and references speak to individuals and then she uses those in her answers to their questions. I watched her during breaks in the show and then for a couple of minutes after the show do just that with the audience members. So, I'm looking forward to joining this conversation as I sit down next to Jodi.

Clara and Jodi welcome me to the table with smiles. Jodi adds as she holds a forkful of salad suspended in mid air, "Clara here just asked me a fascinating question. One that I've only been asked by upper level students before." I can see Clara sit up a little taller when Jodi says this. Nice.

I say, "What's the question?"

Jodi says, "Did the Ancient Greeks and Romans really believe in the existence of the gods and goddesses that are such important parts of their stories or not? That is, did they think the gods and goddesses were truly real or were they symbols or metaphors for…something else?"

I look at Clara. Before I can praise her for the question, she says, "It seems to me that they just used the gods telling them what to do or whatever as an excuse to do things that they knew they shouldn't do or wouldn't be allowed to do under normal circumstances. Like killing people, executing people."

Ahh. Execution. Punishment. Now I get where this is coming from. Her dad's in jail. When he went to trial years back there was a week or so in which the public prosecutor said he would push for the death penalty. But eventually he, the prosecutor, backed away from that. No wonder this is her question. I ask Jodi, "So, what's the answer?"

Jodi chews her salad for a couple of seconds then says, "I'm going to give you an unsatisfying answer. Some did. Some didn't." She's right. That is an unsatisfying answer. She goes on, "Look at the world today. Pick any church or temple or mosque or synagogue. If you could interview the members and were able to get genuine answers I'm willing to bet that some percentage of the community fully believed in their god. I'm also just as willing to bet that some percentage, probably a fairly high percentage, doesn't actually believe in that god but sees the whole religious process as a way to build community and raise children in a framework that teaches them about

148

good and evil, duty and sacrifice, selfishness versus selflessness and so on and so on."

Clara hangs on Jodi's every word. Then she jumps in, "But somewhere along the line there must have been some people who truly believed in the gods, people who had genuine experiences with them, right? Something so influential like a religion doesn't just start from people hanging out asking themselves, 'Gee, I wonder how I can raise my kids and teach them right from wrong?' That makes no sense."

I add, "Who was the first person to speak to Zeus?" Pause. "Or whichever of the ancient gods first had contact with humankind? Is that…known?"

Jodi frowns, "No. Unfortunately that detail isn't known nor do I think it ever will be. While we here in the Western World tend to stop at the ancient greek pantheon when we think of old gods, the truth is there were cultures and religions older than the Greeks that had very similar pantheons and it's clear that the Greeks' beliefs came from those older cultures or, at least, that those older cultures and the ancient Greeks shared an even older, common culture, a set of beliefs from which they both arose. And when you start digging into that territory it becomes an endless search for the first or the original human culture. More diligent scholars than I have spent their entire lives doing just that. That's not my particular cup of tea, thank you very much."

"What's it?" I ask as I don't quite understand Jodi.

"'It' in this context is the origins of humankind and, too, civilization as we know it. Speaking broadly, there are physical remains that tell us that humans physically like us lived for roughly a hundred thousand years before creating anything that looks like what we have now, before coming together to form large communities with division of labor and hierarchical social structures, yada, yada, yada. I won't bore you with those details. So, the question becomes what prompted humans to form civilization in that manner? Since we got along fine - that is we lived for countless generations - without it, why did we create it? Some say that humans always had a version of civilization and we just don't have or haven't found the remains of those ancient ways yet. Others say that there was some world-wide disaster that forced humans to cluster together for safety and that was the impetus for civilization and we've just kept going along with it. Still others say that there are, hmmm, learned figures, ancient sages of unknown origin who taught those lazy, lay about all day humans of ancient times how to farm and make tools and useful stuff like that. Your question," she looks at Clara and then at me, "the way you framed it - who was the first person to speak to Zeus? - would fit in best with that assessment of ancient history." She looks at Clara again, "Although, I sense that you're looking for a somewhat different answer, yes?" Clara nods. Jodi goes on, "You want to know the answer to the really big question. You want to know what the gods or God thinks of us, right? Have we done right in the eyes of the divine? Or have we messed up the whole thing terribly?"

I see the light of understanding spark up behind Clara's eyes. Jodi just put words to something that's been rattling around inside her, Clara's, head for a long time now. Probably for as long as she can remember. Clara doesn't say anything in response. She just nods and blinks away a tear. I ask Jodi, "What do you think the answer is?"

Jodi says, "I think we're all handed our lines and play our parts as best we can and when we get to the other side...that's when we'll know the truth. But we can't know the truth - the big truth, the capital T truth - here, in this life because it will distract us from playing our roles. We'll focus on that instead of focusing on our lives here and now. Which is what we need to do."

I let this sit for a moment. Clara does, too. Then I ask, "So, you believe in the other side? In life or something like it after death?"

Jodi says with a calm certainty, "I do." Pause. "How about you?"

I'm taken back by the question. I wanted to hear her answer. I wanted her to go on at length about why she believes whatever it is that she believes. But now she wants to hear from me. I can feel Clara looking at me. I can't joke my way out of this. Memories flash through my head of their own volition. I think of Benny and his weird abilities. I think of moments when I've felt the presence of my father. And, yes, my mother, too. I think about the UFO in Puerto Santibel. And the one at the movie opening. I think of moments between me and Scott that I know were more than just the two of us in a way that I can't even come close to putting into words. I think of scenes when I was full-heartedly engaged with other actrons, wholly focused on the moment in which something mystical (that's the only word that comes close to fitting) washed over us. A sense of rightness and otherness that was both comforting and confusing. I think of a similar sense, yet less aggressive, a sense that came quieter and easier to me when I've been really deep in meditation. A sense that whispered to me instead of arriving like a gust of wind and leaving just as quickly. This whisper, this soundless whisper, cannot be unheard. Once you've experienced it, it will never leave you. Ever.

I take a breath and say, "I've had experiences that I can't explain. More than one. Far more than one. I think, no, I know that there is more to the world, our understanding of the world than we care to admit. I've experienced moments of…beauty…that have no logical explanation. And I hold out hope that the greater whole that we don't understand and, I suspect, that we can't understand because it simply surpasses us, is…divine, is good in that sense. I hold out hope that there is a greater design and meaning to all that we experience and, like you say, we just need to trust and focus on our own lines, our own roles and let the great stage manager in the sky deal with all the rest."

All three of us are silent for a long moment. Then Clara asks me, "Will you teach me how to believe that? Because I don't. I want to. But I don't."

Jodi looks at me. I can see she's curious as to how I will answer. Gently curious. I say to Clara, "Let's start with meditation and see what happens from there. Okay?"

Clara blinks away tears. Again. Then she stands up, gathering her now empty plate as she says, "Thanks. Both of you. But I have to go now."

Jodi and I are silent as Clara puts her dish in the washing machine then waves at us as she heads out. There's a beat then Jodi says to me, "That one has a lot to deal with."

It hits me in that moment. I say to Jodi, "So you know about her father and…" I don't finish the sentence.

Jodi nods as she keeps her eyes on the door Clara just exited through, "I do. As I was walking around earlier today looking at the beehives, I overheard a couple of the other, younger workers talking. Like young ones do. Casual, heedless of their words. Not intentionally mean but…thoughtless." She looks at me and says, "If this were an ancient Greek play," she waves a hand at me then towards the door to indicate Clara, "I'd say you two were forever linked. I'd say that the gods have tied you together in a knot from which you must untie yourselves." Pause. "Or not, as the case may be. Maybe you just need to be comfortable with the knot. Maybe you simply need to accept the divine link between you and her." Her eyes narrow as she studies my face. "I'd like to stay in touch with you."

"Why?" I say more defensively than I mean to.

"Because I think there's potential for something beautiful, something of beauty between you and Clara," Jodi says as calmly as if she were asking me to pass the salt to her.

"Like what?" I say. This time I'm more curious than defensive. I've always felt a little less than in terms of my education. I didn't go to college. I went to Hollywood. Every now and then I feel that lack of formal education. Not the partying and the new adult drama. No. I had plenty of that during my first years in Hollywood. But sometimes when I'm reading scripts and talking to directors and other actrons and such I realize that there's a detail - a turn of phrase from a famous book, for example - that they picked up on and I didn't. In those moments, I feel - for just a split second, but a powerful split second - like an outsider. I don't like that feeling. Scott often tells me things that he learned about in college. I prod him to tell me more whenever we have the time. Storytime with Scott. I love it. I love it because I love him. I love it because I feel less like an outsider in those moments.

Jodi shrugs her shoulders as she responds, "Only the gods know at this point." Then she excuses herself and puts her dish in the dishwasher. I look around. I don't see Luisa. She must have left a while ago. How long have I been sitting here? It feels both like just a few minutes and for an eternity. Jodi walks over to me and hands me a business card. She says, "If you ever want help interpreting the mixed messages of the divine, give me a call."

I take her card and say, "Thanks." Pause. "I think."

Jodi chuckles, waves goodbye then heads out the door.

43.

It's the middle of the night and I'm dead asleep when my phone starts buzzing. I try to ignore it at first. I was having a really good dream about green chile tiramisu bacon double cheese danish burgers. But the buzzing persists. And persists. And persists. I roll over and flap my hand around on the unfamiliar surface of the nightstand. Finally, I grab my phone and peel open my eyes as I stare at the bright screen in the dark. It takes my eyes a few seconds to adjust to the harsh contrast between the phone and everything else. I see a series of texts from Miley. No words. Just five exclamation points. Three separate texts with five exclamation points. WTF?

I sit up and think, *Miley, if this is more Bad Thad bandwagoning and bus driving I'm going to throttle you.* I stretch my arms out and shake my shoulders to help wake myself up. Part of my brain is still cavorting in the wonderful world of fantasy foods. I grab the top fleece blanket and drape it over my shoulders as I stand up. I look at my phone to make sure I didn't imagine/dream these texts from Miley. I did not. Damn. I walk over to the couch and sit cross-legged on it arranging the blanket around me for what I suspect will be a long and somewhat panicked conversation with Miley. I take several deep breaths. I remember what Scott said to me a few weeks ago, "How about instead of her winding you up, you calm her down?"

Easier said than done. So. Much. Easier.

Part of me holds out hope that this is some sort of Sophie-Miley prank. Maybe they went line dancing after the hot springs and drank a little more than they should have and are all silly and giddy and let's wake up K.C. It's not a big part of me. But it's there and I hope it's right. Because five exclamation points for real means SCANDAL. Or something of equal import, equal intensity, equal annoyingness.

I blink my eyes very deliberately several times then call Miley. She picks up immediately. She's talking a hundred miles an hour, "A friend just called me. A friend from Hollywood. She works in one of the bigger agencies. A good friend. A good business friend. Not like a friend friend. You

154

know what I mean. Anyway, this friend says that she's heard from reliable sources that someone has hacked Shawn Muze's book. The original version of his book. Not from his computers. But from the computers of the publishing company. Or the editor. Or something like that. And this someone is going to leak it out in dribs and drabs. The juicy parts of the book. The parts that the publishers didn't want to let out. The rumors are that people are going to be pissed. That careers will be ruined. That this will be the biggest Hollywood scandal in decades."

Does Miley sound happy? Or is she just excited? Or...??? I ask, "How sure of this source are you? Have any leaks come out yet?" Then, "And what does this have to do with me? Or you? Or whatever?" *Why did you wake me from a wonderful dream to tell me this?* I ask, "Are you...excited about this?"

"Excited. Terrified. Shocked. Confused. I'm all those things and...and...and I don't know what else. This is all too much. Way too much," says Miley.

"You need to take a breath, Miley. Seriously. What happened to all the meditation we've done over the past year? Just remember that. Go back to that," I say more for myself than for Miley. But, yeah, for Miley, too.

"How about you calm her down?" That's Scott's voice in my head.

"How about," I begin, "you tell me what facts, hard facts there are right now. Not rumors. Facts. Let's start there." My brain is starting to focus a bit more. Only a tiny part is still gamboling amongst the waves of the cream puff, licorice, jelly-filled donut sea.

Miley says, "Well, now that you put it that way I don't think there are any facts. Nothing has been, uhhh, certified or actualized or however you say that."

"Proven? Nothing has been proven? Is that what you're trying to say?" I ask.

"Proven?" Pause. "I guess that's the right word. But this isn't a court so not like that," Miley says.

"No, right," I say, gathering my own thoughts now. "Not like that. Right. Okay, so facts are zero. But you feel confident in what your friend friend told you. Yeah?"

"I do," says MIley with more confidence. This is more comfortable territory for her, assessing relationships. More familiar territory than establishing veracity.

"The gist is Muze's book got hacked and bad shit's going to get leaked. Stuff that will embarrass, hurt and/or otherwise damage people's reputations?"

"Correct," says Miley in a very to the point manner.

"Okay," I say again. "So, the question is what do we do now? Is that it?"

"Yes," says Miley.

"It's half past a rat's ass, right now, Miley," I say, using a phrase I heard somewhere long ago and I had completely forgotten about until this very moment because it's been so very long that I've been awake at this hour. I add, "There's nothing that either one of..." Then I get it. Oh. "You want me to call Muze? Is that it?"

"That's...what I was thinking. Yeah," says Miley. She knows I'm going to hesitate so she adds, "I checked. It's early morning in the Caribbean. What with the kid..."

"Lucius," I say.

"...and Muze's get fit, stay fit, forever fit lifestyle he's taken on, I mean, did you see that Men's Health article? He's gone all fitness fanatic now that he's got a kid. Anyway, he'll be awake. He'll be awake and doing like ten thousand pushups. It says so in the article."

"Not ten thousand..."

"Okay, fine, not ten thousand. But he'll definitely be awake."

I mull this over for a moment or ten. I can hear the exasperation growing in Miley with each breath she takes. I have to admit there is a certain logic to this approach. What if there's something in the book about me? Yup. I went right there. Come on. Confess. So would you if you were in my position. What if Muze said something nasty or dismissive or derogatory about me? What if he said I'm a horrible person? A

156

horrible actron? A waste of talent? An entitled bitchy starlet? And these are just off the top of my head.

Okay.

Pause.

"How about you calm…" No, Scott. Stop. I need to think. There is a time and place to be calm. There is a time and place to get amped up. I need to figure out what time and place this is right now. Should I call Muze? He will be awake. I didn't tell Miley but I did see that Men's Health article. It was fifteen hundred pushups, not ten thousand. Modern day Jack Lalane Muze is now. I thought it was adorable. The way he wants to stay healthy for his kid.

Okay. Got sidetracked. Muze will be awake. I can call him to see if he's heard about this hack. Yes. That makes sense. I don't know if he knows. And he should know. So since I know I should reach out to him to make sure he knows. Yup. That works. Then if he did say anything nasty about me he'll feel compelled to tell me when I'm talking to him because he and I have a good enough relationship that way. Hell, I'm his wife's half-sister. That has to count for something. That plus we've been through some stuff together. Some.

Okay. I say to Miley, "Alright. I'll gather myself here and give him a call. I'm going to need some coffee first. So, it'll be a few minutes before I call. Then however long the conversation takes. Then I'll call you back. So, to be safe, let's say an hour. Okay?"

"Oh…kay," says Miley. I can tell she wants a quicker turnaround but there's nothing she can do to speed up the process. She rallies a bit and says, "Okay. Yes. Good. And thanks, K.C."

I didn't think of it until she said that last bit. But then I get it. It's not the words she said. It's how she said them. She said them like she's depending on me. She trusts me and she's depending on me and it scares her a bit. Right. Of course. If Muze says something about me in his book, if somehow my reputation gets destroyed then Miley goes down with me. She's put her acting career aside to be my assistant. It would be hard for her to start that up again if… Oh…kay. Ok. Time to get some coffee.

44.

I throw on some clothes then I encounter the first problem: I don't have any coffee in my cabin. How is that possible? I could have sworn… I don't have time to puzzle this out. I just need to get some coffee. So, where… The main house. Surely, even at this time of night or morning or whatever this dark-enshrouded time of day is there will be coffee in the main house kitchen. Luisa prides herself on the whole old West schtick. A pot of coffee bubbling at all times on the stovetop ready for the ranch hands to sip on whenever they come back from a hard day of ~~driving cattle~~ gathering honey. This makes me laugh as I pull on some ankle boots and pull open the door. Cowboys. Nope. Beeboys. Ha!

Oh, shit. It's cold out there. Okay. Where…? There! I grab the fleece and wrap it around me making sure it doesn't trail in the dirt as I step down from the cabin onto the gravel path. I pull the fleece tighter as the cold, sharp air sniffs out all my exposed flesh. I make a little pocket for my head and cinch the sides around my shoulders and across my chest. I figure I look like some Eastern European woman with a shawl. Except, of course, for the fancy jeans and ankle boots. Ok, so, Faux Old West/European shawl woman. That's me right now.

The sound of my footsteps on the gravel is louder than anything I've ever heard before in my entire life. I feel like I'm in a cartoon and every sound I make is hyper-loud when it needs to be hyper-quiet. Scrunch! Scrunch! Scrunch!. Okay, can I walk in a way that's less loud? Maybe if I step over to the side where there's less gravel? Nope, that's not working at all. Fuck it. Just walk. Stay on coffee target.

My phone!?! Did I bring… yes, okay, it's in my pocket.

I round the bend in the pathway and see the main house a hundred or so yards away. I stop for a moment and look up at the night sky. It's so clear. Clearer than I've ever seen it before. The speckled, glowing band of the Milky Way stretches at an angle across the blackness of space. It takes my breath away. So big. So beautiful. So magical. Each point of light is a star just like our own sun. Each point. A sun. Each point.

I stand there for I don't know how long. I'm perfectly still as I keep my eyes on the heavens above. The heavens. The stars. The infinite expanse of space. I don't feel the cold. I feel locked in place as the world and the Milky Way spin around me. All at once I'm at the center of everything and, also, just one point of existence amongst countless other points of existence. We're all rotating around each other. Turning, ever turning. And ever still. It makes no sense. It makes perfect sense.

So big. So beautiful.

How can all of that be random? How can it all be just...particles in motion?

That doesn't make sense to me. There has to be something else. Something guiding it all.

So big.

So beautiful.

So magical.

At some point, I start walking to the main house again. It's not a conscious decision. It just seems like the thing to do. The moment for stillness has passed. Now it's time to move.

45.

As expected, there is coffee in the kitchen. But it's not in a dented, metal kettle like Hollywood would have it. No, it comes in the form of one of those fancy, sleek, single-serve pod machines. Art deco coffee. That's all I can think as I pop a purple pod into the form-fitting slot, clunk-clunk the side lever and, after making sure there's water inside (sometimes I'm smart!), push the on button. As the machine hums and heats up, I sit down at the long, wooden table once more and pull out my phone. I draw up Muze's number and hover my thumb over the little dot that will connect me with him if I tap it.

I don't tap it. I wait. And wait. And wait. My thumb goes stiff. I still wait.

The coffee machine hisses and fizzles and groans like it's just given up its last bit of life energy to make this single cup of coffee. I put my phone down on the table and walk over to grab the heavy ceramic mug that I found on the sideboard. This one has a very serious looking bison staring out from its side. No more howling coyote. Now I've got a buffalo in my hand.

I take a few initial sips of the purple pod coffee. Not bad. Plus, I can feel the caffeine running through my veins already. I'm sure that's more psychological than physical but whatever. I pick up my phone and swipe up Muze's contact again. My thumb hovers once more. I realize that this moment could be the end of one stage of my life and the beginning of another.

I wait.

So big.

I realize that any moment in my life could be the end of one stage and the beginning of another.

So beautiful.

I tap the screen and my phone reaches out through the electromagnetic ether. It rings once, twice, three times. Shawn picks up. I say, "Hey."

He says, "You heard."

"I did."

"You're good, K.C. I didn't say anything about you. Nothing bad. In fact, I praised you. I said my one regret

160

leaving Hollywood is that I wasn't able to complete the Shadows franchise with you." Pause. "How's that going, by the way."

"MDB has plans for Shadows 3. She, of course, has a different vision for it. But Hugh is focused on other projects right now." Hugh Summers. The writer Shawn brought on a couple of years back. Brought on but kept hidden. Hugh remained writer mysterioso for a while. Until last year when Muze left Hollywood and MDB scooped Hugh up. He's the architect of the Hall-iverse now.

"The Hall-iverse," says Shawn.

"Indeed," I say. "How's Kal and Lucius?"

"Doing mommy and baby yoga on the beach as we speak."

"Ohhhh"

"I know. I look at them and my heart skips a beat. Every time."

"I'm happy for you, Shawn."

"Thanks."

"Is there anything…anything…I should be ready for? From the book?"

"From the book, no. Just bad people getting called on their bullshit. Maddy can handle any blowback in her sleep." He's right. She can. "But…I have a favor to ask."

"Go on."

"Kali's obviously busy. She's no longer overseeing the transition program."

This is the program Shawn established years ago for wards of the state. It provides various support services, resources and, occasionally, money to those who qualify which is pretty much anyone who applies. Shawn's very generous and very wealthy. The transition the program focuses on is from leaving the state's custody to being an independent adult. Kali was part of the program years ago. Then she oversaw it for a while. Now she's not. So…

"I have a team of three set up to keep the program running. All three went through the program. I trust them. But I need a place for them…"

"Consider it done," I say.

"Office space as well as…"

"Whatever they need. Plenty of space left in the tower. More than enough."

"Thanks, Case. Should I have them contact…"

"My assistant. Miley. You met her at a party a few months back."

"Miley? Ohhh. Right."

"She'll coordinate with the property management company and your people."

"Great. Thanks again."

"I'll send you her contact details as soon as I hang up." A thought. "Hey, it was Miley who heard about all this. Then she called me and asked me to call you."

"Sounds like she's on it. I only heard an hour ago."

"Yeah, she is on it. Also, she thinks you walk on water. So, could you call her and tell her yourself what you told me? And add it that I wouldn't know what to do without her?"

"Soon as I hang up, I'll make the call."

"Great. Thanks. Say hello to Kal and Lucius for me."

"Will do. And, great show last night. Now I need to read up on cellular automata. Or maybe I'll have someone do that for rme."

"Oh, thanks. Thanks. For everything, Shawn. Really."

"Least I could do. Really. And…" Shawn pauses for a long moment. He doesn't usually pause. Ever. I wait. "I just want to be sure that you realize I've handed you the baton. You get that, right?"

The baton. He's handed me the baton. Right.

"I do now."

"Good."

I can't resist. "Just to be clear, is this the relay baton or the conductor's baton because if it's the conductor's…"

"If you don't stop, I'll tell Kali that you asked for fashion advice."

I shudder at the thought of being lectured about fashion by Kali. "You're a very mean man, Shawn Muze."

"Sometimes I'm mean. Sometimes I walk on water."

We both laugh at this.

"Okay, Shawn, thanks again. Make that call."

"I will. Thank you, too."

46.

I sit at the table and slowly finish my coffee. I'm not sure whether I'm going to go back to bed or if I'm just going to push through the rest of the day. I rinse out the mug and set it to dry on the sideboard where I found it. The coffee was good. I may have to get me one of those machines.

I walk out once more into the night. This time it feels different. It's still cold. I'm still wrapped up in my fleece shawl. The sky is still dark and infinite and slashed by the Milky Way. But now it feels like I could reach out and touch each and every star. This, of course, is impossible. But being impossible doesn't diminish the sensation, the feeling, the experience of being connected to everything out there. All I have to do is reach out. Maybe that blue star there. Or that yellow one up there. Or that twinkling one. Or...

I stand and stare at the stars one by one for a long while.

Eventually, I head back to my cabin. I'm just inside pushing the door shut behind me when my phone buzzes. It's a text from Scott. It reads, "You've created a monster. A Miley Monster."

I laugh as I call him. He picks up right away saying, "Why did you use your powers this way? Why, oh, why?" he says this in a very melodramatic voice then laughs. It's a good laugh. A relaxed laugh.

"What's she doing?" I can only imagine what a Miley freshly praised and emboldened by Shawn Muze would get up to.

"I woke up to a shriek. I thought she was being murdered. So did the twins. We ran down to her and Sophie's room. Just as we got to the door, she threw it open and ran down the hallway. No. Excuse me. She skipped down the hallway to the stairs and just kept going. Sophie stumbled to the door and told us that Shawn Muze had called her. Called her and thanked her and that's when she erupted. A few minutes later she came skipping up the stairs at the other end of the hallway. She went back to her room and proceeded to recite her entire conversation with Muze - every painstaking detail - over and over and over again. Sophie, to be clear, hates you right now. The twins and I have retreated back to our respective rooms. But Sophie has nowhere to hide."

"Nowhere to run, nowhere to hide," I say absent-mindedly. The coffee, despite a valiant effort, is wearing off. I yawn as I lean against the now closed door.

Scott says, "What's that?"

"A song. From long ago. Nowhere to run. It was part of a school play. Haven't thought of that in years." I yawn again. "Hon, this monster-maker needs to go back to bed. I love you. Tell Sophie I'll make it up to her somehow."

"Of that, I have no doubt," says Scott. "Love you. Get some sleep."

47.

I don't even make it to my bed. I curl up on the sofa and slowly collapse over onto my side tugging my fleece shawl tighter around me. I'm asleep within seconds.

...

...

...

I struggle to sit upright. It takes me three times. My brain is still half asleep. But I just had an idea. A really good idea. A really good movie story idea. I need to get it down before I forget it. I fumble around for my phone before realizing it's still in my pocket. Oh. That's what's jabbing me in the thigh. Right. Now speak into the phone. I say, "Record."

The phone doesn't do anything.

I stare at the phone. The main button is mocking me. Right. The main button. I push it and repeat, "Record." This is how this works, right?

The screen swirls with a fancy, swishy, multi-colored display. Then it bings.

Sleep washes over me like a soporific wave and I lean down on my side.

No! Don't fall asleep. Record your idea. Record your idea. Record your idea.

I say, "..........." Wait. What did I just say? Did that make any sense? Did I record my idea?

Another wave of fatigue - ten times immense (immenser?) than the last one - washes over me. It's all I can do to place my phone down gently before I close my eyes and....

48.

I wake to Clara standing over me looking very concerned. I blink my eyes several times. This does not help nearly as much as I want it to. I mumble something that even I don't understand. Clara says, "Are you okay?" Pause. "You didn't...overdose or something like that, did you?"

Now, I'm offended. But I still can't sit up. I slept on the couch - right! The couch! I remember now! - in a very awkward position and my muscles seemed to have frozen in said position. But there is hope. I smell coffee. Somewhere. Nearby. I manage to extricate one hand from the tight folds of the fleece and hold it up in Clara's general direction. She grabs hold and pulls up. I'm sitting up now. Good. Very good. I mumble louder and more intelligibly this time, "Coffee?????" Yes, this is worth five question marks.

Clara steps around to the other side of the coffee table and I see - Ta Da! - a thermos of coffee and a large mug from the kitchen. Not howling coyote. Not bison. This one has the Black Hills Bee Hives logo on it. A black silhouette of a bumble bee floating over a stylized flower with three sharp, triangular peaks in the background.

I look up at Clara then back at the thermos. See understands implicitly and pours me a very large and possibly magical cup of coffee. She hands it over to me and I take a deep draught of its aroma before swallowing half the contents of the mug. It's only at that point that I lean back on the couch, look up at Clara again and say, "First, no I did not overdose. Heaven forfend!" Where did that come from? Nevermind. Keep talking. "Second, what time is it? And, third...I don't know what third is anymore but it will come back to me."

Clara says, "It's almost ten in the morning. Mar..."

Ah, I remember now. "Third, who sent you?"

"...cus sent me to make sure you're okay and you didn't go off to the big city to buy a Hummer or something."

That comment sounds like Marcus. I can tell by the expression on Clara's face that she realizes the comment is partially poking fun at her, too, for being the receiver of a brand new car. She's not comfortable being involved in the joke. I take another large swallow of coffee then say, "They're just jealous, that's all."

Clara cocks her head at me and says, "Ahhh, yeah, ummm, no. I'm not worried about that. I am concerned that you look like hell right now and you need to be at the prep meeting in a few minutes."

Almost ten. Right. Prep meeting. Right. I look to the door and try to see through it with my sleep-blurred vision. I look back at Clara, "You didn't by any chance bring the golf cart?"

Clara crosses her arms over her chest and says, "Well, I sure didn't want to carry your dead body all the way back there by myself."

She's got a dark sense of humor. I think I like it. But…not sure yet. Need more coffee. I drain the mug, hold it out to Clara as I say, "Another, please." Then I force myself to walk into the bathroom, brush my teeth, pull back and straighten my hair, spritz some deodorant under my shirt then give a few more sprays up and down my body (don't worry, it's biodegradable, pump action, crystal-based, all natural, all kind, all happy happy happy deodorant, no planets were hurt in its making), splash some water on my face, look at myself in the mirror once again, straighten my belt, pull down my sleeves then clap my hands together in front of my face.

By the time I'm outside (yes, I picked up my phone on the way out), Clara is sitting in the golf cart holding the mug out in my direction. I grab it and sit next to her. I hold the mug out to the side as I say, "Let's ride." Clara hits the accelerator, the golf cart lurches forward and I somehow manage to keep all the precious coffee inside the mug. I make that look easy. But it takes years of practice.

The wind in my face, the coffee and the morning sun bring me back to some semblance of normalcy as we drive to Sal's cabin. I look at the mountains in the distance then at Clara. She looks so serious right now. Come to think of it, she's always looked serious. Except for her happy dance yesterday. I say, "Thanks for coming to get me."

Clara asks while keeping her eyes on the path, "Did you not sleep well or…what?'

What did mess with my…oh, right. Miley Monster and Muze Leaks. Right. Okay. I say to Clara, "There was a phone call I had to take. It interrupted my sleep. You know how that is." That's when I remember trying to record my movie story idea. The idea that came to me when I was dead asleep. I pull out my phone and look at the message I recorded. It says. "Seesaw animals foundling." I squint very hard at the screen. Unfortunately, the words do not change. I mouth the phrase to myself, "Seesaw animals foundling. Seesaw animals foundling. Seesaw animals foundling."

Clara gives me a look and says as we round the corner of the main house, "Is that an acting thing? Like a voice warm-up?"

I stare at her totally not understanding her question. I take another very careful as we are still moving sip of coffee. Then my brain engages, "Oh. No. I recorded this last night. An idea came to me when I was sleeping. I tried to get it down before I forgot it."

"Seesaw animals foundling," Clara says flatly. "What does that mean?"

I look her dead in the face and say, "I have no clue."

She pulls up in front of Sal's cabin. I hop out, thank her, she waves and pulls away. I walk up and am about to knock on the door when Sal opens it and says, "Ahhh, right on time as usual. I like that about you, K.C. I really do." He looks me up and down, turns to walk back into the cabin and says over his shoulder, "Let's make sure Greg does an extra special job on you today."

He means, of course, that I look like hell.

Ouch.

I say by way of explanation, "I got a call late last night. Had to take it. There's this…" Wait. If I heard about the Muze book hack last night, shouldn't Sal have heard of it by this morning? Surely one of his multiple minions in the entertainment industry would have informed him by now. If only for curiosity's sake. "…personal thing with my assistant and her boyfriend…" Nice cover, K.C. Playing that spy in Guatemala really did help you be slick. Sometimes. "…so it was this whole weepy, melodrama. You know how that is."

I sit down on the opposite side of the round table from Sal. He peers over the rim of my mug and asks, "Need a refill?"

"Sal, the answer to that question is and always will be yes," I say. He gets back up, grabs the coffee pot, pours me a cup, puts the pot back and sits back down. I say as he does this, "What's the word for today?" This means what's up with the show plans for today? I then ask, "Where's Marcus? He's usually…"

Marcus comes through the door at that point like he's just been blown here by a bad wind rising. He looks first at me then at Sal as he announces, "The bus broke down."

49.

We are silent for several seconds. The bus. The tour bus. The audience and the guests. Working without an audience or guests. Fuck.

Sal chuckles and says to me, "Well, it looks like you're ad libbing tonight. And I do mean the whole night."

"But that's going to be flat like flat earth flat without an audience. I mean you guys are great straight men but..." Sal smiles knowingly at me. He knows this. He knows this far better than I do. I look at Marcus, "Isn't there another bus? A rescue bus?"

"I've been on the phone with the bus company for the past hour. There was a second bus, an in case of emergency bus..."

"A rescue bus," I repeat with hope brimming in my heart.

"...that one broke down, too. The driver was going fast to get to the first bus and went off the road. No one was hurt, thank god, but an axle was broken. So, no rescue bus."

"Can't we hire some drivers and vans or something?" I ask as the hope starts to trickle out of my heart. I really don't want to ad lib a full show. I'm good, yes, but not whole show good. Doing a whole show, unrehearsed, very little prep. That way lies folly. That way lies embarrassing Youtube clip after embarrassing Youtube clip.

Marcus is by the table now. He grips the back of the chair in front of him and hangs his head, "Not that simple unfortunately. You see, the first bus didn't just break down. It was rammed by buffalo." I exchange stunned looks with Sal then we both look back at Marcus. He continues, "Yeah. I know. There was a spontaneous mini-stampede. That's the phrase the bus agent used over and over. He actually sounded excited. Like he'd just seen a double rainbow or a shooting star. Something rare like that. A spontaneous mini-stampede. Lasted for about thirty seconds. A cluster of bison charged across the road where the bus was traveling. Dented the front pretty bad from what this guy says. So bad the tires won't rotate anymore. The people inside were shaken up. A few cuts, a few bumps and bruises. Ambulances were called.

171

The bus company is being very careful about injuries and medical care and all that. So…" he looks at me directly, "even if we could hire drivers and vans or whatnot the audience members and the guests, the librarian guests, are not able to come. They have to stay overnight for observation."

Sal asks, "How are the buffalo?"

"The bus agent," Marcus says with a hint of disbelief, "described them as restless but otherwise unharmed."

Sal repeats, "Restless," as if he's stumbled upon hidden meaning in the word. "Restless."

"What…ahh…who are the other guests we had lined up?" I ask as all memory of those details has suddenly vacated my cranium.

"Well," Marcus says, "we had Professor Whitmore originally scheduled for tonight but that got switched up so we were going to do double librarians tonight. Unfortunately…"

Sal cuts in, "Both librarians were on the bus."

"Both librarians were on the bus," Marcus echoes then hangs his head and pinches his temples with thumb and forefinger. Things are not looking good.

A thought.

Do I dare say it?

Yes.

"If the librarians and the audience can't come here…" I look carefully at Sal and Marcus to make sure they're paying attention. They are. "…then I should go to the librarians and the audience."

Sal and Marcus stare at me for a second. Then they look at each other for several seconds. Then they nod. Sal turns to me and says, "If the mountain will not come to Mohammed then…"

Marcus finishes the saying, "…Mohammed will go to the mountain."

Sal flips into business mode, "Marcus can you get that all set up with the hospital…"

"Hospital and a couple of medical clinics. The bus group was taken to at least three different sites," says Marcus matter of factly.

Sal bites his lip for a second and he thinks out loud, "Can we do two…" Then he shakes his head. "No, choose the hospital. If that only means one librarian then fine. I'll stay here on set in case this all goes to shit. You can cut back to me and I'll improvise…something. I'll talk to Luisa. Maybe she'll agree to be interviewed. Or we can do a slow tour around the beehives and the rest of the property. It's not great material but at least it will fill air time." He looks at me, "Maybe Clara…"

I cut him off, "No. I want Clara with me. Clara and Al. Al to film. Clara to drive. I trust Al. I trust Clara. This is all so quick and slapdash. I need people I trust. I trust them."

Marcus nods. He understands. He says, "I'll send another crew of three down as soon as I get permission from the hospital. As soon as I figure out which hospital. They'll have time to get exterior shots, do some basic advance work so when you, Clara and Al get down there you won't be going in blind."

I nod. Good. That sounds good.

Marcus goes on as he looks at Sal, "Hospitals always…"

Sal finishes the sentence, "…ask to do kids stuff. Sick kids stuff." He looks at me. "They always do."

I shake my head. Sick kids. Shit. I say, "I'll do it. But I don't want it on camera."

"We need to fill the air time…" Marcus starts.

I say, "You'll have me walking in, going to see the librarian. I can milk that. You'll have Sal here directing the whole process. You," I look at him, "should start the show. Make a joke about the stampede. Explain what's happening. Then cut to me at the hospital. Walking in, seeing people, saying hi, interview the librarian then back to you Sal then…"

Marcus says, "Right. That's not nearly a full show."

I keep going, "Sal and Luisa at the beehives. That's sort of been set up by Professor Whitmore talking about them last night. Then, like you said Sal, maybe a little tour then…then…"

Marcus insists, "That's still not enough air time. We need to cut back to you with the sick kids…"

173

"No," I snap. Then, "Sorry. Sorry, Marcus. I get it. I do. We need to do the show right. And I will meet with the sick kids. But I don't want that on air. Okay? I really don't. I don't like using sick kids as some sort of emergency prop. It just doesn't feel right. Not at all. If the hospital wants it, great. I understand. I'm more than happy to meet with the kids. But we don't put it on air. Just…no."

Marcus and I stare hard at each other for several seconds. Finally, Sal says, "Dammit, she's right. It won't look good. We haven't mentioned it yet. We haven't promoted it like we would with charity stuff, like we normally do with charity stuff. We can't even do the whole 'let's surprise the kids' thing. We don't have the time to get anything good set up. Interviews, family visits, background stories. We don't have time for any of that. She's right. They would come off as sad, gloomy props. So, we don't put it on air. Do it. Yes, of course. But don't put it on air."

Marcus takes a deep breath. And another. Then he nods and says, "Okay. So…what then?"

We sit and stare at each other.

Thinking.

Thinking.

Thinking.

"Hey…" a glimmer of an idea comes to me. Sal and Marcus look at me with hopeful eyes. "Dr. Holmes." The brain surgeon. "Does he work at one of the hospitals?"

A moment of hope. But Marcus shakes his head, "No. He was here in the area on tour."

Shit. I thought I had…wait. "What about his grandson? Theo? Was there any follow up on the apology he made to his ex?"

Marcus snaps his fingers, "We did get his contact information. I can call him. See what's going on with that. See if he's still in the area. Still on tour. They would be, what?, coming back from Medora by now? Yes. Yes, I think I have that right. Coming back from Medora and spending the night at…"

Marcus and I stare at each other as we both say loudly, "…the haunted hotel."

Marcus stops but I keep going, "I've stayed there. I can talk about that. I can riff on that. Then bring in Theo and interview him again about what's happening with…with…"

Marcus says, "Rita. His girlfriend's name is Rita. And maybe even have Dr. Arnold…"

"Dr. Holmes," I correct him. Then add, "Yo, Dr. Holmes." Sal and Marcus stare at me. I say, "You know it's funny."

Marcus brushes that off, "Yes, right. Theo and Dr. Holmes. Right. Girlfriend Rita. If we get in touch with them, you can go down early and we can film that segment prior to the hospital, have it ready to go. We can play around with what segment of the show to play that in. If your stuff at the hospital goes well then…maybe…maybe…we won't need that interview. Especially, Sal, if you can go for a while with Luisa and the bee hives. And make it interesting."

Sal takes a sip of coffee then says, "Let's saddle up."

50.

Marcus and I head out of Sal's cabin. I wave at him as I go in the direction of the main house and Luisa while he heads back to his own cabin to make a whole bunch of phone calls. I'll tell Luisa what's going on and why I need Clara for the day. Then Sal will follow up with her later about being interviewed.

The moment is odd. I'm in a rush to prepare for the show but I can't really do anything specific right now except pass on information. It's the old hurry up and wait. By luck I see Luisa, Clara and Kaley in the main house. It looks like Luisa has made them a batch of cookies and this is their mid-morning break. This internship looks more like being a camp counselor than it does like working in a real job. Not that I'm one to talk. My job isn't real. It's all make believe.

I say to Luisa and Clara while Kaley hovers on the edge of my vision, "We need to do some shooting down in the city tonight, down at the hospital. I'll need Clara to drive. We'll be gone into the evening, too, most likely."

Luisa gives me a nod. The more time I spend with Clara, the more time Luisa wants me to spend with Clara. She senses the same connection that Professor Whitmore noted. Joined by the gods. Clara asks, "When do we leave? Why do we need to go down there?" She pulls out her phone to look up directions and asks, "What's the name of the hospital?"

That's when Kaley speaks up, "Dunsmore Medical." We look at her. Right. She's from the area. She'd know the name of the hospital. She goes on, "I have a sister. She's a radiologist. She works there."

I turn back to Luisa and Clara. I say, "That must be it."

Clara taps in the name. Kaley adds, "I can call my sister and get you in touch with people down there. Do you need that?" Pause. "Can I come with you? I'd like to do a background story on this. A follow up piece for my newspaper."

I shake her off, "No, Kaley, not today. We're too busy. It's a bit hectic. Too many balls in the air at once today. You understand."

176

Kaley insists, "I could call my sister and you could interview her. She has a collection of funny x-rays. That would be a good skit for the show."

I saw a stand up comedian use his own x-rays in his act once. It was actually pretty funny. He went through the stages of his life by showing x-rays for injuries he acquired from youth on up. A broken leg (kickball accident), missing teeth (frozen too hard ice cream accident), a knife stabbed through his arm (arts and crafts accident). At one point he showed a scan of his head. There wasn't anything obviously wrong like the other x-rays. Then he pointed to a small black spot and said, "And that's brain cancer."

The next segment of his show was an interesting but not quite ready for prime time dive into his living through treatment for brain cancer, surviving (he called that a "having more life accident") and the whole experience changing his perspective on life. "Before the cancer, I had a totally different job. I worked in insurance. People would call up and I'd laugh at them. Now, you come here and laugh at me. It's really flipped things around that brain cancer." Yeah. Like I said, not quite ready. But still memorable.

There might be... I ask Kaley, "Have you ever seen these x-rays before? Is this something your sister..."

"...Heather..."

"...Heather has done before? Does she have a good selection of x-rays, permission to show them? All that stuff?"

"Oh, yeah," says Kaley. "Heather's part of a hospital outreach program. They go to schools and what not to teach kids safety tips and who to call in case of an emergency. Stuff like that. The x-rays work great with the kids. Seeing a shin bone broken at ninety degrees really gets their attention."

Thinking.

Thinking.

Looking at Clara. She stares back

Thinking.

Looking at Clara. She gives me an almost imperceptible shoulder shrug.

Thinking some more. Librarians, staff, random audience members then funny x-rays. I think that could actually work. I could just about fill a show with that. There'd be no need to cut back here. That, in my opinion, would make the show better. Focus on the hospital only. Go all in on that. Don't dilute it with bees and honey. I'm sure Sal could riff fine with Luisa and this setting. But…

I say to Kaley, "Get your sister on the phone. Let me talk to her. Then, if I think that will work, you can come with us to get your story. Same rules a la MDB apply. Agreed?"

Kaley nods sharply, "Agreed." Then she pulls out her phone and calls her sister. I walk with Clara to the door putting an arm around her shoulder as I say, "I'm going to need you to be my assistant today. That means I need you to stay on top of things for me. My mind, pretty soon, is going to get filled with and distracted by rehearsing the show in my head. Sort of rehearsing. Mental preparation. Running through options in my head. What if I say this about an x-ray? What if I say that? My ad lib brain is going to take over at some point. That's good. That's what I need to do a good show, a good performance. So, what I need you to do is keep me grounded. Get me from point A to point B. We'll most likely be moving around in the hospital. Al's going to go with us, too, to do the camera work." Clara smiles at this. I thought she would. "So, coordinating with him will be a big help. I might," I look her hard in the eye, "I might get a little barky-barky demanding things in the moment. That doesn't mean I'm mad at you. It just means that I need something to happen as quickly as possible. So, can you play that role today? Driver, assistant, taker of phone calls, fetcher of objects and information. Can you do that?"

Clara puts on a serious face then says, "Well, for a day that started with me thinking you were dead, it sure has taken a sudden turn."

There's that sense of humor again. She's opening up a bit more. That line was actually funny. Good. Very good. But it wasn't an answer. I ask, "So, that's a yes?"

"That's a yes," she says back to me.

51.

It's about an hour later. I talked to the x-ray sister. She's excited to be on national TV. Her description of the x-rays sounds like they'll work for a laugh. Then she has some stories about doing her outreach program that we could work in if we have the time and she does well on camera. I'm going to need to be in super observant, super responsive host mode for this show. I don't want to put anyone we interview in an awkward position. I don't want to embarrass them live on TV. Not at all. I do want to get a good laugh from them. Sometimes the latter morphs into the former for people not used to being filmed. I'll have to be very careful about that tonight.

I've talked with Sal and Marcus about wanting to focus the show on the hospital and not cut back to Sal back here. Sal insisted that he be prepped and ready just in case something goes haywire down at the hospital. That makes sense. That's professional thinking, right there. He also insisted that we do the bit with the grandson at the hotel before we go to the hospital. "Even if we don't use it tonight, we can use it on tomorrow's show. Or the day after that. It'll be a good tie back to the start of the week. And," he said firmly, "it'll be a dry run for your impromptu crew. It will give you, Al and Clara a sense of how you'll work together on the fly in the hospital."

Marcus agreed with that. I told him that Clara's acting as my assistant today. He was very good with her. He pulled her aside and made sure Clara had all the contact names and numbers and a sense of what might happen. Let's be clear. The on location filming could go very smoothly. Al is confident in his rig. He's confident in himself. I'm getting more and more comfortable with the whole concept of the show and how to facilitate it as a host. I'm going to keep it light and easy with an aim to showcase all the good that the hospital does while having some fun with another librarian and funny/cautionary x-rays. I can weave all those strands together into one solid show. I can. I'm pretty sure I can.

But with live, on location shoots you just never know. You just never know. Rarely do they go off without any glitches, hitches and hiccups. Very rarely. But, on the other hand, you just make do with what you have and most people out there in television land are very accepting of such complications. If we end up on Youtube for bloopers, well, a little humility isn't necessarily a bad thing.

And now it's time to go.

52.

Clara's driving. I'm in the passenger seat. Kaley's in the back seat. Al is ahead of us in his vehicle filled with his equipment. There's a tension in the car between Clara and Kaley. Under normal circumstances, I'd do something about that. Get them to talk to each other. But not today. I'm using the time in the car to let my mind drift and relax. I'm going to need to be as rested as possible tonight. This is going to be longer and more strenuous than the previous shows. Not overwhelming. But full, busy, one thing after another until it's done. That sort of day. A little nap in the car will definitely help me.

I'm dozing lightly, half asleep when the phrase comes back to me. "Seesaw animals foundling." I let it rest in the center of my head. "Seesaw animals foundling." It was such a good idea. I remember it being good, really good, so good but I don't recall the details of the idea. "Seesaw animals foundling." The car shifts lightly under me as we take a long, gradual turn. My body presses deeper into the seat. I relax more. "Seesaw animals foundling." With an act of ocular will, I crack open one eyelid to catch the time on the car clock. Then I let the eyelid seal closed and I fall asleep.

…

…

…

I come back to the waking world in stages. First there's a sense of movement. My body weight shifting.Then the distinct aroma. New car smell. Right. I'm in the new car. Clara's new car. Then I hear voices. First is Kaley, "She obviously cares for you. Honestly, I didn't expect that."

Then Clara. Short and to the point, "Why not?" Her words have an edge to match the point.

Kaley again, "Ohhh, not that you shouldn't have someone… not that you aren't worthy of… look, I don't mean it like that. I mean it's… I mean… I've been a little stressed lately with this internship. It wasn't the one I wanted and I know I've been stressed about that and I know I can be bitchy when I'm stressed…"

"Can be?" Clara cuts in. Good girl. Hold her feet to the fire.

"Ok. I have been bitchy to you and I want to apologize for that. So. I'm sorry. I am. I got jealous of you and Luisa. She dotes on you. That pissed me off. My mom… And then K.C. here comes along and she dotes on you, too. In my head I was like WTF? Like what about me? I'm right here, too. What makes Clara so special? And I know that's just my mom in my head. My therapist tells me to not let my mom in my head. But she doesn't live with her so…" She trails off.

I wonder how Clara will respond. I hold my not quite asleep face as still as possible. There's a long silence then Clara breaks it, "Apology accepted." Then, "It's funny. I was jealous of you and you were jealous of me."

"Yeah. Really funny. Hardy har har," says Kaley in a self-mocking tone.

Clara giggles then mimics Kaley's tone of voice, "Hardy har har."

Then they both say it louder and in unison, "Hardy har har. Hardy har har. Hardy har har." At the end they both break into genuine laughter.

Something about their laughter jars something loose in my still half asleep brain. The idea comes back to me. I sit upright in the passenger seat, all of a sudden fully awake. At least, I think I'm fully awake. I say, "C. and C., animus/anima, refounding. C. and C., animus/anima, refounding. C. and C., animus/anima, refounding." I stare hard at a surprised but still keeping her eyes on the road and Al's vehicle in front of us Clara. Then I pull out my phone and repeat the phrase three more times to be recorded, double check the spelling and accuracy and relax deeply into the seat letting out a long sigh.

Clara keeps driving. I sit up a little. Kaley asks from the back seat, "Is everything okay?" Then, "What was that?"

I turn to look back at her as I say, "That was an idea I had last night and tried to record in my phone but failed and now it just came back to me. So, I made sure to record it right this time."

"No more seesaws," Clara says.

I say, "No more seesaws. It was supposed to be C. and C. That's Chester and Charlene. Those names refer to a person from history. Hollywood history. I read a book about him a few years ago. I even bought the rights to turn the book into a movie. But I could never figure out exactly how. So, I gave the rights to a director friend. He's taking a shot at it now. He's the one who recommended the book to me. And, ohh, ha! I just remembered. I started reading that book when I was in the haunted hotel a few years ago. That's where we're heading now. Okay. That's weird. When I had the idea last night I had no idea I'd be going to the hotel today. Ha." Meeting Scott, getting my first phone call from Shawn Muze, reading the Chester/Charlene book, my mom's funeral, the bookstore video of me and the bakery girl. All those memories flash through my head. "Yeah, Rapid City does weird things to me. No doubt." I turn to look at both Clara and Kaley. "Get ready. Tonight's show could be really strange."

53.
       Clara shrugs off my comment and asks, "So, what's the idea? What does 'animus/anima refounding' mean?"

       I glance back at Kaley to see if she's taking notes. She's not. I say to her, "This might be a good bit for your story." She pulls out her phone and starts recording. I look forward again and raise my voice a little as I explain, "Chester is a mostly forgotten figure from early Hollywood history. Chester was his public name, persona, identity. The author of the book puts forth an argument that Chester was actually Charlene, a woman who played as a male in public in order to run her business. Which was making film. That is, making celluloid. Making the actual, physical film. Not making A film. Okay. So, one person. Male and Female both. Maybe. According to the author. Animus/anima is a Jungian concept. You two know about Jung?"

       Clara shrugs, "A little."

       Kaley echoes, "Yeah, a little."

       I decide to skip this part, "Not important. It just means that everyone has a male side and a female side. Aspects. A male aspect and a female aspect. There's more to it but that's the essence. So. Chester slash Charlene. Animus slash anima. Early Hollywood history. Deception. Illegal businesses and bribes and threats and all sorts of behind the scenes intrigue. Betrayal. Revenge. The book has it all. That's why I wanted to make it into a movie. But I could never get my head around Chester slash Charlene. I could never quite get how to play that role. It always came off as victimized. A victim-powered revenge story. I don't like revenge stories. So, I could never get it right. He slash she was betrayed. She slash he did seek revenge. Years later. But I always felt like I was missing something, some greater element of the story. That's what refounding means. That's how that ties in. Just like Professor Whitmore sees a version of the world refounded on Aeneas and Dido loving and respecting each other I now see a Hollywood movie business refounded on Chester slash Charlene able to get justice. Justice in a proper manner. Justice and recognition. Go back and change the starting point of Hollywood and we can change all that comes after."

184

Kaley says, "Okay. I think I understand what you're saying. But you can't actually go back and change Hollywood history."

"No," I say, "of course not. But I can change the story we tell ourselves about Hollywood history. I can offer up a different, alternate…pathway, an alternate option, another example. A wonderful What If scenario. No, not wonderful. A…haunting What If scenario. Yes. That's the word. Haunting. As in regrets from the past pushing on the present moment. Pushing and pushing and pushing until things change. Until we make a change."

"What change are you talking about?" Clara asks, "Repaying Chester/Charlene's ancestors? Something like that?"

"No, I'm thinking more…symbolically, I guess. Psychologically. Mentally. I want to shift perception. I want to provide a new lens through which to view Hollywood. Or through which Hollywood views itself. A new way of thinking about Hollywood."

"And what exactly is that new way?" Kaley asks.

"I'm still working on it." Pause. "But I'll get there. With help. I'm going to need a lot of help."

54.

We arrive at the Alexander Houston Hotel a little after 2PM. Clara pulls the car into a parking spot on the opposite side of the street from Heroes Unbound, Scott's comic book store. Former comic book store. He gave it to Sam, his half-brother, when he moved to Wayside. Wayside. Wow, I haven't been there in a while. I miss it. I miss Alonsha's field. I do. But…it wasn't meant to be. We sold for a good price and now we're in an L.A. penthouse. Shudder. I'm still getting used to that. I live in a penthouse. Yup, that still sends tingles down my spine.

I help Al get his equipment out of the car. I task Kaley to help as well. She jumps right in. Clara, a little confused, starts to help, too, but I tell her to call Marcus and get the information for coordinating with Theo and Dr. Holmes (Yo!). Her eyes light up with a mixture of fear and hope. She wants to do well. I can tell. I grab her shoulder and say, "Don't stress. Just focus. Focus." She nods then heads into the lobby.

Kaley is Al's pack animal at this point. She's carrying a shoulder bag on each arm, has some sort of bulky belts fastened around her waist (batteries maybe?) and is carrying light reflectors with both hands. I look at her. She doesn't notice for a few seconds. When she does, she smiles sheepishly at me, lifts the reflectors up in both hands and says, "Anything for the story." I smile back at her then, with a nod from Al who is strapped into his steady cam, we head inside.

The Houston has a strong, old school, back in the day this is how things were done, understated elegance vibe to it. The lobby has sparse, white columns, one each at the four corners. The roof is two storeys high with a frosted glass sky light to filter in the sun. The floor is filled with leather furniture (couches, chairs, love seats) and covered by two, very large oriental rugs. Dark wood coffee tables rest in front of the couches. Smaller versions rest by the sides of the individual chairs. There are a couple of wingbacks here but, I smirk, the ones in Heroes Unbound are better. Yes, I am biased. Very biased.

There is a quiet murmur of activity as we enter. I see Clara at the desk being looked down on by a middle management type. You know the kind. He thinks a name badge and a title makes him superior to others. I can't stand them. But, keep it cool, K.C. Don't rush over just yet. Give Clara a chance to handle this on her own.

Kaley plops down on the end of one of the couches. I stand nearby. Al is looking all around the space. He spends several seconds assessing the sky light and then walking around the furniture looking at the angles and play of the ambient light. I keep an eye on Clara dealing with His Fatuousness. She's remaining calm. He's being dismissive. I'll give it to a count of twenty then I'm going over there to flex my fame-iosity muscles. Fame-iosity. Yes. I made that word up. Just like Shakespeare used to do. Get stuck writing - make up a word. Perfect. Perfect.

Al stands next to me now and points at a wingback and loveseat resting at ninety degrees to each other in the far corner of the lobby. He says, "That could work over there. You on the chair. Theo on the loveseat. Have him at one end and the empty space next to him implying his girlfriend. His missing girlfriend."

The missing girlfriend. That sounds like a true crime story. This is not a true crime story. Unless it's a true crime of the heart story. Ohhh, that's bad. Note to self: do not say that phrase during the show tonight. You'll be tempted but don't do it. I walk closer to the corner that Al has indicated. I can fully pretend to be assessing its potential as an interview spot. But really I'm just getting closer to the desk where Mr. Meddling Manager is once again shaking his head at Clara. Clara is offering her phone to him. She must have called Marcus to get Marcus to convince Mr. This is My Small Domain and I Rule it with an Iron Fist and no young kid is going to come in here and take over. Yeah, I know. That name is too long.

Ohhh, I forgot to tell you. I grabbed my space hoodie before leaving. I'm wearing it over the top of today's cowgirl chic outfit. Right now I have the hood of the hoodie pulled up over my hair and, yes, a huge pair of sunglasses on. No one has recognized me so far. Not that many people have passed through the lobby since we've come in. A handful but besides glancing at Kaley and her literal baggage for a moment they haven't made a fuss. Good. That's good.

I say to Al who has walked over with me to get closer to the corner he thinks will work, "You don't think it would be too noisy in here? Wouldn't a private room be better? We'd have to stop people from coming through here. I don't think they'll go for that."

Al says as he points at the main entrance, "I think this is far enough back from most of the foot traffic that it would work. Actually, I think it would add some...veracity, some real life, hey this is happening right now feel to it. Background noise. I can take a few establishing shots of people walking through. Some are bound to stop. We can set up a line they can't pass. It'll be like a spontaneous audience. Maybe you can interact with them. A little. What do you think?"

An unvetted, spontaneous, random audience. I'm not sure about that. But maybe I'm just being fearful. It would add some authenticity to the "filmed live" element that we do want. The more this recorded segment can match the energy of the live segments the better.

I look up at the main desk. Mr. Stick up His Ass Gatekeeper has Clara's phone pressed to his face and his listening while shaking his head back and forth. Okay, I've just about had it. That's when Clara looks over her shoulder at me. I give her a silent signal with both hands asking if she needs my help. She bites her lip, looks quickly at the manager guy, looks back at me and nods. I stride right over there. I usually don't do this sort of hey, I'm a star and I need you to do this for me stuff but tonight is the exception. One of the rare exceptions. If only the guy just listened to Clara and Marcus then I wouldn't need to do this.

I smile at Clara as she steps aside and I step forward to the desk. I wait until the man's eyes are on me then I flip back my hoodie and pull off my sunglasses. That's when I recognize the manager. He's lost weight. His hair is different. More gray. His cheeks are sagging, not fleshy anymore. His eyes are still sharp, attentive. I didn't recognize him from a distance. But I sure do now.

Yup, it's Daryl.

55.

Quick recap. Daryl hired me as a waitress when I lived in Rapid City. I was in high school. Dad and I spent a couple of years here. Daryl is also the guy who my mom connected with years later when mom wrote her book. Her book about her life but, yeah, about me, too. The last time I heard from, no, about Daryl is when Scott retrieved my mom's diary from him. Daryl sent the diary to Scott's comic book store. The one across the street. And now, years later, Daryl is here working at the haunted hotel.

Great. Just great.

As quickly as I can, I shift into smiley happy mode. I was in pushy bitchy mode. But with Daryl, I know that won't work. I realized as soon as I recognized him that my fame-iosity is going to be counter productive. He tried to blackmail me once. Scott, my real life hero, dealt with that. He's kept those details from me to this day but, yes, there was counter blackmailing threatened. Thinking back on that now, maybe that wasn't the best approach. But…well, you can't change the past. Or…can you?

I say simply, "Daryl. What a surprise."

Daryl eyes me in silence for several moments then says, "Ms. Hingergarten." That's it. Not "hello," not "how can I help you?," not "it's been a while," not even "you and your crew need to leave." Not any of that. Nothing. Nada. Zero. Just "Ms. Hingergarten."

I press on. Gently. "You talked with Marcus, my producer. The producer for Kincaid Live!" Yes, I am dropping Sal's name. Maybe that set of fame-iosity muscles will work with Daryl. Clearly mine won't. It's hard to pull the I'm a star routine with someone who hired you as a waitress back in the day. What did I say about humility? Not going to lie - it doesn't feel good right now.

Daryl nods and hands me back Clara's phone. I glance at the screen. The call is still active. I put the phone to me ear and say, "Marcus, you there?"

"What is going on down there, K.C.? I've been in contact with Theo. He's good to go. He's on the way back from lunch to the hotel as we speak. You don't have to even deal with this manager guy. Just deal with Theo. Keep it simple."

I take all this in as I keep smiling at Daryl. Then I say, "Uh-uh, great, call you back soon." I turn to hand Clara's phone back to her then say, "Get in touch with Theo. He should be here soon." She nods and walks back over to Al. I hold up a finger to Al to let him know I still have to deal with Daryl.

I turn back, smiling again, to Daryl. We look at each other in silence for several seconds. He speaks first, "Your...friends lied. They threatened me and they lied."

The last time I dealt with Daryl...well, Scott dealt with Daryl. Scott and someone he knows here in town who knows stuff about Daryl. That's what Scott told me back then. I was so thankful that Scott handled that situation. So thankful. If Mo were here right now, he'd tell me not to split hairs. Because splitting hairs never works. Fine. But I'm not going to back down either. So...

"You were blackmailing me, Daryl. YOU were threatening and blackmailing ME. That's how that started. In case that detail slipped your mind." I say all this with a smile, with easy, relaxed body language. You never know when someone is filming you from a distance. Or security cams. Or whatever. Best to look as pleasant and calm as possible while I get through this.

"All I was asking for was a donation to the church."

"But you weren't asking. You were threatening."

"I...offered incentive for you to do the right thing."

"You threatened to release embarrassing material about me."

"You needed to be shown the way. To donate to the church. Not that...arts program."

I feel an insult I will not be able to take back rising in the back of my throat. As much fun as I am having with this blunt exchange with Daryl (yes, I admit it, this is fun talking like this - no pretense, no bullshit; I get why MDB operates this way) I don't want to blow it. I swallow the insult and ask, "What happened to you Daryl? What happened to the restaurant manager who hired a freshman high school girl and made her feel safe and listened to her talk about her dreams? Where is that guy? How did he turn into this… this brittle, scared, bitter person before me?" Pause. "You used to love the arts."

Ooops. I didn't quite swallow all of the insult.

Daryl's chin quivers for a moment. Then he clenches his jaw. He clenches his jaw and breathes in and out through his nose as he continues to glare at me. His eyes flash fire. Eventually, he gathers his thoughts and says, "What happened to that sweet, innocent girl I knew back then? What made you turn into a sleazy, alcoholic, cheap, Hollywood sexpot floozy?"

Sexpot floozy? Alcoholic? Wha… Ohhhh. He must have seen the videos of me back in the day. The young starlet, puking party girl phase of my life. But… I've changed since then. But [thinking, thinking, thinking] that was a recent change, a couple of years, maybe more, when I ended up back here in Rapid City, when I met Scott and dealt with Daryl and Mom. Right before Mom died. Ohhh, right. Mom. I get it now. This is Mom. Collateral damage from Mom.

I take a long, very long breath then say, "Daryl, I don't drink anymore. I haven't for years. I know there are videos of me…doing that. But that was years ago. The internet is forever but I've changed since then. I changed because of my mother." I study his face for a moment when I mention mom. He flinches. I can tell he thinks that I should have been better to my mother. He thinks this because somehow she convinced him to think this. That's what she did, after all. She was a master manipulator, that one.

I go on, "I don't know how you and my mom met. Or what the nature of your relationship was. I'm sure you were good to her. I'm sure you were. So…thank you for that. But you need to understand that she was very hurtful to me and to my father…"

"Your father cheated on her," Daryl spits.

Don't defend. Don't get angry. Just speak truth. "Yes. He did. And that's something he dealt with as best he could. I didn't know about it back then but now looking back I can say it weighed on him greatly. Greatly. It…clung to him. He…" An understanding unfolds inside my head. An understanding of my father that I've never had before. It blossoms like a flower that's been waiting for the light of the sun for ages in order to open its petals. "...he didn't think he deserved to be happy. He didn't think he was good enough to be happy." The words ring true. They are true. Damn.

I take a second to recover from this. I regather my thoughts and start over, "My mom and dad… I don't… I'm forever grateful to them. For having me and raising me. As best they could. But I can't keep reliving their lives, their mistakes. I did for a while when I was younger. By drinking and partying and puking. All that stuff that I'm sure you saw online. But I stopped. I realized that I need to live my own life and make my own mistakes. Find my own way." I take another deep breath. I've lost my train of thought. I say, "Look, I don't know what my mother told you about me and dad. I don't know what you know about me now. But I don't think this…" I wave my hand back and forth between the two of us. "...is helping, is doing any good for you or for me."

"She always loved you," says Daryl.

That comment takes my breath away. Part of me wants to believe it. But…

Daryl goes on, "Even when you were doing all that drinking. She always loved you. I didn't understand how. But she did. You didn't take her calls back then. Ever. That's why I told her she should write the book. To let you know that she loved you. She loved you and wanted the best for you. That's what I told her to do. But then the book became this…thing. It became something else. It started spinning out of control. I… I…"

It was Daryl's idea for mom to write the book. He urged her to write a book so she and I could come to some sort of reconciliation. But then mom did mom stuff and turned the good thing nasty. That feels right. That rings true. Then Daryl tried to salvage something good out of the whole scenario by getting me to donate to his church. But he assumed I'd be like mom. He assumed things would spin out of control with me, too. That's why he "provided incentive." Such plans. Such grasping. Such folly. But… Would I have done any differently if I were in his position?

193

…

…

…

Probably not.

Sigh.

I say to Daryl, "Yeah. That's what mom did. That's what happened with her. Things spun out of control. I'm sorry that happened to you. That she did that to you. I should have guessed that, seen that. Years ago. I'm sorry I didn't. I am."

Daryl wipes a tear from the corner of his eye and says, "Thank you." Then he can't hold the tears back anymore. They stream down his face. He searches for and finds a box of tissues under the desk. He takes the better part of a minute to wipe his eyes and steady himself. When he's composed, he says to me, "I miss her." He nods and his chin quivers again. "I know she wasn't perfect. By any stretch of the imagination." He says this last part in a very deep, exaggerated voice. Yes. I can tell. He does know. "But…I miss her. She…lived a life, that's for sure. Quite a life. She and I had good talks. I miss our talks."

I let that wash over me for a few seconds. At the end of her life, my mom had a friend. A good friend. Daryl. I say, "Thank you for missing her." Now, it's my turn to wipe a tear from the corner of my eye. Daryl hands me a tissue. I take it. When I'm ready, I say, "Can we start over, Daryl? I'd like to start over."

Daryl forces a smile on his face. Not because he's angry with me. Because he's sad. He misses his friend and he's sad. He says back to me, "I'd like to start over, too."

56.

So, that happened. Daryl and I are not totally good but better. Better.

Then Theo came back from lunch and we filmed an interview with him. A follow-up interview about his apology to his girlfriend. Ex-girlfriend. Rita. Daryl gave us permission to film it in the back corner of the lobby. Al was right. The lighting there was fantastic. Here's how that went.

As Al directed (he who holds the camera is in charge of the set), I sat in the single chair while Theo sat on one end of the love seat. I started off easy with a couple of simple questions about what he and his grandfather had done since they were last on the show (Only two days ago? Was that only two days ago? My, how time flies.). They had continued on with the tour bus to Devils Tower. You'd be proud of me. I didn't make any alien jokes about Devils Tower. Yes, Scott will be disappointed. Sometimes you need to leave the low-hanging fruit alone. A too obvious joke is often not good.

The tour took them up to Medora for a night to see a performance of "Medora, the Musical." Early this morning they headed back down here to Rapid City. This is the end of the tour for Theo and Dr. Holmes. They fly home tomorrow morning. That's when I ask about Rita, "So, back home. Have you heard anything from anyone about your apology? Has Rita reached out, by any chance?"

A handful of people, including Dr. Holmes, are standing about twenty feet away in the lobby. Clara is doing a very professional job of keeping them back. Daryl has provided us with a velvet rope divider that is working perfectly. Theo tightens his lips in a non-smile/non-frown. He says very gently, "No. She has not reached out. I admit that part of me hoped she would. But she hasn't. And I understand that. I do. I was…neglectful. I missed my opportunity. I'm glad that my grandfather urged me to say something on your show…"

"…this isn't my show. It's Kincaid Live!" I felt compelled to say that. I don't want to ever take credit for someone's else's hard work. Not even a little bit.

Theo goes on, "…ummm, right…which I guess fits with my apology. I don't want any credit or treatment or response from that, from Rita just because I did it on television. I get the drama, the romantic flourish of it all and in the moment it felt good. But I realized later that it could have put pressure on Rita to respond. In a public manner. And that's definitely not what I wanted. Not at all."

Okay. But… "So, why did you agree to come back on the show now then?"

There's the sound of distant thunder and a slight darkening of the natural light. Out of the corner of my eye, I see Al direct Kaley to shift the reflectors to compensate for the change. Theo says with a look towards Dr. Holmes, "My grandfather, who is standing over there, insisted. He says love requires boldness. He told me that if I didn't do this interview and things don't work out with Rita that I would regret it for the rest of my life. So, I had to give it a shot. I had to try."

A thought. I ask, "So, if your positions were reversed, if it were Rita here on the show and you were out there watching, how would you feel?"

Theo taps a finger on his lips for a few moments before responding, "I'd be upset. At first. The whole public pressure element. But then I'd like to think part of me would be flattered. Part of me would be confused. I think at the very least I'd reach out to Rita to talk. Yes, I definitely would reach out to her to talk."

The thunder booms again. Closer this time. There's a flash of lightning. Sunlight flickers and dances through the skylight. The small crowd by Clara lets out a unified "ohhhhhh." I turn directly to the camera and say, "As much as I'd like to say that Sal Kincaid doesn't have the ability to control the weather to make dramatic effects like this…I can't. Sal's been around so long he knows everyone. I'm pretty sure he knows someone who can make it thunder like this."

Al gives me a thumbs up as I turn the focus back to Theo. I say, "Well, since this is being filmed a few hours before it will be aired, maybe even a day before it's aired we won't hear…"

That's when Theo's phone rings. He apologizes profusely. He says, "I'll turn it off right now. So sorry. I thought

I left it in the room. So sorry." He looks at the phone screen and his face goes still.

I ask, "Is it..."

Theo shakes off the question, "No, it's not Rita. It's my mother. And she sent a few texts. It looks important. I think I should..."

He starts to stand up. I wave at him to sit back down, "No. Go ahead and answer. You should always answer the phone when your mother calls."

Theo shifts in his seat away from the camera. Al focuses on me for a moment. I put a mockingly exasperated smile on my face like moms, right? What're you gonna do? Al goes back to Theo who we can overhear saying, "We're good. Yes. Yes, he is. I'm making sure. Yes, he's taking his medication. No. Mom. No. We'll see you tomorrow. Look, I'm on TV right now. No, really. Yes, another interview. Yes, right now. What?"

Theo looks up at me at this point to say, "My mom says hello." I brighten and smile for real at his point. How adorable. Theo repeats the words his mom is feeding into his ear without thinking about them. "She says you should be proud of yourself for doing almost as good a job as Sal Kincaid." When he realizes what he just passed on his face blanches in embarrassment. Al focuses on me. I go from happy, sweet, smiling and how nice of Theo's mom to - when the word "almost" is said - frowny, and dejected like I just got slapped in the face.

Yes, I am playing along. Spontaneous mom humor. You can't fight it. You just have to roll with the punchline. But, also, "almost?" Really? "Almost as good a job." I decide to lean into it. I wave at Theo to get his attention again. His mom is clearly giving him an earful but he's not repeating anything out loud at this point. He's just staring at the floor and nodding. I wave again and say sharply, "Theo. Let me talk to your mom."

Theo holds the phone out from his ear and shakes his head no. Like absolutely no. But I keep waving at him to hand the phone to me. He hesitates. I keep waving. He looks at the phone. All of us can hear his mom's voice coming through. He stands up, leans toward me and drops the phone into my waiting hand. I say as I look directly into the camera, "Hello, this is K.C. Hall."

Mom goes on for a couple of seconds before realizing that I'm talking to her. Then she asks me about my outfit tonight. I say, "It's cowgirl chic. A fitted, fringey black vest over a white top with a large collar. And billowy black pants with ankle boots. Yes, I do like me some ankle boots. You, too, uh-uh, uh-uh." I listen to more mom comments. "Oh. You liked the tuxedo outfit better, did you? That's nice to hear. I liked it, too. But you can't wear something like that every…" Mom interrupts me again. I listen as I give a look of now I understand your pain to Theo. Theo rolls his eyes. Then, "No, ma'am. I'm married. Yes, very married. Yes, I agree, Theo is a very nice young man. Yes, he did make a mistake letting Rita go. But sometimes things don't… No, I haven't met Rita. I'm sure she's a nice young woman. Yes, very nice."

I look up and see Dr. Holmes standing next to my chair. He does not look happy. He doesn't say anything. He just motions for the phone. I hand it to him. He says to his adult daughter, "Vilma, this is your father. Yes. Now, leave us be, you hear. We will see you tomorrow Theo and I. But you need to… My medication and whether I take it or not is none of your business, Vilma. Always butting in you were. Always." The thunder rumbles directly above the hotel now. I look up at the skylight with a look of heaven, please spare us from interrupting parents.

Dr. Holmes hands the phone back to me as he says, "You hang up now." Then he turns and walks back to Clara and the velvet rope without another word. I hold the phone out and Theo takes it from me. I compose myself as does Theo. Then I say, "Well, after all that. I'm not sure what to say."

"Me neither," adds Theo.

The thunder rumbles and lightning flashes. The hotel lights flicker for a moment. I see a pained look on Al's face. I say into the camera, "I think it's pretty clear that Sal wants us to finish up now. Theo, thank you. Dr. Holmes," I give a little wave to him in the small crowd, "thank you. And Theo's mom, wherever you are, I will seriously consider changing my hair style to what you suggested." I shake my head emphatically NO as I say this. I finish with, "Good night everybody from the Alexander Houston Hotel in Rapid City, South Dakota."

57.

Afterwards, I sign a few autographs and chat with the members of the small crowd and say goodby to Daryl. We hug. It's good. It's one of those hugs between people who know that they may never see each other again. So, there's a touch of sadness to it but mostly there's a sense of relief. Deep relief.

I notice the front windows of Heroes Unbound as we head outside to the vehicles. The life size cardboard figures of a Wonder Woman ripoff and a Superman ripoff (Scott didn't want to risk violating any copyright laws when he had a local artist make them so he didn't use the actual characters) are back to back looking out onto the sidewalk doing their static best to entice people into the store. They are busting out of heavy, black, nasty looking chains with a burst of energy. Get it? Heroes Unbound. Yeah, a little on the nose but fun nonetheless. It strikes me that the figures could easily be images of Jung's anima and animus. Yes, very dramatic, very in-shape, very idealized, special effects versions of the anima and animus but images nonetheless. Evocative images. Powerful images. I wonder if any comic book writer has explored that aspect. I'll have to ask Scott. I'm sure he'll know.

I hop in the front of the Forester, strap my seat belt on and close my eyes for just a moment. Kaley loads the back of the vehicle then she and Clara get in at the same time. Clara says to me, "We're heading to the hospital now." I nod acknowledgement without opening my eyes. Kaley offers from the back, "That was an amazing interview, Ms. Hall."

I say "Thank you," absent-mindedly. I don't mean to be dismissive. But my mind is already zooming ahead to what's next. The hospital and the kids. The sick kids.

58.

      I said I didn't want the kids stuff on film and I don't. We didn't film it. Likewise, I won't talk about it much here. But there is something I want to pass along. There was a six year old girl named Henrietta. She's going into heart surgery tomorrow. Surgery that has only a fifty-fifty chance of success. Surgery that will require a long, painful recovery. The look on her parents' face was devastating. I hugged them for a long time. That's all I could do. Words are useless in those scenarios. Or so I thought. But then Henrietta said, "Everybody's life is different. This is my life and I'm going to live it as long as I can."

      Yes, I did break down in tears. Some of the tears were for Henrietta, but not all of them. Some were for Mo. Of course. Some were for my father. Some, yes, were for my mother. Some were for that unknown time in the future that all of us will face.

      I told Henrietta that I would come back to see her when she's healthy enough for visitors. Then I went into the bathroom and cried silently for several minutes. At some point, Clara knocked on the door and said, "We have to get ready now."

      Shakespeare flashes into my head.

      "The readiness is all."

      Henrietta understands that better than most of us ever will.

59.

Marcus and the advance team have done a fantastic job of coordinating with the hospital. I go from room to room, bed to bed to take pictures with the people from the bus accident who are being kept overnight for observation. Some of them clearly have no idea who I am but they want a picture with me because their compatriots are getting pictures with me and they don't want to be left out. When all of that is said and done, we go to do the interview.

We set up in one of the waiting rooms at the end of the hallway. There is one librarian at the hospital. Cale Moncrief. He's from Albuquerque. Ohh, that's good. I know Albuquerque a little. I haven't been back since dad and I moved years ago but I can riff on that with him. Good, that will make the start of the interview easier. So, here goes.

I smile into the camera again, "Welcome everyone…" I go on to set the scenario for the viewers at home: tour bus, buffalo, spontaneous mini-stampede and go. I turn to Cale at that point and say, "Did they at least give you a sticker that says 'I survived a stampede at Custer State Park and all I got was this lousy sticker?' Maybe a t-shirt?"

Cale laughs and shakes his head. Of course not. But he doesn't say anything. His eyes are a little unfocused.

I offer up a soft ball, "So, tell me about yourself, Cale. You're a librarian. From Albuquerque. How did you end up there? Did you grow up there?"

Cale (balding, slightly overweight, shy) says into his chest, "I was a military brat. My parents were in Germany then a couple of other places. Then we ended up in Albuquerque when I was in high school." He falls silent.

I ask, "Did you ever eat at a little restaurant down near the university called, ohh, what was the name, ahhh, El Patio. That's it. El Patio. My dad took me there a couple of times. The food - like so many places in Albuquerque - was fantastic. But what stands out for me was this man with a long, wispy, white beard who played guitar inside the restaurant. The restaurant was in an old house. One of those small, old houses down in that area and the tables were both inside and outside on the patio, duh!, and he would sit inside with his one foot on a small stand so he could balance his guitar just so and he'd play the most beautiful acoustic songs. No singing. Just the guitar. It was magical."

I realize that I've fallen in love with my story memory and need to focus back on Cale. I repeat, "So, ummm, did you ever eat there?"

Cale looks up at me for a half second and says, "No."

Okay. I'll need to work for this interview. "Alright. So, let's talk libraries. What can you tell me about your library, Cale? Tell me something that you deal with that most people wouldn't think about when they think about libraries."

Cale tilts his head up and his lips move but he doesn't say anything. I wait, hoping that something will come to him and he'll speak up. But in the end all he does is look at me and shrug his shoulders. I give Al the eye like "Is this a set up? Did Marcus set me up? Is this a prank?"

Al just shrugs as well. I see Clara shoot me a look then step outside into the hallway.

Okay. Not sure what's going on there.

I look at Cale and say, "Tell me about the mini-stampede. What was that like? Being in the bus when the buffalo charged. I bet that was exciting, yeah?"

Cale looks me in the eye and raises a hand to his lips. For a moment, I think he's going to really open up. But then all he says is, "I didn't see anything. All I know is that I was looking out the window and then there was a rumble and then my head smacked really hard against the window and then I blacked out."

Right. Head injury. Concussion. Staying the night for observation. Maybe this interview wasn't the best idea given the circumstances. I go for empathy at that point, "Right. I'm sure that was disorienting. You do look a little...fuzzy. Maybe we shouldn't do this right now. I'm sure Sal and his crew can arrange another time to have you on the show. I know you said you were fine earlier and the doctors gave the thumbs up and all but you seem a little off right now. I'd feel horrible if this set you back in any way. So, why don't we call this off, okay?"

I look up at Al and he nods. He doesn't want to nod. He doesn't want to end this interview but he sees that we need to.

I say into the camera, "Okay, let's send it back to Sal at the Ranch." Al gives me the signal that we're clear. That's when Clara comes back in the room with a nurse. The nurse comes right over. I stand up and let her have my seat as she talks to Cale while Al follows me out into the hallway with the camera. I realize I'm going to need to do more on the fly work.

Al signals that we have five minutes to set something up. I ask Clara, "What did the advance crew have besides Cale? Weren't there a couple of nurses on stand by? Or the radiologist?" I look at Kaley. She shakes her head. She doesn't know where her sister is.

Clara says, "The radiologist is downstairs. We can do that but we'll still need another segment. The nurses are ready but..." She cuts off and stares at the floor.

I say, "But what, Clara?"

Al says, "We should go do the funny x-ray bit."

Clara says, "No." She takes a breath then says, "No. I don't think we should. I have something better." She stares at me with big eyes. I stare back at her with impatient eyes. She goes on, "When you were with the kids I wandered around a bit. I found some teenagers. One has a broken leg. He had to get pins in it or something. A couple of his friends were there. They were just about to watch Mighty Martie. So, I told them about you being here tonight. They didn't believe me at first but then I showed them a couple of pictures I took at the hotel. They, uhhh, they said they'd be cool with it if you stopped by to talk about the movie with them." She stares at the floor again. "They're probably still watching it."

I roll this possibility around in my head. I look at Al for his feedback. He gives a nod like maybe it could work, let's try it. I say to Clara, "Lead the way." Then, "What time do we have, Al."

"Three and a half minutes," he says.

"Where..." I say to Clara.

She cuts me off, "One floor down." She starts walking to the nearest elevator.

Ok. Here we go.

60.

Let's just cut to the interview with the teens. I'm sitting in the room by the side of Justin's bed. He's the one with the broken leg. A cute, wild-haired, skinny, big smile on a happy face kid. On the other side of the bed his two friends are standing by. Kim and Jake. They are brother and sister. They live a couple of doors down from Justin and his parents. Justin and Jake are fifteen. Kim is fourteen. They were there when Justin went off the bike jump they'd made at the end of their cul-de-sac, lurched sideways in the air and landed badly. There was a very loud snap and then screaming. "Lots and lots of screaming," said Kim with a mixture of empathy and laughter in her face.

Clara has contacted both sets of parents and Marcus has spoken to them and they have given permission for them to be on air. She, Clara, actually did this while I was with Henrietta and the others. In other words, Clara's good at this. She's good at handling things on the fly. Looking for options. Paying attention to her surroundings.

I warm the kids up with some easy questions about how long they've known each other and the details of the bike crash. They are remarkably relaxed with me and in front of the camera. That makes my job easier. Finally, we turn to Mighty Martie. Al focuses on the laptop on the bed. The movie is paused at the scene where I'm in the desert in giant ape form and am learning how to better control my enormous body. In other words, the Flashdance scene.

Once Al pulls out to show us all at once again, I say to the three, "Ok, I need you all to be honest with me. Do you like this movie? Don't tell me what you think I want to hear. Tell me what you think about the movie. Honestly. I'm a big girl. I can handle it." I say this with a playful tone. I find myself genuinely curious what these kids think of my movie and, at the same time, feeling my way through this interview to make it work for the show as best it can.

After the three exchange tentative glances with each other, Justin goes first, "I like the action scenes. They were clever. Not your usual giant monster stuff."

I ask, "So, you like giant monster movies? Have you watched a bunch of them?"

He nods, "I have. You can find so much stuff on Youtube. The old ones. The newer ones I see when they come on streaming."

A thought. "What's your favorite old giant monster movie? Not a recent one. But a black and white one."

Justin pulls the corner of one eye down and the same side corner of his lips up as he thinks about this for a few seconds. Jake cuts in, "Come on. You know the one. We joke about it all the time."

Justin blushes slightly then says, "Okay, yeah. It's The Amazing Colossal Man." Pause. "Do you know that one?"

I don't. I say so, "I don't. Tell me about it. Why do you like it? Why do you two make jokes about it?"

"Well, uh, there's this scene and it's supposed to be serious. But it's actually really funny. To us, anyway. Watching it now. I guess it was serious back when it first came out," says Justin.

Kim adds, "They were just talking about it earlier. Because of Justin's operation."

I can't imagine what the connection between a giant monster movie and an operation for a broken leg could be. I need to know. "What's the scene?"

Justin shrugs. He's a little embarrassed. He doesn't want to say. I look at Jake. He says, "It's near the end when the military is tracking down the Colossal Man. They think they have a way to stop him. It's a drug and…"

Kim, impatient with her brother, says, "It's a giant syringe. They stick a giant syringe into the Colossal Man but he pulls it out and stabs one of the military guys with it and kills him."

"Ohhh," I say. I get it. "So, you joked that the doctors here were going to stick you with a giant syringe before your operation. Was that it?"

The boys chuckle and nod their heads. Kim shakes hers.

I ask her, "Why are you shaking your head?"

Kim looks at her brother and Justin like they're idiots. She loves them but they're idiots. "They say that's why they like Colossal Man. But it's not. They like the romance. I can see it in their eyes when they watch the movie. That's why they like Mighty Martie, too."

Jake protests half-heartedly, "That's not true. I like the investigator. The character trying to piece together what happened after it was all over. His mind sync stuff."

Jake is talking about Gyrin's investigator/pseudo-psychic profiler character. I'm about to say something about that character when Kim responds, "You like the investigator because you like trying to figure people out. You like trying to figure people out because you want to have a girlfriend. I see how you look at..." Kim stops here as Jake flashes her a don't you dare say her name look. Kim pauses for a second then says, "...you know who."

I hesitate. I'm not sure how to negotiate this flare up of sibling...siblingness. Thankfully, now that she's talking it doesn't look like much will stop Kim. She looks up from her brother and over to me as she says, "That's not why I like Mighty Martie, though. I like it because it's like your rainbow videos."

My...rainbow videos? What? I ask, "How is Mighty Martie like my rainbow videos?" I honestly cannot see the connection. I did those videos and that movie so far apart from each other. The videos were ad hoc fun that went viral. The movie was a major studio production.

Kim rolls her eyes upwards as she thinks about her answer for a moment then she says, "Mighty Martie is trying to figure out how to use her new body. Her new, strong, giant body. It's very awkward. She makes a few mistakes. But they are mistakes. She's not evil or bad or trying to hurt people. Which is like you in your rainbow video. When you puke rainbows on people." Here she sings a snippet of the tune from the videos, "Sheeee pukes rainbooooows, sooooo you don't have toooooo."

I flash back to Wayside and the crew when they first showed me that rainbow video. It was after my mom's funeral. It was after my infamous AM LA segment. It was after I'd done

Shadows of the Moon and was waiting for Shadows 2 to start. All that flashes through my head as I ask Kim, "How do you mean? I was like Mighty Martie in the rainbow videos. How?"

Kim looks me seriously in the face. Now I'm the idiot. She says to me, "In Mighty Martie you're a monster who breaks stuff in Hollywood. Not intentionally. You don't want to hurt people. You just want to find your lover and have things work out happy. In the rainbow videos you puke on bad guys. Bad Hollywood guys. You don't want to hurt them. Not really. You just want them to go away so things can work out happy. In Hollywood. In the movie you're a giant ape. Who I think should come back for a sequel because you need a better ending. But anyway. In the movie you're a giant ape. In real life you're a giant rainbow. A happy rainbow trying to make things right in Hollywood. In fact," Kim slings her mini-backpack bag around in front of her, "that's why I bought these sunglasses a while back. I don't wear them. I just keep them in my bag to remind me. To remind me to rainbow up."

She pulls out a pair of cheap, plastic sunglasses. They don't even have lenses in them. They're just costume glasses. Play around glasses. Make believe glasses. They are rainbow colored. They start with red at the top then run through lines of color all the way down to the bottom purple line. Rainbow sunglasses. Kim hands them across the bed to me as she says, "Here. My gift to you."

I take them from her and hold them in my hand for a moment. I don't know what to say. Those rainbow videos. I'd all but forgotten about them. Like all viral videos they had their moment then faded away. I never considered that anyone would take such…hope from them. I mean, they were just simple, silly little videos. I look up at Kim and say, "Thank you. That's very sweet of you." She beams a bright smile back at me. I see Al gesticulating wildly. Right. Keep the interview going. He signals that we need about a minute more. Right. Time to get back to work.

I take the glasses in both hands and make a production out of admiring them, unfolding them and slipping them onto my face. I turn to the three teens and say, "Alright. Well, I think it's time to get a final verdict, a final vote from all three of you.

Ummm, let's do this. And, again, be honest. Like I said, I'm a big girl. I can handle the truth…"

Jake can't help himself. He whispers, "You can't handle the truth." The line from A Few Good Men. The line said by Jack Nicholson's character when…. Whatever. I'm sure you know it. If not, look it up.

Kim pokes Jake in the shoulder when he says the line. Jake winces and gives me the I'm sorry, I'm sorry look. I smile to reassure him that it's all good. I continue on, "I can handle the truth so with, let's see, let's do thumbs. With a show of thumbs, one thumb up for you would maybe go see a sequel to Mighty Martie depending on the trailers and such, two thumbs up being you would definitely go see a sequel to Mighty Martie, one thumb down being don't do a sequel and two thumbs down being no one should watch Mighty Martie ever again because it's such a horrible movie. Ok, got that. Alright. I'm going to cover my eyes and let you give the thumbs without me looking. Okay. Al, our cameraman, will focus on your thumbs. I promise not to look. See, I'm turning away and closing my eyes. Okay. Okay. Let me know when you're done. No, really, let me know when you're done. Is this taking long? It feels like this is taking long. Can I turn around now? Clara? Clara, what's going on?"

I say all that to fill the air time and give the kids a few moments to make up their minds. I sprung the thumbs voting on them and want to give them a little bit to make up their minds. I keep my eyes closed and my head turned. I hope this doesn't look too stupid on live TV. I take a deep breath. I'm actually nervous. I'm nervous about what these three teen kids from Rapid City think about my movie. Ahhhh! Why? Why am I nervous? This is just silly.

Finally, Clara coughs loud enough for me to hear. I say before I turn around, "Okay, that's the signal, right? I'm turning around now." I turn around, drop my hand down and open my eyes. All three kids have shit-eating grins on their faces. So does Clara. I wait a beat then ask, "So, what was the vote?"

Kim, Justin and Jake all exchange glances. Then Kim says, "We are sworn to secrecy. You have to watch the show tonight to find out how we voted."

I look at Clara. She, too, has a shit-eating grin on her face. A very big shit-eating grin. This was her idea. I can feel it. I peer at Al. He's so happy he's almost bursting out of his skin. I look back at the three teens as I say, "Come on. Really? I don't need to know who voted which way. Just tell me how many thumbs up there were. That's all I need to know." Kim holds in a giggle. The boys blush and shake their heads. I look all three of them long and hard in the face. Then I say, "There was at least one thumbs up, wasn't there?" Pause. "Wasn't there?"

End scene.

61.

Al urges us to leave the three teens behind and head out into the hallway. I say to Clara, "You…are in trouble." She laughs because she knows I'm joking. I add, "That was good. That was really good. But there's no way I'm going to be awake when the show airs tonight. So, come on, just tell me. How many thumbs up were there?"

Clara says, imitating Kim from a minute before, "Sorry. I'm sworn to secrecy." Then, to distract me, she says, "We have to go find Kaley and her sister."

Kaley was not in the room with the teens as I asked her to find her sister, the radiologist, and get that all set-up so we could hurry down there during the break and be ready when Marcus needs us to be ready. Marcus wants to keep the live feeling of the show as much as possible. I agree with this even though it makes all this filming down here in the hospital a tad difficult to pull off. But, fuck it, it's just one crazy day. The next couple of days of shows will be a cake walk compared to today. Also, it will make a great chapter in my inevitable autobiography.

Yes, Miley has convinced me to - at some point - write an autobiography. Well, she and Sophie and, to a lesser extent, Sasha. Scott refused to weigh in on the subject except to say, "As long as I look like a genius hero, you can write anything you want about your life." Miley and Sophie laughed at him when he said this. He pointed at them and asked, "And just how do you think you two will come off in this autobiography? Hmmmm?" The crestfallen looks on their faces indicated that they had not really thought about that aspect of the book. Or, if they had, they assumed that I would write glowingly about them. Which, yes, I would. For the most part. That's what I told them as soon as they asked me. Which was immediately after Scott said what he said. To be clear, I emphasized, "For the most part."

Miley tensed up immediately, "What do you mean - for the most part? What other parts are there? All the parts are good. I've never…ohhhh." That's when she remembered her whole recording me without my permission in Puerto Santibel escapade. She said quietly, "Right. There's that." Pause.

"Maybe you shouldn't write an autobiography. It would come off as too self-aggrandizing. You don't want that. You definitely don't want that."

I have no idea if I'll ever write an autobiography. Probably not. But it is fun, every now and then, to think in those terms. What would I include in my own life story? I would definitely include today. In fact, I suspect Rapid City would show up a few times in my autobiography. Hmmmm? Where else? Where else?

We're in the elevator now. Just me, Clara and Al. Apparently, the radiologist office is on one of the lower floors. Like below street level lower. I close my eyes as the elevator descends. I run the two interviews through my head: Cale, the teens. Cale: ummm, ooops, that didn't work. I hope he feels better. The teens: I enjoyed that. I think that came off as genuine. It was genuine and I think it will show through as genuine. But, sometimes, it's hard to tell. You just don't know until you see it play on screen.

I open my eyes as the elevator slows. I see Clara staring at her phone. I see Al doing the same. Al and Clara look at each other. I say, "What? What is it?"

Clara and Al look at each other for a second longer then Al gives Clara a nod. Clara turns to me and says, "We're done. We don't need to film anymore. Marcus says Sal wants to use the whole interview in the hotel tonight followed by the teens segment we just did and then he wants to include an interview with Luisa as they walk around the ranch. Sal says he'll do the opening and closing of the show to round it all out. So...we're done."

I feel a tremendous weight fall off my shoulders. I lean against the wall of the elevator. If I could press myself into it and disappear, I would. Today has been a scramble. I knew it would be. I was ready to keep going. But now that I don't have to, I want to collapse. My legs feel like jelly. I take a few deep breaths and say to Clara and Al, "Thank you both for all you did today. I couldn't have done it without you. Honestly. Thank you."

They say thank you to me and so on and we wander out into the hallway looking for the radiologist office and Kaley.

That's when another text from Marcus comes through to Clara and Al. I wait a moment as they read it. Clara looks at me with a question on her face as she says, "Marcus says there's something you need to see on the hotel interview tape."

62.

We find Kaley and her sister, Janelle the radiologist, a minute later. We sit and chat with Janelle for a few minutes. I do the usual take a selfie and sign an autograph. This time, though, was the first time I ever signed an x-ray. It was one of Janelle's own from when she broke her leg a few years back. She keeps it on hand as a little good luck charm. That's what she said. I'm not quite sure how that works but there you go.

I thought Janelle would be upset that she didn't get to be on the show but she was relieved instead. "I don't do well in front of cameras. I tense up and my face gets all squishy."

I asked her, "Then…why did you agree to be interviewed?" I'm curious that way. Being in front of the camera is so second-nature to me now that I forget it's not for most people.

Janelle looked at Kaley as she responded, "I just wanted to help out this one." Kaley looked away from her sister's glance. I could tell this is a dynamic that they've been playing out for years. Janelle added, "She's the youngest of us and sometimes she gets forgotten about. So, when I can, I make sure she gets included." Janelle gave my bicep a grateful squeeze as she said, "Thanks for including her in all this today."

We said goodbye and headed out to the vehicles. I don't want to admit that I was distracted the entire time interacting with Janelle but I was. I was distracted by what Marcus saw on the hotel interview tape. Was it something bad? It couldn't be. Otherwise they wouldn't use the whole interview like they're planning to do. What would be bad in this situation to begin with? I can't even wrap my head around that.

We're out front of the hospital about to load the equipment into Al's vehicle when Clara's phone buzzes with another text. Just Clara's phone. Not Al's. She reads the text then says to me as she looks up at the hospital, "Kim and the boys say they can see us from their window." She puts a hand up to shield her eyes from the exterior lamps as she scans the rows of windows. It takes us a few seconds. Al spots them first. He points and says, "There. Go three levels up from just above the main entrance and then five rows over to the right. You can just see them waving."

Kaley, Clara and I say at the same time, "Oh, yeah." We take a minute to wave up at them, swinging our arms back and forth so they can see that we see them. A moment later, Clara's phone buzzes again. She laughs then shows us a picture of us taken from the window by Kim. The four of us are slightly blurry, slightly small but definitely waving. Clara texts a response back, gets another in return and says, "Kim and the boys say thanks and to let them know the next time we're in Rapid City."

We bundle into the cars after loading up the equipment. I admit that I'm relieved today's show is over. I am, also, curious about the hotel tape. Curious with a touch of anxiousness. What could it be? I stand by Al's car window. He's in the driver's seat. I'll be in the Forester with Clara and Kaley just like when we drove down here. He rolls down the window and says, "So, you'll follow me back to the ranch?"

I nod, "Yeah. Sounds good. Let's go a little slower than when we came down. It's dark now, well, darkish and I'm worried that Clara doesn't have much night time driving experience."

Al looks at me with an odd expression on his face.
I say, "What?"

He says, "I understand your concern. But, after today, it's obvious that Clara is a very capable young woman. But, sure, I'll keep it to the speed limit." He smiles then adds, "K.C. Hall, mother hen. Who knew?" Then he rolls up his window and revs his engine so he can't hear my response. Which is good because I didn't have one. I wanted to have one but I didn't have one.

63.

When we're on the road, I text Marcus myself saying, "So…what do I need to see on this clip?"

It takes him a minute - I'm sure he's busy getting the show completely ready for broadcast tonight - but he sends me the footage. It's about twenty seconds long. It's the end of the interview with Theo. Dr. Holmes is on the phone with Theo's mom, his daughter, then he hands the phone back to me. Theo and I exchange a line or two. The thunder rumbles and the lights flicker. That's when I see it. When the lights flicker. Behind my chair are two, pale and (yes) ghostly figures. One looks vaguely female. The other looks vaguely male. They are standing (hovering?) behind my chair and looking down on me. They are there then gone in a split second. The thunder rumbles, the lights flicker, the figures appear, then they are gone.

I play the clip a dozen times. Part of me wants to believe. Part of me wants to dismiss this as merely a trick of the light. A trick of the light mixed in with some pareidolia which is just a fancy way of saying the brain sees things that aren't really there. It's the thing the brain does when it sees two small pancakes and one large pancake near each on a plate and "Mickey Mouse" flashes into your head. Or when you see faces in the shapes of clouds. It's the human tendency that Picasso played with when he juxtaposed a bicycle seat and handlebars to make them look like a bull's head. It's the taking of stimulus from out there and overlaying memories from inside your head to create something meaningful. A meaningful image. A meaningful experience.

Yes, this was another lecture from Scott.

Yes, I pretended I didn't like this one but secretly I did.

It made me wonder how much of watching movies and TV, the actual in the moment experience, is pareidolic in nature. I may have just made up that word: pareidolic. Maybe. Not sure. That is, how much of a viewer's experience is shaped by her bringing all her previous, mostly unconscious associations/memories to the film (or show or whatever) that she is currently watching. When you watch a mystery show you're not just watching that mystery show. In one sense, you're watching all the mystery shows you've ever watched before. Our memories and experiences of similar situations bubble along just below the surface of consciousness when we watch a film. We unconsciously compare and contrast the film in front of our eyes with all the films we have stored in our heads. Our memories are constantly shaping our present moment experience.

Now, I could go on and ad lib from this point. I could talk about how we live in an era of a wealth of images. Manufactured images. Fictional images. More so than any other point in human history. I could also talk about the evolutionary importance of facial recognition. I could talk about how we as cave people needed to be able to identify faces as friend or foe, wild or tame. I could talk about visual literacy versus literary literacy. That is being fluent in decoding images versus being fluent in decoding words.

I could talk about all those things but you and I both know that would simply be me not wanting to address the question at hand which is this: were those ghosts my parents?

64.

Clara notices me staring at my phone and, more to the point, being quiet and focused. Thinking, thinking, thinking. She says, "What're you looking at? The hotel interview?"

I feel like I'm surfacing after a very deep dive in the ocean as I look at her and say, "Ummm, yes. Yes, Marcus sent me the hotel clip."

Kaley leans forward to be part of the conversation. She says, "What does it show?"

I hesitate for a brief moment but then I hold my phone such that Kaley can see it and Clara, too, with quick glances as she keeps driving. Kaley emits a little "ohhh" when the ghost figures appear. I play the clip a few more times so Clara can catch the moment. She does. She doesn't say anything. She just looks at me. She's studying my face to see if she can figure out my reaction to this.

Clara looks out the windshield as she asks me, "So…what do you think?"

I take a while to answer. Eventually, I say, "It's my parents. It has to be my parents."

Clara grips the steering wheel harder and blows out a long breath between pursed lips. Kaley offers from the backseat, "So, you believe in ghosts then?"

I say, "I guess I do. If you had asked me a couple of hours ago I might have said no. But, then again, I might have said yes. I've seen some strange things. I've seen videos like this online or on those ghost hunter shows. I'm sure you all have, too. But this," I hold my phone up, "is different. It's different when it happens directly to you. I mean, sure, it could be a trick of the light. I'm sure some people will say that. But that's an awful specific trick of the light, don't you think?"

"So, your parents…" Kaley starts to ask then trails off.

I finish for her with a quick glance at Clara, "…are both dead. For a few years now." I stop there. I don't need to say anything more.

Kaley says, "I've never had someone I know…I've never known someone who's died." Her voice is soft, sincere. She's opening up to me and Clara. It feels as if she's admitting

218

a failure, a shortcoming about herself. Here's this knowledge that other people have and I don't and I'm lesser for it.

I don't want her to feel that way. I say, "Well, don't wish for…"

But Clara interrupts, "Hold on to that. Hold on to that as long as you can. Because at some point you will know someone who passes, who dies. And at that point you'll want to remember this time now, when you didn't know anyone dead."

I look at Clara. I think, at first, that she's talking about her father and my father. But then I realize that there's someone else in her life. That there was someone else in her life. There's so much about her that I don't know. But I don't want to ask or press. She'll talk about it when she wants to. So, instead, I turn to look at Kaley and say, "Clara's right. Hold on to this, what you have now."

Kaley says softly, "Okay."

Clara says, "Back to ghosts." Pauses, bites lip, "Do you think they are around all the time or just sometimes?"

I say, "I don't know. I do know there are lots of books out there that talk about that. Mediums and ghost hunters and stuff like that. But I don't think you can say one way or the other. I don't think you can say all ghosts do this or all ghosts do that. I mean ghosts are people, were people and people do different things, right? So, why would we all do the same thing when we die? That sounds very boring."

At that moment, Scott calls.

65.

     I tell him I'm in a car with Clare and Kaley. I have the two of them say hello. He has Sophie, Miley and the twins say hello back. I ask him where they are and he says, "Still in Steamboat. We've had a restful day. We'll leave early tomorrow. I want to show the kids (he calls all of them kids) Custer State Park just like I showed you that one time." There's a collective groan in the background. I can tell they're partially teasing him and partially really don't want to get on the road early tomorrow. Scott forges ahead, "But that's not why I'm calling. I'm calling because we went to the hot springs here and it's amazing. It's got all this really cool stone work and one of the masons was there setting up a new pool and I started talking to him and I told him about Alonsha and he says he can FIX..." Scott emphasizes that word, "...Alonsha. FIX her! He says he has a special resin epoxy solution that he's developed over the years working at the hot springs that will work just fine."

     A fear flashes through my head. "You aren't going to leave Alonsha there, are you? That's not your plan, right?"

     Scott says, "No. No, no, no. I had the mason, Charlie, I had him show me and Jaxson how to do the repair. It's actually quite simple."

     Jaxson says in the background, "Really very simple. Very simple."

     Sophie chirps in, "I'm an excellent mason. An excellent mason."

     I laugh and say, "Hey, Sophie."

     I hear a rustling of the phone then Sophie's voice comes through loud and clear, "Hey, Case. Before I forget, I need to talk to you about a couple of offers I got recently."

     "Did they see you on Hollywood Boot Camp?" I ask. "Or is this from one of your auditions?" Sophie has been going on auditions for the past few months. Hollywood Boot Camp provided a little buzz for her and she wants to see where she can take it. Like I told you earlier... Or, maybe I didn't. I can't remember now. It's been a long day. Anyway. Sophie came in third on Hollywood Boot Camp. I have never seen someone so upset about coming in third in a competition. To be clear,

Sophie was the viewers' favorite. We know this from the online voting. But the other two players, Brendan and Anna, were meaner and lied more and they convinced the judges with their lies that they were better. It was a whole thing. For a while. Then other stuff happened. Anyway.

Sophie says, "I'm not sure. That's why I want to talk to you. One of the offers is from a company that one of the Boot Camp judges works for. So, I think that's good. But…"

But she's not sure. Right. "Okay. Yes, we'll go over stuff when you get here. Is there a deadline? When do you have to respond?"

"By Tuesday next week. I'm pretty sure I know which offer I want to take but I just want to run it by you and…maybe MDB first." Pause. "I told them I'm on the road and will let them know when I get back to L.A."

Scott starts singing "On the Road Again" in the background. I ask, "Where are you all? What are you doing?"

"We're driving out of town a bit to a ranch that offers stargazing as an activity. They have telescopes and such set up. Jaxson discovered it online."

Jayson says loudly at that point, "No, he didn't, I did."

Jaxson says, "Yes, he found it but I booked our session tonight."

I smile as I hear their voices. I can just see them all piled into Missy Von Van driving along a country road. I realize at that point that I haven't heard from… "Is Miley there?"

Silence.

"Is Miley there?" More silence. "Where is Miley? What's going on?"

Silence. Then Sophie says, "She may or may not be out on a date with a certain mason from the hot springs. We can neither confirm nor deny said date. We have been…"

I finish her sentence for her, "…sworn to secrecy. Yeah, yeah, yeah. Tell me something I haven't heard before." I laugh for a moment then add, "Okay, great to hear from you all. I had a really strange day. Watch the show tonight and we'll talk tomorrow. Bye."

Clara, ever observant Clara, asks with a smile on her face, "Why do people like to keep secrets from you?"

I play into the joke, "I don't know. I'm really such a sweet person. It makes no sense whatsoever."

Kaley joins in, "But they aren't really." Clara looks at her in the rearview. I turn my head to look at her. She goes on, "Telling someone that you're keeping a secret from them is not keeping a secret from them. It just isn't. A true secret is one you don't know about."

Ahhh. Right. I say, "So, what Miley and you, Clara, and the teens did earlier today is…"

"They're just teasing you," says Kaley.

Clara says, "Yes and no. It is teasing but it isn't just teasing." She gives me a quick look then stares out the windshield again, "It's because we feel safe with you, K.C. We all know your story. Everyone knows your story. You've been through some stuff. And you're still here. You're still here and you're still smiling. So, we feel safe enough to tease you. That's what it is."

"Ohhh," I say as I turn to look out the window on my side and do my best to blink away the tears that have suddenly formed at the corners of my eyes. "Ohhh…" I say again. "…kay." I turn back to Clara. She flicks her eyes in my direction. I say, "Well, okay then." Pause. It's my turn to look out the windshield now. "Rapid City. What is it about this place?" I say this more to myself than to Clara and Kaley.

Kaley responds anyway, "It's not Rapid City. It's the Black Hills. They're magical. Powerful and magical." She says this like a resident sharing local knowledge with the tourists. You take this road to get there. Don't eat at that place. Go see the statues of the presidents. Make sure to see the fountain, it's amazing. And, oh yeah, the Black Hills are magical and powerful. They just are.

66.

When we get back to the ranch, I talk about the show with Sal and Marcus. They say they have it all under control. I ask about tomorrow and the next day, specifically about the tour buses and the guests we may or may not have on hand due to them. No, I don't want to run around the next two days like I did today to pull off the show. I will if I need to but I don't want to. Sal assures me that he has checked with the local experts and the likelihood of spontaneous mini-stampedes over the next two days is very low. He's teasing me, of course. I glower at him. Not now, Sal. Not now. He sees this and says, "Seriously, I've checked with the bus companies and made sure there are back ups in place. Buses, vans, elephant caravans. We're all set."

Elephant caravans? I wonder...ohhhh. That's more teasing. It took me a second to realize that. I must be more tired than I realized. I wipe a hand across my face and say to Sal and Marcus, "Okay. You have everything in hand. I'm tired. I'm going to go take a nap."

As I head out the door of Sal's cabin, Marcus asks, "Hey, do you want to see how the kids voted on Mighty Martie? I can show you the clip."

I hesitate for a moment. Part of me does want to see the clip. But not now. Not now. I say, "I'll wait 'til later. Thanks."

I head to the main house. Luisa is there. She gives me a big hug and a bigger bowl of chicken noodle soup. She says, "There's some elk in there, too. For extra goodness." I thank her and take the bowl. She looks me in the eye and says, "You look dog tired. Here, let me put this in a bowl with a lid and you can take it back to your cabin. Would you like that?"

Yes, I would like that. I nod.

Luisa pulls out the pyrex container and pours the soup into it. She says, "You know I had the nicest time talking to Sal today. He says it's going to be on TV tonight. He wanted to talk about your father but I told him no we can talk about the ranch, my family, the bees and whatever else he wants to talk about but not your father. I told him that it's time to move past that with you. That's why he wanted to talk about your father."

He wanted to get to know you better. So, I told him he should talk to you then. He should interview you on the show. Silly man. Sometimes you Hollywood people just think too much."

She hands me the pyrex bowl with a thick, cloth napkin on top. The napkin is wrapped around a soup spoon that's large enough to use as a weapon. She says, "Anything else? Crackers? Chips? A salad?"

I shake my head. Now that my duties are done for the day I feel like a robot powering down its systems one by one. If I don't make it back to the cabin I'll be stuck wherever I am when the shut downs complete. I say, "Thanks, Luisa." I head out the side door and walk back to my cabin. It takes forever. But I'm okay with it. I don't have to rush right now. I don't have to push. I don't have to be…anything. I can just take my time, get back, eat some soup and fall asleep.

I'm about two thirds of the way to the cabin - I can see it down on the left side of the gravel path now - when my phone buzzes. Sigh. What now? I pull it out of my pocket. It's a message from Scott. It's a picture of Randolph. Oh, Randolph! My little lion king! I've missed you. I've been so busy I haven't even thought about him. Scott has been in charge of that aspect of our lives. Randolph, of course, is back in the penthouse. Scott hired a pet-sitting service to look after Randolph since both of us are away from L.A. right now. The picture shows Randolph on his back in the sun completely relaxed. The text with the picture says, "Zoom in on his face." So, I do. I see the little pink tip of his tongue sticking out. That's what cats do when they are completely and totally safe and relaxed. They let their tongues stick out.

I text back, "I'm going to eat some soup then go full Randolph."

Scott laughs at my text and sends back, "You deserve it."

67.

The sleep was wonderful. Even better than the soup and the soup was pretty damn good. But since I went to bed earlier than normal I've woken up earlier than normal. It's 5:32AM. It's still dark out. I peer outside the window. There's the slightest of slightest hints of sun on the horizon. I check my weather app. The sunrise doesn't happen for over an hour. But there's no way I'm going to fall back asleep. I am rested and wide awake.

Maybe I should go for a walk. The silence, the quietude that is present here on the ranch is something that simply doesn't exist in L.A. Anywhere. No matter how much meditation you do or how much sound proofing you're surrounded by when you're doing voice over work, there's always a background buzz, a low-level tension in the air, in the water, in the ground itself. I've enjoyed being away from that out here on the ranch. That's why I want to go for a walk. But maybe there are bears out there. Huh? Why didn't I think of that the other morning? Because no coffee, that's why. So, yeah, bears or other critters that would freak me the fuck out if I stumbled across them all by myself in the time before the sun. Yes, I am being dramatic. But how many Hollywood stars can you name that have bear scars across their faces? Right. Exactly zero. So, yes I'm being dramatic and paranoid but I have a good reason to be dramatic and paranoid.

This is one of those times I wish I could turn into a giant ape. Or, at least, a medium-sized ape. A medium-sized ape with fur to withstand the cold outside and big enough to scare away the bears. Rarrhhhh! That was my medium-sized ape, go away bear growl. Thanks, yeah, it is pretty good.

Of course, now I'm thinking of Mighty Martie which has me thinking of the teens yesterday which has me thinking of last night's show. I do want to see what the kids said about Mighty Martie. Now that I'm rested my curiosity is back. Okay, so enjoy the quietude or watch the clip from the show? Of course, I'll admit, that will lead me to watching the whole show. Like I said, my curiosity is back. So…quietude or… Wait, avoid critters (can't forget that part) and enjoy quietude outside or watch the show here inside? What to do? What to do?

[Note for Scott: Invent a superhero called Quietude Dude whose power is the ability to put anyone in a cone of silence for several minutes. I could definitely use Quietude Dude with Miley sometimes. Okay, most of the time. Love her, do I but overwhelming she can be. Thanks, yeah, that was my Yoda impression. *It is* pretty good, thank you! See, Scott, it is good. You don't know.]

Clearly, I need coffee in order to make this decision. Wait! Last time I looked… Oh, thank god! The magic coffee elves (i.e. production assistants) have done their job and I am fully restocked with coffee. Several pods are stacked neatly by the machine. I usually prefer making whole pots because, yes, left to my own devices in the course of a morning I will drink a whole pot of coffee but we're not going to tell anyone that are we? No, we are not.

But the cabin is set up with a pod machine. Not the purple pod machine that's in the main house kitchen. Another pod machine. Hmmmm, coffee pods. Pod people. Coffee pods. Pod people. What? Pod people. From Invasion of the Body Snatchers. The version from the 1970s. Ohhh, you should watch that. Anyway. Back to my train of thought. Coffee pod. Pod people. Coffee…pod…people. That should totally be a commercial. I can see it now. People walking around in the morning like zombies, then they have their coffee pods, then they turn from black and white zombies to full color, awake and alive people. Reverse zombie transformation. Ohhh! There it is. It was right in front of us all this time. How do you fight off zombies? Throw coffee on them. Now, that needs to be a movie. A funny, sci-fi, horror movie. Say this part in your head with a deep, resonating, movie trailer voice. Ready? Okay. Here it is, "In a world which has been stripped of coffee…"

Stripped? No, that's bad. Let's start over.

"In a world without coffee [insert horrified screams here] comes a hero to save us all. [insert scenes of people dragging their asses to work, pushing mindlessly into crowded elevators, walking into closed doors, dropping their purses and briefcases, falling asleep at the wheel [note: no bad car crashes, just funny car crashes - running into hydrants, knocking over donut stands and such]] A hero born of the Earth [insert shot of a hand thrusting up out of the ground as loose, rich, loamy soil falls away] A hero named Coffee Dude! [insert a guy in a giant coffee bean costume....]

No, that doesn't work. Let's do that again.

"A hero named Coffee Queen!"

Yes, that's better. The alliteration is a little on the nose but whatever.

[insert image of strong, fit woman in a very stylish superhero outfit (think Givenchy power suit, along those lines, something like that, I'll figure out the details later)]

[show Coffee Queen flying over the masses ambling through the city streets below as she sprinkles them with magic coffee pods, once the pods touch them they all come alive and awake, once again turning from black and white to full-color (I know, Wizard of Oz, you just can't escape the Wizard of Oz, it's so influential)]

[Coffee Queen flies off into the distance as the entire city turns fabulous rainbow colors. She lands on a majestic mountaintop and plants a flag emblazoned with the CQ logo and her little Toto-like dog barks happily at her feet...]

No, no little dog. Coffee Queen needs something bigger, something with more umph than a little dog. So.... Ahhhh!

[Coffee Queen lands on a majestic mountaintop and plants a flag emblazoned with the CQ logo with one hand while resting her other hand on top of her pet bison. Her pet bison named...]

What would be a good name for Coffee Queen's pet coffee bison? Hmmmm.

Thinking, thinking, thinking.

Ah!

[Coffee Queen lands on a majestic mountaintop and plants a flag emblazoned with the CQ logo with one hand while resting her other hand on top of her pet bison. Her pet bison named Beanie]

...

227

...

...

Okay, let's pinky swear right now to never tell anyone else - especially Scott, or Sophie, or Sasha, or, god forbid, Miley - about this idea. Never ever ever.

Although, now that I think about it, those magic beans Jack traded for - clearly those were coffee beans. So obvious. Why didn't I see that before?

Okay, I'm done now.

68.

I'm sitting on the porch, wrapped once more in my fleece blanket, coffee mug in one hand and phone in the other. This is my compromise. I experience quietude, avoid critters, enjoy coffee and watch the show - all at once. Right here on the porch. It's perfect.

I draw up the show on the phone. Marcus sent me a link to the entire show. Because that's what he does. He's a very good producer. Yes, I do scroll to the segment with the teens in the hospital room. But I don't scroll right to the end of the segment to see their thumb votes. I admit I was tempted to. But I didn't. I watch the whole interview. It works. I'm glad to see that it works. At least, to my eyes it works. I'll ask Clara and Kaley what they think of it when I see them this morning. Luisa, too. And, yes, Sal and Marcus. But I already know they think it works because they made it part of the show. But, yeah, I'll ask them for feedback. It works but maybe there's something I could have done to make it better.

Okay, here's the end bit with the thumbs. I'm off screen. Al has centered the camera on the kids hands which they are holding out over Justin's casted leg. Clara is holding out her hands, too. Their hands are flat, fingers spread at first. Then they ball into fists with their thumbs sticking out. They twist their wrists so their thumbs swing from totally up to totally down. They do this very quickly, several times. Then Justin, Jake and Kim stop both their hands in the thumbs all up position. But Clara has withdrawn her hands. Al zooms out to show Clara making a heart shape with her hands and framing my turned away head inside the heart. Al holds that image until I start asking if I can turn around then he zooms out to show the whole scene.

Ohhh…Clara…ok. Hold on. I need a minute.

69.

I'm watching Sal and Luisa walk around the ranch while they talk about bees and the Black Hills when MDB sends me a text, "FYI: you should let her know in case she hasn't seen this yet."

There's a link in the text. I tap it. It takes me to a story on one of the lesser tabloid websites. It's titled, "When the K.C's away, the Miley will play." Oh, shit. There are blurry pictures of Miley at what I assume is the hot springs. She's in a bathing suit. She's chatting with a cute guy. I assume that's the mason she went on a date with. They get closer and closer as they talk. The mist from the hot springs swirls around them. It's all very romantic. The article is too clever by half drivel about Miley, "a minor movie star and K.C. Hall's personal assistant for the past year," making the moves on this small town guy. It's all salacious innuendo. Just bad writing. Thankfully, the article is short and there aren't any pictures of them out on a date. Just the pics from the hot springs.

I text MDB, "Thanks for the heads up. I'll call her soon."

MDB sends back, "I saw the show last night."

That's it. That's all she sends. I wait for a moment. Nothing. Just when I'm about to respond with a "Well, what did you think?," MDB sends me three thumbs up followed by a heart emoji.

Clever. Very clever, MDB. Very clever indeed.

I text back, "Har, Har, Har."

That's when she calls. I pick up. She launches right into it, "Honestly, and if you tell anyone this I will kill you…"

I interrupt, "So, you're swearing me to secrecy."

"…call it what you will. That moment with the girl doing the heart around your head…priceless. Just priceless. Who is she by the way?"

I tell her. MDB knows all the details of Clara's connection to me. She just didn't realize heart-finger girl is Clara. MDB and I have shared stuff with each other over the past year. There weren't any long, serious, deep and real conversations. Just short exchanges, questions asked and answered back and forth as we traveled from here to there and back again. We've both pieced together mosaic-like images of each other over that time. We've filled in the details of our backgrounds bit by bit. We needed to. If we're going to make this production company work, we need to know each other and trust each other. Trust does not come easily to either of us. But, we're working on it. So far, so good.

I add, "And I also ran into Daryl, too." I wonder for a split second if MDB will remember who Daryl is.

She gasps then says, "That fucker! Really? What did you say?" I tell her that I took a page out her book and spoke very bluntly to him. She says, "Oh, I'm so proud of you. I wish I could have been there to see that. How did it end up?" I tell her. She's silent for a moment then says, "You had a very busy day yesterday, Mrs. Langle." She knows I love being called "Mrs. Langle" simply because no one knows me as "Mrs. Langle." It's a little shared secret between us. She goes on, "You must have been running around. The ranch, the hotel, the hospital then back to the ranch. All that ad hoc filming. Huh. Last night's show is even more impressive now that I think about it." Pause. Did my heart just melt a little? She goes on, "Which brings me to a bigger point. You've been pushing yourself hard this past year, K.C. And, yes, before you say it, I've been pushing you hard. I've been pushing myself hard and I've been pushing you hard. And you've been pushing yourself hard. Which is good in some ways but I suspect will hurt us if we do it too much. I like to think I learned a few things when I stepped away from the business for those few years. I'd like to think that. But if I'm honest with myself this past year I got sucked right back into the craziness. I did. And, yes, I enjoyed it. But we can't keep doing things this way. We need to take a break. We need to…to…"

I say, "…pace things out." Hearing this sentiment from MDB is simply glorious. I've been wondering how to broach this with her. I have been pushing myself and I would keep pushing myself more and more and more in order to make this all work. But she's right. That tactic will eventually come back to bite us in the ass. We'll burn out. I'll burn out. I'll flame out tremendously and in a not very graceful manner. Worst of all, the tabloids will eat it up. They're just waiting for me to fuck up big time. They are. And that's not paranoia. That's just how things are in Hollywood. Not just with me. With all movie stars. That's just how it is.

"Yes!" MDB says, "Pace things out. Yes. I like that phrase. I've always been a big believer in striking while the iron is hot. But, guess what, we have the iron now. We can make it hot when we want to make it hot. We can strike when the time is right for us. We've laid the groundwork. We have the contracts in place. We have the writer in place. The main one. You're geared up and ready to go. The rest will…"

"The rest will unfold before us," I say.

MDB agrees again, "Yes! The rest will unfold before us. I like that. Maybe you should write your autobiography, K.C." I shared that detail with MDB, too.

"Someday," I say. "But not right now. Right now, I need to call Miley."

"Yes, you do. Tell her it's not a big deal. Tell her I just didn't want her to be blindsided by it," MDB says.

"I will. And thanks. For everything," I say.

MDB is silent for several seconds. Then she says, "Gyrin says hello."

Change of subject. Okay. "Say hello back for me. How's he doing with the whole…"

"…with the whole his mother just fired him thing? Actually, I think he's relieved. He won't come out and say it. But I can feel it. He's been happier these past few days."

"Ohhh, he's staying with you?" I ask, a little surprised.

"Yes, he is. He'd been living with a woman, gave up his own place. Then when I fired him, she dumped him. Looks like she was just using him to get on Curated Worlds. Ha. Ooops. Sorry, kid."

MDB said "Ooops." She gets that from me. She's rubbing off on me and I'm rubbing off on her. "Does he have any plans?" I ask.

"He's thinking about doing a documentary. But that's all he's told me. I don't even know what it's about. You know how he is. Especially with me," she says.

"I do," I say. "Well, I really should call Miley now…"

"Good. Do that and have a good rest of the week out there. We'll do lunch when you get back. Bye."

70.

It's a while later when I call Miley. I want her to be awake when she gets this news. First I text her the link. Then I text her, "Call me when you've read this." She calls a couple of minutes later. Her voice is surprisingly chipper, "Apparently, I'm playing while you are away. That makes me the mouse and you the cat. I knew you had a special connection to Randolph but come on."

I chuckle at her joke then ask, "So, you're okay with this?" I realize as I ask this question that I don't know if this is the first time Miley has appeared in a tabloid story. I suspect it is but...

"I find myself amused. No. Diverted. Isn't that the Jane Austen line? But not excessively. Only mildly. I am mildly diverted. Compared to the on rushing encounter with the splendors of nature and majestic herds of bison we are to see today, how could this trifle of a story at all upset me?"

"Wow, someone's in a good mood," I say.

Sophie says in the background (they are riding in Miley's car behind Missy Von Van and the boys), "There's a good reason for that."

I wait. Will Miley offer up the reason or will I need...

"Thad texted me this morning. He saw the story and he reached out to make sure I'm okay."

Huh. So... "Does this mean you're pro Thad now? I don't have to worry about getting five alarm texts from you when I work with him?"

"I can make no promise regarding my future behavior, Ms. Hall. All I can say to you is that I shall do my best to comport myself as a lady should," says Miley in her best Jane Austen voice.

"Comport? Really?" I joke.

"It is far, far better to comport than to forfend," Miley retorts.

Forfend? Wait. Did I mention that to her? I thought... Nevermind. I say "Okay. Fine. I'm glad you're handling this well. Have fun with the buffaloes," I say then hang up.

The sun is up. The critters have scittered back into the forests. It's time for breakfast.

71.

I kept breakfast minimal (coffee and a few bites of some egg dish Luisa whipped up) as I want to work out in a little bit. I'm going to do a circuit of the gravel paths that spider web the ranch. It will feel good to literally stretch my legs after sitting and riding around in the car so much yesterday.

I stop by Sal's cabin after breakfast to check in on the show. Tonight's line up includes the Creative Writing professor, Lyell Capriti, more interacting with the audience (there have been no mini and/or maxi-stampedes this morning) and then Sal says, "Marcus and I are thinking about having you in the guest role at some point. Playing around with me having you on my show during K.C. Hall Week. What's the term Marcus used? Meta? He said it would be somewhat meta." Pause. "Do you know what he means by that?"

"'Meta' is the term creative people use when there isn't quite the right word to use," I say. "It usually has some element of bending back on itself. Of reflecting itself. So, K.C. Hall is a guest on K.C. Hall Week. Meta. The same would be true if I had a show if it were Sal Kincaid Week and I interviewed you. Sal on Sal Kincaid week. Meta."

Sal stares at me. At first, I think he doesn't understand my explanation but then I realize he's pondering something else. He takes a very slow and deliberate sip of coffee then asks me, "You ever think of that? Having your own show?"

No. No, no, no.

No. Definitely not.

Ok, maybe.

I cross my arms over my chest and look down at the floor like a little girl caught by the teacher making fun of him behind his back when he's at the whiteboard. Sal is patient with me. He takes a couple of more sips of coffee as I decide how to respond. Finally, I say, "Valery Ostonyay…do you know her?" Sal nods. Of course he knows her. He knows everyone. "She and I had an exchange years ago. It was short, quick. Right before I did an interview with her. She's so beautiful. Stunning. And such a presence in front of the camera. I told her she should have been a movie star. She told me that I should be a TV host." I clear my throat. "A whole bunch of stuff happened right after that. I was busy. I'm always busy. Irons and striking while hot and so on." Sal nods and sips. "But I confess that Valery's comment stuck in the back of my head. Like that odd stain on a wall that you never noticed before. You've lived in a place for years and never noticed it. Then someone points it out to you and all of a sudden you can't not notice it. You see it every time you pass through the room. It's just there. It doesn't move or change or go away. And you can't rub it off or you'll damage the wall and you figure since you didn't notice it that other people won't notice it and whatever, there's other things to do. So many other things to do." I look into Sal's eyes. "But, of course, the stain is still there. Waiting. Like a question unanswered."

Sal takes another sip of coffee then asks with a very straight face, "So, is that a yes or a no?"

I sigh. "Sal…that's a maybe somewhere down the line I'd like to explore the idea but right now - career-wise - is not the time."

He says, "Fair enough. Just so you know, somewhere down the line," he winks at me as he repeats the phrase I just used, "I'll be retiring. I need to swear you to secrecy…"

Really? More secrecy? What is up with this?

"…on that, of course. But keep that in mind. A few years. Maybe. Most likely. Doing the show is constant. Constant work. But it's also steady. The same location. The same crew. Year in, year out. You make contacts. You tell a few jokes. You have some fun. It's…"

He pauses here and mists up. Just for a moment, his eyes get watery.

"…the best job in the world," he finishes.

I take that in and then say, "Thank you for sharing it with me."

Sal blinks his eyes several times, takes another sip and says matter of factly, "Marcus has got some shenanigans going for tonight. I'm not sure what. But be prepared."

"Shenanigans?" I say playfully. "Well, I shall do my best to comport myself properly." Oooops, now Miley's rubbing off on me. "Okay, thanks, I'm going for a run."

72.

The run is glorious. I didn't push myself. I kept a nice, easy pace. Yes, I paced it out. Good for me. Maybe, just maybe, not all workouts need to be full on, get after it, go big or go home explosions of activity. I like those workouts. No. I love those workouts but every now and then I just want to go for a good run. Or a good stretch. Or a good hike.

Wait.

Did I just admit that I like hiking now?

No. That can't be. I can't ever admit that to Scott. Because if I do then he'll plan so many hiking trips for us. And…no, just no. So, I'm swearing you to secrecy on that. Yeah, that's right. The tables have turned.

Anyway. The run cleared my head. I mulled over what shenanigans Marcus might get up to. I ran a few different scenarios through my head. Slime? Would he slime me like that Nickelodeon show back in the day? Would he do a "This is Your Life?" bit with me? I did go to high school for a couple of years in this part of the world. Maybe he tasked his magical elves to dig up embarrassing stuff from that part of my life. Or maybe he's got his hand on some tapes from my early auditions from way back in the day. Ugh. Those would be cringeworthy. I'm sure everybody would get a kick out of it. But, yeah, cringeworthy.

So, I have no idea what Marcus is up to. I'll just have to wait and see.

Ahhh, the run did spur some joke ideas. I know how you love my jokes. The entire world loves my jokes. That's a known and well-established fact. No, you don't get to hear them now. I'm going to use them in my monologue this evening.

Okay, fine. Since you're so curious let's just cut to the monologue.

73.

Lights, camera, cowboy chic outfit #3 (the tux stands on its own), action.

"Hello, America and all the ships at sea. Yes, that is a Walter Winchell reference. It's for all those people of a certain age. If you're not of a certain age, look him up. He was the original gossip columnist. Modern day gossip columnist. The one who started it all. Ahhh, if only...if only that had never started. Anyway, we don't have time to dive into that because we have guests to get to and, more importantly, we have jokes to tell. I...have jokes to tell. Last year I shared my tachyon joke with you. Yes, yes, I know you loved it by how much you groaned in the audience and so many frowny face emojis were plastered across the comments section. Insert sad trombone sound here. Oh, sorry. I shouldn't have read that line out loud. Keeley J." I turn to the cardboard cutouts of the band, "that's for you. You were suppo..."

A very loud, sad trombone sound surges out of the speaker behind the cut outs.

"Ahhh, you know what they say about comedy. Timing is..."

Another, much louder sad trombone sound washes away my voice.

I look over at Sal and Marcus and simply shake my head at them. They, of course, pretend to be innocent, completely innocent, nothing, they know nothing.

I turn back to the camera, "Fine. Just fine. I can tell what kind of night it's going to be. First, we'll be talking to Lyell Capriti, a professor of Creative Writing. I'm curious about that. How does one teach others to be creative? That, actually, has been on my mind for a few years now. But I'll save those details for later. After Professor Capriti, we'll chat up the audience. I don't think we need to talk about Mighty Martie anymore, not after last night's show. So, we'll let the fine people here tonight come up with some new questions for me and go with that."

I hold up a finger, "But first, the thing you've all been waiting for. It's K.C.'s Home Grown Joke Time." I hold up both my hands, fingers splayed like this is the most exciting thing to ever happen to me. "I'll start with a little inside baseball joke. A specialized joke. This one is inside Lord of the Rings. Not baseball. Lord of the Rings. So, get that frame of reference in your head. Okay. Here we go. What do you call the breath of evil?"

Wait.

Wait.

Wait for it.

"The Sigh of Sauron."

VERY SAD trombone sound.

"Get it? Not EYE of Sauron. SIGH of Sauron. Okay, fine. Not even one person that time. Fine. No LotR fans in the audience? That must be it. Fine. Okay, here's the next one. What do you call a dripping clock in South America?"

Wait for it.

Wait for it.

"El Salvador Dali."

Silence. Keeley J. plays the sound of crickets chirping.

"You see, it's funny because there's a country called…"

A very loud game show buzzer sounds. I look over at Sal and Marcus. Sal is holding up a placard with a map on it. The map shows El Salvador and surrounding countries. There's a big arrow pointing to El Salvador. Marcus is holding a placard that states simply, "El Salvador is located in CENTRAL America. NOT South America."

I read Marcus' placard and look at the map. I turn back to the camera and sheepishly say, "You'll have to forgive me. I didn't go to college. Sometimes I mix things up. Well, I guess that leaves just the last joke. The last joke is always the best." I look nervously into the camera. "Right. Right? The last joke is always the best?" I turn to Sal and Marcus. They're stone faced. Marcus is holding his hand above a large button as if he's ready to buzz me off stage. I turn back to the camera and nervously adjust my bolo tie. Yeah, Greg insisted on the bolo tie tonight. Not my favorite style but whatever.

I exhale forcefully and raise my hands out again as I say, "Okay, last one, here goes. What do you call…hold on…you'll need to know a little about animal taxonomy to get this joke. The technical names of animals. Not the common names. There. Perfect. This joke can't fail now. No way. No way, no way, no way. Okay, without further delay, here it is. What do you call a buddhist surrealist camelid?"

Wait for it.

Wait for it.

I lean in a little closer to the camera and stage whisper, "You'll also need to know how to spell a certain animal's name." I turn to look at Marcus. He's pretending to struggle to keep his hand from smashing down on the buzzer. I turn back to the camera, "Technical name spelling jokes. Those are always the best. Always." I step back to my original spot on stage.

Wait for it.

Wait for it.

I'm doing jazz hands as I say the punchline, "Salvador Dalai Llama." I smile big and goofy. I'm waiting for the torrent of laughter from the audience. But, of course, nothing comes, nobody laughs. I drop my hands down and say, "It's funny because llamas are camelids and the Dalai Lama…"

That's when Marcus hits the buzzer several times in a row. I put my hands on my hips as I turn to him. Then I point a stern finger in his direction as if I'm going to tell him off. But I don't. I don't because the theme music from Big Fin X starts playing. I look from side to side, up and down, all around. The music gets more intense. It's a cross between the Jaws theme and the music from Psycho. I do my best to look terrified. Playfully terrified as I scan the surroundings looking for the threat. Then a person in a pale gray bodysuit with a huge shark head resting on his shoulders comes racing out of the audience at me. The man (Is it a man? I can't tell) opens and closes the jaws of the shark head menacingly as he chases me around the stage a couple of times. I go off screen to the right. The shark guy chases me. Then I pop up right in front of the camera to say, "We'll be right back."

Cut to commercial.

74.

When we come back, I'm sitting at the desk and Professor Capriti is sitting in the chair next to the desk. I have him introduce himself and name the university he works at then I make a link between him and Professor Whitmore. It's always good to make links between guests when you can. It helps the audience weave the shows together in their heads, make it a connected whole. "So, professor, a couple of nights ago I had one Professor Whitmore on. She's a Classics professor. All that old stuff. You're a Creative Writing specialist. Back in the olden days the people believed in the Muses. Not just "the muse" like we say today. Oh, I was inspired by the muse. No, they had very specific Muses. Nine Muses. Isn't that right?"

Professor Capriti is a portly, middle-aged cherub of a man. His round, bald head glistens under the lights. His round belly strains against his too tight, plaid vest. His eyes are two black points behind his circular, wire-rimmed glasses. He looks like Santa Claus' bookish cousin. He folds his hands atop his belly as he replies, "Yes, that is indeed true. There were nine muses in ancient times. Both the Greeks and the Roman, ummm, trafficked in such a belief. Nine goddess muses."

"Oh," I say, "the muses were goddesses. I didn't know that. I thought they were just, ummm, spirits, I guess. I didn't realize they qualified as goddesses."

Capriti adds, "Yes, goddesses. Full-fledged goddesses. There were, ahhh, many, many buildings - temples and such - erected in their names. Sometimes all the muses. Sometimes just one specific muse. Yes, just like the temples for other gods and goddesses."

A thought. I say, "That reminds me of a question one of my smart friends…" I pause here and look into the camera. I say with a slightly defensive tone, "Yeah, I have smart friends." I turn back to Professor Capriti, "Ahhh, my friend asked the other day did the ancients really believe in all these gods and goddesses or were they more metaphorical, or allegorical. A way to refer to events and dynamics and patterns that they didn't have the scientific knowledge back then to understand? The god of thunder because they didn't understand the weather, for example. Or the god of the ocean because that, too, was a mystery to them? What can you tell us about that?"

"Ummm, not a whole lot, I'm afraid. You'd have to talk to Professor Whitmore or someone like her to get that answer. Creative Writing is my field. I know about the ancient muses that way. Not because I specialize in ancient beliefs and culture."

The sad trombone sound echoes on stage again. I give my death stare to the Keeley J. cardboard cutout. I turn back to Professor Capriti, "Of course. Right. My mistake. Creative Writing. Right. I'm not sure if you know this professor but I've dabbled in a little creative writing myself. My jokes are just the tip of the iceberg in that regard." I mug for the camera here.

"That would make for a very small iceberg then," Professor Capriti says with a completely deadpan face.

It takes me a second to realize he's just zinged me. "I've worked on a couple of scripts...hey! Was that...did you...now, professor, I'm trying to be nice to you here. Very small iceberg. That...that hurt a little, professor. I'm not going to lie."

Capriti lights up with an impish smile. I can see he's having the time of his life making fun of me on national television. This is a story he'll tell his grandchildren. Fine. I can get behind that. He keeps smiling. He couldn't stop if I paid him to. I add, "Okay, let's cut to the chase. Tell me about teaching creative writing. How does that work? And, frankly, why should the audience care?" I say that last line a little harshly. It's a push back against his making fun of me. A playful push back. He tilts his head slightly in my direction as if to say, "Touche." Good. He gets it. This is all in good fun.

He says, after drawing a contemplative breath, "Writing is fundamental. That is to say, it has been part of human life for ages now. Yes, the ancient historians can tell you of times in the far past when humans didn't write. But, let's be honest, the interesting stuff only started when we began writing. And we've kept writing ever since. Sooo much writing. In so many different forms, different languages for different reasons.

Technology advanced and we have all these wonderful cameras and films and so on. But despite the existence of these other modes of communication, writing, in my humble opinion, still dominates. Phot-ography. Vide-ography. Film-ography," He says these words emphasizing the last few of syllables. "All of those media refer back to writing. That's the 'graphy' part of their names. So, even when we use different technologies, our minds are linked unconsciously back to writing. Because writing is fundamental."

I hadn't thought of that. But it's true. Point for Capriti. I say, "Fair enough, fair enough. I see here on my card that you contend that anyone can be taught how to write creatively. Do I have that correct? You think anyone," I jerk my thumb in the direction of Sal and Marcus, "even a certain pair of knuckleheads that shall not be named can be taught to write?"

Capriti is in his wheelhouse now. He says, "To be clear, I not only think anyone can be taught to write creatively, I insist, in fact, it is my goal to teach as many people as I can to write creatively. Because, once again, writing is fundamental. Once you develop a facility with writing in the creative vein, you will find other areas of your intelligence building up, strengthening, integrating. More than anything, creative writing is a synthetic process. A process that draws on all elements of your life and brings them together, fuses far flung and previously unconnected details into something new, something novel." He pauses here and looks directly into the camera. I suspect my dear professor is an avid local theater participant back in his hometown. He's virtually chewing the scenery now. He says adroitly, "Now, the writing may not be any good. There's no guarantee of that, unfortunately. But it will be creative. It is important to draw a distinction between being creative and being good or interesting or of high quality. Those qualities can come later, can be developed but that is a different process than spurring creativity. It's related, of course, but different."

I ask, "Okay. I'll bite. How does one get good at writing creatively? How does one, say, write a novel that's interesting, that's popular, that's a best seller?"

Capriti says as if he's been waiting for me to ask this very question, "One word: discipline. You must work your craft. Just like you would spend time to develop any skill or profession. You must put in the time and work at it and get feedback and be open to change, be coachable, be willing to adapt and grow and stretch yourself." He says this all right into the camera then turns melodramatically to me as he adds, "I imagine the same is true with acting, yes? Has that been your experience?"

I nod and smile, smile and nod as I say, "Oh, lord yes. I was almost completely inexperienced when I landed in Hollywood. I absolutely had to work at getting better at it. Absolutely."

Capriti stifles a giggle as he looks over at Sal and Marcus. What...

Marcus holds up a hand like a student asking a question. I play to the moment, unsure what's happening but willing to go with it. Sal did say there would be shenanigans tonight. "Yes, Marcus? What do you have for us?"

"The prosecution would like to enter into evidence..."

I interrupt, "The prosecution? What..."

The Law and Order "dun-dun" sound comes from the cardboard cutouts.

I forge on, "...the heck are you..."

Dun-dun.

"...talking about over..."

Dun-dun. Dun-dun. DUN-DUN!

I stare hard at the Keeley J. cutout for a long moment. I open my mouth to continue my question and...

DUN-DUN, DUN-DUN, DUN-DUN.

I hold up a finger and open my mouth like I'm going to say something but then think better of it. Instead, I point to Marcus and say simply, "Go on."

"The prosecution would like to offer into evidence the following witness statements regarding the defendant's, one Ms. Hingergarten, alleged acting abilities back at the time of the, ummm, violation."

I can't help myself, "Violation?!?"

DUN-DUN

At this point I bang my head down on the desk a few times then say, "Fine, fine, go ahead. Show me what you've got."

I study the monitors to see what the audience at home is watching. To my genuine surprise, Jon appears on screen. Yes, Jon. He's walking on a beach with hands clasped behind his back. He's turned to the side looking into the camera as if he's in the middle of a heartfelt conversation. He nods sagely then says, "Yes, when she got to Hollywood, Ms. Hingergarten was...well, there's no other word for it. She was a ham. She was bad. She was all the things you could think of that make for bad acting rolled into one. There were so many things that she did wrong when she acted, that is, when she tried to act. So many things. But...one does stand out. Ms. Hingergarten suffered from O.G. Yes, I know. It's hard to hear. Even harder to say. Ms. Hingergarten had a serious case of Over-Gesticulation."

Oh. No.

I know where this is going. Back in the day, Jon helped me become better at acting. I listened to him. I followed his advice. I even went to watch him work on a set one time. On set for one of the early Big Fin films. That was early in my career. You couldn't even call it a career at that point. I had done a couple of background roles. A little voice over work. Mo (ahhh, Mo) sent me down to watch Jon. This was before I knew Mo and Jon were a couple. Mo was secretive that way. Private. I knew Jon simply as another of Mo's clients who Mo convinced to help me out.

Dammit. I know exactly where this is going. I know what Marcus is going to show next.

When I was down there on set, I watched Jon and the other actrons work. I did. I was so very serious back then. Focused and serious and desperate to figure out a way to make this Hollywood thing work. Because I had nothing else. It was Hollywood or bust. I didn't want to bust. I refused to allow myself to bust. Thus, serious, focused, studying, thinking, hard thinking, lots of scowling, lots of questions. Lots and lots and lots of questions. Yes, I can admit that I gave Miley a run for her money back then. That is, back then I asked as many questions of Jon as Miley asks me these days. So, yeah, don't tell her. Secrecy and swearing and…you get the idea.

Swearing. I know where this is going. I know what clip Marcus is going to show. There will be a lot of swearing. By me. Inside my head when they show this.

Back to the set in Mexico with Jon when I was young and clueless. Jon did his best to tell me to lighten up. But I brushed off his silly, very un-serious advice. Couldn't he see I was being serious? I was focused. I was there to learn about the craft of acting. Who was he to tell me to be less serious? Why was he wasting my time? I have half a mind to call Mo and complain. In fact, I did call Mo and complain. All he said to me was, "Trust him. He knows what he's talking about. One day, he's going to be a director and a damn good one."

Begrudgingly, I listened. But only because I couldn't change my flight out. I had to stay there for a few more days. So, I decided to learn what I could, which I was very sure was not going to be that much. Stupid Big Fin movie. I should have known better.

That night, Jon knocked on the door of my cabana (yes, an actual cabana). I opened the door. I was not happy. I was working on a script. He told me to put the computer down and come with him to the set. I resisted. Because that's what I did back then. Fine. You can call it sulking if you want to. I prefer resisting. Whatever. But Jon wore me down and my script sucked anyway so I went with him. He told me as we approached the bar set (Jon's character was a bit of a drunk and most of his scenes were filmed on that set) that he thought I had talent but I needed to get out of my own way. I remember distinctly that I scoffed at him. Full on, dismissive, what does his guy know scoff. That's when he grabbed me by the shoulders and looked me in the eye as he said, "You're in Hollywood. You're learning to be an actress. Lighten the fuck up, for god's sake."

I tried not to laugh. I really, really, really didn't want to laugh. But I did anyway. It was only a short, quick laugh. There then gone again. But Jon smiled and said, "Ok, good. There is a sense of humor in there. Thank god. I was starting to doubt myself there. Good. Now. Here we are. At the bar. Sit there. Yes, just like my character did in the scene earlier today. You watched that. I saw you watching me with your serious face. Which is good. You do need to be serious about this. Learning how to do this. But you don't need to be so glum. It looks like someone put seaweed in your shorts. Come on. Lighten up. Smile. No, you're on set now. You're acting now. I'm going to be over here. I have this camera. See," He waved his smartphone at me then showed me its screen. He was indeed filming me. I nodded and got very serious. He yelled at me instantly, "No. No, no, no. Stop that right now. Right this instant. Give me a smile instead. No. Not…no. You look like you just smelled a fart. That's not a…for goodness sake. Here. Stand up. Step way from the bar. Swing your arms around in circles. Just do it, missy. Trust me. You'll thank me when this is all done. Swing your arms. Good. Now nod your head up and down as big as you can go. A few more times. Good. Now swing your arms again but smaller circles. Now nod again but smaller nods."

Jon led me through this process of starting out with big, broad movements then gradually smaller and smaller movements for several minutes. Arm swings, head nods, smiles, finger points, elbowing imaginary person next to me, picking up a glass from the bar, standing up from the chair, sitting down in the chair, walking into the bar, walking out of the bar, turning my head as if someone just called my name, pretending to laugh, and, finally, knee slaps (yes, actual slapping of the knee). Then he said, "Do you dance?" I nodded. I had taken the usual dance classes growing up and a few more since I'd been in Hollywood. I wasn't good by any means but I knew the moves. "Okay, good. I'm going to run you through a few standard moves and we'll do them all big at first then gradually work our way down to doing them smaller and smaller and smaller. Okay? A nod or a smile or a 'yes' would be helpful. Okay, great. Good to know you're still inside there somewhere. Ready? Let's start."

That is what Marcus showed the national television audience right then and there. A montage of Jon working me through my paces as a young and clueless actress. Of course,

247

Marcus selected only the big versions of all the movements and gestures and reactions that Jon asked me to do. Only the hyper-exaggerated versions. The Over-Gesticulated versions. Waving hello with my hand way above my head and big, big, bigger than you can believe eyes. Walking into the bar like I was marching in a parade. Turn my head when called as if I'd heard the most dramatic thing ever. Sitting down on the barstool as if my legs had just been cut from under me. Jazz hands like no one has ever jazz handed before. So much shaking of the hands. SO. MUCH. SHAKING. AND. JAZZING.

I cover my face in embarrassment. Part of my brain says silently inside my head, "Jon will pay for this." Another part of my brain says, "This is effing hilarious. See how far you've come, Case? See how far? You're so much better now."

When the clip ends (yes, it felt like it went on forever), I look over at Marcus. He's beaming. So is Sal. After a couple of false starts that he can't finish because he's laughing so hard, Marcus finally says, "The prosecution rests."

DUN-DUN.

I look into the camera and say, "We'll be back shortly. After I've killed my producer." Then I smile bigly. Oh so bigly.

75.

When we come back, Marcus, Sal and I are standing at three gameshow-esque contestant stands on one side of the stage. Professor Capriti is standing a few feet across from us holding index cards in his hands like he's Alex Trebek. Marcus whispered to me as the contestant stands (buzzers included) were being set up, "Capriti is a decent actor. We rehearsed this earlier. He's going to take the lead when we come back from commercial." Which, of course, since we're filming this a few hours before it's aired isn't an actual commercial break but we pretend it is to keep the show as authentic as possible for the viewers.

Capriti announces to the crowd and the camera, "Welcome back to Write for Your Life, the gameshow which pits our contestants against each other in a battle of creative skills. You know our contestants. You know they're all tied up. This round will decide who wins tonight on [melodramatic stare into the camera] Write…for Your Life." He then snaps the index cards in his hands and looks over at us, "Contestants, when I give you the signal, you will have half a minute - thirty thin seconds - to write a flash fiction piece on the topic I have here in my hand. You must write at least eighty words and no more than one hundred. Fewer than eighty disqualifies you. More than a hundred also disqualifies you. Are you clear?" Sal, Marcus and I nod our heads and ready our hands over the keyboards in front of us. Capriti snaps the index cards again as he says, "Okay, tonight's flash fiction topic is…"

Capriti stares at the camera again. A drum roll sound issues out from the cardboard cutouts. "…Mighty Martie or Big Fin: who is the better movie monster? And…go!"

All three of us type hurriedly away. I was not prepared for this tonight. But I have been prepared for this for several years now. Not this - in particular. But this - in general. The on-demand unleashing of creativity. This is how I imagine it was for royal entertainers in ancient times. A feast, some food, some wine, some drunkness, a turn of the royal head to the clever one, the far too clever one standing nearby and then a demand, "Entertain us! Now! Tell us a story! Give us a joke!

Go on! Do it or I'll cut off your head!" Yes, this royal personage has a bloody streak, one akin to Carrol's Queen of Hearts. Anyway. I can't think about that now. I have to type.

As I sense the thirty seconds coming to an end, I risk a glance at the other two. Sal and Marcus are on either side of me at the stands so I flick my eyes to one side then the other. Sal finishes his story with a tap of his middle finger and then pulling back of both hands as if the story he's just written is radioactive and/or spiked with razors and will either burn or slice his hands if he's not careful. On the other side, Marcus's hands rest calmly and still just above his keyboard. He's either blanking out or he finished early. Finished early? How could he? I'm still throwing words up onto the screen. What's my word count? Dammit! One hundred and eight. I have to get rid of that last sentence. Hurry, hurry, hurry. Backspace, backspace, backspace.

Bzzzzzzztttttttt!!!

That's the buzzer. Ok, I think I got it under the limit. I don't know if it will make sense but at least I won't be disqualified. I look up at Professor Capriti. He's smiling into the camera. I look at Marcus and Sal. Sal smiles whimsically back at me. Marcus shakes his head dismissively. Dismissive of himself, that is. Of himself and his story. Me? I shrug. I honestly don't know if what I just wrote makes any sense at all. But I enjoyed writing it.

Capriti has finished mugging for the camera and is now standing next to Sal as he says, "First, Mr. Kincaid, I need to thank you once again for providing me this opportunity. My colleagues simply couldn't believe it when I told them I was going to be on your show performing like this. Well, all I can say now is I hope they believe their own eyes." Once again he faces the camera directly and smiles, smiles, smiles. Lord, I hope I don't come off like that when I turn to the camera. No, I don't. At least, I don't think so. No, I know I don't because Marcus and Sal (and Miley and Scott and Sophie) would have let me know if I did. It's not that Capriti looks bad, per se. He just comes off a little desperate. A little too "look at me." You need some "look at me" to host the show, for sure. But not that much. Not that much.

"Now, this test was not a pure test of creative writing. There was a specific topic which you three were tasked to write about. That, I've found over the years of teaching, can both help and hinder the creative flow. Which, Mr. Kincaid, do you think it did for you?"

Capriti tilts the long, thin, handheld microphone he's been holding since the start of this segment towards Sal. Sal says, "I think the topic confused me more than anything. So, I guess it hindered me. But I think I did alright anyway."

Capriti says, "Well, let's take a look. Show us your story."

Sal pushes a button next to his keyboard and his story flashes up on the monitors and on the screens of people across the nation. That is, it will when we actually broadcast the show. Here's what Sal wrote:

> There once was a man from Phuket
> Who had a golden tick-et
> That let him ride a giant shark
> Across the seas to the Met
> There on stage he saw a Gorilla
> Giant and clothed like a Viking
> Singing the last aria of the season
> An ode to the goddess of Bison
> The shark, left outside in the street,
> Got jealous and stormed the stage in heat
> -ed anger, he struck the Gorilla with an
> Envelope Manilla and back they went
> To the Phillipines, all reconciled, to live the

dream

Capriti reads Sals work out loud then notes, "Ninety words. Well done, Mr. Kincaid. Well done indeed. Some classic imagery. Some modern imagery. Playful. A touch of Gilbert and Sullivan in there, too. Well done, indeed."

All I can think as Capriti praises Sal is, *Stop kissing his ass. He didn't even answer the question.*

Then, of course, Capriti comes to me, "Now, K.C. Hall, let's see what you wrote."

My text flashes up on screen. Here it is:

251

"In the eternal battle between Giant Shark and Giant Gorilla, we are all losers. Locked for ages in mortal combat have these two titans been. But now and here we have an opportunity to help free them from this adversarial adversarying. We the people can raise our voices and tell them that we love both of them, that we want both of them, that we care for both of them. There's enough love to go around for everyone. So, put down the tree trunk club, blunt your razor sharp teeth and instead give each other a hug. Because hugs make..."

Capriti pinches his face when he comes to the end of my story. He looks at the word count and says, "One hundred words on the nose, so, I guess, well done in that regard. But unfortunately you didn't finish your last sentence there. And that looks like it was going to be the big conclusion to your piece which is more of an appeal than an argument. An appeal to the audience. And without that last bit, the whole thing falls flat, K.C." He looks up at me as he leans far too casually against my contestant stand. He's so very full of himself right now. This chance to be in the spotlight has fed his ego a little too much. Like stuff yourself on Thanksgiving dinner too much. Anyway. Whatever. Just get through this bit then Capriti will be gone.

I smile tightly back at Capriti. I want to say something clever. But I'm freezing up. Thankfully, Sal leans over and adds, "I think you should ask her what her last line is."

Capriti stands up straight when Sal speaks. He nods and smiles at Sal. He'd do anything Sal told him to do. Anything. So, he turns to me and says, "What was your last line going to be?"

I smile at Sal as I lean towards the now proffered microphone and say, "The last line was 'Because hugs make giants of us all.'" Capriti winces when I say the line. I confess, so do I. I erased that line and was going to put in something new but I ran out of time. I did not stick the landing. I did not end the story well.

Capriti once more pinches his face then says, "A little twee, don't you think? And, also, a little self-serving. You want the public to love both shark and ape. In other words you want the audience to love both of your movies. Hmmmmm."

That last "hmmmm" comes with a tone of heavy disdain. It takes a great deal of self-control to not spit venom back at Capriti. In my head (and, thankfully, ONLY in my head) I respond, *Look, Professor Prick, be glad I don't stab you here on stage with that microphone. Yeah, there we go. We need a new version of Clue. It was Scarlet Starlet on stage with the microphone. She killed Professor Prick. I can see it now. Professor Prick's body on the floor with blood oozing out of...*

Marcus sees the tension building behind my eyes and says to draw Capriti's attention to him, "Ugh. My story didn't even come close to either of those two. I guess that's why I'm a producer and not a performer like Sal and K.C."

I exhale and let all board game murder imagery vanish from my head as I turn to Marcus next to me. Capriti moves down to Marcus' stand and says, "Let's see what you have and we'll let the studio audience decide."

Marcus' text flashes up on the monitor. Here's what he wrote.

Shark. Gorilla.
Gorilla. Shark.
Shark. Gorilla.
I don't know what to say.

Gorilla. Shark.
Shark. Gorilla.
Gorilla. Shark.
I can't choose between the two.

Maybe if I mix them up.
Shorilla. Gark.
Gark. Shorilla.
Shorilla. Gark.
Nope. That doesn't work.

Choosing sucks.
This story sucks.

I'm not good at this.
Typing words, typing words, typing words.
I'm done.

Uff, that's bad, I think and keep to myself. I pat Marcus on the back comfortingly. He knows his story is bad. We all know his story is bad. It's hard to be bad in front of an audience. I feel for him.

Capriti offers up with an exaggerated nod and forced earnestness, "There's a certain honesty to your work, Marcus. And honesty in creative pursuits is important. It's often overlooked or dismissed…" He shoots a look at me when he says this. What the…? Then he looks to the audience, "Don't you agree? Honesty is important in creative pursuits. Especially in creative pursuits. Yes. Yes it is. Can we get a round of applause for Marcus' honesty."

The audience feels put on the spot. They respond with a smattering of half-hearted claps. Capriti takes a couple of steps closer to them as he juices them for more, "Yes, good, yes, let's cheer on Marcus' honesty." There is another round of clapping, slightly larger than the previous smattering. A smattering and a half. I look at Sal and then at Marcus. They know this is not going well. We know this is not going well. Capriti is forcing it. Sal whispers to me, "I've got this."

He walks out from behind his contestant stand and waves to the crowd as he walks up behind Capriti. The clapping swells up genuinely. The audience loves Sal. I mean, who doesn't? Idol of millions, that one is. For a moment, Capriti thinks he's generating the boost in applause. He blushes. Big time. Then Sal gives him a side hug and deftly takes the microphone from him as he says to the audience, "Thank you, Professor Capriti. Watch out, Pat Sajak. There's a new host around. Let's hear it for Professor Capriti. Yes, yes, thank you. When we come back, K.C. and Big Fin will have a little sit down and we'll take some questions from the audience. You won't want to miss it."

76.

Marcus bundles Capriti off-stage and begins handling him. Sal whispers to me as those two walk off together, "Give some of them an inch and they get nasty."

Oh, thank god. Sal senses it, too. I say to him, "What was that about? Did I piss him off somehow?"

Sal shakes his head, "No. Nothing like that. People - some people - are just jealous. They don't show it most of the time. But when the spotlight is on them, it seeps out. They can't help it." He shrugs, "That's just how it is. I've seen it a million times now. It's nothing you did."

I breathe a sigh of relief. Sal knew exactly what to tell me. For a moment there, I thought I had done something wrong. But I didn't. That was all Capriti. Okay. Good. Another sigh. I ask Sal as Marcus and Capriti are now well out of earshot, "So, what's up with this Big Fin sit down? Is this more of Marcus' shenanigans?" I'm not worried. Just curious.

Sal smiles and says, "No. Not Marcus. This one's on me." Then he walks away.

Ummmm…??? I wonder, should I be a'feared? No, Sal would never do anything bad.

Right?

77.

I'm back behind the desk. Marcus and Capriti are wandering around the ranch. Sal assures me I won't have to deal with him anymore. I wait for the signal then read the introduction on the monitor, "Welcome back everybody. Professor Capriti has been whisked away on a game show emergency, I'm afraid to say. But that's okay because we now have the star of My Dinner with Big Fin...Big Fin!"

A thought, *Did Sal actually reach out to...*

At that point, the person in the gray bodysuit and wearing the Big Fin shark head walks onto stage, waves at the studio audience then sits down next to the desk. The audience loves this. I'm not quite sure why. But they do. They are actually giving Big Fin a standing ovation. I think maybe, yes, now I'm feeling a little jealous. But I don't want to come off like Capriti did. So, when the applause dies down I turn to whoever is inside this costume and just say it, "Wow, that was quite the entrance. I think I'm a little jealous of you."

Big Fin holds both his hands on either side of the giant and awkward shark head as he nods in the affirmative. What is this? What is Sal getting at here? Is this going to be a silent interview? Will I have to do all the talking? Only one way to find out. I say to Big Fin, "Welcome, welcome. Have you, uhhh, let's see. Should I ask you just yes or no questions? Is that how this is going to work?" A thought. I turn to the cardboard cutouts of the band, "Or maybe your voice will be supplied by..."

That's when the person in the Big Fin costume pulls the giant shark off his head and reveals his face to me. Except, it's not a he. It's a she. It's Sarai. I blurt out, "Oh, so the introduction wasn't lying. It is you. The star of My Dinner with Big Fin. Sarai..." All of a sudden, I blank on her last name.

Sarai sees me blanking and jumps in, "...Sullivan. It's actually different than when I met you. I've taken my mom's maiden name. Her family name. I'm Sarai Sullivan now."

I say to the crowd, "Sarai Sullivan everybody. Wow. I have to admit I did not think that was you in the costume. I thought all the shark stuff, all the Big Fin stuff was just Marcus and Sal messing around. But it is actually you. Wow. We

256

haven't seen each other since we did the Dinner video. Wow. Okay. So, let's start there. How have you been doing? What have you been up to? How's…"

I was going to ask, "How's your mother?" But I stopped myself. Because Sarai's mother, Kathryn Sullivan (aka Pak Wong, aka Carina) is the person who almost blew up the filming of Big Fin X. Almost. Very almost. But that's in the past. I don't want to focus on that. Sarai, though, sees that's what I was about to ask and once more finishes my sentence for me, "…my mother? She's good, actually. Really good. She is living down in Puerto Santibel now, believe it or not. So, I've been splitting my time the past while. A few months up here. Well, the L.A. area. Then a few months down there. With mom."

I have to ask, "She's living in Puerto Santibel?"

"Yes, in fact, she never really came back - except for a couple of weeks - to the United States." Sarai pulls a face, "There were some, ummmm, legal issues that developed out of all that stuff that happened down there so she, on the advice of her lawyer, slipped out of the country…" Sarai moves one hand in the air like a fish swimming through water as she says this bit. "…and headed back to Puerto Santibel. She's been there ever since. Yeah." She does the hand gesture again and smiles then winces. I can tell things with her mom are still a little tender. That's when I realize I am jealous of her. Not of the applause she got when she came on stage as Big Fin. I'm jealous that she gets to interact with her mom. Because her mom is still alive. And mine is not. Wow, that's not ever going to go away, is it? Unless…

I shake off the idea that just popped into my head.

But it pops right back in.

I shake it off once more.

It comes right back.

Ok. Here we go.

I hold up a finger to Sarai and say, "Excuse me. There's something… Haaaa…" I let out a deep exhale. I feel something release deep in my chest. Really? Am I going to do this here? Now? Really?

Yes. I am.

257

I look into the camera and say by way of preamble, "I met Sarai and her mom a while back when I filmed Big Fin X…" some applause from the studio audience "…thank you, yes, but that's not the point of this. I met Sarai and her mom and I admit back then in the midst of everything that went on I found myself a bit jealous of Sarai and her mom. I did. I found myself for the first time missing my mom. That is, not being angry at my mom. Just missing her. I suspect many of you watching know about my mom and I and how we were estranged when she passed. We were estranged for much of my life, most of my life actually. I won't go into all those details. They aren't important now. Seeing Sarai here right now…" I turn to Sarai. "…it is good to see you again…" I turn back to the camera. "…brought all that back to me, that moment on the beach and with the ghost thing that happened in the hotel yesterday which I have no idea if that was real or a trick of the light or a trick of something else but it does, all of this coming together right here and now in this moment makes me want to say…" deep, deep, deep exhale "…Mom, wherever you are, I miss you."

A wave of emotion, of several emotions - some good, some bad, all powerful - washes through me. I keep looking into the camera. I blink away tears as fast as I can. None of them roll down my cheeks. But they do well up in the corners of my eyes. Saria reaches across and squeezes my hand. I squeeze back as I keep looking into the camera. I take a deep inhale to replace the exhale, shake my head once, twice then turn back to Sarai, "Okay," I squeeze her hand then let it go, "okay. Now that's over. Over for now. Okay. Sarai, why don't you tell me what you've been up to since I saw you last."

78.

The show ended and I went back to my cabin. I needed some alone time. The show wasn't hard. Not at all. Any show that pretty much follows the original plan and can be filmed in one place - I'll never call those shows hard ever again. Sure, Capriti was annoying but Marcus and Sal handled him. I'm just tired. Worn out. The moment about mom took it out of me. Not in a bad way. But in a "finally I admitted that to myself" way. Things are shifting inside. In a good way. But I need time to let them shift.

So, I got a plate of food - fried chicken and the fixins! - from Luisa in the main house then headed back to the cabin. I'm biting into my second drumstick when Scott et al calls (yes, Scott told me what "et al" means). Scott said, "So, guess what?" Before I can guess, he says, "We're staying at the haunted hotel. That was the deal I had to make with these guys in order to get them to spend time at Custer State Park. I wanted to see the sunset there. It was so beautiful, Case. So beautiful. I wish you'd been there."

Before I can respond Sophie grabs the phone from Scott and says, "We're really going to need to talk when I get there. Things are heating up a bit. Is that what Hollywood people say when they start to get offers? Things are heating up. I think I may be in a bidding war. I think people are bidding for me to do their projects. I think I'm a hot commodity right now."

I say, "That's amazing, Sophie. Really. I can't wait to hear about it. Now…"

"I know, I know. I'll hand the phone back to Scott. I just wanted to tell you before you two got all mushy and lovey dovey."

"I do not…" The phone changes hands again. But it's not Scott who has it. It's Miley.

"You really do get mushy with Scott. Just admit it, Case. It's adorable so admit it. Now, before I hand the phone back to him I need to tell you that I'm going to start auditioning again." Pause. She doesn't say anything. I don't say anything.

Finally, I say, "That's good. I'm happy for you. But...I will miss you. As my assistant. Do you want to... That is... When exactly..."

I used to pride myself on not having a personal assistant. That, in hindsight, was stupid of me. But there you go. Sometimes, I'm... You know the rest. This past year with Miley as my assistant and MDB in charge of my professional life (well, co-in charge, along with me) has been fantastic. It's been stable and fun and good. No surprises. No drama. Aside from discovering I have a half brother and Sasha and I drifting apart and now that I know what was going on there - a little - even that seems low key drama compared to prior years. So, I'm happy for Miley. But I'm sad that she'll no longer be my assistant. That's what I'm trying to say to her here. Trying and not succeeding.

Miley jumps in, "You're tongue-tied. You rarely get tongue-tied. That means one of two things. Either you're very tired. Seems possible. Or you're going to miss me terribly and you don't quite know how to say that. Which is sweet and is, also, true for me, too. So, I don't know how this will go. If I'll get picked at any of my auditions or not. No one knows. But Sophie and I have made a pact to support each other as we go through this process. She's nailing it, of course. Because she has the whole martial arts, laser-focus training plus the I'm just a small town girl from Arizona thing going on. People eat that shit up, I'm telling you. But you already know that. That was part of your appeal back in the day. At least, I imagine it was. Not Arizona. But Albuquerque. Or Rapid City. Or wherever it was in Oregon you lived. That whole thing. Hmmmm, now that I think about it, having lived in so many places probably helped you in some way. Meeting people from different parts of the country. That had to help. I'm not sure how. But I'm sure it did. Anyway, back to brass tacks. I don't want to fully stop being your personal arranger just yet. So, I'll stay on half time. Or partially in some way. We can figure out those details when we get back to L.A. I'll stay on long enough to train and supervise the next personal arranger..."

"Arranger?" I ask, partially to stall Miley. This is the first time she's referred to her that way. I'm curious as to why she's doing that. But really I just need a moment to reflect on Sophie and Miley starting their careers. I remember when I went on my first…

"Yup, that's my new term. I decided I don't like 'assistant.' It just doesn't feel right. So, I'm calling myself a 'personal arranger' now. It's more accurate and reflective of my actual…"

"It's semantic bullshit," I hear Jaxson call out in the background.

"Ignore him," sighs Miley like a world-weary traveler facing yet another annoying but minor complication on her multi-stage journey. "So, yes, we'll figure out the details when we get back to L.A. Before that, though, we'll see you up there tomorrow night. We'll get there before night time. I do want to see the whole honey operation. You should really make a joke about honey trap on the next show. Isn't that what spies called using women to lure men into giving up secrets? And vice-versa, I suppose, too. A honey trap? I'm sure I read that somewhere. Go on. Workshop that, as US actrons like to say. You have my permission to use that joke on national TV. After all you've done for me, that's the least I can do for you. Oh, got to go. Sophie's calling to me. Bye!"

The phone changes hands again. Scott says softly, "You okay there? I know Miley leaving…"

All I can think of is Scott wrangling this crew for the past few days on the road. I cut him off to say, "You've earned your stripes this week, huh?"

It takes him a moment to understand my meaning then he says, "They've all been a bit much at times. But I'm glad we did this. Really glad. The only thing that I wish were different is you being here." Okay, now I do feel mushy inside. Scott adds, "But we'll see you tomorrow so…"

Before I realize what I'm saying, I ask him, "Scott, am I crazy to keep doing this? All this?"

Scott is silent for several seconds. Then he says, "What exactly do you mean, Case?"

"I mean I could retire right now. You and I could take the money we have right now and buy a place and settle down and live our lives, go on road trips, start a family, bake cookies, you could write your graphic novels, I could write…whatever I wanted to write and…and we could do whatever we wanted whenever we wanted. No more AM LA. No more Hollywood drama. No more traveling to shoot on location. No more…of any of that. We could do that right now. I could drop the mike with that news on tomorrow night's show and end my career that way and walk away."

"What about…MDB and the Hall-iverse and all the stuff you two have planned for these next few years?" There's a touch of hope in Scott's voice. But there's concern, too.

I say, "I know. Which is to say I don't know. I don't know how that would all work out. This idea just popped into my head. I haven't figured anything like that out. But it would work out some way. I'd be done in Hollywood. That's the whole point. Hollywood things like that wouldn't matter anymore. I'd apologize to MDB. She'd be mad. Really mad. But she's indestructible. She'd get over it. And then we could be together like we were in Wayside for those few months." Pause. "I miss those months, Scott. I miss how much we were together back then."

Scott says, "You're right, Case. I miss our time in Wayside, too. I do. And if you decide this is what you want to do, I'll be behind you fully. I need you to know that."

Pause.

Long Pause.

Very Long Pause.

Finally, I say, "But…"

"But," Scott begins, "I don't want you to run away from Hollywood. That's not quite the right word but it's the best I can come up with right now. There are people - MDB, Miley, Sophie to a lesser extent, and others like Mac - who are depending on you, who you have agreements with. But, you're right, shit happens, things change and if you quit today they would figure something out. So, that's there and it needs to be considered but that's not what I'm worried about. I'm worried about you, how you would feel, say three years down the line, five years down the line, ten years down the line. Would you want to ever get back into Hollywood in some fashion? I think…well, it doesn't matter what I think. It matters…"

262

"Tell me what you think," I say to Scott. "Tell me."

"I think…" Scott takes a deep breath then continues, "I think you have unfinished business. I think you're at a place of success in your career that most never reach. I think that scares the shit out of you. I know there are times it scares the shit out of me so it has to scare the shit out of you. I think you've handled it so far better than most, if not better than anyone…so far. I think it's very tempting when you're at this high point to want to jump off. I think you're very, very good at working your way to the top but you don't know what to do now that you're at the top. The same things that got you here might not work to keep you here. I think part of you realizes you need to change things up. Joining with MDB and leaving Sasha's company was part of that. A big part. But only part. I think you've been so focused for so long on how to get here that you never really thought about what you would do when you got here. Sure, you'll make more movies. Sure, you'll make more shows. And they'll be good. And people will enjoy them. Don't ever lose sight of that, Case. You bring people joy. You make people happy with your work. You do. You're not the only one, no, of course not, and, sure, if you stopped there would be others to do that but do you really want to stop, like stop stop? Or do you want to try something different? Stretch yourself creatively? Do the Hall-iverse, yes. But maybe add some new challenge in there? Maybe…ohhhh."

"Ohhhh?" My heart skips a beat. "Ohhhh what?"

Scott says, "I, ahhh, I walked away from the girls when I took the phone from them. So we could talk privately. I thought I was far enough away from them. But I just turned around and they are staring at me in a way that I don't know how to describe. I think they just heard everything I just said to you which I'm sure was not what you wanted and it most definitely is not what I wanted. Ahhhh, Miley would like to talk to you but if you don't…"

Fuck. He's right. I wanted this to be only between him and me. But it's not now. Fuck. I say, "Hand her the phone…no, wait, just put me on speaker. Is it just you three? Are the twins there?" Do I want the twins to be there?

There's a clicking sound then Miley says, "It's just us three. The twins just went over to Scott's old comic book store. So, yeah, just us three."

"Okay, good," I say. I take a moment to gather my thoughts then I begin, "Look, Miley, Sophie, I'm just having a moment here. Really. There's nothing to worry about..."

"That's a lie," says Miley bluntly. Sophie adds a very strong "mmmmm hmmmm" in the background.

"No, look, it's been a long-ish week. I've missed Scott. And you, too, of course and I just need..."

"K.C. Hall Hingergarten Langle whatever your name is, stop lying," says Miley. "Just stop, please. All three of us know you, K.C. Please don't lie to us. I can tell by how seriously Scott was talking to you that this isn't just a moment. So, don't say that again. Okay?"

"Okay," I say.

"Good. Now...now you've done so much for all of us that I really have no right to ask you to do anything more but I'm going to do just that. I'm going to ask you to keep acting. I'm going to ask you to not quit or retire or take a hiatus or whatever you want to call it. Please don't, Case. Just don't. I know that's not fair of me. But tough shit. Scott's right. I will never say that again in front of him ever so you know that I'm serious when I say it now. Scott's right. He's right. You're scared about what's next. You are at the top. Everyone will be gunning for you. That's just how Hollywood is. That's just how life is. But if you step away from it all now, you'll regret it. You will. You'll second guess yourself straight on to crazy. You will. I know you enough to know that. Maybe that will take three years. Maybe that will take five years. Maybe that will take three months. Who knows? But it will happen. You'll see a story about Josie or some other actron in a role that you'd know you would have done such a better job with and you will eat your own heart out and you'll end up driving Scott crazy because all he'll want to do at that point is go camping and look at buffalo and stare a sunsets and bullshit like that. And you'll be all no let's go visit our dear friends Miley and Sophie in Laguna Beach or wherever we have a fabulous home together. And Thad, too. Yes, Thad will be there. You better

264

believe it. Scott will resist because he knows as soon as you set foot in Hollywood again you'll want to act again and you'll be so eager you'll take whatever is offered to you first which will be some crappy remake of something or other and when that comes out you'll say to Scott ohhh, I can do better than that and the whole process will start all over again. You know that's true. I know that's true. Sophie knows that's true. Scott knows that's true. Hell, Randolph knows that's true. So…don't do that. Stay. Keep acting. Find some meaty roles. Make the Hall-iverse…my god, if you walk away from the opportunity to have a whole creative universe built around you I swear I will pull your hair out the next time I see you…anyway, find something, some element to challenge yourself with. That's your…huh, I see it now. I know what your problem is. Your problem is that it's all too easy for you. Oh, look at me, I made another blockbuster movie. Ohhh, my ape movie didn't do so well. I think I'll quit now. What!?! It was just one mediocre movie! But it should have done better. Everything I do needs to be awesome. Dammit, K.C. If I acted that way with you, you would smack me across the face…"

"No, I would smack you across the face. Ummm, metaphorically. Not actually. But yeah," says Sophie. Then she adds, "There would be so many burpees. So many. And I don't even want to think about what Sasha would do to you. My god!"

"Yeah!" says Miley with renewed vigor. "Yeah! So, so…so eat your fucking tiramisu, get some sleep and shut the fuck up about wanting to retire!"

Silence.

Miley said that with such gusto. That's the loudest I've ever heard her say anything.

More silence.

Then Scott says in a calm and even manner, "I agree with Miley."

A split second later, Miley erupts once more. This time she's ecstatic that Scott agrees with her. "Hell yeah, Hingergarten! Take that you…you…you…"

Silence again. Miley doesn't finish her sentence. She doesn't need to. Her meaning is more than clear.

I take a deep breath and say, "Okay. I hear you. I hear all of you. I do. And you're right. I would get the hankering…"

"Hankering?" asks Sophie.

"Hey, I've spent the week on a ranch. I can say 'hankering' if I want to say 'hankering.' Anyway, I would at some point want to come back to Hollywood. I had not thought of that before and you all are right about that. So, if that's true then, yes, I might as well stay and keep on doing my thing for now. So I guess I should say thank you for pointing that out to me."

Silence. Then Sophie says, "Go on. Say it."

Uff. Okay. I say, "Thank you, Sophie. Thank you, Miley. Thank you, Scott. My dear, sweet…"

"That's enough of that mush-head," Sophie says jokingly but with a little edge in her voice. Ha!

"Fine. Fine. I do have one more thing to say before I hang up." I say this with a hint of mystery in my voice. I know Miley can't resist a mystery.

"What's that?" asks Miley.

"I'm going to hang up and then I'm going to call Thad and tell him all about his future home in Laguna Beach with you and Sophie," I say.

"Don't you…"

Click.

Oh, that felt good. That felt really good.

Now, time for more fried chicken.

79.

When I get up the next morning. I see a few texts from Professor Whitmore. It starts with, "I watched the show last night. WTF Capriti? I'm so angry with him. I personally apologize on behalf of professors everywhere. Also, for the past few days I've had a couple of lines of dialogue bouncing around in my head. Dialogue between Dido and Venus. Just a couple of lines. I don't know what to do with them. Or what they could turn into. Maybe you can figure it out. Here they are."

The next text from her has the lines:

Dido: I forbid Cupid's Arrow. I live and love on my own terms and with as much intensity as any who have been envenomed by Cupid's potion.

Venus: With this stance of chosen abandon, you embody my very spirit - the only way to give of oneself is to give all of oneself. I freely lend you my strength for all your endeavors.

A third text from Whitmore states, "I imagine this happening at the point in the Aeneid where Venus sends Cupid to make Dido fall in love with Aeneas, thus the arrow reference. So, Dido chooses her own love and life and throws off the influence of the gods (in this case, goddess). In doing so, Venus is so impressed that she essentially gives Dido her blessing to do as she wants. Maybe you can use that in a movie or show or something. Take care, Whitmore."

As I go for a run (I woke up later than yesterday, the sun is just about up, the sky is clear, the air is fresh, if I didn't go for a run it would be a tragedy), these lines bounce around in my head. *I forbid Cupid's arrow. I forbid Cupid's arrow. I forbid Cupid's arrow. This stance of chosen abandon. This stance of chosen abandon. This stance of chosen abandon. Is to give all of oneself. Is to give all of oneself. Is to give all of oneself.*

My blood pulses through my veins. The lines pulse through my head. The cool morning air fills my lungs. I pass the main house and head out on a large loop of gravel that leads down to the long driveway and then back. The rhythm of my strides is hypnotic. I feel my body waking up. I feel alone with the world.

I keep running.

I settle deeper into the movement. My shoulders relax. My arms swing more freely. The tension in my neck warms and dissolves. I am no longer making myself run. No longer forcing my muscles to contract. My body has taken over. It now carries me along with it as we run. Together we run. Together in motion we are free. This, this right here, this state of effortless action, of flow, of joyous synchrony is what I love about a good workout. It's also what I love about acting. When I'm on it the lines flow from me as my character and I are one. Then the other actrons in the scene respond in kind. We are ourselves. We are our characters. We have embodied their spirits, their essences in our bodies and, momentarily, brought them to life. We are multiplied. We are made greater.

I never lose myself in a character. I find myself. I find greater aspects of myself. Greater potentials. Greater wisdom. Greater grief. Greater anger. Greater peace. Once I let go of a character, once the acting is done, I am more centered and, yes, more myself.

I freely lend you my strength for all your endeavors.
I freely lend you my strength for all your endeavors.
I freely lend you my strength for all your endeavors.

That is what I do with the characters I portray. That is what the characters do for me. It's a synergistic process. A mutual reinforcing. A mutual expansion of our energies. But it must be freely chosen by both participants. Or it simply won't work. Or the combination will tend toward destruction rather than creation. Things will fall apart instead of coming together. Forced union is no union at all.

After going around the loop path seven times, I round the corner of the main house and head back towards my cabin. I don't think about it. I just do it. My body knows what to do. I come to the spot in the path where I stopped the other morning. I stop again. No thinking, just doing. I stop, turn and look towards the rising sun. The horizon is bathed in fresh light. I close my eyes and let that light wash over me. I welcome it with a silent prayer.

80.

When I get out of the shower, I see MDB called then left a text. It says, "Call me." I call back when I'm dressed and walking over for breakfast. MDB picks up and I say, "Good morning."

MDB says, "More like a strange morning. Have you heard what's happened?"

"No, I have not," I find myself saying this without the slightest degree of tension or apprehension. That's a big change for me. Usually, a call that starts like this would put me on edge, make me nervous. But not today. And, I suspect, not ever again.

MDB launches into it, "Three studio execs resigned yesterday. One from GMG. One from Parastar. One from Traveling Roadshow."

Resigned from Hollywood? Yesterday? There must be something in the air, I think. "Huh? Which ones?" I ask. MDB rattles off the names. I barely register them. I'm sure I've heard them before. But it's no one I've ever worked with. I ask, "Did they do this together for some reason? Is this like a protest? Or are they starting a new company together or something?" I ask out of curiosity. Curiosity, not concern.

MDB says, "No. At least, so far no. You know how these egos are. They want every announcement they make, every memo they send celebrated to the high heavens. They love to have stories written about their majestic creative genius. BUT…" MDB says that word like a grenade exploding, "…not this time. This time it was simply put out on twitter by all three. Early in the morning. Simple, basic, bland, short statements saying 'effective immediately I have chosen to retire from the company for personal reasons, I wish to thank everyone, blah, blah, blah.' That's it. Nothing else. They aren't even in L.A. right now. Some internet sleuth who tracks flights and airport cameras or something like that posted pictures of them getting on planes yesterday. All three left yesterday. Separately. Different destinations. As far as the hacker could tell. Not one of them is in town. And it looks like none of them have plans on returning anytime soon. Sooooo…"

I know what MDB's going to say. I beat her to the punch(line), "You think this is Muze's book."

"YES!" Another word explosion. "It has to be. It just has to be."

"Have you heard from Shawn?" I ask.

"No," MDB says. "Have…"

"No, I haven't. I called him when the news about his book being leaked, hacked, whatever but I haven't heard anything from him since."

"Ok. Well. I guess that's good," says MDB.

I can tell by her tone of voice that she wants to ask me something. I say to her, "Is there anything you want to…"

"Please tell me you don't have any deep, dark, nasty secrets that you can be blackmailed with," says MDB. "I know that you don't. I know that. But after this morning, I just need to hear you say that. These resignations have put me a little on edge. I've just come back into the business. We're just starting up the Hall-iverse. I…confess that I'm still finding my way after having been gone for so many years. Things are the same, yes. But they are different, too. I can't quite put my finger on what it is but there's something different going on these days. That worries me. Soooo…"

I smile as I say, "Besides being a closet tiramisu addict, drinking far too much coffee, occasional bouts of self-doubt, occasional bouts of wanting to chuck it all in, occasional moments when my head gets so big and I am convinced, absolutely that I am god's gift to acting and, oh yeah, can't forget these, occasional moments of knocking down ex-lovers who confront me outside the soundstage I'm working on, no, I do not have any deep, dark, nasty secrets blackmailers can use against me."

MDB says, "Oh, thank god! Thank god. Thank you, K.C. I know I'm being a bit of a drama queen this morning but I did really need to hear you say that. I'm…ahhhh…I'm looking…ahhh…."

I know what she wants to say. I, also, know that she can't say it. Not yet. We're still getting used to working together. So, I say it first, "I'm counting on you, MDB. Going

270

forward with the next stage of my career, I'm going to need you in my corner."

MDB is silent for several seconds then she says, "Thank you, K.C. I'm going to need you, too. I have such plans. Such plans."

"Ohhh!" I say as a thought crystallizes in my head. "There is one thing. I have a project I want to direct. Write and direct."

"Oh, lord. Another actress turned director," MDB says with a bounce in her voice. She's teasing me. "Are you sure you…"

"I'm very sure. We'll go over the details when I get back," I say.

"You do realize your schedule is pretty full for the next…" MDB cautions.

"I do. That's okay. It's going to take me a while to get the script just right. And for the people I want to…get some experience. So, yeah, no rush. But I needed you to know because we're in this together. Whatever this is, we're in it together."

MDB says, "I can't wait to hear all the details."

Then we hang up and I head into the main house.

81.

Luisa made huevos rancheros this morning. Heaven! She insists I sit down while she prepares a plate for me. A girl could get used to getting served like this. Maybe Luisa can show Scott how to make huevos. Hmmmm. I look up the Hollywood resignations on my phone as I wait. There's not much online. Yet. Just a couple of blurbs. Hmmmmm.

Luisa puts the plate in front of me. Let me just say, if you've never had huevos rancheros in your life, you don't know how good breakfast can be. I pick up my fork and linger over the first taste of egg-y, spicy, cheesy, fresh tortilla-y deliciousness. That's when Clara comes into the kitchen. She's studying her phone. When she sees me, she says, "Did Professor Whitmore send you those lines, too?"

I swallow and say, "Yes, she did. I didn't know she sent them to you. She didn't mention that."

Clara looks at her phone again, "I think she sent them to me after you." Pause. "I think." She sits down across from me. She has no choice. Luisa will not let her out of the kitchen until she eats a full plate of food. I can tell by Clara's face that she's not used to being mother henned this way. That makes two of us. But I'm old enough to enjoy it. Clara isn't there yet.

Clara's lips move as she reads the lines Whitmore sent us. I wait for her to look up from her phone. When she does, I ask, "So, what do you think?"

She sighs, "I'm not sure. It's better for Dido, yeah. She's empowered. She's her own woman now. But the whole Venus lending her power thing is a bit too much for me."

"That stuff is all over those old stories. The gods and goddesses intervening, choosing sides, working against each other, complaining to Zeus. You know that, right?" I ask.

Clara looks at me like I'm an idiot, "Yes. I know that." She doesn't like having her intelligence questioned in the slightest. Okay. Noted. Before I can say anything else, Clara offers a half-hearted admission, "Well, I know that now. I looked up the Aeneid after Whitmore was here." A flash of anger distorts her face, "What was up with Professor Crappy last night anyway?" I shrug and lift another forkful of paradise into my mouth. Clara says, "Just goes to show you that being educated is no guarantee of being nice, right?"

I say, "Indeed. No guarantee." Another forkful. This is really good.

"Sooo," Clara pinches one eyebrow down as she tilts her head up to think. She's back on the original subject now. "Soooo, what would those lines do for the whole duty vs. love, responsibility to the whole, the greater cause vs. personal desires and wishes theme of the Aeneid?" I fix Clara with a steady stare. She shrugs and says, "Yeah, that comes right from a website." Another shrug. "But it's still interesting. I mean it's Aeneas who is quote duty-bound unquote in the Aeneid. It's his freakin' story after all. But, also, it's not his story. It's pretty much Roman propaganda. Oh, we're so awesome. Look, we were founded by the Trojans. Which doesn't make sense to me. The Trojans lost, right? Why was it so great to be founded by the losers? I need to look that up. No, I'll ask Whitmore. She'll explain it to me better. But If Dido..." now Clara's back to the original question. No transition. She just jumps right back. "...is all empowered now, taking Whitmore's lines, then what would she do? Would she stick to her duty of being the Queen of Carthage? Or would she maybe sail off after Aeneas since she abandoned herself to love or whatever?" Clara's face betrays a deep distrust of such love and its accompanying abandon. So young. She studies my face as she asks, "What do you think?"

I linger for a moment over another forkful of the huevos. Then I put my fork down and say, "I think it's a false choice. I think there is no true duty without real love. Duty comes from outside. It's imposed on you. By the gods or parents or society. Love - when it's done right - comes from the inside. It's natural. It's organic. It flows out of you. Sooo..." I know what I want to say but I can't find the right words.

Clara waits as I search for them. Then she says, "So, how do you balance those two? How do you choose between them?"

All of a sudden this moment feels very important for Clara. And me, too.

I say, "You don't choose. You can't choose. That's what I'm trying to say. It's a false choice as in you can't make the choice. That is, you can't avoid duty and you can't avoid love. They will always be in your life in some form or another. So, you have to bring them together. You have to join them. Otherwise, they'll tear you apart. You have to…" More searching for the right word. "…marry them together. Join them. Find the place, the spot or the way that your duty and your love fit together."

Clara nods and says. "Love comes from inside. That's Whitmore's change. And what you just said. No outside arrow bullshit. Dido's love is her own love, her own choice. And if what you just said is true - there's no true duty without love as part of it - then…then…let's see. How would Whitmore put that?"

I pause here to think that through. Clara puts her phone down on the table between us so we can both look at Whitmore's lines together. There's a certain, deliberate, stilted rhythm to them. A hint of the faux original poetry translated into modern prose creating an awkward cadence. Awkward but memorable. Like a person on the street interview being carried out in Shakespearean couplets. There's an incongruency to the words as they strike your ear. They do not slip into your mind. They push.

I take a breath, pretend I'm auditioning and say Whitmore's lines out loud to get a better sense of them, "I forbid Cupid's Arrow. I live and love on my own terms and with as much intensity as any who have been envenomed by that cherub's potion." I didn't like the repetition of Cupid's name so I changed it to 'cherub.'

Before I can say Venus' lines, Clara jumps in, "With this stance of chosen abandon, you embody my very spirit - the only way to give of oneself is to give all of oneself. I freely lend you my strength for all your endeavors."

As the words come to me, I add, "One cannot have true duty without love. Such a vessel is full of holes through which a life's blood will leak. Love makes duty whole. Duty makes love steadfast."

274

I look at Clara. She looks at me. For a split second, I am looking into the eyes of Venus. For a split second, she is looking into the eyes of the Queen of Carthage. Clara and I lean back from each other and the table. She looks at me. I look at her. She's just Clara. I'm just K.C. She says, "That's bullshit."

I say, "Yeah. But it's also true. Life's like that."

"How do you tell the difference then?" Clara asks with a hint of sadness in her voice. A hint she does her best to cover up. So young.

I look her in the eyes and say, "Sometimes you just have to experience things in order to understand them. I know that sounds like a cop out or a dismissal. But it's true. Sometimes I'm… Sometimes you don't understand why you're doing something or even what you're doing until you've done it. Then everything becomes clear."

82.

A little while later, I'm in Saul's cabin again and all three of us - Marcus is here, too - are going over tonight's show. The last show of the week. I'll admit I'm tired. For some reason this week of shows has taken it out of me. Tired but not burnt out. There's a difference. I wouldn't have changed a thing about this week. Well...maybe a couple of things. But you know what I mean.

Sal can see this in my face. We're at the table going over the guest list - which is minimal as Marcus has more "secret stuff" planned for me - when Sal says, "You're happy this is the last one until next year, aren't you?"

I nod and say, "No doubt. Yes." Pause. "I don't know how you do it. Honestly. Week in, week out."

Sal smiles and sips his coffee - he's taken a liking to the Highland Grog flavor - but Marcus is the one who answers, "He does it with a support staff of thousands. And, of course, the best producer on the West Coast."

Sal quips, "Mmmmm, West Coast of Tasmania, maybe." He and Marcus share a laugh. I can tell they've been telling each other versions of this joke for years now. Sal adds, "And it's not thousands. You know I don't like huge crews. Fifty. Tops."

Marcus rolls his eyes at me then says in a more serious tone of voice, "Doing the show on the road like this is more difficult. We don't have all the crew out here with us. We're not anywhere near as familiar with the surroundings, the infrastructure, the likelihood of mini-stampedes - things like that." We all laugh for a moment. Marcus goes on, "So, that has made this a much more fly by the seat of our pants experience out here than a regular, in studio week would have been. You get that, right? I wouldn't want you to think that every week of the show is this chaotic."

I say, "I do get that. But thanks for saying it. There have been moments when it's all felt held together by spit and duct tape." I bite my lip and bob my head to the side, "Which, if I'm honest, isn't necessarily a bad thing. I tend to thrive in those scenarios. Running around, slapping things together, ad libbing like you said a few days ago, Sal." Another bob of the head, "But this time around, I'm starting to see the benefit, the big benefit of having the structure in place, the support staff, the familiar surroundings, all that."

Sal waits a beat, takes another sip of coffee then says, "So, tonight, Mac is your only guest. You comfortable doing two whole segments with just him?"

"I am. Easily. He and I have worked on Stack Life for a while now. We can shoot the shit for that long, no problem," I say.

Sal looks at Marcus, "You want to give any hints about what else you have up your sleeve for tonight?"

Marcus beams, "Nope. Except to say that you'll like it. I'm sure of that." Then he winks at me.

Okay, now I'm not so sure.

83.

It's a bit later. Greg has just done me up for the show. I'm wearing a tan, suede jacket and pants combo over matching cowboy boots. You can barely see the boots as the pants are long and a bit flared by the heel. Greg tried once again to get me to wear a matching hat but I refused. I'm not big on hats. They make me look funny. I have a black blouse woven through with shimmery, shiny, sparkly threads. That provides a hint of buckaroo sparkle. Just a hint.

I pull out my phone to check for messages from Scott et al. They should have been here by now. He did send me a couple of messages earlier saying the twins were impossible to pull away from the comic book store and the girls were sleeping in really late so they left Rapid City much later than planned. I sent him back a frowny face emoji. He sent back "Soon." As in, we'll see each other soon.

There are no messages. So, I call him. He picks up right away. But his voice is rushed and tense, "Hey, uhhh, sorry, hold on. Uh, whoa. Okay. So, we're running even later than I thought. There was a miscommunication about gas. As in…as in nevermind because it's too stupid to mention. I'll just say that Miley is never allowed to drive any of our vehicles ever again. Especially not when she's caught up with Thad."

"I am not caught up with Thad," yells Miley from somewhere behind Scott. "What does that even mean? Caught up?"

Sophie adds, "It means you didn't pay attention to how much gas we had and we ran out. THAT'S what that means."

"Whatever. I drive electric now. I don't pay attention to gas stations," snarls Miley.

'WE KNOW," says everyone else at the same time.

I can't help but laugh. Scott says, "So, yeah, we'll be there. But I'm guessing it will be after you're finished filming the show. Maybe an hour or so after." Pause. "Sorry about that."

He's sorry because I did want him to see me do the show in person. Last year I was so nervous about being on Kincaid Live! that I asked Scott to not come to the studio during the filming. I wanted to keep home and the show

278

separate. He was fine with that. This time around, though, I wanted him to see what it's like when I do the show. Tonight was supposed to be that night. Dammit, Miley! But, whatever, he'll be here later and I can show him around then. Yeah, I will most definitely show him around.

84.

As I finish up with Scott, Sasha sends me a text, "Got a moment, Gorilla Girl?"

I frown at the new nickname. I text back, "A quick one. And let's go back to pipsqueak. Your other nicknames for me so far suck."

She calls a few moments later, "My nicknames for you do not suck. Just because you don't like them doesn't mean they suck."

"That's precisely what it means. Nicknames have to work for both people involved otherwise they just become insults." I say this with a very authoritative tone.

Sasha replies, "Ohhhhh, boss lady voice. Okay, okay. Back to pipsqueak then."

"Good," I say then laugh. "What's up?"

Sasha says, "You heard about the resignations?"

"I did. MDB touched base with me," I say.

"Good. So, now, Connor…" Sasha stops talking here. I can tell she's waiting for me to react to the mention of my half-brother/her fiance.

"Connor, yes. I do think I've heard of him," I say by way of making light of the situation.

"Okay, good. Connor now has a chance to move up at GMG. So, that's good. But he wants me to join GMG fully, too. That's actually part of his pitch to the board. Which is flattering and all but…"

"Sasha - no!" I find myself saying before I realize it. I attempt to backtrack, "I mean, think about it. Think about it very seriously. I mean would you and Kelsey…"

Sasha says, "That's the thing. If I joined GMG fully, I'd have to let go of my stake and my role in Kelsey's and my business. We've been working closely with GMG - as you know…"

"Uh-uh," I say.

"But this would be a full on move for me to become part of GMG. A Vice President."

"Shit!" I say. "Vice President. Of what?" There are so many vice presidents at the Hollywood studios that they have areas of focus or specialty or whatever. Sometimes the titles match what the person actually does at the studio. Sometimes not and the title is merely to indicate that the person has clout in the system, that he or she can make things happen.

"Vice President of New Talent Development," says Sasha with a very proud voice.

"I like it," I say. Because I do. I think Sasha would be great at spotting up and coming talent. Writers, actors, directors, what have you. She's got a good sense for that. But... "Okay. So...why are you calling me?"

Sasha pushes back, "Nope. You first. Why did you say 'no' so quickly just a moment ago."

"Because..." Thinking, thinking, thinking. "Because you've been with Kelsey for so long." That's true but that's not it. Thinking, thinking, thinking. "Because once you're Vice President you and I and MDB might, well, we might end up working against each other. I...I don't want that. Not...now."

Silence. Neither Sasha and I say a thing for several seconds.

Finally, Sasha says, "I don't want that either." Pause. "But it might happen." Pause. "So, we'll have to promise to be civil and good with each other." Pause. "Such a radical thought out here in Hollywood." Pause. "Are you sure this has nothing to do with Connor?"

There it is. I want to say no. I really do. But...

"Okay, maybe it does have something to do with Connor. Or, as Big T would correct me, my unresolved feelings regarding Connor. I am happy for you Sasha. Both of you. And I can even imagine a time when I get to know Connor and we're all good and everything. But...that time is not now. It's not here. It's not yet and it's going to take some work. So, when you said you and Connor and GMG and all that it felt like he was taking you away from me. Which is silly, I know. But true. I feel like we're just starting to come back together. I don't want to lose you again, Sash. I don't."

More silence. But not as long this time.

After a few seconds, Sasha says, "Okay. Listen, pipsqueak, I don't want to lose you either. So, I promise right now to not let that happen. I understand what you're saying about you and Scott. I get that. I do. But I need you to put that aside for just a moment because I called you for another reason as well. A related reason. As Vice President of New Talent Development, I've reached out to Sophie…"

"What!?!" I say angrily. Wait. Why am I so angry about this? Shouldn't I be happy for Sophie? I should. I really should. And I am. But… Okay, take a breath. Calm down. This can work. It can. "Sorry, Sash. I'm just having an irrational moment here. It's not you."

"She told me she told you about getting offers but not that one of the offers was from me and GMG," Sasha says in a very calm and deliberate way.

"Yes, that's true. She did tell me. We were going to talk when I got back to L.A.," I say. Also in a very calm and deliberate manner.

"Right. She let me know that. But this thing with the resignations - did you know anything about that? Those rumors about…"

"…about Muze's book being behind it all? No, I don't know anything about that. Honestly. And blissfully so."

"…okay, anyway, the resignations have shaken things up here. People are scrambling a bit. The situation is…fluid. So, I need to have a decision from Sophie by the end of tomorrow. Not just Sophie. I've reached out to others. But you don't know any of them. And it felt weird dealing with Sophie without looping you in so…here we are…"

"So…" I say as I let all this tumble through my brain. "So…you are leaving your business with Kelsey? Does she know this?"

"Yes, she does. And, yes, that was hard. But she understood. Mostly. That will take time, too. But that's my issue not yours," Sasha says firmly.

"So…" Thinking, thinking, thinking. "I'm happy for Sophie. Really. She'll be good. You know that already. But…" Ahhh, here it is. I see it now. "…there's a project I have in mind that I'd like her to do. But it won't be ready for a couple of years. At least. Maybe longer. I need to write it and then I'm going to direct it. But I want Sophie for the role. One of the main roles. And…well, I have someone else in mind for the other main role but I'm still…it's all still in the very earliest stages. Sooo…"

"So you want to know if I'll be okay with Sophie working on your project once she's with GMG officially. Well, that's going to be up to her and her agent…"

"Her agent?" For a second, I'm confused. "Oh, right. You won't be her agent anymore. Once you sign with GMG. Huh. Do you think she'll stay with Kelsey?"

"No idea," says Sasha. Then, "You know what we're doing right now, Case?"

"No, what?" I ask.

"We're doing that thing that we hated when other people did it with us when we were new in the business. Planning stuff out for them. Figuring out their careers as we would like them to be WITHOUT TALKING TO THEM."

Shit. She's right. "You're right. We're turning into the people we didn't like. Mo held me back. You saw through that. And who was that guy who tried to…"

"Let's not talk about THEM anymore," says Sasha. "In fact, let's agree that we do things up front. That we do things differently. That we don't do the usual Hollywood bullshit now that we're in positions to do that sort of stuff."

"Okay. Yes. I like that. Agreed." Pause. "So, how will we do things?" It's one thing to want to change the way things are done. It's an entirely different thing to create new ways of doing things.

"Fuck if I know," says Sasha. Then we both laugh. Shit. It's been a long while since I've laughed like this with Sasha. Too long.

"I have to go now, Sash. When I see Sophie tonight, we'll call you together. How does that sound? We'll call you together and figure things out," I say.

"Make it tomorrow morning. I've got a date with my fiance tonight. Ha," she says. Then, "I missed you, pipsqueak."

"I missed you, too. Let's…let's not let that happen again. No matter how much yelling and/or therapy it takes. Agreed?"

"Agreed."

85.

It's showtime. For the last time this week. I won't bore you with my monologue. I'll cut right to the chase with Mac. You haven't seen him in a long time, have you? Good. There's lots to catch up on. I introduce him and he walks out on stage. He's wearing his usual on set get up: jeans, sneakers, a long sleeve t-shirt (this time covered by a loose-fitting leather jacket (his one sartorial acquiescence to being a guest) and a baseball cap. Except for the jacket, he looks exactly like he does when I see him on the set of Stack Life up in Hamilton, Canada. Also, he's carrying a small, gift-wrapped parcel. I give him a hug. A good one. Because he's one of the good ones.

We sit down and let the clapping subside. I say, "Mac Waid. Mac Waid, Mac Waid, Mac Waid. It's good to see you."

He smiles and lifts the gift-wrapped package in both hands to present it to me. "It's good to see you, too, K.C. So good that I brought you a present." I take the package from him and undo the bow as he goes on, "It's from Camile's." He turns to look at the camera. "Camile's is a bakery in Port Dover Canada. A few years back, K.C. and I did some location shooting there for Stack Life…" there's a quick burst of applause, "…thank you, yes, and at some point, understand this was K.C.'s first season on the show, in fact it was the start of the shooting for the second half of that season, we'd taken a bit of a hiatus for various reasons, anyway, K.C. stumbled across this bakery and bought it out of all its goodies and brought them all to set for the crew and other actors to share."

Another burst of applause. I finish unwrapping and opening the box. It's a huge slab of tiramisu. It looks perfect. Mac produces two forks from his jacket pocket, unwraps them from their plastic sheath and brandishes in the space between us as he continues to talk directly to the camera, "For those of you who haven't read the articles about K.C. where this has been mentioned, the simple fact is this. K.C. is a wee bit obsessive. I have to say 'wee bit' to make this personality trait of hers sound cute and adorable. But in truth it's a wee bit more than a wee bit. Which is good. Because that drive is what makes her such a good actress, such a hard worker. But it also makes her a bit, more than a wee bit, compulsive when it comes to certain foods. Tiramisu, especially tiramisu from Camile's Bakery in Port Dover, is one of those foods."

Mac looks at me and ceremoniously hands me one of the forks. I take it from him with a bow. I ready my fork in one hand. He readies his fork in one hand. I turn to the camera and say, "Okay, that's our show for tonight. I'm done. I'm going to be eating tiramisu for the rest of the evening." Then I wave as if it's the end of the show. The end credits music issues forth from behind Keeley J and the rest of the cardboard cutouts. Mac and I stab our forks into the exceptionally large, rectangular mass of tiramisu. I can't imagine how it kept its shape during the trip from Camile's to the ranch. But somehow Mac pulled it off. After we both take our first bites and mug for the camera with our full mouths, I slowly start to pull the tiramisu closer to me. Mac sees this right away and slowly starts to pull the tiramisu back towards him. We engage in a minor tug of war for a few seconds then cut to commercial.

When we're back, the tiramisu is halfway gone. We've slowed down a bit because we have to actually talk to each other now and, like I said, it's a huge piece. We look each other in the eyes and slowly lay down our forks like two gunfighters agreeing to a truce. This gets a chuckle from the audience. I lean back in my chair and say, "Thank you for that, Mr. Waid. You always did have a sense of what was needed on set. And, to be clear, there is no bad time for tiramisu. Not ever."

Mac says, "It was the least I could do. Truly. I was in Port Dover last week and went to Camile's. As I was standing in line I heard a couple of customers talking about the time you bought out the store. You're a local legend up there. So, like I said, it's the least I could do."

I look down at my cards. I don't really need them. I could easily talk to Mac for hours. But I suppose I should hit the points Marcus wants me to hit. I look up and say, "So, do you want to share the big news regarding Stack Life or…"

Mac says, "I think maybe it's better coming from you."

I defer, "I'd feel a little awkward I think if I were the one to…"

285

"I don't believe that for a second, K.C. Hall. Go on, tell the world," Mac insists.

I pretend to not want to make this announcement. But that's all a lie. I really do want to make this announcement. I turn to the camera, "Stack Life has been nominated for a Best Streaming series Emmy." This gets a big burst of applause from the crowd.

Mac jumps in, "Actually, Best Drama series. They don't distinguish between streaming and broadcast shows."

I look at him, "Really? I thought they did." He shakes his head. I turn back to the camera, "Well, I guess I better say that again. Stack Life has been nominated for Best Drama series." Another, even bigger burst of applause from the audience. I like this crowd. I turn back to Mac, feeding off the playful energy of the audience. I say, "I do...worry every now and then about the show."

Mac knows me well enough to realize I'm setting up a joke. He plays right along, "Ohhh, how's that? Is the showrunner just too devastatingly handsome? Is that it?"

Mac, of course, is the showrunner. I laugh then drop into my fake serious voice again, "No. Sure, that's true but no that's not what concerns me. It's...well, it's the example the show is setting for the youth of the country." I furrow my brow and look down in shame.

Mac gently grabs hold of my hand and asks in a very concerned voice, "Oh, yes. Right. And what example is that?"

I look up at him and say quietly, "All the reading and...all the murders." I clench my fists and pound them lightly on the desktop as I say, "We show so many people reading and there are so many murders on the show..."

"Two murders. There have been just two murders. Three seasons. Two murders," Mac says to the camera.

"But, Mac..." I plaster a hand to my forehead in over-dramatic, Southern Belle style, "...even one murder is too many. We can't keep scaring the youth of our country away from the libraries. I don't want them to think that reading leads to murder."

A quick series of very deep, very ominous bass notes come from the band cutouts. I look at Mac nervously. He grabs my hands in desperation. Then we break into laughter. Mac says, "I've actually had a number of emails from librarians throughout the country who say they've noticed an increase in the numbers of people using their facilities. They say they get questions about Stack Life all the time. They swear our little show…"

"Nominated for Best Drama Series," I blurt out again.

"…is bringing more and more people back to the libraries all over the country." Pause. "And Canada, too." I'm not sure why but something about the way he said that last line - And Canada, too - cracks me up. I can't help but laugh. Once I start laughing he starts laughing which makes me laugh more which, of course, makes him laugh more which… You get what's happening.

I wave to the camera. Marcus cuts to another commercial break.

86.

I'd like to say Mac and I are over our giggle fit when we come back. But we're not. We are eating tiramisu again in an effort to quelch our laughter but that tactic is not working that well. Not at all. Through a series of snorts, chortles and forkfuls of tiramisu I manage to ask Mac, "So, what else do you have for us, Mr. Handsome Showrunner?"

This question sends us into another, uncontrollable fit of silliness. Keeley J and the cutouts (hey, that's not a bad band name - The Cutouts) start playing the Benny Hill Show music. You know what I'm talking about. This, of course, only makes Mac and I laugh some more. After a half minute or so I catch my breath enough to say, "No, come on, be professional, seriously, what else do you have to tell us?"

Mac sits up straight. He's doing his best to hold it together. I can see his shoulders shaking as he struggles to not laugh. He takes a deep, deep breath and forcefully blows it out. His shoulders shake some more then he manages to say with a straight face, "I do have a bit of news for you. I have been, ummm, negotiating with your business partner behind your back, so to speak."

"MDB?" I ask without laughing. Okay, there was a little laughter.

"Yes, Ms. DuBont herself. She wanted me to surprise you with this so here goes." He takes another deep breath then says, "Stack Life will be, officially, we've figured out the plot details as well as the real life who owns what rights to what details and so, yes, Stack Life will officially become part of the Hall-iverse starting next season."

My jaw drops open. I had no idea MDB was working on this. I had no idea this was possible. I love working with Mac. One of my complaints about launching into the Hall-iverse was that I wouldn't get to work with Mac anymore. MDB picked up on that. She must have. She picked up on that and made this happen. Did I mention my jaw dropped open. I'm speechless.

Mac sees this and continues on, "So, yes, we will get to keep working with each other. For at least a few more years."

I don't have any words. So, I stand up, lean over and hug him. Mac manages to stand up as I'm holding onto him.

He whispers into my ear but the applause is so loud that I can't make out what he's saying. Finally, I let go of him and we're standing there at the desk and he says to me, "But that's not the only surprise for tonight." He looks to Marcus just off stage and yells to him, "Okay, I think it's time."

87.

At that point, Marcus looks off to his side and waves. Wait, where's Sal? Sal is usually standing with Marcus. I've been laughing so hard with Mac that I haven't noticed he's not there until just now.

Marcus keeps waving. Waving like he's directing a vehicle or… He is directing a vehicle. It's one of the golf carts. Sal is driving it right up next to the stage. And he's not alone. Miley and Sophie are sitting on the back seat. Yes, the golf cart has a back seat. It's a big golf cart.

What…? How…?

Mac grabs my forearm and walks me over to Sal and the girls. He says to me, "They've had this planned all along. They've been just down the road the past day or so. All that stuff about gas and delays and whatnot…that was all a lie." He squeezes my arm. "Don't be too mad at them." Then he kisses me on the cheek as Sal waves at me to sit down next to him.

I do so but I keep my eyes on Miley and Sophie. They have shit-eating grins plastered to their faces and they are avoiding making eye contact with me. I notice then that they are wearing suede outfits that look very much like mine and holding small bouquets of flowers.

Wait!

No!

How…?

Sal eases the golf cart away from the stage and down the gravel path out to the field with the large tent. It's dusk now. Twilight has settled on the ranch, the fields and the mountains in the distance. The tent with all its support poles and ropes strung with bright white lights looks like a cluster of stars descended from the sky. I gasp when we round the corner and I see it. Miley and Sophie do, too. Sal says to me, "It is beautiful, isn't it?"

I want to stare at it forever. I see waiters carrying trays of food and glasses of wine into the tent. It's not a huge tent. It holds about a hundred people, I guess. And we, Scott and I, had invited maybe a total of fifty people for the reception which was supposed to happen tomorrow. A small reception/celebration of our marriage which we haven't had time to do this past year. Nor the inclination. We didn't want to do it in L.A. That didn't feel right. That doesn't fit us as a couple. So, when the plans for the show week being shot on location on Luisa's ranch crystallized, we knew we wanted to make our reception part of it. Our reception. Not...whatever this is.

A shock of fear lances through me. I ask Sal, "Where are the cameras? I don't..."

Sal puts a hand on my shoulder and reassures me, "No cameras. None of tonight is being filmed. We filmed the set up of the tent earlier this week and some behind the scenes stuff with these two and the rest of the crew earlier today. That's what people will see for the last few minutes of the show when they watch tonight. We will show one long distance shot of the tent like this because it does look so fabulous. But that's it. Everything that happens in there tonight will be private."

"Everything...???" I ask.

Miley and Sophie can't contain themselves anymore. They squeal with excited laughter then Miley says, "You're getting married again, you doofus. Scott's parents and brother are here. We're here." Sophie adds, "The Twins. We even pried Hannah away from her loverman in Wyoming. Elena, too. The whole Wayside crew. Also, MDB and Gyrin. They came in this afternoon. Plus, a certain witchy friend of yours..."

"Sasha's here?!?" I yell.

Miley says, "Sasha is here because she's your maid of honor, duh!"

Sophie adds as she points at Miley, "She's an excellent arranger. Excellent."

I look back and forth between Miley and Sophie as I say, "I really want to hug you guys, well, no, first I want to yell at you then I want to hug you." Pause. "No. Seriously." That's when they start to tear up. They blink their eyes furiously and wipe at the corners to stop the tears from ruining their makeup.

A thought. I ask, "What about...?"

Miley cuts me off, "Connor is not here. We ALL decided that was not... appropriate. Sasha understands. Really. You

291

and Connor and Sasha and Scott can get to know each other back in L.A. Tonight's all about you and Scott."

Sophie adds, "Annnndddd one other little thing." She looks at Miley. Miley is confused for a second then she remembers. She says, "Oh, yeah! You and Scott and one other thing."

"What other thing?" I demand of them. They hold their hands over their mouths. They aren't going to tell me. I look to Sal. He points towards the tent as he says, "You'll see it when we pull around the corner here."

I face forward. Sal guides the golf cart in a wide, banking turn around the end of the tent. Out of the corner of my eye, I notice more busy waiters. Then I see a standalone trellis. With an arch covered in flowers. Scott is standing to one side of the arch. He's wearing a suit whose color matches my outfit. MDB is standing there, as well. Miley stage whispers, "MDB is the officiant."

Of course, she is. Then I notice Sasha standing across from Scott's brother. Maid of honor and best man. All wearing outfits that match mine in color. This has been planned for a while. I'm so overwhelmed. And happy. And confused. And happy. And...so many emotions.

Sophie says, "Hold on, hold on...there!" Her hand lances out over my shoulder. She's pointing to a spot just behind MDB, just behind the trellis. For the second time tonight, my jaw drops open.

It's Alonsha.

Alonsha completely whole and back to her original spherical shape. There are five, large, flaming torches arranged in a semicircle behind her. She's shining, shining, shining. She looks so beautiful. She looks like she belongs exactly there. So perfect. Sal pulls the golf cart up to the space between the lines of chairs that face the wedding party. That's what this is: my wedding. A real wedding. I wave to Scott's parents sitting on one side. Then I see Jon sitting on the other side and I wave to him. That's when I see Josie, too. OMG! They must have been planning this for so long! Mac slides into a seat next to Josie. He's just run all the way over here. I wave at Josie. She starts crying. No! Stop that! You'll make me cry.

That's when I realize it's too late. I am crying. In a blur of tears and joy, I see Hannah, Elena, Sarai, Clara and the twins sitting in the second row of chairs. I look up at Scott. From him to me it's about fifty feet. I can see his smile. I can see his tears. Dammit, we're all crying now. The girls hustle over to stand behind Sasha. She looks back at them to make sure they are in the exact right place. I wave at her. She waves at me. Sal walks around the front of the golf cart and holds his arm out to me. Music comes from somewhere. The wedding march. Sal says, "If I may have the honor."

I stand up and loop my arm through his. We pause for a moment at the gap between the rows of chairs. He looks down at me and says, "Whenever you're ready." I nod at Sal then look at Scott. He smiles back at me. I say to Sal as I keep looking at Scott, "I'm ready."

And that's how I got married.

...

...

...

Again.

88.

Henrietta survived the heart surgery. Her parents say she's doing well. There's months of recovery ahead but she's smiling and playing with toys and telling them not to worry anymore.

I found this out on the flight back to L.A. from the Dakotas.

The same flight Valery Ostonyay called to tell me about some concerning rumors.

Or should I say disturbing rumors?

That all depends on whether the rumors turn out to be true or not.

And I won't know that until I get back to L.A. and do some investigating of my own.

But I'll save all that for the sequel.

Thank you for reading my book.
If you liked it, please leave a review.
If you have a question, visit my website:
www.cameronmcvey.com
For my other books, go here:
Amazon.com: Cameron McVey: Books, Biography, Blog, Audiobooks, Kindle
If you're ever in Steamboat Springs, CO and need to relax,
Check out Strawberry Park Hot Springs
https://strawberryhotsprings.com/

Made in the USA
Columbia, SC
01 December 2022

72376481R10163